# THE
# UNBOUND

# THE
# UNBOUND

## AN ARCHIVED NOVEL

VICTORIA SCHWAB

**HYPERION**
New York

First Edition
1 3 5 7 9 10 8 6 4 2
G475-5664-5-13319

Printed in the United States of America

This book is set in Perpetua and Clarendon.

Designed by Tyler Nevins

Library of Congress Cataloging-in-Publication Data
Schwab, Victoria.
The unbound: an Archived novel/Victoria Schwab.—First edition.
pages  cm
Summary: Starting her junior year at Hyde School, Mackenzie Bishop,
a Keeper tasked with stopping violent Histories from escaping the Archive,
becomes the prime suspect when several people vanish without a trace.
ISBN 978-1-4231-7820-0 (hardback)
[1. Future life—Fiction. 2. Dead—Fiction. 3. Supernatural—Fiction.
4. Libraries—Fiction.] I. Title.
PZ7.S39875Un    2014
[Fic]—dc23        2013035335

Reinforced binding

Visit www.un-requiredreading.com

SUSTAINABLE FORESTRY INITIATIVE   Certified Sourcing
www.sfiprogram.org
SFI-00993

THIS LABEL APPLIES TO TEXT STOCK

*To Patricia—*

*for the shoulder, the ear, and the unwavering faith*

*In three words I can sum up everything*
*I've learned about life: it goes on.*
—Robert Frost

# ONE

**M**Y BODY BEGS for sleep.

I sit on the roof of the Coronado, and it pleads with me, begs me to climb down from my perch on the gargoyle's broken shoulder, to creep back inside and down the stairs and through the still-dark apartment into my bed—to *sleep*.

But I can't.

Because every time I sleep, I dream. And every time I dream, I dream of Owen. Of his silvery hair, his cold eyes, his long fingers curling casually around his favorite knife. I dream of him dragging the jagged side of the blade across my skin as he murmurs that the "real" Mackenzie Bishop must be hidden somewhere under all that flesh.

*I'll find you, M,* he whispers as he cuts. *I'll set you free.*

Some nights he kills me quickly, and some nights he takes his time; but every night I bolt up in the dark, clutching my arms around my ribs, heart pounding as I search my skin for fresh cuts.

There aren't any, of course. Because there is no Owen.

Not anymore.

It's been three weeks, and even though it's too dark to make out anything more than outlines on the night-washed roof, my eyes still drift to the spot—a circle of gargoyles—where it happened. Or, at least, where it *ended*.

*Stop running, Miss Bishop. There's nowhere to go.*

The memory is so vivid: Wesley bleeding out on the other side of the roof while Owen pressed the blade between my shoulders and gave me a choice that wasn't really a choice because of the metal biting into my skin.

*It doesn't have to end like this.*

Words, promises, threats that hung between us only long enough for me to turn the key in the air behind his back and make a tear in the world, a door out of nothing, to nothing—to *nowhere*—and send him through.

Now my eyes find the invisible—*impossible*—mark. It's barely a scratch on the air, all that's left of the void door. Even though I can't *see* the mark, I know exactly where it is: the patch of dark where my eyes slide off, attracted and repelled at once by the out of place, the unnatural, the *wrong*.

The void door is a strange, corrosive thing.

I tried to revisit that day, to read what happened in the statues on the roof, but the memories were all ruined. The opening of the void had overexposed them like film, eaten through solid minutes—the most important of my life—and left only white noise.

But I don't need to read the images in the rocks: I *remember*.

A stone crumbles off a statue on the far side of the roof and I jump, nearly losing my balance on top of the gargoyle. My head is starting to feel heavy in that dangerous, drifting-off way, so I get down before I *fall* down, rolling my neck as the first slivers of light creep into the sky. I tense when I see it. I am in no way ready for today, and not just because I haven't slept. I'm not ready for the uniform hanging on my chair, or the new face I'll have to wear with it. I'm not ready for the campus full of bodies full of noise.

I'm not ready for Hyde School.

But the sun keeps rising anyway.

Several feet away, one of the gargoyles stands out from the others. Its stone body is bundled in old cushions and duct tape, the former stolen from a closet off the Coronado lobby, the latter from a drawer in the coffee shop. It's a poor substitute for a boxing dummy, but it's better than nothing—and if I can't sleep, I might as well train.

Now, as dawn spills over the roof, I gingerly unwind the boxing tape that crisscrosses both my hands, wincing as the blood returns to my right wrist. Pain, dull and constant, radiates down into my fingers. It's another relic from that day. *Owen's grip like a vise, tightening until the bones crack and the knife in my fingers clatters to the Narrows floor.* My wrist would probably heal faster if I didn't spend my time punching makeshift dummies, but I find the pain strangely grounding.

I'm almost done rolling up the tape when I feel the familiar scratch of letters on the piece of paper in my pocket. I dig the slip out and in the spreading light of day I can just make out the name in the middle of the page.

*Ellie Reynolds. 11.*

I run my thumb over the name, as if expecting to feel the grooves made by the pen, but the strange writing never leaves a real impression. A hand in the Archive writes in a book in the Archive that echoes its words onto the paper here. Find the History, and the name goes away. (No lasting mark. I thought of keeping a list of the people I'd found and returned, but my grandfather, Da, would have told me there's no point in dwelling. *Stare too long at anything,* he'd say, *and you start to wonder. And where does wondering get you? Nowhere good.*)

I head for the rusty rooftop door. Finding Ellie Reynolds should keep me busy, at least until it's a more acceptable hour to be awake. If I told my parents how I'd been spending my nights—half in nightmares and half up here on the roof—they'd send me to a shrink. Then again, if I told my parents how I'd spent the last four and a half years of my life—hunting down and returning the Histories of the dead—they'd lock me in a psych ward.

I make my way down four flights of concrete stairs, intensely aware of the silence and the way my steps knife through it. At the third floor, the stairwell spits me out into a hall adorned with worn yellow wallpaper and dusty crystal lights. Apartment 3F waits at the far end, and part of me wants so badly to go home and sleep, but another part of me isn't willing to risk it. Instead I stop halfway, just past the metal cage-like elevators at the spot framed between an old mirror and a painting of the sea.

Next to the painting, I can make out the crack, like a ripple in the wallpaper, simultaneously pushing and pulling my gaze. It's a pretty easy way to tell if something doesn't belong, when your eyes can't quite find it because it's something you're not supposed to see. Like on the roof. But *unlike* on the roof, when I slide the silver ring off my finger, the discomfort disappears and I can see the shape crystal clear in the middle of the crack.

A keyhole.

A door to the Narrows.

I run my fingers over the small, dark spot, hesitating a moment. The walls between worlds used to feel like they were made of stone—heavy and impenetrable. These days, they feel too thin. The secrets, lies, and monsters bleed through, ruining the clean lines.

*Keep your worlds apart,* warned Da. *Neat and even and solidly separate.*

But everything is messy now. My fear follows me into the Narrows. My nightmares follow me out.

I fetch the leather cord from around my neck, tugging it over my head. The key on the end shines in the hallway's artificial light. It isn't mine—isn't Da's, that is—and the first time I used it to open a Narrows door, I remember feeling bitter that it could so easily replace my grandfather's key. As if they were the same.

I weigh this one in my palm. It's too new and a fraction too light, and it's not just a piece of metal, but a symbol: a warning that keys and freedom and memories and lives can all be taken away. Not that I need a reminder. Agatha's interrogation is carved into my memory.

It had only been a few days. Enough time for the bruises to color on my skin, but not enough for my wrist to heal. Agatha sat there in her chair, smiling pleasantly, and I sat in mine, trying not to let her see how badly my hands were shaking. I had no key—she'd taken it—and no way out of the Archive without it. The problem, as Agatha explained it, was that I'd seen behind the curtain, seen the system's cogs and cracks. The question was, should I be allowed to remember? Or should the Archive carve out everything I'd ever seen and done within its jurisdiction, leaving me full of holes, free of the weight of it all?

*Given the choice,* I'd told her, *I'd rather learn to live with what I know.*

*Let's hope you're making the right choice,* she'd said, placing the new key in my palm. She curled my fingers over it and added, *Let's hope I am, too.*

5

Now, standing in the hall, I slide Agatha's key into the mark on the yellow wallpaper and watch the shadows spread out from the keyhole, soaking like ink into the wall as the door takes shape. When it's finished forming—its edges marked by light—I will myself to turn the key. But for a second, I can't. My hand starts to shake, so I tighten my grip on the key until the metal bites into my skin and the pain jogs me free, and then I shove open the door and step through into the Narrows.

As the door closes behind me, I hold my breath the way kids do when they pass a graveyard. It's superstitious—just some silly hope that bad things won't happen unless you breathe them in. I force myself to stand there in the dark until my body recognizes that Owen's not here, that it's just me and, somewhere in the maze of halls, Ellie Reynolds.

She turns out to be a simple return, once I finally find her.

Histories are easier to track down when they run, because they cast memories like shadows over every inch of ground they cover. But Ellie stays put, huddled in a corner of the Narrows near the edge of my territory. When I find her, she goes without a fight, and it's a good thing—as I lean back against the dank wall, it's all I can do to keep my eyes open. I drag myself back toward the numbered doors that lead home, yawning as I reach the door with the Roman numeral I chalked onto its front. I step back into the Outer, relieved to find the third floor hall as quiet as when I left it. It's too easy to lose track of time in the Narrows, where clocks and watches don't work, and today of all days, I can't afford to be late.

Sunlight is flooding through the apartment windows as I inch the door closed and cross the living room, steps masked by the sound of coffee brewing and the low hum of the TV. Below the date and time stamp on the screen—six fifteen a.m., Wednesday—a news anchor prattles on about traffic and the sports roundup before changing gears.

"Up next," he says, shuffling papers, "the latest on a crime that has everyone stumped. A missing person. A scene in disarray. Was it a break-in, an abduction, or something worse?"

The anchor delivers the line with a little too much enthusiasm, but something about the still frame hovering behind him catches my attention. I'm halfway to the TV when the muffled sound of my parents' footsteps in their room reminds me I'm standing in the middle of the apartment, still wearing my black, close-fitting Keeper clothes, at six in the morning.

I duck into the bathroom and snap on the shower. The water's hot, and it feels wonderful. The heat loosens my shoulders and soothes my sore muscles, the sound of the water filling the room with white noise, steady and soothing. My eyes drift shut, and then . . .

I sway and catch myself the instant before I fall forward into the wall. Pain zings up my bad wrist as I push off the tile and swear under my breath, snapping the lever to cold. The icy water hits my skin, the shock of it leaving me miserable but awake.

I'm towel-clad and halfway to my bedroom, the Keeper clothes bundled beneath my arm, when my parents' door opens and Dad pops out. He's clutching a coffee mug and exuding his usual air of underslept and overcaffeinated.

"Morning," I mumble.

"Big day, sweetheart." He plants a kiss on my forehead, and his noise—the static every living person carries with them, the sound of their thoughts and memories—crackles through me, the images themselves held back only by the Keeper's ring on my finger. "Think you're ready?" he asks.

"Doubt it," I say, resisting the urge to point out that I don't have a choice. Instead, I listen to him tell me I'll rise to the challenge. I even manage to smile and shrug and say "I'm sure" before escaping into my room.

The cold water may have been enough to wake me up, but it's hardly enough to prepare me for the school uniform waiting on my chair. Water drips from my hair into my eyes as I consider the black cotton polo—long-sleeved, piped with silver, and sporting a crest over the chest pocket—and the plaid skirt, its pattern made up of black, silver, green, and gold. Hyde School colors. In the catalog, boys and girls study under hundred-year-old oaks, a wrought-iron fence to one side and a moss-covered building to the other. A picture of class and charm and sheltered innocence.

I reach for my newly charged cell phone and shoot Wesley a quick text.

> I'm not ready for this.

Wesley Ayers, who labeled himself in my phone as *Wesley Ayers, Partner in Crime*, has been gone for almost a week; he left right after his father's wedding for a "family bonding edition" honeymoon. Judging by how often he's been texting, I'd say he's opted out of most of the bonding.

A moment later, he texts back.

> You're a Keeper. You hunt down the animated records of the dead in your spare time. I'm pretty sure you can handle private school.

I can picture Wesley tucking his hands behind his head as he says it, one brow arching, his hazel eyes warm and bright and lined with black. I chew my lip as a small smile breaks through. I'm trying to think of something clever to say back when he texts again.

> What are you wearing?

My face flushes. I know he's just teasing me—he saw the uniform before he left—but I can't help remembering what happened in the garden last week, on the day of the wedding. The way his lips smiled against my jaw, his now-familiar noise—that cacophony of drums and bass—pressing through me with his touch before I could find the strength to tell him no. The hurt in his eyes once I did— so well concealed that most people wouldn't even notice. But I did. I saw it in his face as he drew back, and in his shoulders as he pulled away, and in the corners of his mouth as he told me it was fine. *We* were fine. And I wanted to believe him, but I didn't. I don't.

Which is why I'm still standing here in my towel, trying to think of what to text back, when I hear the apartment's front door open and slam. A second later, a breathless voice calls my name, and then there's a knock on my bedroom door. I toss the phone aside.

"I'm getting dressed."

As if that's an invitation, the door starts to swing open. I catch it with my palm, forcing it shut again.

"*Mackenzie,*" my mom says with a huff. "I just want to see how the uniform fits."

"And I'll show you," I snap, "just as soon as I'm *wearing* it."

She goes quiet, but I can tell she's still standing there in the hall beyond the door. I pull the polo over my head and button the skirt. "Shouldn't you be down in the café," I call, "getting ready to open?"

"I didn't want to miss you," she says through the wood. "It's your first day. . . ."

Her voice wavers before trailing off, and I sigh loudly. Taking the hint, she retreats down the hall, her footsteps echoing behind her. When I finally emerge, she's perched at the kitchen table in a Bishop's apron, flipping through the pamphlet on Hyde School dos and don'ts. (Students are encouraged to be helpful, respectful, and well-mannered, but discouraged from makeup, piercings, unnaturally dyed hair, and raucousness. The word *raucousness* is actually in the pamphlet. I highlighted the bits I think Lyndsey will like; just because she's an hour away doesn't mean she can't get a good laugh at my expense.)

"Well?" I ask, indulging my mom with a slow twirl. "What do you think?"

She looks up and smiles, but her eyes are shining, and I know we've entered fragile territory. My stomach twists. I've been doing my best to think *around* the issue, but seeing Mom's face—the subtle war of sadness and stubborn cheer—I can't help but think of Ben.

My little brother was killed last year on his way to school, just a couple of weeks before summer break. The dreaded day last fall when I went back to class and Ben didn't will go down as one of the darkest in my family's history. It was like bleeding to death, except more painful.

So when I see the strain in Mom's eyes, I'm just thankful we've gained the buffer of a year, even if it's thin. I allow her to run her fingers over the silver piping that lines the shoulders of my polo, forcing myself to remain still beneath the grinding sound that pours from her fingers and through my head with her touch.

"You'd better get back to the coffee shop," I say through clenched teeth, and Mom's hand slips away, mistaking my discomfort for annoyance.

She manages a smile anyway. "You ready to go?"

"Almost," I say. When she doesn't immediately turn to leave, I know it's because she wants to see me off. I don't bother to protest. Not today. Instead I just do a quick check: first the mundane—backpack, wallet, sunglasses—and then the specific—ring around my finger, key around my neck, list in my . . . No list. I duck back into my room to find the piece of Archive-issued paper still shoved in the pocket of my pants. My phone's there, too, lying at the foot of my bed where I tossed it earlier. I transfer the slip—blank for now—into the front pocket of my shirt and type a quick answer to Wesley's question . . .

What are you wearing?

Battle armor.

. . . before dropping the phone into my bag.

On our way out, Mom gives me the full spiel about staying safe, being nice, playing well with others. When we reach the base of the lobby's marble stairs, she plants a kiss on my cheek (it sounds like breaking plates in my head) and tells me to smile. Then an old man calls over from across the lobby, asking if the café is open, and I watch her hurry away, issuing a trill of morning cheer as she leads him into Bishop's.

11

I push through the Coronado's revolving doors and head over to the newly installed bike rack. There's only one bike chained to it, a sleek metal thing marred—Wes would say *adorned*—by a strip of duct tape on which the word *DANTE* has been scrawled in Sharpie. I knew a car was out of the question—all our money is feeding into the coffee shop right now—but I'd had the foresight to ask for the bike. My parents were surprised; I guess they figured I'd just take the bus (local, of course, not school; Hyde wouldn't deign to have its name stenciled on the side of some massive yellow monstrosity, and besides, the average student probably drives a Lexus), but buses are just narrow boxes crammed with bodies full of noise. The thought makes me shudder.

I dig a pair of workout pants out of my bag, tugging them on under my skirt before unlocking Dante. The café's awning flaps in the breeze, and the rooftop gargoyles peer down as I swing my leg over and push off the curb.

I'm halfway to the corner when something—some*one*—catches my eye, and I slow down and glance back.

There's someone across the street from the Coronado, and he's watching me. A man, early thirties, with gold hair and sun-touched skin. He's standing on the curb, shielding his eyes against the sun and squinting up at the old hotel as if it's intensely interesting. But a moment earlier as I zipped by, I could swear he was looking at me. And even now that he's not, the feeling lingers.

I stall at the corner, pretending to adjust the gears on my bike as I watch him not-watch me. There's something familiar about him, but I can't place it. Maybe he's been to Bishop's while I was on shift, or maybe he's friends with a Coronado resident. Or maybe I've never seen him before, and he just has one of those familiar faces. Maybe I just need sleep. The moment I let in the doubt, it kills my conviction, and suddenly I'm not even sure he was looking at me in the first place. When he crosses the street a moment later and vanishes through the front doors of the Coronado without so much as a glance my way, I shake it off and pedal away.

The morning is cool, and I relish the fresh air and the wind whistling in my ears as I weave through the streets. I mapped out the route yesterday—drew it on my hand this morning to be safe—but I never look down. The city unfolds around me, a vast and sunlit grid, a stark contrast to the dark tangle of corridors I'm used to.

And for a few minutes, as the world blurs past, I almost forget about how tired I am and how much I'm dreading today. But then I round the corner and the moment ends as I find myself face-to-face with the moss-slick stones, ivy-strewn walls, and iron gates of Hyde School.

# TWO

M Y FAMILY is about to run away.

Ben's been dead for almost a year, and our home has somehow become a house, something kept at arm's reach. They say the only way around is through, but apparently that's not true. The other option, I know now, is to turn and run. My parents have started packing; things are vanishing, one by one, into boxes. I try not to notice. Between struggling to survive sophomore year and keeping my list of Histories clear, I've done a pretty good job of ignoring the Ben-shaped hole—but eventually even I can't help but see the signs.

Mom quits another job.

Dad starts going on trips in his most collegiate suits.

The house is more often empty than full.

And then one day, when I'm sitting at the kitchen table, studying for finals, Dad gets back from a trip—an interview, it turns out—and places a booklet in front of me. I finish the paragraph I'm reading before letting my gaze wander over to the glossy paper. At first glance it looks like a college packet, but the people splashed across the cover in studious poses wear uniforms of black and green and silver and gold, and most of them look a shade too young for university. I read the name printed in gothic capitals across the top: *HYDE SCHOOL.*

I should say no. Blending in is hard enough in a school of fifteen hundred, and between the Ben-shaped hole and the Archive's ever-filling page, I'm barely keeping up my grades.

But Dad has that horrible, hopeful look in his eyes, and he skips the speech about how it will "enrich my academic portfolio," doesn't bother to tell me that it is "a smaller school, easier to meet people," and goes straight for the kill. The quiet, questioning, "It will be an adventure."

And maybe he's right.

Or maybe I just can't stand our home-turned-house.

Maybe I want to run away, too.

I say yes.


*I should have said no.*

That's all I can think as I straddle the bike and stare up at Hyde School. The campus is tucked behind a wrought iron fence, and the lot in front is filled with fancy cars and peppered with students who look like they came straight out of that catalog Dad brought home last spring. There is a bike rack, too—but the only students around it are clearly freshmen and sophomores. I can tell by the color of the piping on their uniform shirts. (According to the brochure, freshmen are marked by a glossy black, sophomores by green, juniors by silver, seniors by gold.)

I hover at the edge of the lot, leaning the bike against a tree as I dig out my phone and reread Wesley's text.

I'm pretty sure you can handle private school.

Letting my gaze drift back up, I'm not so confident. It's not the uniforms that have me thrown, or even the obvious old-money air—I wouldn't be much of a Keeper if I couldn't blend in. It's the fact that I could count the number of students here in less than a minute if I wanted to. There are few enough to make me think I could come to know their names and faces. Which means they could come to know mine. My last school was large enough to afford a certain degree of anonymity. I'm sure there *was* a radar, but it was easy to stay off it—and I did. But here? It's hard enough keeping my second life a secret with only a few people to con. In an "intimate atmosphere"—the brochure's words, not mine—people are going to notice if I slip up.

*What difference does it make?* I tell myself. *Just a few more people to lie to.*

It's not like I'll be selling different lies to different crowds here. I just have to convince everyone of one simple thing: that I'm normal. Which would, admittedly, be easier if I'd slept more than a couple of hours at a time in the last three weeks, and if I weren't being haunted by the memory of a History who tried to kill me. But hey. No such thing as a perfect scenario.

Most of the students have gone onto campus by now, so I cross the lot, chain Dante to the bike rack, and tug off the workout pants from underneath my skirt. When I get to the front gate, I can't help but smile a little. A massive metal *H* has been woven through the bars. I snap a photo on my phone and send it to Wes with the caption *Abandon all hope, ye who enter here* (the inscription on the gates of Hell in Dante's *Inferno*, and Wesley's favorite passage). A moment later he responds with a single smiley face, which is enough to make me feel a little less alone as I step onto campus.

Hyde is made of stone and moss, most of the buildings laid out around a quad. It's all linked by paths and bridges and halls—a miniature version of the university where Dad works now. (I guess that's the idea behind a college preparatory school.) All I can think as I make my way down a tree-lined path to the administration building, with its ivy-strewn facade and clock tower, is how much Lyndsey would love it here. I send her a text telling her so, and a few seconds later she texts back.

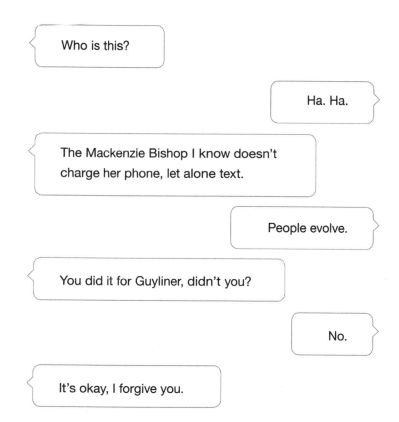

Who is this?

Ha. Ha.

The Mackenzie Bishop I know doesn't charge her phone, let alone text.

People evolve.

You did it for Guyliner, didn't you?

No.

It's okay, I forgive you.

I roll my eyes and pocket my phone before taking a last, deep breath and pushing open the doors of the admin building. I'm deposited in a large glass lobby with corridors trailing off in several directions. I manage to find the main office and retrieve my final schedule and room assignments from a woman with a frighteningly tight bun, but instead of backtracking, I'm then sent through a separate set of doors that lead into a large hall crowded with students. I have no idea what to do next. I do my best to stay out of the way as I internally repeat the phrase *I will not pull out a map, I will not pull a map, I will not pull out a map.* I studied the layout of campus, I really did. But I'm tired. And even with a solid sense of direction, it's like the Narrows, where you have to learn the grid by moving through it.

"It's one building over, second hall, and third room on the left."

The voice comes from right behind me, and I turn to find a senior (gold stripes trace across the black of his uniform) looking down at me.

"Excuse me?"

"Precalc with Bradshaw, math hall, room 310," he says, pointing at the paper in my hands. "Sorry, didn't mean to look over your shoulder. You just seemed a little lost."

I fold the paper and shove it back into my bag. "That obvious?" I ask, trying to keep my voice light.

"Standing in the middle of the admin building with a class schedule and a daunted look?" he says. "Can't blame a guy for wanting to help." There is a kind of warmth to him, from his dark hair and deep tan to his broad smile and gold eyes. And then he goes and ruins it by adding, "After all, the whole thing does have an air of 'damsel' to it."

The air ices over.

"I'm not a damsel." There's no humor in my voice now. "And I'm really not in distress, if that's where you were going next."

He flinches; but instead of retreating, he holds his ground, his smile softening into something more genuine. "I sounded like an ass just then, didn't I? Let me start again." He holds out a hand. "I'm Cash."

"Mackenzie," I say, bracing myself as I slide my hand into his. The sound that fills my head is loud—the noise of the living is *always* loud—but strangely melodic. Cash is made of jazz and laughter. Our hands fall apart and the sound fades away, replaced a moment later by the first bell, which echoes through the halls from the clock tower.

And so it begins.

"Let me walk you to class," he says.

"That's not necessary."

"I know. But I'd be happy to do it all the same."

I hesitate, but there's something about him that reminds me of Wes—maybe the way he stands or how easily he smiles—and at this point I'd probably attract more attention by saying no; people are already casting glances as they hurry past us to class. So I nod and say, "Lead the way."

Within moments I regret it.

Having Cash as an escort not only results in a halting pace—he stops to say hello, hug, or fist-bump *everyone*—but also more attention than I ever wanted to garner, since he introduces me every single time. And despite the fact that the first bell's already rung and the halls are emptying, everyone takes the time to say hello back, walking with us a few feet while they chat. By the time Cash finally guides me through one of the elevated halls that bridge the buildings into the math hall and deposits me at room 310, I feel dazed from the attention.

And then he just disappears with little more than a smile and a "Good luck!"

I don't even have a chance to thank him, let alone ask for a clue about where I'm headed next. Sixteen pairs of eyes shift up as I walk in, sporting the usual spectrum of interest. Only the teacher's attention stays trained on the board as he scribbles out instructions below the header *Precalculus*. Most of the seats are already taken; in some strange and twisted version of the high school dynamic, I'm left with the back row instead of the usually shunned front. I slide into the last empty seat as the teacher starts, and my chest finally begins to loosen.

Waiting for something to start is always worse than when it does.

As the lesson begins, I'm relieved to find that underneath the moss and stone and uniforms, school still kind of feels like school. You can dress it up, but it doesn't change much from place to place. I wonder what class Lyndsey has first. She'll be sitting in the front row, of course. I wonder who will sit next to her on the left, who will reach over and doodle in the margins of her books when she's not looking. I start to wonder what Ben would be studying, but then I catch myself and turn my thoughts to the equations on the board.

I've always been good at math. It's straightforward, black-and-white, right and wrong. Equations. Da thought of people as books to be read, but I've always thought of them more as formulas—full of variables, but always the sum of their parts. That's what their noise is, really: all of a person's components layered messily over one another. Thought and feeling and memory and all of it unorganized, until that person dies. Then it all gets compiled, straightened out into this linear thing, and you can see exactly what the various parts add up to. What they equal.

*Tick. Tick. Tick.*

I notice the sound in the lull between two of Bradshaw's explanations. It's a clock on the back wall, and once I start to notice it, I can't stop. Even with Bradshaw's expert projection (I wonder if he took a speech class or used to act, and how he ended up teaching precalc instead), there it is: low and constant and clear. Da used to say you could isolate the sounds in the Narrows if you tried, pluck out notes and pull them forward, letting the rest sink back. I tug on the *tick tick tick*, and soon the teacher's voice fades and the clock is all I can hear, quiet and constant as a pulse.

*Tick. Tick. Tick.*

*Tick. Tick.*

*Tick . . .*

And then, between one tick and the next, the lights go off.

All at once the whole set of soft fluorescents on the ceiling flickers and goes out, plunging the classroom into darkness. When the lights come back on, the room is *empty*. Sixteen students and a teacher all gone in a blink, leaving only vacant desks and the ticking clock and a knife resting, gentle as a kiss, against my throat.

# THREE

"**O**WEN."

It comes out barely a whisper, my voice tight with fear. *Not here. Not now.*

He lets out a low breath behind me, and then I feel his lips brush against my ear. "Hello, M."

"Don't—" I start, but the words die as the knife presses into my throat.

"Look at you," he says, using the metal to lift my chin. "Putting on a show. Smiling and nodding and trying to pass for normal."

The knife falls away, and a moment later he's there—rounding my chair, clucking his tongue as he perches on top of the desk in front of mine, hunched forward, resting his elbows on his knees. His silvery hair is swept back, and his eyes hang on me, wild and wolfish and blue.

"Do they know you're broken?" he asks, twirling the blade between his fingers. "They will, soon enough. Should we show them?"

I grip the desk. "You don't exist."

"And yet I could break you," he says softly, "in front of all of them. Crack you open, let them see all the monsters you're made of. I could set them free. Set *you* free." He sits up straight. "You don't belong here."

"Where do I belong?"

In a blink he's gone from the other desk and standing next to mine. He rests the knife against my desk, its tip inches from my ribs. His other hand comes down on my shoulder, holding me in my chair as he leans close and whispers, "With me."

He drives the knife forward and I gasp and jerk upright in my seat, catching my rib cage on the edge of my desk as the bell rings. Owen is gone, and the room is full of students scraping their chairs back and hoisting their bags onto their shoulders. I sag back again, rubbing my ribs, then haul myself to my feet and slide my too-blank notebook into my bag, trying to shake off the dregs of the nightmare. I'm almost to the door when Mr. Bradshaw stops me.

"Miss Bishop?" he says, straightening his desk.

I turn back to him. "Yes, sir?"

"Did I bore you?"

I cringe. "No, sir."

"Well, that's a relief," he says, adjusting his glasses. "I do so worry about boring my students."

"Oh, you shouldn't," I say. "You're a very good speaker. Drama training?"

I curse myself before the words have even left my lips. Mouthing off in the Archive is one thing, but Mr. Bradshaw's not a Librarian, he's a teacher. Luckily, he smiles.

"I'll assume then that, despite outward appearances, you were listening to my lecture with rapt attention. Still, perhaps in the future you could listen with your eyes open. Just so I know for sure."

I manage a weak smile, a nod, and another "Yes, sir" before heading into the hall in search of Literary Theory and Analysis—I don't see why they can't just call it English. But before I can orient myself, someone clears his throat loudly. I turn to see Cash leaning against the door, waiting. He's got a coffee in each hand, and he holds one out to me.

"Still trying to play the knight?" I ask, reaching reflexively for the cup.

"Your English class with Wellson is on the other side of the quad," he says. "Five minutes isn't enough time, unless you know the way."

As soon as I take the coffee, he sets off down the hall. It's all I can do to keep up and not spill the drink all over myself as I swerve to avoid being hit by shoulders and the noise that comes with them.

"Before you ask how I knew about Wellson," he says, "I don't have a thing for preying on new students." He taps the side of his head. "Just a photographic memory."

"That has to come in handy in a school like this."

His smile widens. "It does."

As he leads me through the building, I try to commit the route to memory.

"You'll learn it backward and forward in no time."

I'll have to. One of the "innovative learning tactics" mentioned in the brochure is the scheduling. Semesters at Hyde are made up of five classes: three before lunch, two after. Every other day the schedule is reversed, so whatever class came first goes last, last first, etc., etc. So Mondays, Wednesdays, and Fridays look like this: Precalc, Literary Theory, Wellness, (lunch), Physiology, Government. Tuesdays and Thursdays look like this: Government, Physiology, Wellness, (lunch), Literary Theory, Precalc.

The brochure contained a lengthy, case study–supported explanation of *why* it works; right now it feels like just another hoop to jump through.

Cash leads the way through a set of doors, out onto an inner quad that's ringed with buildings. Then he veers down a path to the right. Along the way, he drinks his coffee and cheerfully tosses out fun facts about Hyde: It's been around since 1832; it used to be two schools (one for guys and one for girls), but they consolidated; one of the founders was a sculptor, and the campus is studded with statues, fourteen in all, though the number is always up for debate. Cash rambles on, waving whenever someone shouts his way (which is surprisingly often) without so much as a pause in his speech.

Luckily he doesn't stop to chat with anyone this time, and we reach my class right as the second bell rings. He smiles triumphantly, turning away—but not before I can say thanks this time. He offers a salute that sweeps into a bow, and then he's gone. I finish my coffee, trash the cup, and push the door open. Students are still taking their seats, and I snag one two rows back as a middle-aged woman with strikingly good posture—I assume she's Ms. Wellson—writes in perfect print across the board. When she steps aside and I see the words, I can't help but smile.

*DANTE'S INFERNO.*

It is summer, and I'm searching for a coffee shop beneath layers of dust, while Wesley Ayers sits backward on a metal chair. I can see the outline of a key beneath his shirt. The shared secret of our second lives hangs between us, not like a weight, but like a lifeline. I clean, and he rescues a book from a pile of sheets beside the chair.

"What have we here?" he asks, holding up the text.

Dante's *Inferno.*

"Required reading," I tell him.

"It's a shame they do that," he says, flipping through the unread pages. There's a reverence in the way he handles it, his eyes skimming the words as if he knows them all by heart. "Requirement ruins even the best of books."

I ask him if he's read it, and he says he has, and I admit I haven't, and he smiles and tells me that books like this are meant to be heard.

"I'll prove it to you," he says, flashing me a crooked smile. "You clean, I'll read."

And he does. That first day, and for the rest of the summer. And I remember every word.


When the bell rings again, I've aced a pop quiz—the other students didn't even have the decency to look annoyed when Ms. Wellson announced it—and gone a whole class period without a nightmare, thanks to Cash and his coffee. I expect to find him waiting for me in the hall, but there's no sign of him. (I'm surprised to feel a small pang of disappointment as I survey the stream of students in black and green, silver and gold, and come up empty.) The silvers and golds, however, all seem to be heading in the same direction, and since I know from the brochure that juniors and seniors all have Wellness—which as far as I can tell is just a pretentious way of saying *gym*—together before lunch, I decide to follow the current.

It leads out and across the lawn, beyond the ring of buildings to another majestic structure, this one all ancient stone and gothic accents. I finally catch sight of one of the sculptures Cash mentioned, a stone hawk perched on the mantel over the doors.

"The Hyde School hawk," he says, appearing beside me out of nowhere, and a little out of breath. "It's our mascot. Said to represent insight, initiative, and ingenuity."

A cluster of junior girls are on the path several feet ahead of us; as Cash talks, one of them looks back and rolls her eyes. "Cassius

Arthur Graham, I keep telling you, you can't woo girls with school facts. Hyde history is never going to be a turn-on."

I feel my face go warm, but Cash doesn't color at all, only smiles broadly. "It may surprise you, Safia, but not *all* of us open our mouths with the sole intention of getting into someone's pants."

Her friends laugh, but the girl's eyes narrow with the kind of irritation usually reserved for exes and younger siblings. Judging by her features—she has the same dark hair as Cash, hers pulled back into a ponytail, and the same gold eyes—I'm guessing she's the latter. Cash's comment seems to have hit a nerve, because Safia links her arm through her friend's, shoots back a short string of nasty words, and hurries into the Wellness Center. Cash shrugs, unfazed.

"Sister," he confirms as we pass through the doors. "*Anyway*, sorry I was late. Mr. Kerry went off on one of his tangents—be glad you've got a year before you're subjected to him—and kept us after. Have I sacrificed my knighthood? Or did my valiant display in the face of fire-breathing dragons just now win me some credit?"

"I think you can keep your shield."

"What a relief," he says, nodding toward his sister as her ponytail vanishes into the locker room. "Because I think I'll need it later."


By the time I find my locker, preassigned and prestocked with workout shorts and a T-shirt—I cringe at the sight of short sleeves, thankful I'm largely bruise-free (if not scar-free) at the moment— I've knocked into three different girls by accident and managed to avoid several dozen others. School is like a minefield: so many people, so little personal space. Locker rooms are even worse, but I make it through with only a dull headache.

I watch the other girls peel off their necklaces and rings—what little jewelry Hyde allows—and stash them in their lockers before getting changed. I'm not about to relinquish my ring, but I fumble with the key around my neck, knowing it will draw more attention. If someone calls me out on the necklace, they're bound to demand the rest of my jewelry comes off, too. I slide the key over my head and set it on the shelf, feeling too light without it.

I'm just tugging on my workout shirt when I hear someone shout, "Come on, Saf!"

"I'll be right there," comes a now-recognizable voice. I look over to see Safia lacing up her sneakers at the end of the bench. She doesn't look up, but there's no one else around, so I know she's talking to me when she speaks.

"You know it's his job, right?" she asks, cinching her shoes.

"Excuse me?"

She straightens, tightening her ponytail before leveling her gaze on me. "My brother is a school ambassador. Showing you around, making you feel welcome—it's just another one of his duties. A *job*. I thought you should know."

She wants it to sting, and it does. But hell if I'll give her the benefit of letting it show.

"Well, that's a relief," I say brightly. "He's been so clingy, I was starting to think I'd led him on." I shut my locker firmly and stride past her. "Thanks," I add, patting her shoulder as I go. (It's worth the sound of ripping metal in my head to feel her tense beneath my touch.) "I feel *so* much better now."


The outside of Hyde's Wellness Center may sport the same old stone-and-moss facade as the rest of campus, but beyond the locker rooms—which act as gatekeepers to the gym—the inside is all whitewashed wood and glass and steel. There are smaller rooms branching off to one side and a pool branching off to the other, but the main training room is a massive square. It's subdivided into quadrants by black stripes on the floor and ringed by a track. I can't help but brighten a little at the sight of the glittering equipment. It's a pretty big step up from my makeshift gym on the Coronado roof.

I hug the perimeter, taking in the scene. A group is playing volleyball, another jogging around the track. Half a dozen students are breaking into fencing bouts; Safia stands with them, fastening her glove and flexing her sword. I've never fenced before, but I'm half tempted to try, just for the chance to hit her. I smile and take a few steps toward her when a shout goes up from the far side of the room.

On a raised platform near the edge of the massive center, two students are sparring.

They're standing in a kind of boxing ring minus the rope—both seniors, judging by the gold stripes that mark their gym clothes where the fabric peeks out from behind the pads. The gold is all I can see, since the rest of them is buried beneath padding; even their faces are masked by the soft helmets. A handful of students—I can just make out Cash among them, a fencing mask tucked under his arm—and a burly middle-aged teacher stand around, watching as the two boys bounce on their toes, punching, kicking, and blocking. The shorter of the two seems to be working a lot harder.

The taller one moves with fluid grace, easily avoiding most of the jabs. And then, between one blink and the next, he acts instead of reacts, thrusting one foot forward and low before planting his shoe at the last moment, turning on it, and delivering a round-house kick to the other boy's head.

29

The boy ends up on his back, dazed but unhurt. I doubt anyone else noticed his opponent slowing his motion just before his foot connected, easing the blow. The teacher sounds a whistle, the students applaud, and the victor helps the defeated to his feet. He gives the shorter boy a quick pat on the back before the loser hops down from the platform.

I've managed to make my way across the fitness hall while watching the bout, and I've just reached the edge of the group of spectators when the victor gives a theatrical bow, clearly relishing the attention.

Then he tugs his helmet off, and I find myself looking up at Wesley Ayers.

# FOUR

WESLEY AYERS is the stranger in the halls of the Coronado.

He is the Keeper in the garden who shares my secret.

He is the boy who reads me books.

He is the one who teaches me how to touch.

And today, he is the guy on the stone bench, wearing a tux.

It's the end of summer, and we're sitting in the Coronado garden. I'm perched on one of the benches in workout pants and a long-sleeve shirt pushed up to the elbows, and Wesley is stretched out on the other in his best black and white. There's only an hour or two left until his father's wedding, but he's still here.

Something is eating at him, I can tell. Something has been since he showed up, and I stupidly assume it's just the fact that he hates his father's fiancée, or at least what she means for his family. But he doesn't offer any of his usual acerbic remarks, doesn't even acknowledge the wedding or the tux. He just slumps down onto his bench and starts reciting the last of my required reading as if it's any other day.

And then, somewhere between one line and the next, his voice trails off. I glance over, wondering if he's asleep, but his eyes are neither closed nor unfocused. They're leveled on me. I return the look.

"You okay there?" I ask.

A smile flickers across his face. "Just thinking."

He sets the book aside and pushes up from his bench, smoothing the front of his rumpled tux as he closes the gap between us.

"About what?" I ask, shifting to make room as he settles down beside me. He comes close, close enough to touch, his folded arm knocking against my shoulder, his knee against mine. I take a breath as his rock band sound washes over me, loud but familiar.

"About us."


At first, I barely recognize him.

Wesley's hazel eyes are free of the eyeliner I've seen him wear all summer; his hair is still black, but instead of standing up, it's stuck to his forehead with sweat; every bit of silver is missing from his ears. All his little quirks are stripped away, but he's got those proud shoulders and that crooked smile, and his whole face is lit up from the fight. Even without the bells and whistles, it is still undeniably Wesley Ayers. And now that I see him, I don't know how I didn't see him earlier.

Maybe because Wesley Ayers—*my* Wesley—is supposed to be on some beach, bonding with his family.

*My* Wesley wouldn't be here at this stuck-up school, wouldn't lie to me about going here, and certainly wouldn't look like he *belongs* here.

"Who's next?" he asks, eyes glittering.

"I am," I shout back.

The spectators—all boys—turn collectively, but my gaze

is leveled firmly on Wes. The corner of his mouth tilts up. Of course he's not surprised to see *me*. He's known for weeks where I was enrolled. He never said anything. No "Oh great, we can stick together." No "Don't worry, you won't be alone." Not even a "Well, what a coincidence." Why? Why didn't he tell me?

"Now, young lady, I don't think—" starts the burly gym teacher as I approach the platform and begin strapping on pads.

"I signed the waivers," I cut in, tugging on forearm guards, wondering if there even *are* waivers for this class. It seems like that kind of school.

"It's not about that," says the teacher. "This is hand-to-hand combat, and it's important to match the students in terms of——"

"How do you know we're not well matched?" I shoot back, cinching down a shin guard. "Unless you're assuming that because I'm a girl." I look the teacher in the eyes. "Are you assuming that, sir?" I don't wait for him to answer. I step up onto the platform, and he doesn't stop me, which is good enough.

"Give the guy hell!" shouts Cash as I pull the helmet on.

*Oh,* I think, *I will.*

"Hey, you," says Wesley as I meet him in the center of the platform.

"Hey, you," I mimic bitterly.

"I can explain—" he starts, but he's cut off by the sound of the whistle.

I kick forward hard and fast, catching Wesley high in the chest before the shrill metallic cry has even stopped. The crowd gives a gasp as he falls, hitting the floor for only a moment before rolling over and pulling himself to his feet. I attack with another kick, which he blocks. Out of the corner of my eye, I can see we're gaining a crowd. He throws a punch, which I dodge, followed by

33

an uppercut, which I don't. The wind rushes out of my lungs, but I don't let it stop me from grabbing his fist and his wrist—pain thrumming up my own—and turning fast, flipping him over my shoulder.

He should hit the mat flat on his back, but somehow he twists midair and lands in a crouch, elegant as a cat. In a blink he's up again and closing the gap between us. I arch back just in time to avoid a hit and recover fast enough to see an opening—left side, stomach—but I don't take it. It's been three weeks since Owen stabbed Wesley. Even though it doesn't show in his stance, I know it still hurts him. I've seen the laughs cut short by a wince, the ginger way he stands and sits.

My hesitation earns me a swift kick to the chest, and I've got just enough time to hook my foot behind his knee and wrap my hand around his chest plate before I go down, taking him with me. I hit the mat hard and brace myself for Wesley's weight to land on top of me; but his palms hit the floor before his body hits me, and he manages to catch himself.

He hovers inches over me, breathing hard. Then his mouth quirks into a crooked smile, a *familiar* smile, and he knocks his helmet playfully against mine.

"Miss me?"


**The garden is silent except for the sound of my pulse.**

**Wesley leans across the stone bench and brings his lips featherlight against my temple. Then against my cheekbone. Against my jaw. A trail of kisses that makes me suck in a short breath, because the only time Wesley has ever kissed me—truly kissed me—he did it to read my memories. That**

was an angry kiss, forceful and firm. But these kisses are different. These kisses are cautious, hopeful.

"Wes," I warn.

His forehead comes to rest against my shoulder. "You sound like thunderstorms and heavy rain, did you know that?" He lets out a soft, low laugh. "I never liked bad weather. Not until I met you."

His voice has its usual easy charm, but now it's also threaded through with longing.

"Say something, Mac."

Wesley's body rests against mine. The combat padding acts as a buffer, and for a moment all I hear are the sounds of his breathing and my heart. How strange. It's so . . . quiet. I've gotten used to the sound of Wesley's noise—learned to float in it instead of drowning—but even the relative quiet of the familiar can never match this. His body on mine. Simple as skin.

My pulse quickens, and I have to remind myself that I pushed him away. *I* pushed *him* away. Now, looking up through Wes's face mask into his eyes—his lashes darkened with sweat—I will myself to do it again.

"What are you doing here?" I hiss, trying to hide the hurt in my voice.

"This might not be the best time to—"

"Tell me."

He opens his mouth. "Mac—"

And then the whistle blows.

"All right, enough of that," calls the teacher. "Both of you, up."

Wesley closes his mouth but doesn't move. I realize my hand

is still hooked around his chest plate, holding him there. I let go quickly, and he winks before springing to his feet. He offers me his gloved hand, but I'm already standing. I tug my helmet off, smooth my hair, and scan the crowd of students that gathered while we fought.

They stare at me and seem . . . stunned. Confused. Impressed. But they *stare*. Great. More eyes.

"We'll talk later," says Wes under his breath. "Promise." Before I can reply, he's heading for the edge of the platform and tugging off his gear.

"Hey, wait," I call after him. He hops down, and I'm about to follow when the burly gym teacher bars my path.

"One of you has to stay on," he says as Wesley tosses his equipment into the pile. Cash slings an arm around his neck and says something I can't hear. It sends both of them into laughter. Who is this boy? He looks so much and nothing like my Wesley.

"Normally it's the winner," the teacher continues, "but truth be told, I'm not entirely sure who won that match."

I'm about to say that I don't want to stay on, but Wesley is already weaving through the crowd, and the next student, a stocky junior, is hoisting himself onto the platform. I don't want the teacher to think I'm beat after a single fight, so I sigh, readjust my helmet, and wait for the whistle as Wesley's form vanishes from sight.

Wesley lifts his forehead from my shoulder and shifts his eyes to meet mine. "Please, say something."

But what can I say? That when Wesley touches me like this, I think of the way Owen forced me back against the

Narrows wall, twisting my want into fear as he tightened his grip? That when I feel Wesley's lips and my heart flutters, I think of him kissing me in the Coronado hall, reading me, and then pulling sharply away, eyes full of betrayal? That when I think of what I feel for him, I see him bleeding to death on the roof—and the pain that comes with caring about him is enough to stop me cold?

What I say instead is this: "Life is messy right now, Wes."

"Life is always messy," he says, meeting my gaze. "It's supposed to be."

I sigh, trying to find the words. "Two months ago, I'd never met another Keeper. I didn't have someone in my life I could talk to, let alone trust. And maybe it's selfish, but I can't bear the thought of losing you now."

"You're not going to lose me, Mac."

"You walked away," I say softly.

His brow furrows. "What?"

"When you found out about Owen, you walked away. I know you don't remember it, and I'm not blaming you—I know it was my fault for lying—but watching you go . . . I've been alone in this for so long, and I've always managed because I've never had anyone. But having you and losing you . . . For the first time, I *felt* alone, Wes. Having something and losing it, it's so much crueler than never having had it."

Wesley looks down at his hands. "Does it make you wish we'd never met?"

"No. God, no. But what we have now is still new to me. The sharing, the trust. I'm not ready for more." *I'll just ruin it,* I think.

"I understand." His voice is soft, soothing. He plants a

light kiss on my shoulder, like a parting gift, and pulls away.

"It's all new to me, too, remember?" he says a few minutes later. "I'd never met another Keeper before you. And having you in my life is terrifying and addictive, and I'm not going to lie and tell you it doesn't make my heart race. It does." I wonder if he can feel my own pounding pulse through my noise as he tangles his fingers through mine. "But I'm here. No matter what happens with us, I'm here."

He lets go and slumps back into the corner of the bench. He doesn't pick up the book, just tilts his head back and stares up at the clouds. Silence settles over us, heavier than usual.

"Are we good, Wes?" I ask.

"Yeah," he says, flashing a smile that's almost strong enough to hide the lie. "We're good."

By the time I finish showering, the locker room is mercifully empty, no prying eyes to watch as I loop the key back over my head, tucking it under my collar. My chest loosens as soon as the weight settles there. It feels wrong to be without it, even though this key isn't really mine.

I'm tugging on my polo when I feel the scratch of letters like a pin through my shirt pocket. I dig my list out to find a name:

*Harker Blane. 13.*

But I'm nowhere near my territory—I don't even know whose territory Hyde School falls in, or where the nearest Narrows door is hidden, and even if I could find it, my key wouldn't work, since

I'm not authorized to use it here—and I've got half a day of school to go, so Harker will have to sit tight. I don't like to make Histories wait; the longer they do, the more they suffer, and the more dangerous they get. I will Harker to hold on and hope he doesn't start to slip.

My stomach growls as I hoist my bag onto my shoulder and set out to find lunch.

Instead I find Wesley. At least, the newest version of him.

He's sitting cross-legged on a stone bench halfway to the dining hall with a book in his lap. He looks like a stranger. He's missing the black polish that usually graces his nails, his hair is swept neatly back, and he looks . . . *elegant* in his uniform, all black but for the gold thread tracing the edges.

I see him, but he doesn't see me—not at first—and I can't help but stare. Only his silver ring and the faint outline of his key beneath his polo mark him as the same guy I met this summer. It's like he's wearing a disguise, only it fits so well that I wonder if my Wesley—the one with spiked hair and lined eyes and that constant, mischievous smile—was the act. My stomach twists at the thought.

And then his eyes drift up from the book and settle on me, and something in him shifts again, and suddenly I see both of them at once: the affluent student and the edgy boy who likes to fight and fits his rock band noise so well. He's still under there somewhere, my Wes, but I can't help but wonder as he hops down from the sculpture and straightens, waiting for me to reach him: how many faces does Wesley Ayers have?

"I was hoping you'd come this way," he says, putting the book away and slinging his bag onto his shoulder.

"I don't know any of the other ways."

"Come on," he says, tipping his head down the path. "I'll show you."

We start walking toward the dining hall, but then we reach a split. Even though I can see the highly trafficked main building rising on our right, Wes veers left down a narrow, vacant path. Despite my rumbling stomach, I follow. I can't stop looking at him, focusing and unfocusing my eyes to find both versions.

"Go ahead." He keeps his eyes on the path ahead. "Say it."

I swallow. "You look different."

He shrugs. "Hyde has a dress code. They discourage eccentricity, which is unfortunate since, as we both know, I'm quite a fan." He looks at me then, as intensely as I'm looking at him. "You look tired, Mac. Are you sleeping?"

I shrug. I don't want to talk about it.

I mentioned my nightmares a while back, but when they didn't go away I decided to stop talking about them. It's bad enough having my parents coat me with their worry. The last thing I need is someone who knows the truth pitying me. And maybe Wes would have bad dreams, too, if he could remember that day; but he has a twenty-four-hour stretch of black in his mind and only my account and a scar from Owen's knife to go on. I envy him until I remember that I wanted to remember. I chose.

"Is there anything I can do to help or—"

"How long have you been back?" I cut in. "Or did you even go away?"

His brow furrows. "I got in last night. Haven't even had a chance to unpack, let alone come by and check on you. Or Jill. You been keeping an eye on the brat for me?"

I ignore his deflection. "Why didn't you tell me you went to school here?"

He shoves his hands in his pockets and shrugs. "At first it was just a reflex. I didn't know how to handle the fact that you were going to cross more than one of my paths, so I kept it to myself."

"I get that, Wes, I do." The Archive teaches us to break our lives into pieces and to keep those pieces secret, separate. "But what about later?" I ask, the words barely a whisper. "Is it because of what happened in the garden?"

"No," he says firmly. "It doesn't have anything to do with that."

"Then why?" I snap. "You spent the last few weeks reading me books you already knew because you read them here last year. You watched me stress out about this place, and you never spoke up."

His mouth twitches playfully. "Would you believe me if I said I just wanted to surprise you?"

I give him a long, hard look. "Well, you succeeded. But I have a hard time believing you lied to me for weeks just to see the look on my face—"

"I didn't lie," he says shortly. "You never asked me where I went."

The words hit like a dull punch. I didn't ask that specific question, he's right. But only because Wesley never wants to talk about his life. It's not that I don't want to be a part of his; I've just grown used to him being a part of *mine*.

"I told myself," continues Wes, "that if you asked, I'd tell you. But you didn't. You made an assumption, and I didn't correct you."

"Why not?"

He pulls his hand from his pocket and runs it through his hair. It's so strange to see it move through his fingers—soft, black, ungelled. I want to touch it myself, but I stifle the urge.

"I don't know," he continues. "Maybe I thought if you knew I went here, you'd think differently of me."

"But why would I judge you for going here?" I ask, gesturing down to my uniform. "I go here, too."

"Yeah, but you hate it," he snaps, coming to a stop. "You don't even know this place and you hate it. You've spent weeks dreading it, mocking it. . . ." I cringe, regretting the time I decided to don a posh accent and do a dramatic reading of a few key passages from the handbook. "But I grew up here. I didn't choose it, and I can't help it, but I did. And I was afraid you'd judge *me* if you knew." He laughs nervously, his eyes focused on the path instead. "Big surprise, Mac, I care what you think of me."

I feel the heat spreading across my face as he adds, "But I'm sorry. I knew you were stressed about Hyde, and I could have made it better and I didn't. I should have told you."

And he should have. But I think of all the times I kept things from Wes in the beginning, either out of habit or fear, and how it took him nearly dying and the Archive stealing his memories for me to finally tell him the truth. I feel my anger diminishing.

"So you have a preppy schoolboy alter ego," I say. "Anything else you want to tell me?"

The relief that sweeps across his face is obvious—relief that we're okay—but he doesn't miss a beat. "I really hate eggplant."

"Seriously?" I ask.

"Seriously," he replies, bouncing a little on his toes. "But I also hate explaining that it's because of the name and the fact that I grew up thinking it was a plant made of eggs, so instead I just tell people I'm allergic."

I laugh, and his smile broadens—and just like that, my Wesley is back. Doling out jokes and crooked grins, eyes glittering even without the makeup.

We start off again down the path.

"I'm happy you're here," I say under my breath, but he doesn't seem to hear me. I raise my voice, but instead of repeating myself, I simply ask, "Where are we going?"

He glances back and quirks a brow. "Isn't it obvious?" he asks. "I'm leading you astray."

# FIVE

A DOZEN STRIDES LATER, the tree-lined path dead-ends at a stone courtyard. It's raised a few steps off the ground, each of its four corners marked by a pillar. Three students are lounging on the platform, and in the very center of it stands a statue of a man in a hooded cloak.

"It's the only human sculpture on campus," explains Wesley, "so it's probably meant to be Saint Francis, the patron saint of animals. But everyone calls him the Alchemist."

I can see why. Standing in his shrouds, the statue looks more like a druid than a priest. His elbows are tucked in and his palms are turned up, his head bowed as if focusing on a spell. The mystique is only slightly diminished by the fact that his stone hands are currently holding aloft a pizza box.

"This," says Wes, gesturing to the platform, "is the Court."

The students look up at the sound of Wesley's voice. One of them I've already met. Cash is sitting with his legs stretched out on the stairs.

"Mackenzie Bishop," he calls as we make our way up to the platform. "I will never again make the mistake of calling you a damsel."

Wesley frowns a little. "You two have met?"

"I tried to save her," says Cash. "Turned out she didn't need my help."

Wesley glances my way and winks. "I think Mac can take care of herself."

Cash's smile is surprisingly tight. "You seem awfully friendly toward a girl who just kicked your ass. I take it you know each other?"

"We met over the summer," Wes answers, climbing the steps. "While you and Saf were off boating in—where was it, Spain? Portugal? I can never keep the Graham family excursions straight."

It's brilliant, watching Wesley work other people, twisting the conversation back toward them. Away from himself.

"Don't be bitter," says Cash. "You know you've got an open invitation."

Wesley makes a noncommittal sound. "I don't like boats," he says, retrieving a slice of pizza from the statue's outstretched arms, nodding for me to join him.

"The *Saint-Marie*," says Cash with a flourish, "isn't just a *boat*."

"So sorry," says Wes, mimicking the flourish. "I don't like *yachts*."

I can't tell if they're joking.

"I see you've already begun defacing our poor Alchemist again," adds Wes, waving the pizza slice at the statue.

"Just be glad Safia hasn't *played dress-up* with him," says a girl's voice, and my attention shifts to a pair of students sitting on the platform steps: a junior boy sitting cross-legged, and a redheaded senior with her head in his lap.

"Very true," says Cash as the girl shifts up onto one elbow and looks at me.

"You've brought a stray," she says, but there's no malice in her voice, and her smile quirks in a teasing way.

45

"She's not a stray, Amber," says the boy she's been using as a pillow. "She's a junior."

He looks up at me then, and my stomach drops. There's a silver stripe across his uniform, but he looks like he can't be more than fifteen. He's small and slim, dark hair curling across his forehead, and between the pair of black-framed glasses perched on his nose and the notes scribbled on the backs of his hands, he looks so much like my brother that it hurts. If Ben had lived—if he had been given five more birthdays—he might have looked just like this.

He looks away and I blink, and the resemblance thins to nearly nothing. Still, it leaves me shaken as I head up the steps and join Wesley by the statue. He grabs a soda from the Alchemist's feet and gestures toward the other students.

"So you've met Cassius," he says.

"Dear god, please don't call me that," says Cash.

"That's Gavin with the glasses," continues Wes, "and Amber is in his lap."

"Amber Kinney," she corrects. "There are two gold Ambers at Hyde and one silver, and it's not a name that lends itself to shortened forms, trust me, so if you hear someone use the name Kinney—which I hate, by the way, never do it—that's me."

I take a soda. "I'm Mackenzie Bishop. New student."

"Of course you are," says Gavin, and I blush until he adds, "Because it's a small school and we know everybody else."

"Yeah, well, you can call me Mackenzie or Mac, if you want. Just not Kenzie." Kenzie was Da's word; it sounds wrong on everyone else's lips. "Or M." M was the name I'd dreamt of being called for years. M was the version of me that didn't hunt Histories or read memories. M was the person I could have been if I hadn't joined the Archive. And M was ruined by Owen when he whispered it in my ear like a promise, right before he tried to kill me.

"Well, Mackenzie," says Gavin, emphasizing each of the three syllables evenly, just the way Ben did, "welcome to Hyde."


"Mackenzie, will you help me?"

We're sitting at the table, Ben and I, while Mom hums in the background, making dinner. I'm twirling my silver ring and reading a passage for my freshman English class, and Ben's trying to do his fourth-grade math, but it's not his best subject.

"Mackenzie . . . ?"

I've always loved the way Ben says my name.

He was never one of those kids who couldn't speak, who skipped syllables and squeezed words down into sounds. By the time he was four, he prided himself on pronouncing everything. Mom was never *Mama*, Dad was never *Daddy*, Da was never *Da* but *Da Antony*, and I was never *Muh-ken-zee* or *Mc-kin-zee*, and certainly not *Kenzie*, but always *Mah-Ken-Zee*, the three beats set like stones in order.

"Will you show me how to do this problem?"

At nine, even his questions are precise. He has this obsession with being a grown-up; not just wearing one of Dad's ties or holding his knife and fork like Mom, but putting on airs, mimicking posture and attitude and articulation. He has the makings of a Keeper, really. Da didn't live long enough to see him taking shape, but I can see it.

I know I already took Da's spot, but I often wonder if the Archive could make a place for Ben, too.

It's a selfish wish, I know. Some might even call it a

wrong wish. I should want to protect him from everything, including—no, *especially*—the Archive. But as I sit there, turning my silver ring and watching Ben work, I think I might give anything to have him beside me.

I get why Da did it. Why he chose me. I get why everyone chooses someone. It's not just so that someone takes their place. It's so that—at least for a little while—they don't have to be alone. Alone with what they do and who they are. Alone with all those secrets.

It is selfish and it is wrong and it is human, and as I sit there, watching Ben work, I think that I would do it. I would choose him. I would take my little brother with me. If they'd let me.

Of course, I never find out.


In truth, Gavin looks very little like Ben. I know because I've been staring at him—and then trying not to stare—for the last fifteen minutes. Luckily, between a long shower and the walk with Wes, fifteen minutes is all I have before the bell rings.

It turns out that even though we're a grade apart, Amber and I have Physiology together. She tells me on the way how it's all part of her pre-premed plan, how her grandmother was some incredible war surgeon behind the blood-slicked camp curtains, and how she has steady hands just like her. Between the Court and the science hall—marked by a statue of a snake—I discover my favorite thing about Amber Kinney.

She likes to talk.

She likes to talk even more than Lyndsey, and as far as I can tell it's not out of a need to fill the quiet so much as a simple lack of filter between her brain and mouth—which is fine with me, because she's surprisingly interesting. She tells me random facts about the school, and then about each member of the Court: Gavin won't eat anything green and has a brother who sleepwalks; Cash speaks four languages and tears up at sappy commercials; Safia— because apparently Amber is actually *friends* with her—used to be so shy she barely spoke, and still hasn't quite figured out how to speak *nicely*; Wesley is a sarcastic flirt and allergic to eggplant and . . .

Amber trails off. "But you already know Wesley," she says.

"Not as well as you'd think," I say carefully.

Amber smiles. "Join the club. I've known Wes for *years*, and there are times I still don't feel like I *know* him. But I think he likes it that way—an air of mystery—so we all let him have his secrets."

I wish everybody felt the way Amber Kinney does about secrets. My life would be a lot easier.

"So," I say, "Wesley's a flirt?"

Amber rolls her eyes and holds the door open for me. "Let's just say that air of mystery tends to work in his favor." I feel the heat creeping into my face as she glances my way. "Don't tell me you've already fallen for it."

I chuckle. "Hardly." And that much is true. After all, it's not Wesley's *secrets* that make my pulse climb. It's the fact that we have the same ones. Or, at least, most of the same ones. I can't help but wonder, after the shock of seeing him here, what else I don't know.

His voice echoes in my head: *You didn't ask.*

We reach the Physiology room and snag two seats side by side as the bell rings. A surprisingly young woman named Ms. Hill walks us through our syllabus, and I spend the next few minutes flipping through the textbook, trying to figure out which bones

Owen snapped inside my wrist. It's funny—looking at the maps of bone and muscle and nerve, the diagrams of body flexion and movement and potential—how much of this I've learned already. More through trial and error and application than assigned reading, but it's still nice to find that some of the knowledge translates. I run my fingertips lightly over the illustrated fingers on the page.

I make it through the lecture, and Amber points me in the direction of my last class: Government. It's taught by Mr. Lowell, a man in his fifties with a mop of graying curls and a soft, even voice. I'm prepared to have to stab myself with my pen to stay awake, but then he starts talking.

"Everything that rises will fall," he says. "Empires, societies, governments. None of them lasts forever. Why? Because even though they are the products of change, they become resistant *to* change. The longer a society survives, the more it clings to its power, and the more it resists progress. The more it resists progress—resists *change*—the more its citizens demand it. In response, the society tightens its grip, desperate to maintain control. It's afraid of losing its hold."

I stiffen in my seat.

*Do you know why the Archive has so many rules, Miss Bishop?* Owen asked me on the roof that day. *It's because they're afraid of us. Terrified.*

"Societies are afraid of their citizens," echoes Mr. Lowell. "The more a society tightens its grip, the more the people fight that grip." He draws a circle in the air with his index finger, going around and around, and each time he does, the circle gets smaller. "Tighter and tighter, and the resistance grows and grows until it spills over into action. That action takes one of two forms."

He writes two words on the board: *REVOLUTION* and *REFORM*.

"The first segment of this class," says Mr. Lowell, "will be dedicated to the language of revolution; the second segment will be dedicated to the language of reform." He erases the word REFORM from the board.

"You've all heard the language of revolution. The rhetoric. For instance, a government can be called corrupt." He writes the word corrupt on the board. "Give me some other words."

"The government is rotten," says a girl at the front of the class.

"The company is abusing power," says a boy.

"The system is broken," adds another.

"Very good, very good," says Mr. Lowell. "Keep going."

I cringe as Owen's voice echoes in my head. The Archive is a prison.

"A prison," I say, my voice carrying over the others before I even realize I've spoken out loud. The room quiets as the teacher considers me. Finally he nods.

"Rhetoric of imprisonment and, conversely, the call for freedom. One of the most classic examples of revolutionary thought. Well done, Miss . . ."

"Bishop."

He nods again and turns his attention back to the class. "Anyone else?"

By the time school lets out, my edges are starting to fray.

The morning coffee and lunch soda can't make up for the days—weeks, really—without sleep. And having Owen in my head for most of last period hasn't helped my nerves. A shaky yawn escapes as I push open the outer doors of the history hall and step into the afternoon sun, abandoning the crowded path for a secluded patch of grass where I can stop and soak up the light and clear my head. I free my Keeper list from my shirt pocket and am relieved to see that there's still only one name on the page.

"Who's Harker?" asks Cash over my shoulder. I jump a little at the sound of his voice, then unfold the paper slowly, careful to seem unconcerned.

"Just a neighbor," I say, tucking the paper back into my pocket. "I promised to pick up some info on the school for him. He's thinking about it for next year." The lie is easy, effortless, and I try not to relish it.

"Ah, well, we can swing by the office on the way to the parking lot." He sets off down the path.

"You really don't have to escort me," I say, following. "I'm sure I can find my way."

"I have no doubt, but I'd still like—"

"Look," I cut him off. "I know you're just doing your job."

He frowns, but doesn't slow his pace. "Saf tell you that?" I shrug. "Well, yes, okay. It's my job, but I chose it. And it's not like I was assigned to you. I could be imposing my assistance on any of the unsuspecting *freshman*. I'd rather be accompanying you." He chews his lip and squints up toward the summer sun before he continues. "If you'll let me."

"All right," I agree with a teasing smile. "But just to spare those other unsuspecting students."

He laughs lightly and waves to someone across the grass.

"So," I say, "Cassius? That's quite a name."

"Cassius Arthur Graham. A mouthful, isn't it? That's what you get when your mother's an Italian diplomat and your father's a British linguist." The ivy-coated stone back of the main building comes into sight. "But it's not nearly as bad as Wesley's."

"What do you mean?" I ask.

Cash gives me a look, like I should know. Then, when it's obvious I don't, he starts to backtrack.

"Nothing. I forgot you two haven't known each other that long."

My steps slow on the path. "What are you talking about?"

"Well, it's just . . . Wesley's name isn't really Wesley. That's his middle name."

I frown. "Then what's his first name?"

Cash shakes his head. "Can't say."

"That bad?"

"*He* thinks so."

"Come on, I've got to have *some* ammunition."

"No way, he'd kill me."

I laugh and let it drop as we reach the admin building's doors. "You guys seem close," I say as he holds them open for me.

"We are," says Cash with a kind of simple certainty that makes my stomach hurt.

With Wes haunting the Coronado halls all summer, I just assumed that he lived the way I did: at a distance. But he has a *life*. Friends. Good friends. I have Lyndsey, but we're close because she doesn't make me lie. She never asks questions. But I should have asked Wes. I should have wondered.

"We grew up together," explains Cash as we make our way toward the glass lobby. "Met him at Hartford. That's the K-through-eight that leads into Hyde. Saf and I showed up in the fourth grade—third for her—and Wes just kind of took us in. When things started going south with his parents a few years back, we tried to return the favor. He's not very good at taking help, though."

I nod. "He always bounces it back."

"Exactly," he says, sounding genuinely frustrated. "But then his mom left and things went from bad to worse."

"What happened?" I press.

The question jars him, and he seems to realize he shouldn't be sharing this much. He hesitates, then says, "He went to stay with his aunt Joan."

"Great-aunt," I correct absently.

"He told you about her?"

"A little," I say. Joan was the woman who passed her key and her job on to Wesley. The one the Archive cut full of holes when she retired just to make sure its secrets were safe. The fact that I've heard of Joan seems to satisfy something in Cash, and his reluctance dissolves.

"Yeah, well, he was supposed to go stay with her for the summer," he says, "to get away from the divorce—it was brutal—but Hyde started back up in the fall, and he wasn't here. Our whole sophomore year, it was like he didn't exist. You have to understand—he didn't call, didn't write. There was just this void." Cash shakes his head. "He's loud in that way you don't really notice till he's gone. Anyway, sophomore year comes and goes without him. And then summer break comes and goes without him. And finally junior year comes around, and there he is at lunch, leaning up against the Alchemist like he never left."

"Was he different?" I ask as we reach the office door at the mouth of the glass lobby. That was the year he became a Keeper.

Cash stops with his fingers on the handle. "Apart from the black eye I gave him? Not really. If anything, he seemed . . . *happier*. And

I was just glad to have him back, so I didn't pry. Wait here, I'll grab you some prospective student pamphlets."

He vanishes into the office, and I glance absently around the hall. It's covered in photographs—though *covered* suggests chaos, and these are all immaculately hung, each frame perfectly level and perfectly equidistant from the others. Each one has a small, elegant date etched into the top. In every picture, a group of students stands, shoulders touching, in several even rows. Senior classes, judging by the gold stripes in the more recent color photos. The years count backward along both walls, with the most recent years here by the mouth of the lobby and the older ones trailing away down the hall. Like most of the posh private schools, Hyde hasn't always been coed. As I backtrack through the years, the girls vanish from the group photos, appearing in their own set and then disappearing altogether, along with the reds and blues and golds, leaving only boys in black and white. I let my eyes wander the walls, not knowing what I'm looking for until I find it. When I do, everything in me tenses.

He could have gone to any of the schools in the city, but he didn't. He went here.

In the frame marked *1952*, several dozen boys stand in rigid rows, stern, well-groomed, elegant. And there, one row down and several students in, is Owen Chris Clarke.

His silver-blond hair registers as white in the colorless photo, and that, plus the shocking paleness of his eyes, makes him look like a flare of light in the wash of black uniforms. The ghost of a smile brushes his lips, like he knows a secret. And maybe he does. This would have been before—before he graduated, before he was made Crew, before Regina was murdered, before he brought her back, before he killed the Coronado residents and jumped from

55

the roof. But at the time of the photo, he was already a Keeper. It shows in his eyes, in his taunting smile, and in the hint of a ring on the hand resting on another student's shoulder . . .

"You ready?"

I pull away from the photograph to find Cash standing there, holding a short stack of pamphlets.

"Yeah," I say, my voice a little shakier than I'd like, as I cast another glance at the photo.

*You and I are not so different.*

I frown. So what if Owen went here? He's gone. This is nothing more than a faded photograph, a glimpse of the past—a perfectly reasonable place for a dead boy to be.

"Let's go," I say as I take the papers.

Cash walks me out.

"Where's your car?" he asks, surveying the parking lot, which has already emptied out quite a bit.

I cross to the bike rack and give Dante a sweeping gesture. "My ride."

He blushes. "I didn't mean to assume—"

I wave him off. "It's like a convertible, really. Wind through my hair. Leather seats . . . well, seat." I dig my workout pants out of my bag and tug them on under my skirt.

He smiles, gold eyes drifting down to the sidewalk. "Maybe we could do this again tomorrow."

"You mean school?" I ask, unlocking the bike and swinging my leg over. "I think that's the idea. Doesn't work very well if you only go once." I try to say it straight-faced, but the smile slips through.

Cash breaks into a warm laugh as he turns to go. "Welcome to Hyde, Mackenzie Bishop."

His easy joy is contagious, and I feel myself still grinning as I watch him retreat through the gates. Then I look back out over the parking lot and all the warmth goes cold.

The man from this morning, the one with gold hair and gold skin, is leaning back against a tree at the edge of the lot, sipping coffee out of a to-go cup, and he's looking at me. This time he doesn't even try to hide it. The sight of him is like a brick through a glass window, shattering the mundane. It's a reminder that life couldn't be further from normal. Normal is a thing I might dream about, if I weren't too busy having nightmares.

There's one thing scarier than the fact I'm being followed. And that's *who* is following me. Because there's only one possible answer: the Archive. The thought makes my blood run cold. I can't imagine it's a *good* thing, being tailed by Crew. And that's exactly what he is. What he has to be.

The way he sips his coffee and shifts his weight and his unguarded body language create an illusion of boredom that's dampened only by his gaze, which is sharp, alert. But that's not what gives him away. It's the confidence. A very specific and dangerous kind of confidence. The same kind Owen had.

The confidence exuded by someone who knows they can hurt you before you hurt them.

The golden man's eyes meet mine, and he smiles with half his mouth. He takes another sip of his coffee, and I take a step toward him just as a horn goes off in the parking lot. The sound steals my attention for a second, even less, but by the time I look back at the man, he's gone.

Great.

I wait a second to see if he'll reappear, but he doesn't, and I'm left with only a sinking feeling in my stomach and the nagging question: *why* is the Archive having me followed?

The worry eats at the last of my energy as I pedal home. By the time I get there, my vision is starting to blur from fatigue. When I dismount, the world rocks a little. I have to stand still a moment, wait for the dizziness to pass before I drag myself through the doors and up the stairs.

I want sleep.

I need sleep.

Instead, I go hunting.

# SIX

**I** STIFLE ANOTHER yawn as I step out of the stairwell and into the third floor hall, grateful that Harker's still the only name on my list. After stashing my skirt in my schoolbag and shoving that behind a table halfway down the hall, I straighten my ponytail in the mirror above the table and fetch the key out from under my collar. The transformation is complete: student to Keeper in under a minute.

Across from the mirror is a painting of the sea, and just beside that is a crack in the wall. A seam where the worlds don't quite line up. No one else sees it, but I do, and when I tug off my ring, the crack becomes clearer, the keyhole tucked into the fold. I slot my key, and the Narrows door blossoms like a stain, the faded wallpaper darkening as the frame presses against the surface. A thread of light carves the outline of the door, and I turn the key, hear the hollow click, and step through into the dark. I'm lifting my fingers to the nearest wall, about to read the surface for signs of Harker, when I think I hear it.

Humming.

My heart starts to race as I pull away from the wall and turn toward the noise, panic flooding through me. And then between one pulse—one step—and the next, the world disappears.

Everything goes away.

Goes black.

And then, just as suddenly, it comes back— *I* come back—and the humming is gone and my head is killing me and I'm running. Sprinting. *Chasing.* A boy sprints several yards ahead of me.

"Harker, stop!" The words tumble out before I even realize they're mine. "There's nowhere to run!" I add, which isn't strictly true, since we're both covering plenty of ground. There's just nowhere to run *to*.

My lungs are burning and my legs ache and I don't have enough sleep in my bones for this, but adrenaline fills in the place where sleep should be as the Narrows echo with the sounds of the hunt. Heavy breath and pumping limbs and shoes hitting hard against the concrete, his as he flees, mine as I chase.

And I'm catching up.

The kid loses a stride when he looks back, and then another when he takes a corner too fast and slides into the wall. Harker springs off, keeps going. I cut the corner sharp, too, shoes skidding a fraction on the slick ground of the Narrows, but I know these halls, these walls, these floors, and I'm off again, closing the gap.

He's between one sprinting step and the next when my hand finally tangles in his collar, catching him off balance. I pull hard, and Harker goes sprawling backward to the floor, a few feet from the nearest Returns door, marked by a white chalk circle shaded in. He starts to scramble away, but I haul him to his feet and pin him back against the wall as I get my key into the lock and turn. The door opens, showering us both in glaring white light.

I get a good look at his eyes as they go wide—the pupils wavering, about to slip—right before I shove him into the glaring white, but it's not until after he's through the door, the light is gone, and I'm left alone in the dark with my slamming pulse that I process the look he gave me and realize what it was.

*Fear.*

Not of the Narrows or of the glaring Returns, but of *me.*

It's like being doused with cold water, that thought, and it leaves me feeling breathless and dizzy. I bring a hand up to the wall for balance. A shallow pain draws my eyes to my arm, and for the first time I see the scratches there, raked across my skin, and a sick feeling spreads through me.

When did this happen?

When did Harker fight back?

I rack my brain, trying to rewind my own mind, trying to remember when he scratched me, or what made him run in the first place, or how we met, and panic coils around me as I realize that I *can't.*

I remember stepping through the door and into the Narrows. I remember the sound of humming, and then . . . nothing. Nothing until halfway through the chase. The time between is just *missing.* I squeeze my eyes shut, scrambling for the memories and finding only a blur. I sink down to the floor and rest my forehead against my knees, forcing air into my lungs.

One of Da's lessons plays in my head, his voice low and steady and smooth: *Keep your head on, Kenzie. Can't think straight when you're all worked up. Histories panic. Look at all the good it does them.*

I take another breath and try to calm down. What was I doing? I was reading the walls . . . I was about to read the walls when I heard the humming, and then . . . and then I lick my lips and taste blood, and just like that, the memories rush back.

*Someone was humming.*

*Just like Owen used to do. My heart started to race as I followed the melody through the halls. It sounded so much like humming at first, but then it didn't—the Narrows does distort things—growing louder and*

61

*harsher until it wasn't anything like humming, wasn't music at all, but a hard and steady* thud thud thud.

*Harker kicking a door halfway down the hall, so loud he didn't hear me coming until I was there behind him, head pounding, and then he spun and, before I could even lie my way into his good graces, caught me off guard with his fist.*

It comes back like still frames, glimpses in a strobe.

*My hand tangled in his shirt.*

*Shoving him back.*

*A mess of thrashing limbs.*

*His shoe coming up against my stomach.*

*His hands clawing his way free.*

*Both of us running.*

I feel sick with relief. The memory's shaky, but it's there.

As I pull the list from my pocket and watch Harker's name bleed off the page, one question claws its way through my spinning thoughts: why did I black out in the first place?

If I had to guess, I'd say sleep. Or rather, the lack of it.

This—blacking out, losing time, whatever it is—happened once before. A few days after Owen. Last time—which was the first time, and I'd hoped the *only* time—I hadn't been sleeping, either. I was so tired, I could barely see straight. One moment I was trying to talk down a History, a teenage girl, and the next I was alone in the hall and my knuckles were raw and her name was gone from my list. When I finally calmed down, the memories came back, blurry and stilted, but there. She'd already slipped, thought I was someone else. Called me M (probably Em, like Emily or Emma). That's all it had taken to make my hands shake and my heart race and my mind skip. A sliver of Owen.

I told myself then it wasn't a big deal. It only happened once—unlike the nightmares that came every night like clockwork— so I didn't tell Roland. I didn't want him to worry. Da used to say you had to see patterns, but not go looking for them, and I didn't want to make something out of nothing. But Da also used to say that one mistake was an accident, but two was a problem.

As I look down at the scratches on my arms, I know.

This is officially a problem.

I will myself to get back to my feet. I consider the door beside the one I just sent Harker through, the one marked with the hollow white circle I use to denote the Archive. I should tell Roland. And I will—later. Right now, I have to get home. Last time I lost a minute, maybe two, but now I can tell I've lost more than that. I dig my nails into my palms, hoping the sting will keep me awake as I head back for the numbered doors.

The key dangles from its cord around my wrist, and I swing it up into my grip and slide the teeth into the lock on the door that leads back to the third floor. It opens, the hall beyond nothing but shadow from this side, and my shoe is halfway through when I hear a familiar voice on the other side and jerk back sharply, heart hammering in my chest.

Stupid, stupid mistake.

The doorway isn't visible to normal people. If I'd passed through into the Coronado, I would have walked straight through the wall itself—at least it would have appeared that way—and into my mother.

"It's going well, I think. . . ." The Coronado may be lost from sight, but her voice reaches through the veiled space, muffled, yet audible. "Right, it takes time, I know."

I can hear her coming down the hall, nearing the Narrows door as she talks, the long pauses making it clear she's on the phone. And then her footsteps stop right in front of me. Maybe she's looking in the mirror across from the invisible door. I think of the schoolbag stashed behind the table under the mirror, and hope she hasn't discovered it.

"Oh, Mackenzie?"

I stiffen, until I realize she's answering the person on the line.

"I don't know, Colleen," she says.

I roll my eyes. Her therapist. Mom's been seeing Colleen since Ben died last year. I'd hoped the sessions would end with the move. Apparently, they haven't. Now I brace my hands on either side of the doorway and listen to one half of the conversation. I know I shouldn't leave the Narrows door open, but my list is clear and my curiosity is piqued.

"It hasn't come up," says Mom. "Yes, okay, I haven't *brought* it up. But she seemed better. Seems. Seemed. It's so hard to tell with her. I'm her mother. I should be able to tell, and I can't. I can tell something's wrong. I can tell she's wearing this mask, but I can't see past it." My chest tightens at the pain in her voice. "No. It's not drugs."

I clench my teeth against a curse. I hate Colleen. Colleen's the one who told Mom to throw out Ben's things. The one time we met face-to-face, she saw a scratch on my wrist from a pissed-off History and was convinced I did it to myself to *feel things*.

"I know the symptoms," says Mom, ticking off a list that pretty well sums up my current behavior—evasion, moodiness, troubled sleep, being withdrawn, inexplicable disappearances . . . though in my defense, I do my best to explain them. Just not using the truth. "But it's not. Yes, I'm sure." I'm glad she's sticking up for me, at

64

least on this front. "Okay," she says after a long pause, starting down the hall again. "I will. I promise." I listen to her trail off, wait for the jingling sound of her keys, the apartment door opening and closing, and then I sigh and step out into the hall.

The Narrows door dissolves behind me as I slide my ring back on. The skirt and the bag seem undisturbed behind the table, and in a few short steps I've transformed back into an ordinary Hyde School junior. My reflection stares back at me, unconvinced.

*I can tell something's wrong. I can tell she's wearing this mask, but I can't see past it.*

I practice my smile a few times, checking my mask to make sure it's free of cracks before I turn down the hall and head home.

That evening, I put on a show.

I picture Da clapping in his slow, lazy way as I tell Mom and Dad about my day, injecting as much enthusiasm into my voice as I can without tipping my parents from pleasant surprise to suspicion.

"Hyde's pretty incredible," I say.

Dad lights up. "I want to hear all about it."

So I tell him. I'm basically feeding the pamphlet propaganda back to him, line by line, but while I may be amping up the excitement, the sentiment isn't a total lie. I *did* enjoy it. And it feels good to tell something that even vaguely resembles the truth.

"And you'll never guess who goes there!" I say, stealing a carrot as Mom chops them.

"You can tell us during dinner," she says, shooing me away with a pile of placements and silverware. "Set the table first." But she smiles as she says it.

Dad clears some books from the table so I can set it and retreats to the couch to watch the news.

"Who's closing the coffee shop tonight?" I ask.

"Berk's got it."

Berk is Betty's husband, and Betty is Nix's caretaker. Nix is ancient and blind and lives up on the seventh floor and won't come down because he's wheelchair-bound and doesn't trust the rickety metal elevators.

Berk and Betty moved into one of the vacants on the sixth floor two weeks ago after Nix finally succeeded in lighting his scarf on fire with his cigarette. I was shocked—not about the fire, that was inevitable, but that they would move in for him, not being related in any way. But apparently Nix was like a father to Betty once, and now she's acting like a daughter. It's sweet, and it all worked out because Berk—who's a painter—was looking for a social fix, and Mom was looking for a hand at Bishop's. She can't pay him yet, but he doesn't seem to mind. He only asked to be able to hang his pieces in the coffee shop for sale.

"I'll take him down some dinner later," says Mom, setting aside a plate.

I'm carrying water glasses to the table when the headline on the TV catches my attention, and I look over Dad's shoulder at the screen. It's the same news story from early this morning, about the missing person. A room in disarray flashes across the screen, and I'm about to ask Dad to turn the volume up when Mom says, "Turn that off. Dinner's ready."

Dad obediently clicks the TV off, but my eyes linger on the blackened screen, holding the image of the room in my mind. It looked familiar. . . .

"Mackenzie," Mom warns, and I blink, losing the image as I turn to find my parents both already at the table. They look like they've been waiting.

I shake my head and manage a smile. "Sorry. Coming."

But sitting down turns out to be a bad idea.

The moment I do, the fatigue catches back up, and I spend most of dinner rambling about Hyde just to stay awake. As soon as the dishes are cleared, I retreat to my room in the name of homework, but I've barely gotten through a page of reading before my eyes unfocus, the words on the paper blurring together. I try standing, then I try pacing while holding my textbook, but my mind can't seem to grab hold of anything. I feel like my bones are made of lead.

My gaze wanders to the bed. All I can think of is how much I want to lie down . . .

The book slips through my fingers, hitting the ground with a soft thunk.

. . . how badly I want to sleep . . .

I reach the bed.

. . . how certain I am . . .

I tug back the covers.

. . . that when I do . . .

I sink into the sheets.

. . . I won't dream of anything.

# SEVEN

**T**HE ROOF IS full of monsters, and they are all alive.

They perch on stone claws and watch with stone eyes as Owen stalks me through the maze of bodies.

"Stop running, Miss Bishop," his voice echoes across the rooftop.

And just like that, the concrete floor crumbles beneath me and I plunge seven stories through the bones of the building to the Coronado lobby, hitting the floor so hard my bones sing. I roll onto my back and look up in time to see the gargoyles tumbling toward me. I throw my hands up, bracing for the weight of stone. It never comes. I blink and find myself in a cage made from the broken statues, a web of crossing arms and legs and wings. And standing in the middle is Owen, his knife dangling from his fingers.

"The Archive is a prison," he says calmly.

He comes toward me, and I scramble to my feet and back away until I'm pressed up against the stone bodies. Their limbs jerk to life and shoot forward, grabbing my arms and legs, snaking around my waist. Every time I struggle the limbs tighten, my bones cracking under their grip. I bite back a scream.

"But don't worry." Owen runs a hand over my head before tangling his fingers in my hair. "I will set you free."

He draws the flat side of the knife down my body, bringing

the tip to rest between my ribs. He puts just enough weight on the blade to slice through my shirt and nick my skin, and I squeeze my eyes shut, trying to get away, trying to wake up, but the hand tangled in my hair tightens.

"Open your eyes," he warns.

I drag them open and find his face inches from mine. "Why?" I growl. "So I can see the truth?"

His smile sharpens. "No," he says. "So I can watch the life go out of them."

And then he drives the knife forward into my chest.

I sit up in the dark, one hand clutching at my shirt, the other pressed over my mouth to stifle the cry that's already escaped. I know it's a dream, but it is so terrifyingly real. My whole body aches from the fall and the gargoyles' grip, and the place on my chest where the knife drove in burns with phantom pain.

My face is damp, and I can't tell if it's from sweat or tears or both. The clock says twelve forty-five, and I draw up my knees and rest my head against them, taking a few slow, steadying breaths.

A moment later, there is a knock on my door.

"Mackenzie," comes my father's quiet voice. I look up as the door opens and I can see his outline in the light spilling from my parents' bedroom into the hall behind him. He comes to sit on the edge of my bed, and I'm grateful to the dark for hiding whatever is written across my face right now.

"What's going on, hon?" he whispers.

"Nothing," I say. "Sorry if I woke you guys up. Just had a bad dream."

"Again?" he asks gently. We both know it's been happening too often.

"It's no big deal," I say, trying to keep my voice light.

Dad tugs his glasses from his face and cleans them on his T-shirt. "You know what your Da used to tell me about bad dreams?"

I know what Da used to tell *me*, but I doubt it's the same thing he told my father, so I shake my head.

"He used to tell me there were no bad dreams. Just dreams. That when we call them good or bad, we give importance to them. I know that doesn't make it better, Mac. I know it's easy to talk like that when you're awake. But the fact is, dreams catch us with our armor off."

Not trusting myself to speak, I nod.

"Do you want to . . . talk to someone about it?" He doesn't mean talk to him or talk to Mom. He means a therapist. Like *Colleen*. But I've got more than enough people trying to get inside my head right now.

"No. Really, I'm fine."

"You're sure?"

I nod again. "Trust me."

My heart sinks, because I can see in my father's eyes that he wants to, but doesn't. Da used to say that lies were easy, but trust was hard. Trust is like faith: it can turn people into believers, but every time it's lost, trust becomes harder and harder to win back. I've spent the last four and a half years—since I became a Keeper— trying to cling to my parents' trust, watching doubt replace it little by little. And doubt, Da warned, is like a current you have to swim against, one that saps your strength.

"Well, if you change your mind . . ." he says, sliding to his feet.

"I'll let you know," I say, watching him go.

He's right. I should talk to someone. But not Colleen.

I listen to the sound of his receding steps after he's closed the door, and to the murmur of my mother's voice when he returns to their room. I let the whole apartment go quiet and dark, and only when I'm sure that they're asleep do I get up, get dressed, and sneak out.

I step into the Archive, and I shiver.

My sleep hasn't been the only thing affected by Owen and Carmen's recent attack. The Archive has changed, too. It has always been marked by quiet, but where the lack of noise used to feel peaceful, now it feels coiled and tense. The silence is heavier, enforced by hushed voices and warning looks. The massive doors behind the antechamber's desk have been pinned back like butterfly wings, held open to make sure that the newly installed sentinels have full visibility and immediate access to the atrium and the network of halls beyond. The two figures are the most striking addition—and the most loathsome. Dressed in solemn black, they flank the entrance to the Archive. The sentinels are Histories, like everyone else who works within the Archive walls; but unlike the Librarians, they wear no gold keys and do not seem fully *awake*.

Roland told me that they've been implemented in every branch in his jurisdiction, though he himself had no say in the matter of their presence. The order for increased security came from over his head. I'm guessing that means it came from Agatha.

Agatha, the assessor, who I haven't *seen* again since the interrogation, but whose presence seems to haunt this place the way Owen's haunts me.

Roland wasn't happy about it. As far as I can tell, no one was. The Librarians are not used to feeling watched. Agatha can claim the sentinels are there in case of another Owen; the fact is, they're also there in case of another *Carmen*. It's one thing to be betrayed by a known traitor. It's another to be betrayed by someone you thought was a loyal servant.

The sentinels' eyes follow me as I step through into the antechamber.

I force myself not to look at them. I don't want them to see that they give me the creeps. Instead I focus on the desk and how relieved I am to see Lisa sitting there behind it with her black bob and her green horn-rimmed glasses. Lately it feels like a gamble every time I step through. Will I be met by Roland's calm gray eyes or Lisa's cautious smile, or will I be confronted with Patrick's disapproving glare? Or will Agatha herself be waiting?

But tonight, I'm lucky enough to have Lisa. Her head is bent forward over the Archive's ledger, and I can't help but wonder who she's writing *to*. The book that always sits on the desk holds a page for every Keeper and every Crew in the branch, the partner to the paper in my pocket, and its thickness is a strange reminder that even though I often feel alone, I'm not. I'm only one page in a thick old book.

Lisa stops writing and looks up long enough to see my tired eyes. The strain of the past few weeks shows in her eyes, too, the way they flick to the figures behind me before coming back to me. She gives me a nod and says only, "He's in the atrium, toward the back."

Bless her for not making me stand there and state my business in front of the sentinels, who may look like statues, but no doubt hear and see everything that happens here and feed it all back to Agatha.

I mouth the words *thank you* and round the desk, passing through the archway and into the atrium. The central room is still as grand as ever, the high, arching ceilings and stained glass of a church, broken by aisles of shelves instead of pews, ten halls branching off like spokes.

I cross the vast hall in silence and find Roland tucked in between two aisles, his red Chucks a spot of color on the pale floors. His back is to me, head bowed as he looks over a folder. There's tension in his shoulders, and I can tell from his stillness that he's stopped scanning the page and is now staring past it, lost in thought.

I've had four and a half years to study Roland's postures and moods, ever since Da offered me into his care and he accepted. The constancy of him—his tall, thin, unchanging form—has always been a comfort, but now it's also a reminder of what he is. The Archive tells us that Librarians don't change as long as they're here, their suspended age a trade for their time, their service. And up until a few weeks ago, I bought it. And then Carmen told me the truth: that Roland, along with every other Librarian who staffs the Archive, comes not from the Outer, but from the shelves here. That they are all Histories, those of past Keepers and Crew woken from their sleep to serve again. It's still so hard for me to believe that he's *dead*.

"Miss Bishop?" he says without looking up. "You should be in bed." His voice is soft, but even at a whisper I can hear the lilt in it. He closes the folder before turning toward me. His gray eyes travel over my face, and his brow furrows.

"Still not sleeping?"

I shrug. "Maybe I just wanted to tell you about my first day of school."

He hugs the folder to his chest. "How was it? Learn anything useful?"

"I learned that Wesley Ayers goes there, too."

A raised brow. "I assumed you already knew that."

"Yeah, well . . ." I say, trailing off into a yawn.

"How long has it been, Mackenzie?"

"Since what?"

"Since you slept," he says, looking at me hard. "Really slept."

I run a hand through my hair and tally up the time since the rogue History of a deceased Crew member tricked me into trusting him, stole my key, threw me into a Returns room, stabbed Wesley, tried to kill me, and nearly succeeded (with a Librarian's help) in tearing the entire branch of the Archive down. "Three weeks, two days, and six hours."

"Since Owen," says Roland.

I nod and echo, "Since Owen."

"It's showing."

I cringe. I'm trying so hard, but I know he's right. And if he can see it, Agatha could, too.

My head starts to hurt.

Roland cranes his neck, looking up at the stained glass that interrupts the highest part of the walls and trails like smoke onto the ceiling. The Archive is always bright, lit by some unseen source, but the shifting light beyond the windows is an illusion, a way to suggest change in a static world. Right now, the windows are dark, and I wonder if Roland sees something in them I don't, because when his eyes sink back to mine he says, "We have some time."

"For what?" I ask, but he's already walking away.

"Follow me."

# EIGHT

I'M THIRTEEN, covered in blood, and sitting cross-
legged on a table in a sterile room. I've been a Keeper for
less than six months, and this isn't the first time I've landed
in the medical wing of the Archive. Roland stands out of the
way, arms crossed over his chest while Patrick prepares a
cold pack.

"He was twice my size," I say, clutching a bloody cloth to
my nose.

"Isn't everyone?" asks Patrick. He's only been at the
branch a couple weeks. He doesn't like me very much.

"You're not helping," says Roland.

"I thought that's exactly what I was doing," snaps Patrick.
"Helping. You called in a favor, and here I am, patching up
your little pet project off the books."

I murmur something unkind behind the cloth, one of the
many phrases I picked up from Da. Patrick doesn't hear it,
but Roland must, because he raises a brow.

"Miss Bishop," he says, addressing Patrick, "is one of our
most promising Keepers. She wouldn't be here if the council
had not voted her through."

Patrick gives Roland a weighted look. "Did they vote her
through, or did you?"

Roland's gray eyes narrow a fraction. "I would remind
you who you're speaking to."

Patrick lets off a short sigh like steam and turns his attention back to me, pulling the cloth from my grip to examine the damage over his glasses. It hurts like hell, but I try not to let it show as he presses the cold pack against my face and repositions my hand over it.

"You're lucky it's not broken," he says, peeling off a pair of plastic gloves.

Roland winks. "Our girl, she's made of steel."

I smile a little behind the cold pack. I like the idea of that. Being a girl of steel.

"Hardheaded," says Patrick. "Keep it iced and try not to get punched in the face again."

"I'll do my best," I say, the words muffled by the cold pack. "But it's so much fun."

Roland chuckles. Patrick packs up his things and leaves, muttering something that sounds like *useless* under his breath. I watch him go.

"You threw your arms up when the History took a swing at you," says Roland casually. "Is that what happened?"

I look down and nod. I should have known better. Da taught me better, but it was like two different lessons, in practice and in truth, and I wasn't ready. Da said the right moves have to be like reflex, not just learned but known, and now I see why. There was no time to think, only act. React. My arms came up and the History's fist hit them and they hit me. Heat spreads across my cheeks, even under the cold pack.

"Hop down," he says, uncrossing his arms. "And show me what you did."

I get off the table and set the cold pack aside. Roland throws a punch, slow as syrup, and I bring my arms up, crossed at the wrists. His fist comes to rest lightly against them, and he considers me over my raised hands.

"There is no right pose to strike, no position to take. The worst thing you can do in a fight is stop moving. When someone attacks, they create force, movement, momentum, but you'll be okay as long as you can see and feel the direction of that force and travel with it." He puts some weight behind his fist, shifting to one side as he leans forward. I let myself shift to the same side and back, and his fist slides away. He nods. "There we go. Now, better get that ice back on your face."

Steps echo in the hall beyond the room, and Roland's gray eyes flick to the door.

"I should go," I say, taking the cold pack with me. But when I get to the door, I hesitate. "Do you regret it?" I ask. "Voting me through?"

Roland folds his arms across his chest. "Not at all," he says with a smile. "You make things infinitely more interesting."


"Where are we going?" I ask under my breath. Roland doesn't answer, only leads me out of the aisle and down the sixth hall that branches off the atrium. The Archive is a network of mismatched spaces, branching and intersecting in a system only the Librarians seem able to comprehend. Every time I follow someone through the maze, I struggle to keep hold of my bearings as I count the turns. But tonight, instead of guiding me on a winding path across landings, down corridors, through rooms, Roland goes straight, straight to the very end of the very long hall and through a smaller set of doors set into the end.

We end up in another hallway, one much shorter, narrower, and dimly lit. He hesitates, glancing around to see and hear if we're alone.

"Where are we?" I ask when it's clear that we are.

"Librarians' quarters," he answers before setting off again. Halfway down the hall, he reaches a simple dark-paneled door and stops. "Here we go."

The door opens into a cozy room with pale striped walls, sparsely furnished with a daybed, a low-backed leather chair, and a table. Classical music whispers from a device on the wall, and Roland moves through the small space with the comfort of someone who knows every inch of it.

He crosses to the table and absently drops the folder he's been carrying into a drawer before pulling something shiny from his pocket. He runs his thumb over the surface once before setting it on top of the table. The gesture is at once worn and gentle, reverent. When he pulls his hand away, I see that the object is a silver pocket watch. It's old, and I can't keep my pulse from quickening when my eyes settle on it. The only objects that come into the Archive arrive on the bodies of Histories. Either he snagged the watch from a body or it came in with his.

"It doesn't work anymore," says Roland, sensing my interest. "Not here." He gestures to the daybed. "Sit."

I sink onto the soft cushion and run a hand over a black blanket folded on the bed beside me. "I didn't think you needed sleep," I say, feeling awkward. It's still so hard to process the idea that he's . . . not alive.

"Need is a strange thing," he says, methodically rolling up his sleeves. "Physical needs make you feel human. The lack of them can make you feel less so. I don't sleep, no, but I rest. I go through the motions. It provides a psychological relief rather than a physical one. Now try to get some rest."

I shake my head, even as my body begs me to lie down. "I can't," I say quietly.

Roland sits down in the low-backed leather chair opposite, his gold Archive key gleaming against the front of his shirt. Keeper keys unlock doors to the Narrows; Crew keys unlock shortcuts in the Outer; Archive keys unlock Histories, turning them on and off like appliances, not people. I wonder what it would feel like to turn a life off with a single twist of metal. I remember Carmen holding hers out to me, remember the pins-and-needles numbness that shot up my hand when I tried to wrap my fingers around it.

"Miss Bishop," says Roland, his voice drawing my attention up. "You have to try."

"I don't believe in ghosts, Roland. But it's like he's haunting me. Every time I close my eyes, he's there."

"He's gone," says Roland simply.

"Are you sure?" I whisper, thinking of the fear and the pain that follow me out of my nightmares. "It's like there's a part of him that dug its nails into my head and held on. I see him when I close my eyes, and he feels so *real*. . . . I feel like I'm going to wake up and he'll still be there."

"Well," says Roland, "you sleep, and I'll keep an eye out for him."

I laugh sadly, but don't lie down. I need to tell him about the blackouts. It would be so much easier *not* to tell him—he's already worried, and it will only make things worse—but I need to know if I'm losing it, and since I'm the one shot through with nightmares and missing moments, I don't think I'm the best judge.

"Something happened today," I say quietly. "In the Narrows."

Roland steeples his fingers. "Tell me."

"I . . . I lost time."

Roland sits forward. "What do you mean?"

"I was hunting, and I . . . It was like I blacked out." I roll my bad wrist. "I was awake, but one minute I was one place, and the next I was somewhere else, and I couldn't remember how I'd gotten there. It was just blank. It came back, though," I add, "after I calmed down."

I don't say how shaky the memory was and how I had to fight to recover it.

Roland's gray eyes darken. "Is this the first time?"

In response, my gaze escapes to the floor.

"How many times?" he asks.

"Just once. A couple weeks ago."

"You should have told me."

I look up. "I didn't think it would happen again."

Roland shoves up from his chair and begins to pace. He should tell me it's going to be okay, but he doesn't bother lying. Bad dreams are one thing. Blacking out on the job is another. We both know what happens to a member of the Archive if they're deemed unfit. There is no such thing as a leave of absence here.

I look up at the cream-colored ceiling.

"How many Keepers lose their minds?" I ask.

Roland shakes his head. "You're not losing your mind, Mackenzie."

I give him a skeptical look.

"You've been through a lot. What you're experiencing, it

sounds like residual trauma and extreme fatigue, paired with the influx of adrenaline, are triggering a kind of tunnel vision. It's a feasible reaction."

"I don't care if it's feasible. How do I make sure it doesn't happen again?"

"You need rest. You need to *sleep*," he says, a note of desperation working its way into his voice as he slumps back down in his chair. His gray eyes are worried, a paler version of the fear that flashed through them when Agatha first summoned me to be assessed. "Please try."

I hesitate, but finally nod, slide off my shoes, and curl up on the daybed, resting my head on the folded blanket. I consider telling him that I think I'm being followed, too, but I can't will the words out.

"Do you regret it yet?" I ask. "Voting me through?"

His mouth twitches, but I don't hear his answer, because my body is already betraying me, dragging me down into sleep.


When I wake, the room is empty, and for a split second I can't remember where I am or how I got here. But then I hear the whisper of classical music from the device on the wall and remember that I'm in the Archive, in Roland's quarters.

I blink away sleep, marveling at the fact it doesn't cling to me. No dreams. No nightmares. For the first time in days. Weeks. I allow a small, breathless laugh to escape. My eyes burn from the sheer relief of a few hours' sleep without Owen and his knife.

I fold the blanket Roland let me borrow and return it to the corner of the daybed before getting up. I switch the music off as I pad across the cloisterlike space. Behind a door left ajar on the far wall, I find several versions of his self-assigned uniform: slacks and sweaters and button-down shirts. I look around for a clock even though I know there isn't one. My eyes go to the silver pocket watch, still on top of the side table. It doesn't work, but I find myself reaching absently for it when my attention slides to the drawer beneath.

It is barely ajar, just enough for me to see another glint of metal, and when I take the drawer in both hands and slide it open—the wood utters a soft hush—I find two worn silver coins and a notebook no larger than my palm. I lift the notebook. The paper edges are yellowed and fragile, and when I peel the cover back, I find a date written in elegant script in the bottom corner.

*1819*

The next several pages are filled with notes too small and old to read, and mingled with them, pencil sketches. A stone facade. A river. A woman. The name *Evelyn* runs in his careful script under her throat.

The journal sings beneath my fingers, brimming with memories, and I hesitate to put the book back. Roland has always been a mystery. He never wanted to talk about the life he'd left behind, the one he claimed he'd go back to when he was done serving. But now I know he didn't leave a life behind at all, not willingly, and he'll never go back to it.

The question "Who is Roland?" has become "Who *was* Roland?" and before I can stop myself, I close my eyes and reach for the thread of memory in the notebook. I catch hold, and time turns back. It rolls away, and darkness ripples into an alleyway at night: a young, smudged Roland standing beneath a pool of flickering lamplight. He's cradling the notebook in one hand as he shades in the woman's hair with a short stub of pencil and pins a slip of paper to the opposite page with his thumb. As he draws, letters bleed onto the slip. A name. He snaps the notebook shut and checks his pocket watch, three Crew lines spreading like a shadow across the inside of his wrist.

The sound of voices draws me out of the memory, and I set the notebook back into the table drawer as the door groans a little under someone's weight, but doesn't open.

I hold my breath as I ease the drawer shut and step toward the door and the voices on the other side. When I press my ear against it, I can hear his melodic voice and just the edges of Lisa's soft, even tone. And then my chest tightens as I realize they're talking about *me*.

"No," says Roland quietly, "I realize it's not a permanent solution. But she just needs time. And rest," he adds. "She's been through a lot."

Another murmur.

"No," replies Roland. "It hasn't come to that yet. And it won't."

I force myself away from the door as he echoes, "I know, I know."

When Roland comes back into the room, I'm sitting on the floor, lacing up my shoes.

"Miss Bishop," he says. "How are you feeling?"

"Like a new person," I say, getting to my feet. "How long was I out?"

"Four hours."

Four hours, and I want to cry. How mended could I feel with eight? "It's amazing," I say. "The difference. To be free of Owen for a night."

Roland crosses his arms and looks down at them. "You could be free of him for longer." His gray gaze slides up. "You don't have to live with it, the weight of what you've been through. There are options. Alterations—"

"*No.*" *Alterations.* The word for when the Archive carves out memories from someone's mind. Cuts their life full of holes. I think of Wesley, missing a day of his life. I think of his great-aunt, Joan, stripped of years when she retired, just as a *precaution.*

"Miss Bishop," he says, reading my disgust, "alterations are not carried out solely on those who leave, or those who need to be kept in the dark about the Archive's existence."

"No, they're also for those deemed unfit—"

"And for those who *want* to forget," counters Roland. "There's no shame in it, Mackenzie. Wanting to be free of certain memories. The bad ones."

"The bad ones?" I echo. "Roland, they're all tangled up. Isn't that the idea? Life is messy. And even if it weren't, I said no." The truth is, I don't trust them to stop with the memories I'm willing to lose. And even if I did, it feels like running. I need to remember. "We've had this conversation already."

"Yes, we have, back when you were only fighting bad dreams. But if you keep having tunnel moments—"

"Then we'll handle it," I say, making it clear the conversation is over.

Roland's shoulders slump, his arms falling back to his sides. "Very well." He lifts his silver watch from the side table and slips it back into his pocket. "Come on, I'll lead you out." I notice, as I follow him, that the halls don't seem to shift around us. Unlike the twisting corridors of the stacks, the path to the Librarians' quarters is a straight and steady line.

We reach the front desk, and I cringe when I see Patrick sitting there. His eyes flick up, cold behind their black-framed glasses, and his mouth draws into a tight line. Roland anticipates a remark and speaks first.

"It's come to my attention that Miss Bishop's predecessor did not adequately prepare her before his demise."

"Pray tell," says Patrick, "in what ways is she lacking?"

I frown. Nobody likes being talked about like they're not in the room, especially when the talk centers on their shortcomings.

"Stillness," says Roland. "She's more than competent when it comes to combat, but lacks the patience and conservation of energy that comes with proper training."

"And how do you plan to assist her?"

"Meditation," answers Roland. "It'll benefit her, anyway, when she makes Crew and—"

"*If* she makes Crew," corrects Patrick, but Roland continues.

"—and she's a quick learner, so it shouldn't take long for her to pick it up. In the meantime, when she comes, send her back." He straightens, flaunting his full height. "And do it without interrogation, please. I'd like to make the most of *everyone's* time."

I forget sometimes what a good liar Roland is.

Patrick considers us both, clearly trying to pick apart the ruse, but in the end his mouth only twists into a mean smile, his eyes hanging on me as he addresses Roland. "If you think you can teach Miss Bishop to be quiet and still for once, then best of luck."

I bite my tongue as Roland nods to us both and vanishes back into the atrium, leaving me alone with the sentinels and Patrick, who appraises me coldly. Neither one of us has forgotten that he was the one who summoned Agatha in the first place. That he petitioned to have me removed. Now he says nothing, not until I've passed between the sentinels to the Archive door and my key is slotted in the lock. Only then does Patrick add a low but audible, "Sleep tight."

I'm halfway back to my numbered doors, trying to swallow the bad taste Patrick always leaves in my mouth, when my eyes drift to a chalk marking on the wall.

It's not on one of the doors, but on a stretch of dark stone. I drew it two and a half weeks ago to mark the spot where it happened. Some days I walk past it, but others I stop and force myself to remember. To *relive*. Roland would be furious. I know I should be moving on, should be doing everything I can to put the memory behind me, or let the Archive take it away, but I can't. It's already scarred into my mind a dozen ways, all of them twisted, and I need to remember—not the nightmarish distortions that have followed, but what actually happened. I need to remember so I can be better, stronger. Da used to say mistakes were useless if you tried to forget them. You had to remember and learn.

My hand drifts to the wall, and I barely have to reach before the memories rush up beneath my fingers. I spin them back, away, until I find that day—and even then, past the blinding light of the Returns door being thrown open, past our tangling bodies and the key and all the way back to the moment when I thought I had a chance. I know exactly where it is and when to stop, because I've watched the scene so many times, studying his strength and my weakness. Watching myself lose.

I drag the memory to a stop and hold it there, in the second before the fight starts. Owen's hand is outstretched as he asks for the ending of the story; my hand is about to reach for my hidden knife. I know what's going to happen.

And then it does.

There is no sound, no color, only a blur of motion as I go for the knife against my leg and Owen lunges forward. Before my blade can reach his chest, his hand closes around my wrist. He slams it back into the wall, forcing his body against mine.

Phantom pain drifts into my fingers as I watch his grip tighten. The knife tumbles to the floor. I try and fail to get free as he catches the blade and spins my body back against his, the glinting metal coming to rest beneath my chin.

He frees the final piece of the story—and with it the final piece of his key—from my pocket and shoves me away so he can assemble it. I don't run. I don't do anything but stand and watch and cradle my broken wrist. Because I still think I'm going to win.

I attack and manage to send the knife skating into the dark— even manage to send Owen backward, too. But then he's up again, catching my leg and slamming me back onto the hard floor. I curl in on myself in pain, struggling to force air back into my lungs.

It's obvious now that Owen was playing with me.

My recovery is too slow, but he waits for me to get to my feet. He wants me to believe that if I can, I stand a chance.

But when I finally summon the strength, he is there: too fast, a blur as he wraps his hand around my throat and pins me against the nearest door. I watch myself gasp and claw at his grip as he reaches up and takes hold of the key wrapped around my good wrist, snapping the cord with a single sharp tug. He unlocks the door behind me and showers both of us in glaring white light. I watch him lean in, watch his lips move, and I don't need sound to know what he's saying. I remember just fine.

"Do you know what happens to a living person in the Returns room?"

That's what his lips are mouthing. And then, when I don't answer—can't answer—he adds, "Neither do I," before he shoves me backward into the blinding white, closes the door, and walks away.

My hand slips from the wall. A now-familiar numbness spreads through me in the memory's wake.

The Owen in my nightmares is drawn in color and sound, and even when I know I'm dreaming, it feels so unbearably real, here and now and terrifying. But watching us this way, I don't feel any of the fear. Frustration and anger and regret, maybe, but not fear. This scene is faded and gray like an old movie, so clearly a moment in the past. It doesn't even feel like *my* past, but one that belongs to someone else. Someone weaker.

I think of Roland's offer—of letting the Archive go in and hollow out everything that Owen touched and ruined—and I can't help but wonder if this is how I'd feel about him after that. If he were only this, a memory in someone else's life, would he be able to hurt me in my sleep? Or would I be free?

I shove the thought away. I'm not going to run away. That isn't the way to be free. And I'm never going to let the Archive into my head, when it would be so easy for them to erase more of me. Erase everything.

I need to remember.

# NINE

I FETCH THE discarded book from my bedroom floor and manage to finish the reading for my government class as the Thursday morning sun peeks over the horizon. *At least it will be fresh in my mind,* I reason as I pack up my school bag. As long as I can get through three chapters of lit theory and a section of precalc during lunch, I'll avoid falling behind on the *second day* of school.

Dad knocks short and crisp on my door and says, "Up!" and I do my best to sound groggy as I call back and zip my bag closed. I'm halfway through the living room when the TV catches my eyes. It's that *same* story. Only this time, in addition to the photo of the trashed room, there's a title in bold on the bottom of the screen.

## Retired Judge Phillip Missing

A photo goes up beside the anchor's face, and I get a sinking feeling in my stomach. I recognize the room now, because I *know* the man they're talking about.

I met him two days ago.

Mr. Phillip likes to keep things neat.

I notice before he even lets me in. His welcome mat is straight, and the planters on the porch are evenly spaced, and when he opens the door I can see the order carrying through into the entryway, where three pairs of shoes are lined up, laces out.

"You must be from Bishop's," he says, gesturing to the box tucked under my arm. It has a blue cursive *B* on the top. Until school starts, Mom has me running deliveries as payment for the new bike. Not that I mind. The fresh air helps me stay awake, and the riding helps me learn the city grid—which isn't a grid at all here on the edges, but a mess of veering streets and neighborhoods, apartments and parks.

"Yes, sir," I say, holding out the box. "A dozen chocolate chip."

He nods and takes the box, patting his back pocket and then frowning a little. "Wallet must be in the kitchen," he says. "Come on in."

I hesitate. I was raised not to take candy from strangers or climb into vans or follow older men into their homes, but Mr. Phillip hardly looks threatening. And even if he is, I'm willing to bet I could take him.

I roll my wrist, listening to the bones crack as I cross the threshold. Mr. Phillip is already in the kitchen—which is clean enough to make me think he doesn't use it—arranging the cookies on a plate. He leans in and inhales, and his eyes turn sad.

"Something wrong?" I ask.

"Not the same," he says softly.

He tells me about his wife. She's dead. He tells me how, before, the house always seemed to smell like cookies. He doesn't even like to eat them. He just misses the smell. But it's not the same.

We stand there in this unused kitchen, and I don't know what to do. Part of me wishes Mr. Phillip had never asked me to come in, because I don't need his feelings on top of mine. But I'm here now and I might be able to fix him, or at least glue a couple pieces back together. Finally I hold out my hand.

"Give me the box," I say.

"Excuse me?"

"Here," I say, taking the empty container from his hands and dumping the tray of cookies inside. "I'll be back."

An hour later I'm there again, and instead of a box I'm holding a Tupperware of cookie dough: about twelve cookies' worth. I show him how to heat the oven, and I scoop a few clumps of dough onto a sheet and slide the sheet in. I set the timer and tell Mr. Phillip to follow me outside.

"You'll notice the smell more," I say, "when you go back in."

Mr. Phillip seems genuinely touched.

"What's your name?" he asks as we stand on the porch.

"Mackenzie Bishop," I say.

"You didn't have to do this, Mackenzie," he says.

I shrug. "I know."

Da wouldn't like it. He wasn't a fan of looking back, not when time was still rolling forward, and I know at the end of the day I haven't done anything but give a man in an empty kitchen a way of clinging to the past. But people like me can reach out and touch memories with only our fingers, so we can't really fault everyone else for wanting to hold on, too.

The truth is, I get it. If someone could give me back the

way our house felt when Ben was home, even a shred of it, I'd give them anything. People are made up of so many small details. Some—like the smell of cookies baking—we can recreate. Or at least try.

The timer goes off inside the house. Mr. Phillip opens the door, takes a deep breath, and smiles. "Perfect."

Mr. Phillip liked to keep things neat. But on the screen, his apartment is in disarray. The room shown is one I only saw in passing on the way from the entry to the kitchen, an open living room with a wall of windows that look out onto a small, immaculate garden. But now the glass is shattered and the room is trashed, and Mr. Phillip is missing.

I turn the volume up, and the reporter's voice spills into the living room.

"Well-known civil servant and recently retired judge Gregory Phillip is now considered a missing person, as well as the potential victim of an abduction."

"Mackenzie," cuts in Dad, striding through the room. "You're going to be late."

I hear the door close after him, but don't take my eyes from the screen.

"As you can see behind me," continues the reporter, "this room of his house was found in a state of chaos—paintings ripped from the walls, books strewn across the floor, chairs toppled, windows shattered. Are these the signs of a violent struggle, or a robber trying to cover his tracks?"

The camera cuts to a press conference, where a man with cropped reddish hair and a stern jaw issues a statement. A bar across the bottom of the screen identifies him as Detective Kinney. I wonder if he's related to Amber.

"There's no denying the signs of foul play," says Detective Kinney. His voice is low, gruff. "And at this time, we are treating the case as an abduction." The camera cuts back to the still frame of the trashed room, but the detective's voice plays eerily on. "We are investigating all possible leads, and anyone with information should contact—"

I shut the TV off, but Mr. Phillip and the trashed room linger in my mind like echoes. What happened? *When* did it happen? Was I the last person to see him alive? Should I tell the police? What would I tell them? That I helped the man's house smell like cookies?

I can't go to the cops. The last thing I need is more attention. Whatever happened to him, it's tragic . . . but it's got nothing to do with me.

My phone goes off, and I realize I'm still standing in the empty living room, staring at the darkened screen. I dig it out of my bag to find a text from Wesley.

> Got your battle armor on?

I smile, haul my bag onto my shoulder, and text back:

> Can't decide what to wear over it.

The conversation follows me down to the lobby.

> What are your choices?

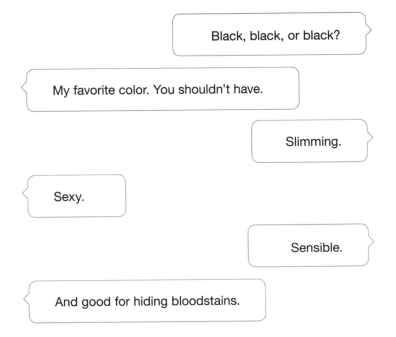

Black, black, or black?

My favorite color. You shouldn't have.

Slimming.

Sexy.

Sensible.

And good for hiding bloodstains.

I smile and pocket the phone as I reach Bishop's. Mom is busy talking to Ms. Angelli, a cat-happy antiques dealer from the fourth floor, and I swipe a muffin and a coffee and head out, feeling more awake than I have in weeks. *Four hours of sleep,* I marvel as I unchain Dante and pedal off.

I keep my eyes peeled for the golden man from yesterday, but he's nowhere to be seen, and I actually start to wonder if he was ever there or if he was just another side effect of the sleeplessness. I hope for the latter, not wanting to think about what the former could mean.

The morning is cool, and I balance my coffee on the handlebars with one hand and steer with the other. As I ride, something fills my chest. Not fear or fatigue, but something lovely and light: hope. I was beginning to think I'd never find dreamless sleep again; but if I could find it in Roland's daybed, then it's possible to find it elsewhere, too. Right now, high on those four small hours of rest, possibility is enough.

When I get to Hyde, I find Cash leaning up against the bike rack, holding two coffees and shooing freshmen away like flies from the spot he's saving me near the front gate. He smiles when he sees me, a broad grin that brightens the morning and helps push any lingering thoughts of Mr. Phillip from my mind. He scoots aside so I can park Dante.

"I wasn't going to wait for you," he explains, "but you see, the schedule flips. I showed you the route for the A block, but not the B block."

"Isn't it just the A block in reverse?"

"Well, yes," he says, offering me one of the coffees. I take it, even though I just finished mine. "But I wanted to make sure you knew that. I didn't want you to think me a negligent ambassador."

"That would be a travesty," I say, tugging off the workout pants beneath my skirt.

"Truly," he says, sipping his drink. "I'm going to lose points as it is for not being able to show you to your morning classes. I'm on the opposite side of campus, and the teachers around here will lock you out if you're late."

"I won't fault you." I get the first pant leg off.

"Good. There are feedback cards around here somewhere, you know."

"I'll be sure to fill one out. . . ." My shoe catches on the second pant leg; when I try to tug it free, my backpack shifts from my other shoulder and my balance falters. Cash's hand comes up to steady me, and his noise—all jazz and laughter and pulse—pounds through my head, loud enough to make me flinch and pull away, toppling the other direction, straight into the metallic rock band sound of Wesley Ayers.

He smiles, and I can't tell if it's my rare moment of clumsiness or the fact I lean into his noise instead of away from it that makes his eyes glitter.

"Steady there," he says as I finally free the fabric from my shoe. I get both feet back on the ground, but his touch lingers a moment before sliding away, taking the thrum of music with it.

"Morning, Ayers," says Cash with a nod.

"Where did you come from, Wes?" I ask.

He tips his head back down the sidewalk.

"What, no fancy car?" I tease.

"Ferrari's in the shop," he shoots back without missing a beat.

"And the Lexus?" chirps Cash.

Wesley rolls his eyes and shifts his attention to me. "Is this one giving you trouble?"

"On the contrary," I say, "he's been a perfect gentleman. One might even say a knight."

"In shining armor," adds Cash, gesturing to his gold stripes.

"He brought me coffee," I say, holding up my cup.

Wes runs a hand through his black hair and sighs dramatically. "You never bring *me* coffee, Cassius."

And then, out of nowhere, a girl swings her arm around Wesley from behind. He doesn't even tense at the contact—I do—only smiles as she puts her manicured hands over his eyes.

"Morning, Elle," he says cheerfully.

Elle—a pretty little thing, bird-thin with bottle-blond hair— actually *giggles* as she pulls away.

"How did you know?" she squeaks.

*Because of your noise,* I think drily.

Wesley shrugs. "What can I say? It's a gift."

"All the cool powers were taken," mutters Cash, half into his coffee.

The girl is still hanging on Wesley. *Perching* on him. Like a bird on a branch. She's chirping on about some fall dance when the bell finally rings, and I realize I've never been so happy to go to class.

It's a good thing I've had two coffees to go with my four hours of sleep, because Mr. Lowell kicks off the day with a documentary on revolutionaries. And whether it's the healthy dose of caffeine or the strange way the subject sinks its nails in, I manage to stay awake.

"The thing to remember about revolutionaries," says Lowell, killing the video and flicking on the lights, "is that, while they may be viewed as terrorists by their oppressors, in their own eyes, they are champions. Martyrs. People willing to do what others won't, or can't, for the sake of whatever it is they believe in. In a way, we can see them as the most extreme incarnations of a society's discontent. But just as people elevate their revolutionaries to the station of gods, avenging angels, heroes, so those revolutionaries elevate themselves. . . ."

As he continues, I picture Owen Chris Clarke, eyes blazing on the Coronado roof as he spoke of monsters and freedom and betrayal. Of tearing down the Archive, one branch at a time.

"But the mark of a revolutionary," continues Lowell, "is the fact that cause comes first. No matter how elevated the revolutionary becomes in the eyes of others—and in his own eyes—his life will always matter less than the cause. It is expendable."

Owen jumped off a roof. Took his own life to make sure the Archive couldn't take his mind, his memories. To make sure that if—when—his History woke, he would remember everything. I have no doubt that Owen would have given or taken his life a hundred times to see the Archive burn.

"Sadly," adds Lowell, "revolutionaries often find the lives of others equally expendable."

*Expendable.* I write the word in my notebook.

Owen definitely saw the lives of others as expendable. From those he murdered to keep his sister a secret, to those he *tried* to murder—Wesley bleeding out so Owen could make a point—to me. Owen gave me the chance to come with him instead of standing in his way. As soon as I refused, I was worthless to him. Nothing more than another obstacle.

If Owen was a revolutionary, then what does that make me? Part of the machine? The world isn't that black-and-white, is it? It doesn't all boil down to with or against. Some of us just want to stay alive.

# TEN

AMBER'S LATE TO PHYSIOLOGY, so she has to snag a seat in the back and I have to spend the period studying the nervous system and trying to stay awake. As soon as the bell rings, I'm out of my chair and standing by hers.

"That eager to get to gym?" she asks, packing up her bag.

"Question," I say casually. "Is your dad a cop?"

"Huh?" Amber's strawberry eyebrows go up. "Oh, yeah. Detective." She hoists the bag onto her shoulder and we head into the fray. "Why?"

"I just saw him on the news this morning."

"Kind of sad, isn't it?" she says. "*I* didn't get to see my dad this morning."

Treading dangerous waters, then. "He works a lot?"

Amber sighs. "On a light day. And the Phillip case is killing him." She almost smiles. "My mom hates it when I use words like *killing* in casual conversation. She thinks I'm becoming desensitized to death. I hate to tell her she's too late."

"My grandfather was a detective, too." Well, a private eye, and mostly under the table work at that, but close enough.

Her eyes light up. "Really?"

"Yeah. I grew up around it. Bound to make you a little morbid." Amber smiles, and I take my shot. "Do they have any idea what happened to that guy, Mr. Phillip?"

Amber shakes her head and pushes the door open. "Dad won't

talk about it around me." She squints into the late morning light. "But the walls in our house are pretty thin. From what I've heard him say, none of it adds up. You've got this one room, and it's trashed, and the rest of the house is spotless. Nothing missing."

"Except for Mr. Phillip."

"Exactly," she says, kicking a loose pebble down the path, "but nobody can figure out why. He was apparently one of the nicest guys around, and he was retired."

"A judge, right? Do they think someone might have been angry with a sentence or something?"

"Then why not kill him?" says Amber, pushing open the gym doors. "I know that's cold, but if you have a vendetta, you usually have a body. They don't have one. They don't have anything. He just vanished. So my question is, who would go to all the trouble to make someone disappear and then leave a mess like that? Why not make it look like he just walked away?"

She has a point. She has a lot of points.

"You're really good at this," I say, following her into the locker room.

She beams. "Crime dramas and years of eavesdropping."

"What are you two going on about?" asks Safia, dropping her bag on the bench. I hesitate, but Amber surprises me by giving a nonchalant shrug and lying through her teeth. "Arteries and veins, mostly."

Saf screws up her nose. "Ewww." She keys in her locker code and starts to change, but Amber smiles and keeps going. "Did you know that veins move around beneath your skin?"

"Stop," says Saf, paling.

"And did you know——" Amber continues.

"Amber, *stop*," says Saf, tugging on her workout clothes.

"—that the brachial artery," she says, poking Saf's arm for emphasis, "is the first place blood goes after being pumped through your heart, so if you sever it, you could conceivably lose all five liters of blood in your body? Your heart would just pump it right out onto the floor—"

"Gross, gross, *stop*," snaps Saf, slamming her locker and storming away toward the gym doors.

Amber looks back at me with a smile after Safia has stormed out. "She gets squeamish," she says cheerfully.

"I can see that." I'd be lying if I said it didn't lighten my mood. "Hey, will you let me know if they find anything?"

She nods a little reluctantly. "Why so interested in the case?"

I flash a smile. "You're not the only one who grew up on crime shows."

Amber smiles back, and I make a mental note to spend more time watching television.

There's a nervous energy in my bones. I want to run—want to *sprint* until it dissipates—but I'm terrified of triggering another tunnel moment, so I spend the first half of gym walking on the track, trying to clear my head. Amber and Gavin are "stretching" on a mat across the room, trying to hide a magazine on the floor between them. Safia is fencing—she's actually *good*, in an obnoxious way—and Cash is on the weight machines with a few other guys. And Wesley is . . . right beside me. One moment I'm alone, and the next he's fallen casually into step next to me. I count the number of strides we walk in silence—eleven—before Wesley feels the need to break it.

"Did you know," he asks, affecting an accent that I think is *supposed* to be Cash's, "that the hawk, which is Hyde's mascot, is known for performing dazzling aerobatic feats to impress prospective mates?"

I can't help but laugh. Wes smiles, and slips back into his own voice. "What's on your mind?"

"Crime scenes," I say absently.

"Never a dull answer, I'll give you that. Care to be more specific?"

I shake my head.

"Bishop! Ayers!" shouts the gym teacher near the sparring platform. "Come show these idiots how to fight."

Wesley knocks his shoulder against mine—a ripple of bass through two thin layers of fabric—and we make our way to the mat and suit up. I roll my wrist, testing.

"Do you really have a Ferrari?" I ask as I cinch my gloves.

He gives me a withering look. "For your information, Miss Bishop," he says, pulling on his helmet, "I don't own a car."

We go to the center of the platform.

"Shocking," I say as the whistle blows.

Wes throws a punch, and I dodge and catch his wrist.

"Waste of gas," he says, before I turn and flip him over my shoulder. Instead of resisting, he moves with the flip, lands on his feet, and throws a kick my direction. I lunge backward. We dance around each other for a moment.

"So you live in walking distance?" I ask, throwing a punch. He catches it—his grip oddly gentle around my bad wrist—and rolls my body in against his, one arm snaking around my shoulders.

"I use the Narrows," he says in my ear. "Fastest transportation around, remember?" He shoves me forward before I can try to flip him again. I spin to face him and catch him in the stomach, on his good side.

"You could only do that if Hyde School was in your territory," I say, blocking two back-to-back shots.

"It is," he says, clearly trying to focus on the match.

I smile to myself. That means he lives nearby—and the only houses nearby are mansions, massive properties on the land that rings the campus. I try to picture him at a party on one of the stone patios that accent many of the mansions, staff flitting about with trays of champagne. While I'm busy picturing that, Wesley fakes a punch and takes out my legs. I go down hard.

The whistle blows, and this time when Wesley tries to help me up, I let him.

"That's how it's done," says the gym teacher, shooing us off the mat. "A little less chitchat would have been nice, but that's the idea."

I tug my helmet off and toss it into the equipment stack. Wesley's hair is slick with sweat, but I'm still picturing him with a butler. And maybe a pipe. On the Graham family yacht.

"What are you grinning about?" he asks.

"What's your real name?" The question tumbles out. There, in the sliver of time after I ask it and before Wes answers, I see another one of his faces. This one is pale, raw, and exposed. And then it's gone, replaced by a thinner version of his usual ease.

"You already know my name," he says stiffly.

"Cash said Wesley is your middle name, not your first."

"Well, aren't you and Cash just thick as thieves?" he says. There's a tightness in his voice. He's a good enough liar to hide discomfort, so the fact that he's letting a fraction of it show makes me wonder if he wants me to see. He strides away across the gym, and I rush to follow.

"And for the record," he says without looking back, "it's still real."

"What?"

"My name. Just because it's not my first doesn't mean it's not real."

"Okay," I say, trying to keep up, "it's real. I just want to know your *full* name."

"Why?" he snaps.

"Because sometimes I don't feel like I know the full *you*," I say, grabbing his sleeve. I drag him to a stop. His eyes are bright, reflecting specks of mottled brown and green and gold. "The other girls here might think your air of mystery is cute, but I know what you're doing—showing everybody different pieces and keeping the whole secret. And I thought . . ." I trail off. *I thought if you could be honest with anyone, it would be me.* It's what I want to say, but I bite back the words.

Wesley squints at me a little. "You're one to talk about secrets, Mackenzie Bishop," he says. But the words are playful. He turns to face me and surprises me by bringing his hands to rest firmly on my shoulders. My head fills with the cluttered music of his noise.

"You want to know my full name?" he asks softly. I nod. He brings his forehead to rest against mine and talks into the small window of space between our lips. "When Crew are paired up," he says, his voice easy and low over the sound of his noise, "there's a ceremony. That's when they have their Archive marks carved into their skin. Three lines. One made by their own hand. One made by their partner. One made by the Archive." His eyes look down into mine. His words are little more than a breath between us. "The Crew make their scars and take their vows to the Archive and to each other. The vows start and end with their names. So," he whispers, "when we become Crew, I'll tell you mine."

And then the bell echoes through the gym, and he smiles and pulls away. "About time," he says cheerfully, heading for the locker rooms. "I'm starving."

Da won't talk about his Crew partner.

He once said he'd tell me anything if I asked the right question, but somehow I never ask the right one to get him to tell me about Meg. He doesn't even tell me her name; I learn it later, after he's gone and I'm packing up his things.

They all fit into one box.

There's a leather jacket, a wallet, a few letters—to Dad, mostly (and one to Patty, my grandmother, who left him before I was born). There are only three photos in with the letters (Da was never very sentimental). The first one is of him as a young man, leaning up against an iron fence, looking lean and strong and a little arrogant—really the only difference between young Da and old Da is the number of wrinkles on his face.

The second one is of him with Mom and Dad and me and Ben.

And the third one is of him with Meg.

They stand close, shoulder to shoulder but for a small gap, Da tilting his head slightly toward hers. His sleeves are rolled down, but hers are rolled up, and I can see, even in the faded photo, the three parallel scars of the Archive carved into her forearm. It's a mirror image of the one etched into Da's skin, the two of them bonded by scars and oaths and secrets.

Neither one of them is smiling in the photo, but they both look like they're about to, and all I can think is that they fit. It's not just the way their bodies nest, even without touching. It's the knowing way they share the space, sensing where the other ends. It's their mirrored almost-smiles, the closest I have ever seen Da to happy. I know so little of this woman, of Da's days as Crew—only that he left. He told me he wanted to live long enough to train me himself (what would have happened if he'd died first? Would someone else have come?), but seeing him—this strange, vibrant, happier version of my grandfather—it hurts to think he gave her up for me.

"Do you think they were in love?" I ask Roland, showing him the photo.

He frowns, running a thumb over the worn edges.

"Love is simple, Miss Bishop. Crew isn't." His eyes are proud and sad at the same time, and I remember that underneath the sleeves of his sweater, he bears the scars as well. Three even lines.

"How so?" I press.

"Love breaks," he says. "The bond between Crew doesn't. It has love in it, though, and transparency. Being Crew with someone means being exposed, letting them read you—your hopes and wants and thoughts and fears. It means trusting them so much that you're not only willing to put your life in their hands, but to take their life into yours. It's a heavy burden to bear," he says, handing the picture back, "but Crew is worth it."

# ELEVEN

I TAKE A LONG, cold shower.

Wesley's touch lingers on my skin. His music echoes through my head. I remind myself as I scrub my skin that we are both liars and con artists. That we will always have secrets, some that bind us and some that cut between us, slicing us into pieces. That we will never see each other whole . . . until we become Crew. But I don't know if I want to be Crew with Wesley. I don't know if I'm willing to let him see all the pieces.

I try to put his promise from my mind. It doesn't matter right now. A world stands between me and Crew: a world of nightmares and trauma and *Agatha*. How do I tell Wesley that I might not make it to the ceremony, let alone the naming? Crew are selected. They are assessed. They are found fit.

If Agatha got her hands on my mind right now, I would never be found fit. Which means I need to keep her from getting her hands on me until I find a way to fix whatever's happening.

I have to hope there is a way to fix it.

A way that doesn't involve letting the Archive inside my head to cut out memories. If I let them in, they'll see the damage Owen did. The damage he continues to do.

I snap the water off and begin to get dressed. The lockers have emptied out by now, but as I slip the key back over my head, shivering a little when the metal comes to rest against my sternum,

Safia rounds the corner, focused on the braid she's weaving with her hair. Until she sees me. Her eyes narrow even more than usual.

"What's that?" she asks as I pull my shirt on over the key.

"A key," I say as casually as I can.

"Obviously," she says, finishing her braid and crossing her arms. "Did he give that to you?"

I frown. "Who?"

"Wesley." Her voice tightens a fraction when she says his name. "Is it his?"

My hand goes to the metal through my shirt. I could say yes. "No."

"They look the same," she presses.

They don't, actually. Wesley's is darker and made of a different metal. "It's just a stupid trinket," I say. "A good luck charm." I hold her gaze, waiting to see if she buys it. She doesn't seem convinced. "I read it in some book when I was a kid. This girl wore a key around her neck, and wherever she went, the doors all opened for her. Maybe Wesley read the same book. Or maybe he kept losing his keys so he put them around his neck. Ask him yourself," I say, because I can tell she won't.

Safia shrugs. "Whatever," she says, tugging on one of her earrings. They look like real gold. "If you guys want to wear ratty old keys, that's your choice. Try not to get tetanus." With that, she turns and strolls out.

My stomach growls, and I'm about to follow her when a sliver of metal catches my eye from beneath the bench. I kneel down and find a necklace: a round silver pendant on a simple chain. The pendant has been rubbed so much that the ornate *B* etched into its front is barely visible. I weigh it in my palm, knowing I should just leave it and hope whoever it belongs to comes looking for it. It's not my problem. But the level of wear on the pendant suggests that it's important to someone. It also means there's a good chance a memory or two has been worn in to it. Object memories are fickle—the smaller the object, the harder for memories to stick—but they're usually imprinted by either repetition or strong emotion, and this kind of token sees a fair amount of both. It can't hurt to look.

I glance around the locker room, making sure I'm alone before I pocket my ring. Instantly, the air in the room changes—doesn't thicken or thin, exactly, but shifts—my senses sharpening without the metal buffer. Curling my fingers over the pendant, I can feel the subtle hum of memories tickling my palm, and I close my eyes and reach—not with my skin, but with the thing beneath it. My hand goes numb as I catch hold of the thread, and the darkness behind my eyes dissolves into light and shadow and, finally, into memory.

A girl—tall, thin, blond, classically pretty—sits in a parked car in the dark, face wet from crying, with one hand wrapped, knuckles tight, on the wheel and the other clutching the pendant at her throat. As I roll time back, the memory skips from the car to a marble kitchen counter. This time, the girl is on one side of the counter clutching her pendant, and a woman old enough to be her mother is on the other, gripping a wineglass. I let the memory roll forward, and a moment later the girl shouts something—her words nothing more than static—and the woman pitches the wineglass at the girl's head. The girl cuts to the side and the glass strikes the cabinet behind her and shatters, and I swear I can feel the anger and the hurt and the sadness worn into the surface of the pendant.

I'm about to rewind further when the sharp slam of the locker room door causes me to drop the thread. I blink, pulling myself out of the past just as Amber rounds the corner. I frown and straighten, slipping the necklace into my shirt pocket and sliding my ring back on as she says, "There you are! We were beginning to wonder if you'd snuck out a back door."

And before I can ask who *we* is, she leads me out into the lobby, where Wes and Cash and Gavin are waiting.

"I'm sorry," I say. "I didn't realize anyone was waiting for me."

"Wouldn't be much of an ambassador—" starts Cash, but Wes cuts in.

"Thought you should probably know where they keep the food."

"The pizza yesterday was my treat," adds Amber. "First day tradition. But the rest of the time we have to make do."

Gavin chuckles, and a few minutes later, once they've ushered me across the lawn to the cafeteria—or the dining hall, as Hyde prefers to call it—I understand why.

"Make do"? Hyde has one of the most extensive kitchens I've ever seen. Five stations, each with a course—each course with a regular, healthy, vegetarian, and vegan option. Appetizer through dessert, and a station dedicated to drinks. The only major failing, I realize as another yawn escapes, is the lack of soda. The lack, in fact, of *anything* caffeinated. My body's beginning to slow, and as I load up my tray I can only hope there's some kind of black market caffeine business happening on campus. I ask Cash as much while we're waiting to check out.

"Alas," he says, "Hyde School is *technically* caffeine-free."

"What about the coffees you brought yesterday?"

"Swiped them from the teacher's lounge. Don't tell."

Looks like I'm on my own. It's not so bad, I tell myself. I'll be fine. I just need to eat something. And eating helps, for a little while, but half an hour later, when our trays are stacked on the Alchemist's outstretched arms and I'm wading through a chapter of precalc, Owen's voice begins to whisper in my head. It *hums*. The song reaches up from the back of my mind, out of my nightmares and into my day, wrapping its arms around me in an effort to drag me down into the dark. I close my eyes to clear it, but my head feels heavy, Owen's voice twisting the melody into words and—

"Is that today's homework?"

My head snaps up, and I find Gavin taking a seat on the step above me. I look down at the open math book in my lap and nod.

"I take it that's not," I say, gesturing to the book in his hands.

He shrugs. "You learn to work ahead here whenever you can. Because at some point, you'll invariably fall behind."

I hold up my own work. "Does that point usually come in the first week?"

He laughs. It's a quiet, gentle laugh, not much more than an exhale, but it brightens his face. He pushes the glasses up his nose, and my chest tightens when I see a set of numbers drawn in Sharpie on the back of his hand. It's such a stupid little thing, but it makes me think of Ben. Ben who drew a stick figure on my hand when I dropped him off at the corner near his school the day he died, who let me draw a stick-figure me on his hand to match before I let him go.

So many students make notes on their skin; so few of them look like my brother. "Mackenzie," says Gavin, articulating each syllable.

"Yeah?"

"It's not a big deal or anything, but you're kind of staring at me."

My gaze drops down to my work. "Sorry. You just remind me of someone."

He cracks open his book and takes the pen from behind his ear. "Well, I hope it's someone nice."

Ben takes shape behind my eyes—not the way he was before he died, but the way he was the night I brought him back, the night Carmen opened his drawer and I woke him from his sleep. I see his warm brown eyes turning black as he slips, see him shoving me away with the strength not of a boy, but of a History. I see him crumple to the floor, a gold Archive key gleaming from his back, before Roland returns his small body to its shelf. I see the drawer closing and me on my knees, begging Roland to stop, but it's too late, and the bright red Restricted bar paints itself across the drawer's face before the wall of the Archive swallows my brother.

The math problems on the page blur a little. Fatigue is catching up with me, weakening my walls. Everything is beginning to ache.

"Mackenzie?" presses Gavin softly. "Is it someone nice?"

And I somehow manage to smile and nod. "Yeah," I say softly. "It is."


I can't breathe.

Owen's hand is a vise around my throat.

"Hold still," he says. "You're making it worse."

He's pinning me to the cold ground, one knee on my chest, the other digging into my bad wrist. I'm trying to fight back, but it doesn't help. It never helps. Not here, not like this, when he's taking his time.

And he is. He's carving lines across my body. Ankles to knees, knees to hips, hips to shoulders, shoulders to elbows, elbows to wrists.

"There," he says, dragging the knife from my elbow down to my wrist. "Now we can see your seams." If I could breathe, I would scream. My uniform is dark and wet with blood. It shows up red against the black fabric, like paint—splashed across my front, pooling beneath my body.

"Almost done," he says, lifting the blade to my throat.

And then someone scrapes her chair against the floor and I snap back to English.

Only a few minutes have passed—the teacher's attention is still on the essay she's reading aloud—but it was long enough that my hands are trembling and I can taste the blood in my mouth from biting down on my tongue.

*At least I didn't scream,* I think as I grip the desk and try to shake the last of the nightmare off. My heart is slamming in my chest. I know it's not real. Just my imagination—today the role of Mackenzie Bishop's fears will be played by the History who tried to kill her in a variety of ways. I still spend the rest of the day picturing Roland's room in the Archive—the daybed with the black blanket, the violin whispering from the wall, the promise of dreamless sleep—and digging my fingernails into my palms to stay awake.

By the time school lets out, there are red crescents across both palms, and I shove through the doors of the building and onto the path, gasping for air. I close my eyes and take a few deep breaths. I feel like I'm cracking. Everything aches, the pain drawing itself into phantom lines.

Ankles to knees, knees to hips, hips to shoulders, shoulders to elbows, elbows to wrists.

"Hey, Mac!"

I open my eyes to find Wesley a little ways down the path, a sports bag slung over his shoulder. I must not be hiding the frayed nerves well enough, because he frowns. Cash is only a few strides behind him, talking to another senior guy.

"All good?" asks Wes as casually as possible.

"All good," I call back.

Cash and the other guy catch up. They're both carrying sports bags.

"Hey, Mac," Cash says, shifting the bag on his shoulder. "Think you can find your way without me?"

"I think I can manage," I reply. "The parking lot is that way, right?" I point in the opposite direction of the lot. Cash laughs. Wesley's eyes are still hovering on me. I flash him a smile, Cash knocks his shoulder, and the three head off toward the fields.

I take a last, steadying breath and head through campus to the front gate and the bike rack. I unlock Dante and swing my leg over the bike, and I'm just about to head home when I see a girl in the lot.

I recognize her. It's the girl from the pendant I found in the locker room. The one who clutched a steering wheel in a driveway at night sobbing and dodged the glass her mother threw at her head.

She's a senior—gold stripes—and she's standing with a group of girls in the lot, leaning up against a convertible and smiling with perfect teeth. Every inch of her has that manicured look that so often comes with money, and it's hard to line this girl up with the one in the memories, even though I know they're the same. Finally she waves to the others and strides up onto the sidewalk, walking away from Hyde's campus.

Before I even realize it, I'm following her. Every step she takes away from Hyde seems to weigh her down, changing her a fraction from the girl in the lot to the girl in the memories. I remember the anger and sadness worn into the pendant, and I will myself to call out. She turns around.

"Sorry," I say, pedaling up to her, "this is going to sound really random, but is this yours?"

I pull the necklace from my pocket and hold it up. Her eyes widen and she nods.

"Where did you find it?" she asks, reaching out.

"The locker room," I say, dropping the silver piece into her palm.

Her perfectly plucked eyebrows draw together. "How did you know it was mine?"

*Because I read the memories,* I think, *and you keep bringing your hand to the place where it should be.*

"Been asking around all afternoon," I lie. "One of the seniors in the lot just now said they thought it was yours and pointed me in this direction."

She looks down at the pendant. "Thanks. You didn't have to do that."

"It wasn't a problem," I say. "It seemed like something someone would miss." The girl nods, staring down at the metal. "What's the *B* stand for?"

"Bethany," she says. "I really shouldn't care so much about it," she adds. "It's just a piece of junk. Worthless, really." But her thumb is already there again, wearing away the front.

"If it matters to you, then it's not worthless."

She nods and rubs the pendant absently, and we stand there a moment, awkward and alone on the sidewalk, before I finally say, "Hey . . . is everything okay?"

She stiffens and stands straighter. I can see her mentally adjusting her mask.

"Of course." She flashes me a perfect, practiced smile.

Smiling is the worst thing you can do if you want the world to think you're okay when you're not. Some people can't help it—it's like a tic, a tell—and others do it on purpose, thinking people will buy whatever they're selling if it comes with a flash of teeth. But the truth is, smiling only makes a lie harder to pass off. It's like a giant crack in the front of a mask. But I don't know Bethany, not really, and she doesn't know what I saw. And since she's doing a pretty decent impression of a healthy person—much better than mine—I say, "Okay. Just checking."

I'm about to pedal off when she says, "Wait. I've never seen you at Hyde."

"New student," I tell her. "Mackenzie Bishop."

Bethany chews her lip, and I can imagine her mom yelling at her for such a nasty habit.

"Welcome to Hyde," she says, "and thanks again, Mackenzie. You're right about the necklace, you know. It's not worthless. I'm really glad you found it."

"So am I," I say. I feel like I should say something else, something *more*, but I can't, not without sounding trite or creepy, so I just say, "See you tomorrow?"

"Yeah," she says, "see you."

We head our separate ways. When I reach the main road, I think for a second I see the golden man standing at the corner, but by the time I cross the street and steal a glance back, there's no one there.

I'm just parking Dante in front of the Coronado when I feel the scratch of letters in my pocket and find a new name on my list, but I don't get the chance to hunt it down, because Mom heads me off in the lobby.

"Oh, good, you're home," she says, which is never a good open-ing line, because it means she needs something. Considering she's got a bakery box, a slip of paper, and a frazzled look, I'd say it's a guarantee.

"I am," I say cautiously. "What's up?"

"Last-minute delivery," she says.

My bones groan in response. "Where's Berk?"

She blows a stray chunk of hair out of her eyes. "He's got some kind of art opening, and he already left. I know you've got home-work and I wouldn't normally ask, but with the business being so new, I really need every order I can get and . . ."

A headache is starting to form behind my eyes, but the way I see it, anything that convinces Mom I am *okay* and *normal* and a *good daughter* is worth it. I take the box and the slip of paper from her hands, and she responds in the worst way possible. She throws her arms around my neck, engulfing me in a hug full of breaking glass and twisting metal and boxes of plates being pushed down stairs and all the other piercing sounds that make up her noise. My headache instantly gets worse.

"I'd better get going," I say, pulling away.

Mom nods and bounces back toward the coffee shop, and I drag myself back toward Dante, reading over the slip of paper. Beneath the order name, Mom has drawn a rudimentary map. The delivery is only a few miles away, if her chicken scratch can be trusted, but I've never been to that part of the city before.

For the first time in ages, I get lost.

I zone out a little while riding and end up overshooting the apartment complex by several blocks, and I'm forced to double back. By the time I've found the right building, climbed several flights of stairs—the elevator is broken—dropped off the bakery box to a housewife, and gotten back to my bike, the sun is sinking. My whole body is starting to ache from fatigue.

I swing my leg over the bike and hope Mom's on the phone with Colleen right this moment, telling her how *okay* I am.

But as I speed toward the Coronado, I don't feel very okay. My hands are shaking and I just want to get home and through tonight and back to Roland's room, so I take a shortcut through a park. I don't know the park, but if the map in my head is even close to correct, it'll be faster than the streets.

It *is* faster, until I see a guy crouching in the middle of the path and have to hit the brakes hard to keep from slamming into him. I nearly lose my balance as the bike comes to a jarring stop a few feet in front of him.

The moment I put my foot on the ground, I know I've made a mistake. Something moves behind me, but I don't dare take my eyes off the guy in front of me as he straightens and pulls one hand from the pocket of his hoodie. I hear a metal *snick* sound, and a switchblade flashes in his fingers.

"Hey there, pretty thing," he coos.

I bring my foot back to the pedal, but it doesn't move; I twist in my seat to find a second guy with a pipe threaded through my back wheel, pinning it still. His breath smells like oil.

"Let go," I say, using the tone Da taught me to use with difficult Histories. But these aren't Histories, they're humans—and they're both armed.

One of them chuckles. The other one whistles.

"Why don't you come off that toy and play with us instead?" says the one with the knife. He saunters forward, and the one holding the wheel reaches for my hair. I'm at enough of a disadvantage without straddling a bike, so I dismount.

"See?" says the one with the pipe. "She *wants* to play."

"There's a good girl," coos the one with the knife.

"Good *school*girl," chimes the other.

My pulse is starting to race.

*. . . residual trauma and extreme fatigue, paired with the influx of adrenaline . . .*

"Get out of my way," I say.

The one with the knife wiggles the blade back and forth like a finger, tsk-tsking.

"You should ask nicely. In fact," he says, taking another step forward, "maybe you should beg."

"Get out of my way, *please*," I growl, my pulse thudding in my ears.

The one with the pipe chuckles behind me.

The one with the knife smiles.

They keep shifting so I can only see one of them at a time. When I try to cheat a step to the side, the pipe appears, barring my path.

"Where you going, sweetheart?" says the one with the knife. "The fun hasn't even started yet."

They're both closing in.

My head is pounding and my vision is starting to blur, and then the one with the pipe shoves me forward into the one with the knife, and he grabs my bad wrist *hard*, and the pain shoots through me like a current—and then it happens.

The world stops.

Vanishes.

Goes black.

A long, lovely, silent moment of black.

And then it comes back, and I'm standing there in the park, just like before, and my head is killing me and my hands feel damp, and when I look down at them, I see why.

They're covered in blood.

# TWELVE

THE MAN with the knife is lying at my feet.

His nose is broken. Blood is gushing down his face, and one of his legs looks like it's bent at the wrong angle. His switchblade is jutting out of his thigh. I don't remember stabbing him or even touching him, but my hands say I did. My knuckles are torn up, and I have a shallow cut on one palm—probably from the switchblade. At first, I'm only aware of how numb I feel and how slowly time is moving. And then it slams into me, along with the pain radiating across my hands and through my head. *What have I done?* I close my eyes and take a few steadying breaths, hoping the body will just disappear—this will all just disappear—but it doesn't, and this time the breathing doesn't help me remember. There's just more panic and a wall of black.

And then I hear sounds of a struggle and remember the guy with the metal pipe, and I turn to see him being strangled by the golden man.

The golden man is standing there with his arm calmly wrapped around the thug's throat, pulling back and up until his shoes skim the ground. The thug is flailing silently, swinging his arms—the pipe is lying on the path a few feet away—as he runs out of breath. As the golden man tightens his grip, his sleeve slides up and I can see three lines cut into his skin.

Crew marks.

I was right. . . . Oh, god, I was *right*. And that means a member of Crew just saw me do . . . this. I don't even know what I did, but he saw it. Then again, he's currently strangling someone in front of me. But I bet he at least remembers doing it.

The thug stops struggling, and the golden man lets his body fall to the ground.

"I hate fighting humans," he says, brushing off his pants. "You have to work so hard not to kill them."

"Who are you?" I ask.

His brow crinkles. "What, not even a *thanks?*"

"Thanks," I say shakily.

"Welcome. Wouldn't be much of a gentleman if I didn't lend a hand." His eyes drift down to the man at my feet. "Not sure you needed it, though. That was quite a show." *Was it?* He reaches out. "Let me see those hands."

His fingers nearly brush my skin when I jerk away. He's not wearing a ring.

"Ah," he says, reading my distrust. He produces a silver band from his pocket, holding it up so I can see the three lines etched on its surface before he slides it on. This time when he holds out his hands, I reluctantly give him mine. His noise is low and steady as a heartbeat through my head.

"How did you know?" he asks, turning over my hands to check for broken bones.

"Posture. Attention. Ego."

He smiles that half smile. "And here I figured you just saw the marks." He runs his thumbs over my knuckles. "Or, you know, there's the fact that we've met."

I wince as he traces the bones in my hands.

"In your defense," he adds, "we weren't formally introduced."

And suddenly it clicks. When Wesley and I were summoned to the Archive last month to explain how we'd allowed a teenage History to escape into the Coronado, the golden man was there. He came in late and flashed me a lazy smile. When he heard how long Wesley and I had been paired up before we let the History escape—three hours—he actually *laughed*. The woman with him didn't.

"I recognized you," I lie.

"No you didn't," he says simply, testing my fingers. "You thought I looked familiar, but there's a big difference between knowing a face and placing it. Stare at anyone long enough and you'll start to think you've seen them before. The name's Eric, by the way." He lets go of my hands. "And nothing's broken."

"Why have you been following me?"

He arches a brow. "Just be glad I was."

"That's not a good enough answer," I snap. "Why have you been following me?"

Again, that lazy smile. "Why does anyone do anything for the Archive? Because they're told to."

"But why?" I press. "And who told you to?"

"Miss Bishop, I don't think now's the time for an interrogation," he says, gesturing to the bodies and then back to me. I look down again at my blood-covered hands. They're shaking, so I curl them into fists, even though it sends sparks of pain across my skin.

"I want an answer."

Eric shrugs. "Even if it's a lie?"

The man with the knife in his leg begins to stir.

"You should go home now," says Eric, fetching the piece of pipe and wiping the prints with his sleeve before tossing it back to the ground. "I'll take care of these two."

"What are you going to do with them?"

He shrugs. "Make them disappear." He rights my bike and walks it toward me.

"Go," he says. "And be careful."

My hands are still shaking as I wipe them on my shirt, mount the bike, and leave.

On the way home, as my body calms and my mind clears, the memories begin to trickle back in flashes of color and sound.

The crack of bone as my free palm came up under his nose.

The cry and the cursing and the blind slashing of the switchblade.

The snap of his knee as my shoe slammed into the side of it.

The silent moment when the switchblade tumbled from his hand into mine.

The scream as I drove it down into his thigh.

The crunch of my fist across his face as he crumbled forward. Again. And again.

*Seconds,* I marvel. It took only seconds to break so many things.

And even though I couldn't remember at first, I'm not sorry I did it. Not even a little. I *wanted* to hurt him. I wanted to make him regret the way he looked at me, like I wouldn't be able to fight back, like I was weak. I look down at my raw knuckles as I ride. I'm not weak anymore . . . but what am I becoming instead?

"What happened to your hands?" shrieks Mom when I walk into the apartment. She has her phone to her ear and she says a hurried "We'll talk later" to whoever's on the other end before hanging up and rushing over.

"Biking accident," I say tiredly, shrugging off my bag. It's not a total lie, and I'm not about to tell her that I got assaulted on the way back from *her* delivery. She'd implode.

"Are you all right?" she asks, taking my arm. I wince, less from my wounded hands than the sudden high-pitched crackle that comes with her touch. Still, I manage not to pull free as she guides me into the kitchen.

"I'm fine," I lie, holding my hands under the sink while she pours cool water over them. I managed to wipe off most of the blood, but the knuckles are red and raw. "You're home early," I say, changing the subject. "Slow day at the coffee shop?"

Mom gives me a quizzical look. "Mackenzie," she says, "it's nearly seven o'clock."

My eyes drift to the windows. It's halfway to dark. "Huh."

"You were late, and I started to get worried. Now I see I had a good reason to be."

"I'm fine, really."

She cuts off the water and sets to towel-drying my hands, tutting as she unearths a bottle of rubbing alcohol from beneath the sink. It feels nice—not the rubbing alcohol, that hurts like hell, but having Mom patch me up. When I was little, I came home with all kinds of scrapes—the products of more normal childhood escapades, of course—and I'd sit on the counter and let Mom fix them. Whatever it was, she could fix it. After I became a Keeper and started hiding my wounds instead of proudly presenting them, I'd watch her fix Ben, the same worshipping expression in his eyes as she tended to his battle scars.

These days, I'm so used to hiding my cuts and bruises—so used to telling Mom I don't need her and telling her I'm fine when I'm not—that it's a relief not being able to hide an injury. Even if I have to lie about how it happened.

125

Then Dad walks in.

"What happened?" he asks, dropping his briefcase. It's almost funny, in a sick way, their level of concern over a few cut knuckles. I hate to think how they'd react if they could see some of my larger scars, what they'd say if they knew the truth behind my broken wrist. I nearly laugh before I remember that it's not *that* kind of funny.

"Biking accident," I repeat. "I'm fine."

"And the bike?" he asks.

"The bike's fine, too."

"I'd better check it out," he says, turning toward the door.

"Dad, I said it's fine."

"No offense, Mac, but you don't know much about bikes, and—"

"Leave it," I snap, and Mom looks up from her first aid kit long enough to give me a warning look. I close my eyes and swallow. "The paint might be nicked in a couple places"—I had the sense to scuff it up on the sidewalk—"but it'll live to ride another day. I took the worst of it," I say, displaying my hands.

For once, Dad's not having it. He crosses his arms. "Explain to me the physics of this biking accident."

*And doubt,* Da said, *is like a current you have to swim against.*

"Peter," starts Mom, but he puts up a hand to stop her.

"I want to know exactly how it happened."

My heart is pounding as I hold his gaze. "The sidewalk was cracked," I say, fighting to keep my voice steady. "The front wheel of the bike caught. I threw my hands out when I went down, but rolled and caught the street with my knuckles instead of my palms. Now, if the Inquisition and the infirmary are both done," I finish, pulling free of Mom and pushing past Dad, "I have homework."

I storm down the hall and into my room, slamming the door

for good measure before slumping against it as the last of the fight goes out of me. It feels like a poor take on a teen tantrum, but apparently it works.

Neither one of them bothers me the rest of the night.



Roland frowns. "What happened to your hands?"

He's waiting in the atrium, perched on the edge of a table with his folder in his lap. When I walk up, his eyes go straight to my knuckles.

"Biking accident," I say automatically.

Something flashes in his eyes. Disappointment. Roland pushes off the table. "I'm not your parents, Miss Bishop," he says, crossing the room. "Don't insult me by lying."

"Sorry," I say, following him out of the atrium and down the hall toward the Librarians' quarters. "There was an incident."

He glances back over his shoulder. "With a History?"

"No. A human."

"What kind of incident?"

"The kind that's taken care of." I consider telling Roland about Eric, but when I form the words in my head—*someone in the Archive is having me followed*—they make me sound cracked. Paranoid. The worry's already showing in Roland's eyes. The last thing I want is to make it worse. Plus, I can't prove anything, not without letting Roland into my head, and if I do that, if he sees the state I'm in, he'll . . . No, I won't rat out Eric, not until I know what he was doing there or why he's been following me.

"Did our lovely new doormen see your hands?"

"The sentinels? No." Patrick did, though. He didn't say anything, just looked at me like I was that useless kid again. *Bloody nose*

127

*or bloody knuckles, can't hold her own.* If only he knew how the other guy looked.

"Was it another tunnel moment?" asks Roland.

I look down at my hands. "I remember what happened."

We walk the rest of the way to his room in silence. He lets me in, and I see him pull his watch from his pocket and run his thumb over the surface once before setting it on top of the table. Something tugs at me. It's the same set of motions he did last night. The exact same set. It's so hard to think of Roland as a History, but the repetition reminds me that his appearance isn't the only static thing about him.

He gestures to the daybed, and I sink gratefully onto the soft surface, my body begging for rest.

"Sleep well," he says, folding into his chair. I close my eyes and listen to the sound of him making notes, the scratch of letters on paper low and comforting, like rain. I feel myself sinking, and there's a moment—one brief, terrifying moment—where I remember the nightmares that wait. But then the moment is gone and I'm drawn down into sleep.

The next thing I feel is Roland shaking me awake.

I sit up, stiff from the fight and from sleep. I study the fresh bruises that color my hands as Roland moves about the room. The relief at having slept is dampened by dread as I think of the slice of conversation I overheard beyond the door.

*It's not a permanent solution.*

Roland's right. I cannot keep doing this. I cannot come here every night. But it's the only place the nightmares don't follow me.

"Roland," I say softly. "If it keeps getting worse . . . if *I* keep getting worse . . . will Agatha . . . ?"

"As long as you keep doing your job," he says, "she can't hurt you."

"I want to believe you."

"Miss Bishop, Agatha's job is to *assess* members of the Archive. Her greatest concern is making sure that things run smoothly, that everyone is doing his job. She is not the bogeyman. She cannot just sweep down and snatch you up and take your mind away. Even though she'd like you to think that."

"But last time—"

"Last time you confessed to involvement in a *crime*, so yes, your future was left to her discretion. This is different. She cannot even look inside your mind without permission, let alone take your memories."

"Consent. How forward-thinking." But something eats at me. "Did Wesley give permission?"

Roland's brow crinkles. "What?"

"That day . . ." We both know which day I'm talking about. "He doesn't remember it. Any of it." Did he want to forget? Or was he made to? "Did he give the Archive permission to take those memories?"

Roland seems surprised to hear this. "Mr. Ayers was in very bad shape," he says. "I doubt he was conscious."

"So he couldn't give permission."

"That would have broken protocol." Roland hesitates. "Maybe it wasn't the Archive's doing, Miss Bishop. You know more than most what trauma does to the mind. Maybe he does remember. Or maybe he's chosen to forget."

I cringe. "Maybe."

"Mackenzie, the Archive has rules, and they are followed."

"So as long as I don't grant Agatha permission, I'm supposedly safe? My mind is my own?"

"For the most part," says Roland, perching on the edge of his chair. "As with any system, there are ways around and through. You're not the only one who can *grant* permission. If you denied Agatha access to your mind and she had good reason to believe it harbored guilt, she could petition the board of directors. She wouldn't do it, not unless she had a strong case—evidence that you had committed a crime or that you could no longer perform your job or be trusted with the things you know—but if she had one . . ." He trails off.

"If she had a strong case . . ." I prompt.

"We mustn't let it come to that," says Roland. "Every time the board has granted her access to someone's mind, they've been found unfit and been removed from service. Her record means she won't make the request lightly, but it also means the board will never deny her if she does. And once she has access to your mind—through your permission or theirs—anything she finds there can be used against you. If she found you unfit, you would be sentenced to alteration."

*"Execution."*

Roland cringes, but doesn't contradict me. "I would challenge the ruling, and there would be a trial, but if the board stands behind her, there is nothing I can do. It is very literally in the directors' hands. You see, only they are authorized to carry out alterations."

Da only told me one thing about the board of directors, and that's that you never want to meet one of them. Now I understand why.

Roland frowns, deep in thought. "But it will not come to that," he adds. "Agatha is the one who pardoned you in the first place. I doubt she's looking for reasons to reverse that decision."

I think of Eric following me. *Someone* told him to. "Maybe Agatha's not," I say, "but what if someone else is? Someone who disagreed with her ruling? Like Patrick. Would he go this far? And if someone handed her a case, would she overlook it?"

"Miss Bishop," says Roland. "These are not the thoughts to be filling your head with right now. Don't give her a reason to question her ruling. Just do your job and stay out of trouble, and you'll be okay."

His words are calm, but his voice is laced with cracks and his brow is furrowed.

"Besides," he adds softly, crossing to the side table to fetch his watch, "I promised your grandfather I would look after you." He slides the silver watch into his pocket. "That's a promise I intend to keep."

As I follow him out the door and through the twisting, turning halls, I can't help but remember that he made a promise to the Archive, too, the day of my initiation.

*If we do this, and she proves herself unfit in any way,* said a member of the panel, *she will forfeit the position.*

*And if she proves unfit,* said another, *you, Roland, will remove her yourself.*

# THIRTEEN

**R**OLAND LEAVES ME at the mouth of the antechamber. I nod at the Librarian behind the desk—we've only met in passing—but she doesn't even look up from the ledger, and again I find myself thinking that the book is very large and I am only one page. How many of those pages belong to Keepers? How many to Crew? And why have I never seen any of them in the Archive? I grew up here. Did no one else? Am I really so different? Is that why Patrick hates me?

The eyes of the sentinels follow me out.

On my way home, I dispatch a name on my list with little pretense. The boy takes one look at my battered knuckles and shrinks away, but doesn't run, and I'd be lying if I didn't say that, for once, the fear in his eyes felt gratifying. It is so much easier to handle him with intimidation than by spinning tales and earning trust.

I roll the stiffness from my shoulders as I return home and shower. I'm out and pulling on my uniform when there's a knock on my bedroom door, and Dad calls out, "You better hurry up or we're going to be late."

I finish tugging on my shirt and nearly forget to tuck the key under my collar before opening the door. "What are you talking about?"

Dad flashes his keys. "I'm driving you to school."

"No, you're not."

"I don't mind," he says.

"I do."

He sighs and heads for the kitchen to fill his travel mug with coffee. "I thought you might be nervous about riding your bike."

"Well, I'm not." I frown and follow. "And isn't there a saying about horses and getting back on?"

"Well, yes, but—"

"I'll be *fine*," I say, swinging my bag over my shoulder. His eyes go to my knuckles.

"And you're sure the bike's in working shape?"

"The bike is fine, too. But if you're so worried, why don't you come check it out?"

That seems to pacify him a little, and we head downstairs. I duck into the café and grab a coffee and a muffin while he looks over Dante. Bishop's is busy in the morning, and Mom doesn't even see me come or go. Berk passes me a to-go cup and a paper bag and shoos me away.

"Well, it looks all right," says Dad, brushing off his hands as I join him on the curb. "You sure you don't want a lift?"

"Positive," I say, swinging my leg easily up over the bike to show him how comfortable I feel. "See? Just like a horse."

Dad frowns. "Where's your helmet?"

"My what?" Dad's look turns positively icy, and I'm opening my mouth to say I don't need it when I realize that that's probably a bad line after last night; instead I tell him where it's been since the day he bought it for me. "Under my desk."

"Don't. Move." Dad vanishes back through the doors and I sigh and stand there, straddling the bike with my coffee balanced on the handlebars. I give the street a quick scan, but there's no sign of Eric. I don't know whether that makes me feel better or worse, now that I know he's real. I still don't know why he's been following me.

Maybe it's standard procedure. A checkup. Or maybe he's looking for evidence. Cracks.

Dad reappears and tosses me the helmet. I pluck it out of the air and snap it on. At least it's not pink or covered in flowers or anything.

"Happy now?" I ask. Dad nods, and I pedal off before he can decide the coffee on my handlebars is a safety hazard.

The morning's cool, and I breathe deeply and try to shake off Roland's worry and Dad's distrust as the world blurs past. I'm halfway to school when I round the corner and hop onto a stretch of sidewalk that lines a park, stretching ahead a couple of blocks to form a straight and empty path. In a moment of weakness—or cockiness, or fatigue, maybe—I let myself close my eyes. It's nothing more than a long blink, a second, two tops, but when I open them there's just enough time to see the runner cut out of the park and into my way, and not enough time to swerve.

The collision is a tangle of handles and wheels and limbs, and we both go down hard on the concrete. My head bounces off the sidewalk. The helmet absorbs the worst of it—I'm sure Dad would be thrilled—and I manage to free my leg from under the bike and get to my feet, pain burning through my sleeve and sweatpants. I decide not to look at the damage.

A few feet away, the runner is slower to recover. He gets to his hands and knees and pauses, checking himself before he stands all the way up. I hurry over and offer my hand since I'm the one who technically hit him, even though he's the one who came out of nowhere.

"Are you all right?" I ask. "Anything broken?"

"Nah, I'm okay," he says, getting to his feet. He's not very old—maybe twenty—and he's a little scuffed, but looks otherwise unscathed. Except for the fact that he's *covered* in my coffee.

He looks down and notices it for the first time.

"Huh," he says. "I smell better than I did before."

I groan. "I'm really sorry."

"I think it was my fault," he says, rolling his neck.

"I know it was," I say. "But I'm still sorry I hit you. You came out of nowhere."

He rubs his head. "I guess I got a little lost in the music," he says, gesturing to the earbuds hanging around his neck. He smiles, but seems a little unsteady on his feet.

"Are you sure you're okay?"

He nods cautiously. "Yeah, yeah, I think so. . . ."

"Do you know your name?"

His brow crinkles. "Jason. Do you know *your* name?"

"I didn't hit my head."

"Well, can *I* know your name?" he asks. I think he might be flirting with me.

"Mackenzie. Mackenzie Bishop." I hold up four fingers. "How many fingers do you see?"

"Seven." I'm about to tell him he needs a doctor when he says, "Kidding. Kidding. What happened to your hands, Mackenzie?"

"A bike accident," I say without thinking. "You shouldn't joke when people are trying to determine if you're okay."

"Wow, how many bike accidents have you been in this week?"

"Bad week," I tell him, righting Dante. The bike's a little bruised, but it'll work; I'm relieved, because if I'd broken it, I don't know what I would have told my parents. Not the truth. Even though it *is* the truth this time.

"You're pretty."

"You hit your head."

135

"That is true. But you're probably still pretty."

"Mm-hmm."

"Mackenzie Bishop," he says, sounding out every syllable. "Pretty name."

"Yeah." I drag my phone from my pocket to check the time. If I don't go, I'm going to be late. "Look, Jason, are you going to be okay?"

"I'm okay. But I feel like we should trade insurance info or something. Do they have that, for bike-body collisions? Do you have bike insurance? If you're getting into this many accidents maybe you should—"

"Do you have a phone?"

He looks at me like he doesn't know what that is. Or why I'm asking.

"A phone," I say again, "so I can give you my number. So you can text me when you get home. So I know you're okay."

He pats his pockets. "I don't run with it."

I shuffle through my backpack and dig out a Sharpie and a scrap of paper and write my number on it. "Here. Take it. Text me," I say, trying to make it as clear as possible that this is a here's-my-number-civic-duty and not a here's-my-number-call-me-hotstuff kind of situation.

Jason takes the piece of paper, and I'm about to get back on the bike when he plucks my phone from my hand and starts typing away. When he passes it back, I see he's programmed his number in with the title *Jason the runner you ran over.*

"Just to be safe," he says.

"Yeah, okay, sure," I reply, and before the moment can get any more awkward, I climb back on Dante—horses, falling off, getting back on, etc.—and pedal off. (I wish Eric could have witnessed my stellar Samaritan behavior and reported *that* back to the Archive, but of course *now* he's nowhere to be seen.) I look back once at the corner to make sure Jason is still standing (he is), and then I head to school.

By the time I get there, the lot is filling up and Wesley is leaning back against the bike rack. Another girl—a silver-striped one this time—is hanging off his shoulder, whispering in his ear. Whatever she's saying, it must be good; he's looking down, chewing his lip, and smiling. My chest constricts, even though it shouldn't because I shouldn't care. He can flirt if he wants to. I hop down from the bike and walk it over. His eyes drift lazily up to find mine, and he straightens.

The girl on his shoulder nearly falls off.

I can't help but grin. He says something, and her flirty little smile fades. By the time I reach the bike rack, she's vanished through the gates—but not before shooting a dark look my way.

"Hey, you," he says cheerfully.

"Hey," I say; then, because I can't help myself, I look around and add, "Where's Cash?"

The blow sticks, and Wesley's good humor thins. Then his eyes wander down to my hands, and it dissolves entirely. "What happened?"

I almost lie. I open my mouth to feed him the same line I've fed everyone else, but I stop. I have a rule about lying to Wesley. I don't do it anymore. I can justify evasions and omissions, but I won't lie outright—not after what happened this summer. But I'm also not going to relive last night here on the steps of Hyde, so I say, "It's a funny story. I'll tell you later."

"I'll hold you to it," he says, and then he looks past me. "There you are. Mackenzie here was beginning to worry."

I turn to find Cash striding up the curb, a set of car keys in one hand and a paper bag in the other.

"Morning, lovelies," he says, opening the bag and producing three coffees in a to-go tray. Wesley's eyes light up at the sight of the third drink. He reaches for it, but before his fingers touch the paper cup, Cash pulls it out of reach.

"You can't say I never do nice things for you."

"Statement retracted."

Cash offers me one of the coffees, and I take a long, savoring swallow, since I only got a taste of this morning's cup before I spilled it all over Jason the runner.

"Sorry for the delay," says Cash. "They kept getting the order wrong."

"How hard is it to make three black coffees?" asks Wes.

"Not hard at all," says Cash. "But the order was for two black coffees"—he takes the second coffee—"and a soy hot chocolate caramel whip." He turns the tray in his hand, offering Wesley the last, fancy drink.

Wes scowls.

Cash continues to hold out the tray. "If you're going to be a girl about these things, you're going to get a girly drink. Now be gracious."

"My hero," grumbles Wesley, reaching for the cup.

"And don't pretend you don't like it," adds Cash. "I distinctly remember you ordering it last winter."

"Lies."

Cash taps his temple. "Photographic memory."

Wesley mumbles something unkind into his soy hot chocolate.

The three of us linger at the gates of Hyde, sipping our drinks and watching the flow of students, enjoying the time before the bell rings. And then Cash breaks the peace with one small question, lobbed at Wes.

"Did you hear about Bethany?"

The coffee freezes in my throat. "The blond senior? What about her?"

Cash looks surprised by the fact I know who she is. "Her mom said she never came home yesterday. They haven't been able to find her anywhere." He looks at Wes. "You think she finally ran away?"

"I guess it's possible," he says. He looks upset.

"You okay?" asks Cash. "I know you two—"

"I'm fine," Wes cuts him off, even though I'd really like to hear the end of that sentence. "Just sorry to hear it," he adds.

"Yeah," adds Cash. "Though I can't say I'm surprised."

"Why's that?" I ask.

Behind my eyes, the memory from the pendant echoes: a distraught Bethany clutching the steering wheel, willing herself to go. But what happened? What led up to that moment?

Cash hesitates, then looks to Wes, who says only, "She was having a hard time at home."

And then, before any of us can say more, the bell rings, and we pour through the gates with the rest of the students. Cash and Wes branch off and the conversation dies, but the questions follow me to class. Did Bethany really run away? Why? And if she did, why did she wait until now? She had all summer. What was it about yesterday?

A darker thread runs through my thoughts.

First Mr. Phillip, and now Bethany.

They both have something in common. *Me.*

A sinking feeling follows me through the halls and into class.

Da said you had to see patterns but not go searching for them. Am I drawing lines where they shouldn't be, or am I missing something right in front of me?


No text from Jason.

I check my phone before Precalc and then again before Lit Theory. Finally, on my way to Wellness, I shoot him a message.

> Did you get home safe?

I try to calm my nerves as I shove my phone and my bag into my locker, aware that the noise in the room is different. It's still loud, still full of slamming metal and the shuffle of bodies and voices, but those voices aren't full of laughter. They're full of gossip, and gossip is the kind of thing told in fake whispers rather than shouts, lending the locker room a kind of false quiet.

I only catch snippets of the gossip itself, but I know who it's about.

Bethany.

Popular girl. Small school. The students are latching on to the story. A clump of juniors thinks she was kidnapped for ransom. Another thinks she ran away with a boy. A handful of seniors echo Wes and Cash, saying they're not surprised, after what happened— but they never say exactly what happened. Instead they trail off into silence. One junior thinks she got pregnant. Another thinks she's dead. A few talk under their breaths and shoot dirty looks at the girls who don't have the grace to gossip quietly.

Whatever the story, one thing's for sure: Bethany is missing.

"I don't think it's that simple," says Amber, turning the corner.

"You can't turn everything into a crime," says Safia, following on her heels. "It's morbid."

They slump down onto the bench beside me while I tug on my workout shirt, wishing it were long-sleeved so I could hide my cut-up knuckles. Instead I shove my hands into the pockets of my workout shorts.

"I'm just saying—there's evidence, and it contradicts."

"Admit it, you just want it to be more dramatic than it is."

"I'd say it's already dramatic enough. Bethany's life was like a bad soap opera."

"Ugh," says Safia, shuddering. "You just said *was.* Like she's dead. Don't do that."

"You're talking about that girl who ran away?" I ask as casually as possible.

Amber nods. "*If* she ran away."

I frown. "What makes you think she didn't?"

"Because that wouldn't be as exciting," says Safia, rolling her eyes.

Amber waves her away. "There's evidence that she was *going to* run away, I'll give you that. But there's also evidence that something happened. That she changed her mind."

"What do you mean?" I ask, closing my locker.

"Well, my dad told me that—"

"They got your dad involved? Already?"

"Not *officially*," says Amber. "But he knows Bethany's mom, so he agreed to look into it."

My chest tightens. Make that two things the cases have in common. Me. And the detective. *It's nothing,* I tell myself as I follow Amber and Safia into the gym. *It's nothing, because I didn't do*

*anything. I was nice. I was helpful. I made two people's days better. And*
*those two people just happened to disappear.*

"Anyway," says Amber, "Bethany's backpack and purse were missing, too. But the car was still there, and there was a suitcase tucked in the back, and the car door was open. Either she was grabbed, or she got halfway through leaving and then decided to just walk away instead."

She and Safia head for the mats, and even though I want to run—want to do something to clear my head and calm my nerves—I follow.

"Which would be smart," Amber is saying, "if she really wanted to disappear, since cars are so easy to track."

"Why is everyone convinced she wanted to disappear?" I ask, sinking down onto the mat. "People keep saying they're not surprised, that it was only a matter of time. What do they mean?"

Amber sighs. "Over the summer, my dad was called out to Bethany's house on a noise complaint. There'd been a screaming match, and when he got there, he found Bethany in the driveway with all her things."

"Back up," says Safia. "You're skipping all the good bits." She turns to me. "Okay, so Bethany's mom is a leech. That's what we call it when you only marry someone for their money. Then Beth's dad's company hits a bump or something, and her mom drops him like that." She snaps her fingers. "Takes as much as she can, including the house, and then turns around and finds this new beau to leech off of. He moves in after, like, three weeks."

"Girls," shouts one of the gym teachers. "More work, less chat."

"Stretching is an essential part of wellness!" Safia shouts back. She proceeds to exaggerate every one of her motions, which almost makes me smile.

"So," she continues, "sleazy dude has been there all of a week when he's home alone with Bethany and takes a go at her."

My stomach turns. "What happened?"

"She did what any self-respecting Hyde School girl would do. She punched him in the face. But when she tried to tell her mom what happened, she said it was *Bethany's* fault."

Behind my eyes the woman pitches the glass at Bethany's head.

"And the sleaze totally twisted it to fit," says Safia. "He claimed Bethany tried to seduce *him*. I'm surprised Bethany didn't leave that night. I know she thought about it."

"Dad reported it, but it was word against word. Nothing happened. *But* he told Bethany to call him if the jerk ever tried anything again. If she didn't feel safe."

"So your dad believed her."

Amber's forehead crinkles. "Of course. He's not an idiot. We all thought Bethany would bail, but she didn't. I guess I get it. She just had to get through this year, and then she'd be free." She shakes her head. "I don't know what happened. But it feels off. And why was that suitcase still in the back?"

Safia chews her lip. "Bethany told Wesley once that she kept a bag ready. In case she couldn't take it anymore. That when it got bad she'd sit out in the car, all ready to go. I heard him tell Cash. That still doesn't explain why she left it."

"Did Wes and Bethany have a thing?" I ask.

Safia arches a perfect eyebrow. "Why? Jealous?"

"I'm just trying to get on the same page."

"They had as much of a thing as Wesley has with anyone," says Amber. "Which is not much."

"He's a jerk and a tease," says Safia, even as her gaze wanders over to the track where he and a handful of other guys are running.

She gets to her feet. "Look, not that this hasn't been morbid, girl-bonding fun, but I've got to scout a date for Fall Fest so I don't die alone. Cheers, kids."

Safia bounces off across the gym. Amber watches her go. She looks as unsettled as I feel.

"You don't think she ran away."

Amber shakes her head. "I know it's really early to jump to conclusions, I just have a bad feeling."

"Is the sleazy guy a suspect?" I ask.

"He alibied out, but it's not like he hasn't bought his way out of trouble before. I just . . . I don't trust anything about this. Do you ever get that gut feeling that something's off?"

"All the time."

"Yeah, well, I have it now. And it's not the car abandoned in the driveway, or the fact her mom and Mr. Sleaze pretended to care she was gone," says Amber, pushing to her feet. "It's something else, and it's going to sound small, or stupid, but she had this neck-lace, and she always wore it."

My blood runs cold. "What about the necklace?"

"They found it on the driver's seat."


Lunch, and still no text from Jason.

I send him another message and lean back against the Alchemist statue in the Court. The rest of the group talks about Fall Fest next week and college applications and the Nazi gym teacher, but I can't stop thinking about Mr. Phillip and Bethany. Two people who went missing right after I saw them.

I grip my phone.

What if it's about to be three? What if it already is?

I try to clear the thought. It's ridiculous. This doesn't have anything to do with me. I didn't *know* these people. We crossed paths. People cross paths all the time. Bethany could have run away. Maybe something spooked her—a call from her mom, a passing car—and she gave up on the suitcase and the car and bolted on foot before she lost her nerve. It's easy enough to disappear if you have the money and the need.

But she wouldn't leave the necklace. She'd leave the house and the car and the life, but not the piece of silver. I know that just from holding it.

So if she didn't leave it, what happened? Another abduction?

"Waiting for a call?"

Wesley sits down beside me. I put the phone away.

"I'm sorry about Bethany."

"Me too," says Wes. "Did you two meet?"

"Once. Do you really think she ran away?"

"Do you think she didn't?"

I take a deep breath. "It's just . . . it's the second time this week someone's gone missing."

"It's a city, Mac. Bad things happen."

"Yeah, I know," I say softly. "But these two bad things have something in common."

"What's that?"

"Me." I look down at my hands. "I think I was the last person to see them. Both of them."

He frowns, and I explain about Mr. Phillip and the cookies, and about Bethany and the necklace. And then I dig out my phone and tell him about the runner this morning.

"So you meet these people, and then they just, what? Vanish? Why? How?"

"I don't *know*. But this is a bad case of coincidence, Wes."

"This is really bugging you, isn't it?"

I tug my sleeves over my hands.

"Look," he says. "It's weird, the way it lines up, but the simple fact is none of this is your fault. You haven't done anything wrong. Pretty sure you'd remember if you had."

A dark pit forms in the center of my stomach.

Would I?


I spend the rest of the day racking my brain for lost time, trying to remember if I've forgotten anything, which is as hard as it sounds. While Mr. Lowell goes on about social unrest, I scour my memory for patches of mental black ice, chunks of missing time, but I can't find any.

I went straight home from Mr. Phillip's.

I went straight home after meeting Bethany.

I came straight to school from the bike accident with Jason.

So why are they disappearing?

"These are the building blocks of revolution," says Mr. Lowell, tapping the board. "It's not enough to engender discontent, to weaken the people's faith. A revolution isn't a game of might so much as a game of skill. There has to be a strategy . . ."

It just doesn't make any sense.

". . . a method . . ."

I don't *know* these people. We just crossed paths.

". . . a plan of attack."

And then a dark thought occurs to me.

What if I'm being set up? What if these people are being targeted *because* I crossed paths with them?

But why?

Roland's words echo through my head.

*For someone to deem you unfit, they would need a case. They would need evidence.*

I swallow hard and dig my nails into my palms. I'm jumping again, drawing threads where maybe I shouldn't; it's getting me so tangled, I nearly miss the simple solution.

Start at the beginning.

Judge Gregory Phillip.

Nobody knows what happened to him, but I can find out. After all, the abduction happened inside his house, in a room with four walls. Walls that I can *read*.

All I have to do is break into the crime scene.

# FOURTEEN

$A$S SOON AS the bell rings, I'm out the doors and making my way toward the parking lot. But I pull up short when I reach the gates and see Eric standing at the corner, past the last row of cars, pretending to read a book. Great. *Now* he shows up.

He hasn't seen me yet, and I shuffle back several feet, bumping into students and getting caught in the tide of their grinding static as I retreat through the gates and out of his line of sight.

I don't know what's happening to these people, but whether or not Eric's looking for proof, the last thing I need is the Archive watching while I break into a crime scene. I leave Dante in its place at the bike rack and go in search of another route home, wondering how long Eric will stick around waiting for me to show.

Mr. Phillip's house is only a few blocks past the Coronado, so I can make it there on foot once I'm home. And luckily for me, I know someone who can get me there.

I just hope he's still *here*.

I weave through the main building with its glass lobby and walls of former students, forcing my eyes to skim over Owen's photo, and check the dining hall and the Court, but both are empty. Then I remember the boys dragging sports equipment toward the gym. Halfway down the path to the Wellness Center, I see a shoe-worn trail branching off the main one, and I follow it around the back of the building to find the outdoor fields.

There in the middle of the green, kicking a soccer ball around with a dozen other seniors, is Wesley.

All the guys are dressed in the same black-and-gold school clothes—half still in full uniform and half only in slacks—all moving and shouting, lobbing good-natured insults, calling for the ball. Even though I only get a look at his shirtless back, I recognize him instantly.

Not just by his height or the slope of his shoulders or the tapering muscles of his back—I vividly remember running my fingers down the curve of his spine, pulling slivers of glass from his skin—but by the way he moves. The fluid ease with which he sways and feints, calm giving way to sudden bursts of speed and dissolving back to calm. He plays the way he fights: always in control.

There's a set of low metal bleachers at the edge of the field, and I hop up onto a bench and dig the phone out of my bag. Still no text from Jason. I take a long, steadying breath, then dial his number. It rings and rings and rings, and as it does, the maybes play through my head.

*Maybe Jason gave me the wrong number by accident.*

*Maybe Bethany dropped the necklace, like she did in the locker room.*

*Maybe Mr. Phillip made enemies.*

*Maybe—*

And then the phone cuts to voice mail and I hear Jason's voice telling me to leave a message, and the maybes come falling down. I slide the phone into my shirt pocket and notice Cash down on the field, less elegant than Wes, and louder. He beams as he steals the ball, bounces it into the air, and drives it toward a makeshift goal. But Wesley is there at the last moment, lunging into the ball's path and plucking it out of the air with his hands. Cash laughs and shakes his head.

"What the hell was that, Ayers?" demands one of the other boys.

He shrugs. "We needed a goalie."

"You can't play all the parts," calls Cash, and for some reason that makes me laugh. It's the smallest sound—there's no way anyone could have heard it—but at that moment, Wesley's eyes flick up past the players to the metal bleachers. To me. He smiles, and punts the ball back into play before abandoning the pickup match and jogging over to the bleachers. A moment later, Cash ducks out, too.

"Hey, you," says Wes, running a hand through his hair to slick it back. Muscles twine over his narrow frame—*Look up, Mac, look up*—and the scar on his stomach is healing fast and well. It's now little more than a dark line.

Before I can tell him why I'm here, Cash catches up.

"Have to admit, Mackenzie," says Cash, "you never struck me as a bleacher girl."

I raise a brow. "What? I don't look like a sports fan to you?"

Wes laughs. "Bleacher girls," he says, gesturing down the metal rows to a cluster of green- and silver-striped girls, eyes trained hungrily on the pickup match and the collection of shirtless and otherwise sweaty seniors. A couple of faces have drifted over to me. Or rather, to Wes and Cash. I roll my eyes.

"No offense, boys, but I'm not here to fawn over you."

Cash clutches a hand to the school emblem over his heart. "Hopes dashed."

Wes brings his shoe up to the lowest bleacher and leans forward, resting his elbow on his knee. "Then what *are* you doing here?"

"I came to find *you*," I say; this time, Cash seems to genuinely deflate a little.

Wes, on the other hand, gives me a strangely guarded look, as if he thinks it's a trap. "Because . . . ?"

"Because you told me to," I lie, adding an impatient sigh for good measure. "You said I could borrow your *Inferno*, since it's a better version than mine."

Wesley relaxes visibly. Now that we're both back in our element—both lying—he knows what to do. And I have to hand it to him. Even without knowing what I really want or where I'm going with this, he doesn't miss a beat.

"If by 'better version,'" he says, "you mean it's marked up based on past pop quizzes, tests, and final exams, then yes. And sorry, I totally forgot. It's in my locker."

Cash frowns and opens his mouth, but Wes cuts him off.

"It's not cheating, Mr. Student Council. Everyone knows they change the tests each year. It's just a very thorough study aid."

"That wasn't what I was going to say," snaps Cash. "But thank you for clarifying."

"Apologies, Cassius," says Wesley, digging his bag out from under the bleachers. "Continue."

Cash toes the grass. "I was just going to point out that Wes copied off me for half that class—"

"Lies," says Wes, aghast. "False accusations, all."

"—so if you want any help—"

"Really, as if I wouldn't find more creative ways to cheat," continues Wes.

"—I'm probably your best bet."

I smile and push to my feet. "That's very good to know."

Wes is still grumbling as the soccer ball gets lobbed our way and Cash plucks it out of the air. "Just here to help," he says brightly, turning back toward the field.

"I'll add it to your feedback card," I call after him as he jogs away. My attention drifts back to Wes, who is standing there, shirtless and staring.

"I'm going to need you to put your shirt back on," I say.

"Why?" he says, arching a brow. "Having trouble concentrating?"

"A little," I admit. "But mostly you're just sweaty."

His smile goes mischievous.

"Ugh no, wait——" I start, but it's too late. He's already closing the gap between us, snaking his arms around my back and pulling me into a hug. I manage to get my hands up as he wraps himself around me, and my fingers splay across his chest, the rock band sound washing over me, pouring in wherever our skin meets. And through his chest and his noise—or maybe *in* it—I can feel his heart beating, the steady drum of it hitting my palms. And as it echoes through my own chest, all I can think is: *Why can't things be this simple?*

I mean, nothing is ever going to be *simple* for us—not the way it is for other people—but couldn't we have this? Couldn't *I* have this? A boy and a girl and a normal life?

He brings his damp forehead against my dry one, and a bead of sweat runs down my temple and cheek before making its way toward my chin.

"You are so gross," I whisper. But I don't pull away. In fact, I have to fight the urge to slide my hands down his chest, over his bare stomach, and around his back. I want to pull our bodies closer and stretch onto my toes until my lips find his. I don't have to read his mind to know how badly he wants to kiss me, too. I can feel it in the way he tenses beneath my touch, taste it in the small pocket of air that separates his mouth from mine.

I force myself to remember that I'm the one who said no. That I'm the thing keeping us apart. Not because I don't feel what he feels, but because I'm afraid.

*I'm afraid I'm losing my mind.*

*Afraid the Archive will decide I'm not worth the risk and erase me.*

*Afraid I will give Wesley a part of me he can't keep.*

*Afraid that if we go down this road, it will ruin us.*

*I will ruin* him.

"Wes," I plead, and he spares me the pain of pulling away by letting go. His arms slip back to his sides and he retreats a step, taking his music with him as he crouches and digs his key out of his bag. He slips the metal back around his neck before he straightens, polo in hand.

"So," he says, tugging the shirt over his head. "Why did you really come?"

"Actually, I was hoping you could give me a ride home."

His brow crinkles. "I wasn't joking, Mac. I don't have a car."

"No," I say slowly, "but you have something better. Fastest way around the city, you told me, and I happen to know it leads right to my door."

"The Narrows?" His hand drifts to the key against his sternum. "What's wrong with Dante?"

"Nothing." *Except for the bike's current proximity to Eric.* I tilt my head back. "It just looks like rain." To be fair, it is kind of cloudy.

He looks up, too. "Uh-huh." Not *that* cloudy. His eyes drop back to mine. "Be honest. You just want to get inside my halls."

"Oh, yeah," I say, teasing. "Creepy corridors are *such* a turn-on."

The corner of his mouth tugs up. "Follow me."

Wes leads me around the back of campus to an abandoned building. *Abandoned* might be too severe a phrase; the building is small and old and elegant and draped with ivy, but it doesn't look anywhere near structurally sound, let alone usable. Wes makes another sweeping gesture at the door set into the building's side.

"I don't understand," I say. "Your nearest Narrows door is . . . an *actual* door?"

Wes beams. "Beautiful, isn't it?"

The paint has all flaked off, and the small glass inserts that once occupied the upper middle have broken and been replaced by cobwebs. Even so, it is strange and lovely. I knew that Narrows doors all started out as real doors—wood and hinges and frames—but over time, walls change, buildings come down, and the portals stay. Every Narrows door I've ever seen has been nothing more than a crack in the world, a seam you can barely see. An impossible entrance that takes shape only when summoned by a key.

But here this is: this small, wood-and-metal door. I tug off my ring, the world shifting subtly around me as I tuck the metal band into my skirt pocket and reach out. Pressing my palm flat against the door, I can feel the strangeness, the hum of two worlds meeting and reverberating through the wood. It makes my fingertips go numb. Wesley fishes his key out from under his polo; he slides it into the rusted lock—a real, metal lock—and turns.

"Anything I should know about?" I ask as the door swings open onto darkness.

"Keep your eyes peeled for someone named Elissa," he says. I cast a last glance around for Eric, then follow Wesley through.

The Narrows are the Narrows are the Narrows.

The fact that Wesley's territory looks and smells and sounds like mine—dark and dank and full of distant echoes, like groaning pipes—is just a reminder of how vast the Archive system is. The only differences are the markings he's made on the doors—I use *X*s and *O*s, but Wes has drawn broad red slashes over every locked door, green checks over every usable one. And of course there's the fact I have no idea where I'm going. It looks so much like my territory that I feel like I should know every turn, but the halls and doors are a disorienting almost-mirror.

"Which way home?"

"*Your* home is this way," he says, pointing down the hall.

"And yours?" I ask.

He gestures vaguely behind him.

Curiosity tugs at me. "Can I see?"

"Not today," says Wes, his voice strangely tense.

"But we're so close. How can I pass up the opportunity to see inside the life of the mysterious Wesley Ayers?"

"Because I'm not offering," he says, rubbing his eyes. "Look, it's a big house. Soulless. And I hate it. That's all you need to know." He seems genuinely annoyed, so I let it go. He's so quick to defend the school, even with all its pretention, but whatever's at his house must be worse. The image of Wesley sitting on some grand patio with a butler shudders and breaks.

He starts walking away, and I follow. We move in silence through the Narrows, our senses tuned to the dimly lit corridors around us. I try to make a mental map of these new halls. It's not enough to know the number of rights and lefts—Da taught me how to learn a space, make a memory of it so I could find my way through in both directions and correct my course if I strayed. It's harder this time, since there's already a nearly identical territory mapped in my head.

"Are you going to tell me what happened to your hands?" asks Wes.

"Nothing I couldn't handle."

"You promised me a story."

"It isn't a very nice one," I say, but I still tell him. His steps slow. Even in the dark, I can see him pale as he listens.

"I would have killed them," he says under his breath.

"I nearly did," I say. I carved Eric out of the story. I don't want Wesley to worry, not until there's a good reason to. Luckily the appearance of the territory wall saves me from having to say more.

The boundary between Wesley's territory and mine looks like a dead end, bare except for the keyhole set into it. It's strange, I think, how separate Keepers are kept. Crew may be paired up, but we're isolated. Each on his own page.

Wes slides his key into the small, glowing mark on the otherwise bare wall; as he does, the door takes shape around the lock, the stony surface rippling into wood. The lock turns over with a soft metallic click, and he pulls the door open to reveal my section of the Narrows. The same—a mirror image—and yet different. More familiar.

I free my own key from under my collar and wrap the cord around my wrist. Wes smiles and gives a sweeping bow before stepping aside to let me pass.

"Be safe," he says, holding the door open as I cross through.

I hear it swing shut behind me; by the time I look back, there is nothing but a smooth stone wall and a tiny keyhole filled with light. A shadow crosses it briefly, and then it's gone, and when I press my ear to the wall, I imagine I can hear Wesley's footsteps fading. I feel the scratch of letters on my list, but I don't pull the paper out. The History will have to wait. It might not be happy or sane, but I'll deal with it when I get back.

I head straight through the territory to the numbered doors, my mind already on Mr. Phillip's house as I slot the key into the first door and step out onto the third floor hall, and stop.

Eric is leaning up against the faded yellow wallpaper, reading his book.

"If I didn't know better," he says, turning a page, "I'd think you were avoiding me."

"Flat tire," I say, sliding my ring back on as the Narrows door dissolves behind me.

"I'm sure." He closes the book and pockets it.

"You know," I say, "there's a word for guys who lurk outside schools."

Eric almost smiles. "When you sneak off, it makes one think you're up to no good."

"When you follow people without telling them why, it makes one think the same."

Eric winks. "How are your hands?"

I hesitate. He sounds like he actually cares. Maybe I was wrong about him. I hold them up for his inspection.

"Good," he says. "Fast healer."

"Comes in handy."

"Thank your genes, Miss Bishop. Your recovery rate comes with the territory, just like your sight."

I look down at my mending knuckles. I'd never thought much about it before, but I guess it makes sense.

Just then, the stairwell door bangs open and a woman strides through, a Crew key dangling from her fingers. She's tall, her black eyes fringed with dark lashes, a black ponytail plunging between her shoulders and down her back, straight and knife-sharp. In fact, everything about her is sharp, from the line of her jaw and her shoulders to her fingernails and the heeled boots at the ends of her long, thin legs. I recognize her from that day in the Archive.

Eric's partner.

"There you are," she says, eyes flicking between us.

"Sako, my love." There's a warmth to his voice that matches the cold in hers. "I've just been educating our young Keeper here. They don't teach them anything these days."

I'm willing to bet I know more than Eric thinks about the ways of the Archive, but I hold my tongue.

"Well, school's out. We have work to do."

Eric smiles, his eyes alight. "Wonderful."

My chest loosens. Wonderful indeed. That should keep him off my tail long enough for me to pay Mr. Phillip's house a visit.

He starts toward Sako, and I'm halfway through letting out a breath of relief when he stops and glances back at me.

"Miss Bishop?"

"Yeah?"

"Do try to stay out of trouble."

I smile and spread my arms. "Do I look like a troublemaker to you?"

Sako snorts and vanishes into the stairwell, Eric on her heels.

The moment they're gone, I duck into my apartment and unearth Da's box of things from the back of my closet, rooting around until I find what I'm looking for: a lock pick set. I ditch the school skirt for a pair of jeans and pocket the metal picks, and I'm halfway back to the front door when my phone goes off.

My heart lurches.

In the second between hearing the sound and digging the phone out of my pocket, all my fears feel suddenly silly.

The text will be from Jason, telling me he's fine, and he's sorry his phone was dead, and that he couldn't find the cord, and I'll realize how much I was making out of nothing, piling theory on theory on theory when for once Da was wrong, and it was in fact all coincidence. Maybe Bethany just found the strength to leave her necklace along with the rest of her life. Maybe Eric was hired to protect me, not get me erased. Maybe Mr. Phillip . . . But that's the problem. There is no explanation for Mr. Phillip.

And the text isn't from Jason.

It's from Lyndsey, just saying hi.

My hope collapses, because there are no easy outs—only more questions. And only one place to go. A place that has to have answers.

I take the steps two at a time all the way down to the lobby. Then I cut right down the hall beside the staircase, through the study, and into the garden. I hoist myself up and over the stone wall, hit the pavement in a crouch, and take off running.

# FIFTEEN

DA AND I are walking back to his house one scorching summer day, eating lemon ices, when he gets a call. His phone makes that certain sound it only makes when he's being called to a scene. Unofficially, of course—Da never does anything on the books—and he hands me the last of his lemon ice and says, "You go on, Kenzie. I'll catch up." So of course I dump both ices and follow at a distance. He makes his way three streets over to a house that's roped off, but clearly unattended. He goes to the back door, not the front, and proceeds to stand there until I get within earshot. Then he says, without turning, "Your ears broken? I told you to go on home."

But when he glances back, he doesn't look angry, only amused. He knows I'm good at keeping my hands to myself, so he nods me up onto the step and tells me to watch closely. Then he pulls a set of picks from his back pocket and shows me how to line them up, one above the other, and lets me press my ear to the lock to listen for the clicks. Da says every lock will speak to you, if you listen right. When he's done, he rests his hand on the knob and says, "Open sesame." The door swings open.

He tugs off his boots and knots the laces and hangs them on his shoulder before stepping in. I do everything he does and nothing he doesn't, and together we head inside.

It's a crime scene.

I can tell because everything is very still.

Still in that undisturbed-on-purpose way.

I stand by the door and watch him work, amazed by the way he touches things without leaving any mark.


From the street, Mr. Phillip's house looks almost normal.

The plants are still in their pots, the doormat still clean and even at the top of the steps, and I'm willing to bet that inside the door, several pairs of shoes are lined up against the wall. But the illusion of calm order is interrupted by the bright strip of yellow tape criss-crossing the front door and the police cruiser parked on the street.

I'm leaning against a fence a few houses down, assessing the situation. There's one cop in the cruiser, but his seat's kicked back and his hat is over his eyes. Halfway down the block a woman is walking a dog; other than that, the street is empty.

There's a high wooden fence jutting out to either side of Mr. Phillip's house, but his neighbor's lawn is open, and I make my way across the street behind the cop car and into the yard, heading for their backyard like it's my own. Luckily, they're not home to contradict me—as soon as I'm out of the cop car's line of sight, I press my ear to Mr. Phillip's fence and listen. Nothing. The wood barely groans as I hoist myself up and over and land in a crouch in the manicured backyard.

Plastic has been taped over the two shattered windows at the back of the house, and the grass beneath them is sprinkled with glass, which is strange itself. Normally in a break-in, the windows would be broken inward, but the glass out here suggests the windows were broken from the inside *out*.

I keep my eyes on the ground, careful to step where others have obviously stepped rather than in the untouched patches.

When I reach the back door, I press my ear to the wood and listen. Still nothing—no voices, no footsteps, no sounds of life. I check the lock, but it doesn't budge, so I pull the set of picks from my backpack and kneel in front of the lock. From there I maneuver the two metal bars until the lock shifts and clicks under my touch.

"Open sesame," I whisper.

I turn the handle and the door falls open. I slip the lock pick set back into my pocket and step inside, tugging the door shut behind me. At first, everything looks normal—a small room with a tiled floor, a pair of shoes neatly by the door, an umbrella in a holder, that same sense of everything in its place. Then I look into the room on my left and see the damage. The plastic on the windows has left the space dark, but even without the light I can make out the debris scattered across the hardwood floor. A set of floor-to-ceiling bookcases are built into the wall opposite the broken windows. Most of the debris seems to have come from there—the shelves are practically empty, and a trail of books and odd trinkets litters the floor, thinning as it nears the windows.

I hold my breath. There's a horrible stillness to the room. It's only been three days, but the air is starting to feel stale. It's eerie—a crime scene without a body, like a movie set without the actors.

I tug off my ring and set it on the table by the door. The air shifts around me, humming faintly with life. I'm just bringing my hand to the nearest wall when something happens.

I let my gaze slide over the room. Near the windows, *it slides off.* My chest tightens. A *shortcut*? Here?

And then a pit forms in my stomach as I realize it isn't a short-cut. Shortcuts—the invisible doors Crew use to cheat their way across space—disturb the air, but they are smooth, and this is jagged, snagging my gaze and repelling it at once. My heart starts to race.

A shortcut wouldn't do that.

But a *void* would.

Voids are illegal, tears made in the world, doors to nowhere. The last—and only—time I saw a void was the day I *made* one. The day Owen broke free and the fight spilled out of the Narrows and into the Coronado, through the halls and up the stairs and onto the roof.

I squeeze my eyes shut and can feel Owen's grip tighten around me, his knife between my shoulder blades, his cold blue eyes full of anger and hate as I lift the Crew key behind his back. I turn the key in the air and there is a click and a crushing wind, and Owen's eyes widen as the void opens and rips him backward into the darkness.

And then it closes an instant later, leaving only a jagged seam in its wake.

A seam, just like the one in front of me now. My pulse pounds in my ears. That's why there's debris and broken glass but no body. Voids only open for an instant, long enough to devour the nearest living thing. A perfect crime, when you consider no one can see the method, the mark.

But who would do this? There's only one tool in the world that can make a void door.

A Crew key.

And then it hits me: Eric.

What was it he said in the park last night?

*What are you going to do with them?*

*Make them disappear.*

Mr. Phillip and Bethany and Jason. They all went missing after

I crossed paths with them. Eric hasn't been following me to look for evidence. He's been *planting* it. Setting me up.

Panic chews through me as I bring a trembling hand to the nearest wall, already knowing what I will find. *Nothing.* The same white-noise nothingness that I found on the Coronado roof that day. Voids cover their own tracks, eat through time and memory and make it all unreadable. But I have to try to see, so I close my eyes and let the memories float toward my fingers. I reach out, taking hold of them and rolling time back. The room flickers into sight. At first it is empty; then, bit by bit, it fills with people: officers and men taking photographs. The images spin away and the room empties again, and for a moment I think I might see something. I can feel the void hovering beyond the quiet.

The memory brushes against my fingers.

And then it *explodes.*

My vision floods with white and static and pain. The room vanishes around me into light, and I wrench my hand away from the door, my ears ringing as I blink away the blinding white.

Ruined. It's all ruined. Whoever did this, they knew they wouldn't show up. They knew the void would hide their presence. But they can't hide the void itself. Not that anyone's going to see *that* evidence. No, the only evidence anyone will see is mine. My prints somewhere in Mr. Phillip's kitchen and on Bethany's necklace, my number in Jason's phone.

I tug my sleeves over my hands and rub any fresh marks from the wall.

And then I hear the car door slam.

The sound makes me jump. I knock into the table by the door, and my silver ring rolls off, hitting the hardwood floor and rolling into the debris as footsteps and muffled voices sound from the front path.

I drop to a crouch and scramble forward, kneeling on an open book. I knock aside a binder and a heavy glass ornament as I grasp for the ring. The smooth metal circle fetches up against a toppled chair, and I grab it and shove it back onto my finger just as the front door opens down the hall. I freeze, but the glass ball continues to roll across the hardwood floor with a steady, heavy sound before coming to rest against the wall.

I hear it, and so do the cops.

One of them calls out, "Hey, someone here?"

I hold my breath, weaving my way silently between pieces of debris toward the wall, where I press myself back against it like it'll do a damn bit of good if they decide to come in.

"Probably just a cat," says the other, but I hear a gun slide from a holster and the heavy tread of approaching boots. They're coming this way. I scan the room, but there's nothing large enough to hide behind, and there are only two ways out: the hall the cops are coming down and the back door I first came through. I gauge how much time it will take to reach it. I don't have a choice.

I take a deep breath and run.

So do the cops.

They're halfway through the house when I crash through the back door. I take three sprinting steps toward the fence and then a wall of a man comes out of nowhere and catches me around the shoulders. The moment I try to twist free, the officer spins me, wrenches my arms behind my back, and forces me to the ground, where he kneels on my shoulder blades. I wince as the metal of the handcuffs digs into my bad wrist. My vision starts to blur and my pulse pounds in my ears, and I have to squeeze my eyes shut and beg my mind to *stay here stay here stay here* as the tunnel moment tries to fill my head like smoke. I force air into my lungs and try to stay calm—or as calm as I can with a police officer pinning me to the ground.

But as he drags me to my feet, I'm still me. It's a thin grip, but I hold on. And then I recognize him from the TV.

Detective Kinney.

He pushes me into the house—around the crime scene—and through the front doors. We're tracking dirt, and it's ridiculous, but I pause to think about how put out Judge Phillip would be just before Detective Kinney slams my back up against the cruiser door.

"Name," he barks.

I nearly lie. It's right there on my lips. But a lie will only make this worse. "Mackenzie Bishop."

"What the hell were you doing in there?"

I'm a little dazed by his force and the anger in his voice. Not a professional kind of gruff, but actual rage. "I just wanted to see—"

"You broke into a private residence and contaminated an active investigation. . . ." I cheat a look to either side, searching for signs of Eric, but Detective Kinney grabs my jaw and drags my face back toward his. "You better focus and tell me what *exactly* you were doing in there."

I should have grabbed something. It's easier to sell the cops on a teen looter than a teen sleuth.

"I saw the story on the news and thought maybe I could—"

"What? Thought you'd play Sherlock and solve it yourself? That was a goddamn *closed crime scene*, young lady."

I frown. His tone, the way his eyes keep going to the Hyde crest on my shirt—it's like he's talking to Amber, not me. Amber, who likes to play detective. Amber, who I'm willing to bet has gotten in the way of work before.

"I'm sorry," I say, doing my best impression of a repentant daughter. I'm not used to being yelled at. Mom runs away to Colleen, and Dad and I haven't had a real fight since before Ben. "I'm really sorry."

"You should be," he growls. One of the cops is still inside, no doubt assessing for damage, and the other is standing behind Kinney, wearing a smug smile. I bet he thinks I'm just some rich girl looking for a thrill.

"This kind of stunt goes on your record," Detective Kinney is saying. "It hurts *everything*, *everyone*. It could sure as hell get you kicked out of that fancy school."

*It could do a lot worse,* I think, *depending on how much evidence you've found.*

"You want me to take her to the station and book her?" asks the other cop, and my chest starts to tighten again. Booking means taking prints, and if they take mine and add them to the system, they'll find a match here at Judge Phillip's, and maybe even on Bethany's necklace—unless she rubbed the marks away.

"No," says Kinney, waving him away. "I'll handle this."

"Look," I say, "I know it was really stupid, *I* was really stupid. I don't know what I was thinking. It will never ever happen again."

"I'm glad to hear that," he says, opening the cruiser door. "Now, get in the car."

# SIXTEEN

D A NEVER LIKED the word *illegal*. Semantics. There was no line between *legal* and *illegal*, he'd say, only between *free* and *caught*.

And I'm caught at the station, handcuffed to a chair next to Detective Kinney's desk. My fingertips are stained black from ink, and Kinney's holding up the page with my prints.

"This right here," he says, waving the sheet, "isn't just a piece of paper. This is the difference between a clean record and a rap sheet."

My eyes hover on the ten black smudges. Then he folds the page and slides it into his desk drawer. "This is your one and only warning," he says. "I'm not going to book you today, but I want you to think about what would happen if I did. I want you to think about the ripple effect. I want you to take this seriously."

Relief pours over me as I drag my eyes from the drawer to his face. "I promise you, sir, I take it very seriously."

The detective sits back in his chair and considers the contents of my pockets on the table in front of him. My cell phone. My house key (he left the one around my neck). Da's lock pick set. And my Archive list. I hold my breath as he takes up the paper, running his thumb against it as his eyes skim the name—*Marissa Farrow. 14.*—before he drops it back on the desk, face up. He takes up Da's lock pick set instead.

"Where did you get this?" he asks.

"It was my grandfather's."

"Was he a deviant, too?"

I frown. "He was a private eye."

"What happened to your hands?"

"Street fight," I say. "Isn't that what deviants do?"

"Don't talk back to me, young lady."

My head is starting to hurt, and I ask for water. While Kinney's gone, I consider the drawer with the page of prints, but I'm sitting in the middle of a police station, surrounded by cops and cuffed to the chair, so I'm forced to leave it there.

Kinney comes back with a cup of water and the news that my parents are on their way.

Terrific.

"Be glad they're coming," scolds Kinney. "If you were my daughter, I'd leave you in a cell for the night."

"She goes to Hyde, doesn't she? Amber?"

"You know her?" he asks, his voice gruff.

I hesitate. The last thing I want is for Amber to hear about this incident, especially since I'll need her case updates more than ever. "It's a small school," I say with a shrug.

"Kinney," calls one of the other officers. He strides toward us.

"Partial prints are back on the Thomson girl's necklace," says the officer.

Thomson. That must be Bethany's last name.

"And?"

"No match."

Kinney slams his fist on the desk, nearly upsetting the cup of water. I almost feel bad for him. These are cases he's never going to close, and I can only hope I catch whoever's doing this before they strike again.

"And the mother's boyfriend?" asks Kinney under his breath.

"We rechecked the alibi, but it holds water."

My gaze drifts down to Kinney's desk. And that's when I see the second name writing itself on the Archive paper.

*Forrest Riggs. 12.*

Kinney's attention is just drifting back to the table when I rattle my handcuff loudly, hoping he reads my panic as natural teenager-in-trouble panic and not don't-look-at-that-paper panic.

"Sorry," I say, "but do you think you could take these off before my parents get here? My mom will have a stroke."

Kinney considers me a moment, then gets up and wanders off, leaving me chained to the seat.

Ten minutes later, Mom and Dad arrive. Mom takes one look at me cuffed to the chair and nearly loses it, but Dad sends her outside, instructing her to call Colleen. Dad doesn't even look at me while Kinney explains what happened. They talk like I'm not sitting right there.

"I'm not pressing charges, Mr. Bishop, and I'm not booking her. This time."

"Oh, I assure you, Detective Kinney, this will be the *only* time."

"Make sure of it," says Kinney, unlocking the cuff and pulling me to my feet, his heavy static only making the headache worse. He hands me back my things, and Dad ushers me away before Kinney can change his mind.

I try to wipe the ink from the fingerprint kit on my skirt. It doesn't come off.

I feel the eyes on me as soon as I'm through the doors and look up expecting to see Eric watching. Instead, I see Sako. She's on a bench across the street, and her black eyes follow me beneath their fringe. Her gaze is hard to read, but her mouth is smug, almost cruel.

Maybe Eric's not the one I should be worried about.

My steps have slowed, and Dad gives me a nudge toward the car. Mom's in the front seat on the phone, but she ends the call as soon as she sees us. Across the street, Sako gets to her feet, and I clear my throat.

"See Dad?" I say, loud enough for her to hear. "I told you it was all just a misunderstanding."

"Get in the car," says Dad.

On the way home, I almost wish I could have another tunnel moment, lose time. Instead, I'm aware of every single second of weighted silence. The only sounds in the car are Mom's heavy sighing and the tap of my phone as I delete the texts I sent to Jason. I can't erase the prints from Judge Phillip's kitchen or Bethany's necklace, and I can't unsend the texts or unmake the calls, but I can at least minimize the evidence. I whisper a silent apology as I erase his number.

Dad parks the car, and Mom gets out and slams her door, breaking the quiet for an instant before it resettles, following us up the stairs and into our apartment.

Once inside, it shatters.

Mom bursts into tears, and Dad starts to shout.

*"What the hell has gotten into you?"*

"Dad, it was an accident——"

*"No,* it was an accident that you got caught. But you broke into a crime scene. I come home and find your schoolbag here and your bike missing, and then I get a call from the police telling me you've been arrested!"

"It doesn't count as an arrest if they don't process you. It was just a conversation with—"

"Where is this *coming* from Mackenzie?" pleads my mother.

"I just thought I might be able to help—"

He throws the lock pick set onto the table. "With those?" he growls. "What are you *doing* with them?"

"They were Da's—"

"I know who they belonged to, Mackenzie. He was my father! And I won't have you ending up like *him*."

I pull back. If he'd struck me, it would have hurt less.

"But Da was—"

"You don't know *what* he was," snaps Dad, running his hands through his hair. "Antony Bishop was a flake, and a criminal, and a selfish asshole who cared more about his secrets and his many lives than his family. He cheated and he stole and he lied. He only cared about himself, and I'll be *damned* if I see you behaving like him."

"Peter—" says Mom, reaching for him, but he shrugs her off.

"How could you be so *selfish*, Mackenzie?"

Selfish? *Selfish?* "I'm just trying to—" I bite back the words before they escape.

I'm just trying to *do my job*.

I'm just trying to *keep everything together*.

I'm just trying to *stay alive*.

"You're just trying to what? Get kicked out of Hyde? Ruin your future? Honestly, Mac. First your hands, and now—"

"That was a bike accident—"

*"Enough,"* snaps Dad. "Enough *lies*."

"Fine," I growl, throwing up my hands. "It wasn't an accident. Do you want to know what really happened?" I shouldn't be talking, not right now, not when I'm tired and angry, but the words are already spilling out. "I got lost coming back from one of Mom's errands, and it was getting dark, so I cut through a park, and two guys jumped me." Mom sucks in a breath, and I look down at my bruised knuckles. "They cut me off . . ." It feels so strange, telling the truth. ". . . and forced me off the bike . . ." I wonder what it would feel like to tell them about my wrist. About Owen and all the different ways he broke me. ". . . and I didn't have a choice . . ."

Mom grabs me by the shoulders, her noise scraping against my bones. "Did they hurt you?"

"No," I say, holding up my hands. "I hurt them."

Mom lets go and sinks onto the edge of the couch, her hand to her mouth.

"Why would you lie about that?"

*Because it's easier.*

*Because it's what I do.*

"Because I didn't want you to be upset," I say. "I didn't want you to feel guilty. I didn't want you to worry."

The anger bleeds away, leaving me bone-tired.

"Well, it's too late for that, Mackenzie," she says, shaking her head. "I *am* worried."

"I know," I say.

I'm worried, too. Worried I can't keep doing this. Can't keep playing all the parts.

My head is pounding, and my hands are shaking, and there are two names on my list, and all I want to do is go to sleep but I can't because of the boy with the knife waiting in my dreams.

I turn away.

"Where are you going?" asks Dad.

"To take a bath," I say, vanishing into the bathroom before anyone can stop me.

I find my gaze in the mirror and hold it. Cracks are showing. There's a glass beside the sink, and I dig a few painkillers out of my medical stash under the counter and wash them down before snapping the water on in the tub.

*What a mess,* I think as I sink to the tile floor, draw my knees up, and tip my head back against the wall beside the tub, waiting for the bath to fill. I try to count the different things Da would give me hell for—not hearing the cops in time, getting caught, taking a full two days to notice I was being set up—but then again, it sounds like Da wasn't as good at separating his lives as he thought.

*He only cared about himself, and I'll be damned if I see you behaving like him.*

Is that how Dad really saw him? Is that how my parents see *me*?

The sound of the running water is steady and soothing, and I close my eyes and focus on the *shhhhhhhhhhhh* it makes. The steady hush loosens my muscles, clears my cluttered head. And then, threaded through the static, I hear another sound—like metal tapping against porcelain.

I open my eyes to find Owen sitting on the counter, bouncing the tip of his knife against the sink.

"So many lives. So many lies. Aren't you tired yet?"

"Go away."

"I think it's time," he says, tapping to the rhythm of a clock.

"Time for what?" I ask slowly.

"Time to stop hiding. Time to stop pretending you're all right." His smile sharpens. "Time to show them how broken you really are."

His fingers flex on the knife, and I spring to my feet, bolting for the door as he jumps down from the counter and blocks my path.

"Uh-uh," he says, wagging the knife from side to side. "I'm not leaving until we show them."

His knife slides back to his side, and I brace myself for an attack, but it doesn't come. Instead, he sets the weapon down on the counter, halfway between us. The instant he withdraws his hand, I lunge for the blade; my right hand curls around the hilt, but before I can lift it Owen's fingers fold over mine, pinning me to the counter. In a blink he's behind me, his other hand catching my free wrist, wrapping himself around my body. His hands on my hands. His arms on my arms. His chest against my back. His cheek pressed to mine.

"We fit together," says Owen with a smile.

"Let go of me," I growl, trying to twist free, but his grip is made of stone.

"You're not even trying," he says into my ear. "You're just going through the motions. Deep down, I know you want them to see," he says, twisting my empty hand so the wrist faces up. "So show them."

My sleeve is rolled up, my forearm bare, and I watch as six letters appear, ghostlike on my skin.

*B R O K E N*

Owen tightens his grip over my knife-wielding hand and brings the tip of the blade to the skin just below the crook of my left elbow, to the top of the ghosted *B*.

"Stop," I whisper.

"Look at me." I lift my gaze to the mirror and find his ice blue eyes in the reflection. "Aren't you tired, M? Of lying? Of hiding? Of everything?"

*Yes.*

I don't know if I think the word or say it, but I feel it, and as I do, a strange peace settles over me. For a moment, it doesn't feel real. None of it feels real. It's just a dream. And then Owen smiles and the knife bites down.

The pain is sudden and sharp enough to make me gasp as blood wells and spills over into the blade's path, and then my vision blurs and I squeeze my eyes shut and grip the counter for balance.

When I open my eyes a second later, Owen is gone, and I'm standing there alone in front of the mirror, but the pain is still there and I look down and realize that I'm bleeding.

*A lot.*

His knife is gone, and the drinking glass is lying in glittering pieces on the counter, my hand wrapped around the largest shard. Blood runs between my fingers where I've gripped it and down my other arm where I've carved a single deep line. There's a rushing in my ears, and I realize it's the sound of the bathwater *shhhhhhhhhh*ing in the tub, but the tub is overflowing and the floor is soaked, drops of blood staining the shallow water.

Someone is knocking and saying my name, and I have just enough time to drop the shard into the sink before Mom opens the door, sees me, and screams.

# SEVENTEEN

GROWING UP, I have bad dreams.

My parents leave the lights on. They close the closet door. They check under the bed. But it doesn't help, because I am not afraid of the dark or the closet or the gap between the mattress and the floor, places where monsters are said to lurk. I never dream of monsters, not the kind with fangs or claws. I dream of people. Of bad people dropped into days and nights so simple and vivid that I never question if any of it's real.

One night in the middle of summer, Da comes in and perches on the edge of my bed and asks me what I'm so afraid of.

"That I'll get stuck," I whisper. "That I'll never wake up."

He shrugs. "But you will."

"How do you know?"

"Because that's the thing about dreams, Kenzie. Whether they're good or bad, they always end."

"But I don't know it's a dream, not until I wake up."

He leans in, resting his weathered hand on the bed. "Treat all the bad things like dreams, Kenzie. That way, no matter how scary or dark they get, you just have to survive until you wake up."

. . .

This is a bad dream.

This is a *nightmare*. Dad is speeding, and Mom is sitting in the backseat putting pressure on my arm and I'm squeezing my eyes shut and waiting to wake up.

It *was* a dream. I was dreaming. It wasn't real. But the cut *is* real, and the pain *is* real, and the blood still streaked across our bathroom sink *is* real.

What's happening to me?

I am Mackenzie Bishop. I am a Keeper for the Archive and I am the one who goes bump in the night, not the one who slips. I am the girl of steel, and this is all a bad dream and I have to wake up.

*How many Keepers lose their minds?*

"We're almost there," says Mom. "It's going to be okay."

It's not. No matter what, it's not going to be okay.

*I'm* not okay.

Someone is trying to frame me, and they don't even have to, because I'm not fit to serve. Not like this. I'm trying so hard to be okay, and it's not working.

*Aren't you tired?*

I squeeze my eyes shut.

I don't realize until Mom presses a hand to my face that there are tears streaming down it. "I'm sorry," I whisper under the sound of her noise against my skin.


Fourteen stitches.

That's how many it takes to close the cut in my arm (the marks on my right hand from holding the glass are shallow enough to be taped). The nurse—a middle-aged woman with steady hands and a stern jaw—judges me as she sews, her lips pursed like I did it for attention. And the whole time, my parents are standing there, watching.

They don't look angry. They look sad, and hurt, and scared—like they don't know how they went from having two functioning children to one broken one. I open my mouth to say something—*anything*—but there's no lie I can tell to make this better, and the truth will only make everything worse, so the room stays silent while the nurse works. Dad keeps his hand on Mom's shoulder, and Mom keeps her hand on her phone, but she has the decency not to call Colleen until the nurse finishes the stitches and asks them to step outside with her. There's a window in the room, and through the blinds I can see them walk away down the hall.

They've made me wear one of those blue tie-waisted smocks, and my eyes travel over my arms and legs silently assessing not only the most obvious damage, but the last four years' worth of scars. Each one of them has a story: skin scraped off against the stone walls of the Narrows, Histories fighting back tooth and nail. And then there are the scars that leave no mark: the cracked ribs and the wrist that won't heal because I keep rolling it, listening to the *click click click*. But contrary to Colleen's theories, the cut along my arm—the one now hidden under a bright white bandage—is the first I've ever given myself.

*I didn't,* I think. *I don't—*

"Miss Bishop?" says a voice, and my head snaps up. I didn't hear the door open, but a woman I've never seen before is standing in the doorway. Her dirty blond hair is pulled back into a messy pony-tail, but her perfect posture and the way she pronounces my name send off warning bells in my head. Crew? Not one I've ever met, but the ledger's full of pages, and I only know a few. Then I read the name tag on her slim-cut suit, and I almost wish she *were* Crew.

*Dallas McCormick, Psychologist.* She has a notebook and a pen in one hand.

"I prefer Mackenzie," I say. "Can I help you?"

A smile flickers on her face. "I should probably be the one asking that question." There's a chair beside the bed, and she sinks into it. "Looks like you've had a rough day," she says, pointing to my bandaged arm with her pen.

"You don't know the half of it."

Dallas brightens. "Why don't you tell me?"

I stare at her in silence. She stares back. And then she sits forward, and the smile slides from her face. "You know what I think?"

"No."

Dallas is undeterred. "I think you're wearing too much armor," she says. I frown, but she continues. "The funny thing about armor is that it doesn't just keep other people out. It keeps us in. We build it up around us, not realizing that we're trapping ourselves. And really, you end up with two people. That shiny metal one . . ."

*The girl of steel.*

". . . and the human one inside, who's falling apart."

"I'm not."

"You can't be two people. You end up being neither."

"You don't know me."

"I know you made that cut on your arm," she says simply. "And I know that sometimes people hurt themselves because it's the only way to get through the armor."

"I'm not a cutter," I say. "I didn't mean to do this to myself. It was an accident."

"Or a confession." My stomach turns at the word. "A cry for help," she adds. "I'm here to help."

"You can't." I close my eyes. "It's complicated."

180

Dallas shrugs. "Life is complicated."

Silence settles between us, but I don't trust myself to say any more. Finally Dallas stands back up and tucks the notebook she brought and never opened under her arm.

"You must be tired," she says. "I'll come back in the morning."

My chest tightens. "They finished stitching me up. I thought I'd be able to go."

"Such a rush," she says. "Got somewhere to be?"

I hold her gaze. "I just hate hospitals."

Dallas smiles grimly. "Join the club." Then she tells me to get some rest and slips out.

Yeah, rest. Since that seems to be making everything better.

Dallas leaves, and I'm about to look away when I see a man stop her in the hall. Through the blinds, I watch them talk for a moment, and then he points at my door. At me. His gold hair glitters, even under the artificial hospital lights. Eric.

Dallas crosses her arms as they talk. I can't read her lips, so I can only imagine what she's telling him. When she's done, he glances my way. I expect him to look smug, like Sako—*the Keeper is digging her own grave*—but he doesn't. His eyes are dark with worry as he nods once, turns, and walks away.

I bring my hand to my chest, feeling my key through the too-thin hospital smock as the nurse appears with two little pills and a white paper cup filled with water.

"For pain," she says. I wish I could take them, but I'm worried that "for pain" also means "for sleep." Thankfully she leaves them on the table, and I pocket them before my parents can see.

Mom spends the rest of the night on the phone with Colleen, and Dad spends it pretending to read a magazine while really watching me. Neither one of them says a word. Which is fine with me, because I don't have words for them right now. When they finally drift off, Dad in a chair and Mom on a cot, I get up. My clothes and cell are sitting on a chair, and I get changed, pocket the phone, and slip out into the hall. The hospital is strangely quiet as I pad through it in search of a soda machine. I'm just loading a bill into the illuminated front of one when I feel the scratch of letters in my pocket and pull out the list as a fourth name adds itself to my list.

Four names.

Four Histories I can't return. Roland's warning echoes in my head.

*Just do your job and stay out of trouble, and you'll be okay.*

I take a deep breath and dig my cell out of my other pocket.

> Hey, partner in crime.

A second later, Wesley writes back.

> Hey, you. I hope your night's not as boring as mine.

> I wish.

I think about typing the story into the phone, but now is not the time to explain.

> I need a favor.

Name it.

I chew my lip, thinking of how to say it.

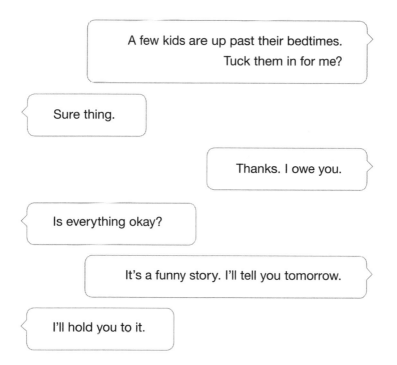

A few kids are up past their bedtimes.
Tuck them in for me?

Sure thing.

Thanks. I owe you.

Is everything okay?

It's a funny story. I'll tell you tomorrow.

I'll hold you to it.

I pocket the phone and the list and dig the soda out of the machine, slumping onto a bench to drink it. It's late and the hall is quiet, and I replay Judge Phillip's crime scene in my head. I know what I saw. The void was real. I have to assume there are two more: one in Bethany's driveway and another wherever Jason vanished. Three innocent people gone. If there's any upside to my being stuck here, it's that no one else should get hurt.

I finish the soda and get to my feet. The local anesthetic has worn off, and the pain in my arm is bad enough to make me consider the pills in my pocket. I throw them away to be safe and head back to my room and climb into bed. I'm not feeling anywhere close to sleep, but I'm also not feeling anywhere close to normal. I think of Lyndsey, who always makes me feel a little bit closer to okay, and text her.

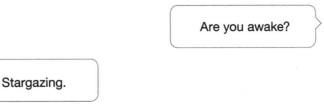

Are you awake?

Stargazing.

I picture her sitting on her roof, cross-legged with a cup of tea and an upturned face.

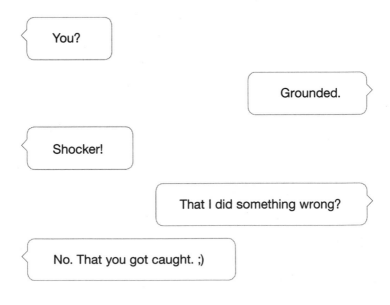

You?

Grounded.

Shocker!

That I did something wrong?

No. That you got caught. ;)

I let out a small, sad laugh.

> Night.

> Sleep sweet.

The clock on the wall says eleven forty-five. It's going to be a long night. I unfold the list in my lap and watch as, over the next hour, the names go out like lights.

# EIGHTEEN

I T HAPPENS AT FIVE A.M.

At first I think it's just another name, but I soon realize it's not. It's a note. A *summons*. The words write themselves onto the Archive paper.

*Please report to the Archive. —A*

I know what the *A* stands for. Agatha. It was only a matter of time. Even with Wesley picking up my slack in the Narrows, he can't cover the incident with the cops, or this. Did Eric tell her I was here? If she knows, then she *knows* I can't answer the summons. Is that what she's counting on? Denying a summons from the Archive is an infraction. Another tally against me.

I'm reading the note for the seventeenth time, trying to decide what to do, when the door opens and Dallas comes in. I force myself to fold the paper and put it away as she says good morning and introduces herself to my parents, then asks them to wait outside.

She sinks into the chair by the bed. "You look like hell," she says—which doesn't strike me as the most professional way to start, but at least it's accurate.

"Couldn't sleep," I say. "They're going to let me go home today, right?" I ask, trying to mask the urgency in my voice.

"Well," she says, tilting her head back, "I suppose that's up to me. Which means it's up to you. Do you want to talk?"

I don't respond.

"Do you dislike me because I'm standing in your way," she asks, "or because I'm a therapist?"

"I don't dislike you," I say evenly.

"But I'm both," observes Dallas. "And most people generally dislike both."

"I dislike *hospitals*," I explain. "The last time my family was in one, my brother had just been killed by a car on his way to school. And I dislike therapists because my mother's told her to throw out all of his things. To help her move on."

"Well then," she says, "I'm afraid your mother's therapist and I wouldn't get along."

"That's a solid tactic," I say.

Dallas raises a brow. "Excuse me?"

"The enemy of my enemy is my friend. It's a good approach."

"Why, thank you," she says cheerfully. "You get away with this a lot, don't you? Deflecting."

I pick at the bandages on my hand. The shallow cuts are healing well. "Most people would rather talk about themselves anyway."

She smiles. "Except therapists."

Dallas doesn't act like a shrink. There's no "How does that make you feel?" or "Tell me more" or "Why do you think that is?" Talking with her is like a dance or a sparring match: a combination of moves, verbal actions and reactions strung together. Her eyes go to my arm. They took the bandages off so it could breathe.

"That looks like it hurts."

"It was a nightmare," I say carefully. "I thought someone else was doing it to me, and then I woke up and it was still there."

"A pretty dangerous twist on sleepwalking."

Her voice is light, but there's no mockery in it.

"I'm not crazy," I whisper.

"Crazy never crossed my mind," she says. "But I was talking to your parents, about Da, and about Ben, and about this, and it seems like you've been exposed to a lot of trauma for someone your age. Have you noticed that?"

Have I? Da's death. Ben's murder. Owen's attack. Wesley's stabbing. Carmen's assault. Archive secrets. Archive lies. Violent Histories. Voids. Countless scars. Broken bones. Bodies. Tunnel moments. Nightmares. This.

I nod.

"Some people crumble under trauma," she says. "And some people build armor. And I think you've built some amazing armor, Mackenzie. But like I said last night, it can't always protect you from yourself." She sits forward. "I'm going to say something, and I want you to listen carefully, because it's kind of important."

She reaches out and brings her hand to rest over mine, and her noise is like an engine, low and humming and steady. I don't pull away.

"It's okay to not be okay," she says. "When you've been through things—whatever those things are—and you don't allow yourself to *not* be okay, then you only make it worse. Our problems will tear us apart if we try to ignore them. They demand attention because they need it. Now, are you okay?"

Before I even realize it, my head is turning side to side. Dallas smiles a little.

"See? Was that so hard to admit?"

She gives my hand a small squeeze, and my gaze drops to her fingers. I stiffen.

Dallas has a dent on her ring finger.

"Divorced," she says, catching my look. "I'm starting to think the mark won't ever fade."

She pulls away and rubs at the spot between her knuckles, and I force myself to breathe, to remember that normal people wear rings, too—and that normal people take them off. Besides, her sleeves are pushed up and her forearms are free of Crew marks.

Dallas gets to her feet.

"I'm going to release you, on the condition that you attend counseling at Hyde. Will you do that for me?"

Agatha's summons burns a hole in my pocket. "Yes," I say quickly. "Fine. Okay."

"Are you sure this is a good idea?" asks Mom when Dallas tells her the news. "I mean, she tried to . . ."

"Not to be crude, ma'am," says Dallas, "but if she'd wanted to kill herself, she would have cut down the road, not across the street. As it is, she's several blocks up."

Mom looks horrified. I almost smile. She's certainly no Colleen.

The nurse rewraps my left arm, and I change back into my school shirt, tugging the sleeve down over the bandage. I can't hide the tape from the glass on my right palm, but that might work to my advantage. Misdirection. The worst of last night's self-pity is gone, and right now I need to focus on surviving long enough to find out who's framing me. *Owen hasn't won yet,* I think, and then I remind myself that Owen didn't do this. I did. Maybe Dallas was right. Maybe I need to stop denying I'm broken and work on finding the pieces.

Speaking of Dallas, she gives me a small salute on the way out and tells me to loosen the armor. The nurse who stitched and bandaged me up seems surprised by Dallas's order to release me, but doesn't question it—only fires off cleaning instructions and tells my parents to keep an eye on me and make sure I get some rest. She leans in and confides in my mother, loud enough for me to hear, that she doesn't think I ever went to sleep.

Great.

There's no sign of Eric or Sako in the hospital lobby or in the lot, and I realize with a sinking feeling that their faces are the only two I'd recognize. I know that a Crew member made the void, but I don't know which one. The Archive keeps its members isolated—each an island—but that means I don't know how many Crew there are in my branch, let alone what they look like.

"Come on, Mac," calls Dad, and I realize I'm standing on the sidewalk staring at the street.

On the drive home, I feel the scratch of more letters in my pocket, and by the time we get back to the Coronado, the summons has repeated itself on the page, the letters darker, as if someone's pressing down harder on the ledger. I turn the paper over and write the words *unable to report*, watching as they bleed into the page. I wait for a reply, a pardon, but the original summons only rewrites itself on the page. The message is clear, but I'm not allowed to close my bedroom door or go to the bathroom without an escort, let alone slip off to the Archive for a good old-fashioned interrogation. I don't even have the excuse of school, since it's Saturday. When I ask if I can go for a walk to get some fresh air, Mom looks at me like I've lost my mind.

And maybe I have, but after an hour of trying to do homework in spite of the hovering and heavy quiet, I can't take it anymore. I break down and text Wesley.

Save me.

Mom won't stop pacing, and Dad finally cracks and sends her down to the café to work off some of her stress. Five minutes after that, there's a knock on the door and Wesley's there with a bag of pastries and a book, looking like himself—well, his summer self: black jeans, lined eyes, spiked hair—for the first time in weeks. When Dad answers the door, I watch the war between what he's supposed to say—*No visitors*—and what he wants to say—*Hi, Wes!* What finally comes out is, "Wesley, I'm not sure now's a good time."

Even though Wes frowns and asks, "Has something happened?" I can tell he's not totally in the dark. If I had to guess, I'd say he's aware of the part where I got picked up by the cops, but not the part where I landed myself in the self-harm section of the hospital. His eyes go to my bandaged hand, and I can see the questions in them.

Dad casts a glance back at the table where I'm nursing a cup of coffee and trying not to look as tired as I feel and says, "Actually, why don't you come in?"

Wesley takes a seat next to me, and Dad stands by the door, clearly debating his next move.

"Dad," I say, reaching out and taking Wesley's hand with my unbandaged one. The steady beat of his rock music fills my head. "Could we have a moment?"

Dad hovers there, looking at us.

"I'm not going anywhere," I promise.

"I'll keep her out of trouble, Mr. Bishop," says Wes.

Dad smiles sadly. "I'm holding you to that," he says. "I'll go down and check on your mom. You've got ten minutes."

When the door closes, Wes gives my fingers a small squeeze before letting go. "Did you hurt your wrist again?" he asks, nodding at my other hand.

I shake my head. "Did Amber tell you?"

"That you got arrested? Yeah."

"It doesn't count as an arrest unless they book you."

Wesley arches a brow. "Spoken like a true criminal. What did you get picked up for?"

"Oh, Amber didn't share that part?"

"She didn't know."

"Ah, well. Remember the guy who disappeared before Bethany? Judge Phillip? I went back to check out his house, since that's where he vanished from. And I might have entered the place using less than legal methods."

Wes hits the table. "You broke into a crime scene *without me*?"

"Be glad, Wes, or we both would have been caught."

"We're a team, Mac. You don't go committing a crime without your *partner in crime*. Besides, if I'd been with you, we probably wouldn't have been caught. I could have stood at the door and made wild bird sounds or something when the cops came back. And if we did get caught, our mug shots would look fabulous."

I can't help but smile at the thought.

"Tell me you at least found something."

The smile slides off my lips. "I did," I say slowly. "A void."

Wesley's brow knits. "I don't understand."

"A void. Like the one on the roof."

"In the middle of Phillip's living room? That doesn't make any sense. The only way there'd be a void there is if someone *made* one. And they'd need a Crew key to do that."

"Exactly." I run my good hand through my hair and tell him about breaking into Judge Phillip's and seeing the void, and the way it made the memories unreadable. I tell him about Eric and

Sako following me. I tell him what Roland said about evidence, and that I know it sounds crazy, but I think I'm being set up.

"You have to tell the Archive," he says.

"I know." I *know*. But tell them what? I know how ludicrous it all sounds. I can see the skepticism in Wesley's eyes, and he's far more forgiving than Agatha will be. I can't just walk in there and announce they have another traitor in their midst. Not after what happened with Owen and Carmen. I need to talk to Roland, but I'll have to get past Agatha first. I know I can't keep ignoring the summonses, but after everything I've put my parents through, I can't just disappear. I think about sending Wesley to the Archive on my behalf, but the last thing I want to do is get him tangled up in this, especially now that Agatha's involved. Besides, we're not really partners. Wesley's not supposed to be helping me.

He looks at me hard. "You didn't feel like mentioning any of this last night?"

I pick at a fraying bit of tape on my hand. "It wouldn't translate well to text," I say. "And I was a little busy."

He reaches out and takes my wrapped hand and runs his fingers lightly over the tape. "What happened, Mac?"

I pull away and roll up my left sleeve for him to see the bandage. I unwrap it so he can see the fourteen little red *X*'s beneath.

"Who did this to you?" he growls.

I wish that were an easier question to answer. I take a breath and hold it for several long seconds before finally saying, "I did."

Confusion flickers across Wesley's face, followed by worry. I go to push my sleeve back down, but he catches my hand and draws my arm closer. His fingers hover over the cut. "I don't understand."

"I didn't mean to do it," I explain. "It started as a dream. Owen was . . . He was the one with the knife, and then I . . ." Wesley pulls me into a hug. He holds me so tight it hurts, so tight his noise pounds through my head, but I don't pull away.

"I don't know what's happening to me," I whisper into his shirt.

Wes pulls back just enough to look at me. "Tell me how I can help."

*Go away,* I think. *Stay away from me and whatever bad is circling.* But I know him well enough to know that he won't. "For one, you could ask Amber not to tell the whole school I got arrested."

"It doesn't count as an arrest unless they book you," echoes Wes, adding, "She won't tell anyone."

"She told you."

"Because she knows I . . ." He trails off.

"You what?"

"She knows I care," says Wes. "About you. By the way, you look like hell. Have you slept at *all* since . . ."

I rub my eyes. "I can't."

"You can't stay awake forever, Mac."

"I know . . . but I'm scared." Words Da taught me never to say. He thought saying it was halfway to surrendering. Now the confession hangs between us. The room settles and thickens, and I can feel the cracks in my armor as it loosens around me.

Wes pushes up from the table. He pours himself a cup of coffee and rests against the counter.

"Okay," he says. "If you're determined to stay awake, I can help. But this"—he gestures down at the spread of precalc and lit theory on the table—"isn't going to do." He digs the physiology book out from the bottom of the pile and flashes me a mischievous smile. "Here we go."

By the time Dad gets back, Wes has managed to cover himself

in an impressive number of Post-it notes, each labeling a muscle (I don't have the heart to tell him we're studying blood flow right now). Dad takes one look at him and *almost* smiles. And when it takes Wes half a dozen tries to affix a yellow sticker to the place between his shoulders, I end up laughing until my chest hurts, and for a while I forget how much trouble I'm in and how tired I am and how much my arm hurts.

I make it to dusk, but even with Wesley's company, I'm starting to fade. Mom is back home and making no attempt to hide the fact that she's hovering. Every time I yawn, she tells me I should go to bed. Tells me I need to sleep. But I can't. I know Dallas said I had to confront my problems, but I just don't have the strength to face another nightmare right now. Especially now that I know I'm capable of doing actual damage to myself. And maybe to others. I would rather be exhausted and awake than a danger and asleep, so I brush off her concern and crack open a soda. It's halfway to my lips when she catches my hand, filling my head with her high, worried static as she pries the can away and replaces it with a glass of water.

I sigh and take a long sip. She passes the soda to Wes, who makes the mistake of yawning as he takes it.

"You should head home," Mom tells him. "It's getting late, and I'm sure your father is wondering where you are."

"I doubt that," he says under his breath, then adds, "He knows I'm over here."

"Mom," I say, finishing the glass of water, "he's helping me study."

"Does he know you're *here* here?" she presses, ignoring me. "Or does he think you're upstairs with Jill?"

Wesley's brow furrows. "Frankly, I don't think he cares."

"Parents always care," she snaps.

"Honey," says Dad, looking up from a book.

They're talking, all three of them, but the words begin to run together in my ears. I'm just thinking about how strange it is when my vision slides out of focus.

The room sways, and I grip the counter.

"Mac?" Wes's voice reaches me. "Are you okay?"

I nod and set the glass down; or at least I mean to, but the countertop's not where I thought it was, and the glass goes crashing to the floor. It shatters. The sound is far away. At first I think I'm about to have another blackout, but those happen fast, and this is slow like syrup.

"What have you done?" Wes snaps, but I don't think he's talking to me.

I close my eyes, but it doesn't help. The world sways even in darkness.

"The doctor said she needed to—"

Everything else is far away.

*"Allison,"* growls Dad. I drag my eyes open. "How could you—"

And then my legs go out from under me, and I feel Wesley's arms and his noise wrap around me before the world goes black.

# NINETEEN

A T FIRST, everything is dark and still.

Dark and still, but not peaceful.

The world is somehow empty and heavy at the same time, the nothing weighing me down, pinning my arms and legs. And then, little by little, the details begin to come back, to descend, rise up, wrap around me.

The open air.

My racing heart.

And Owen's voice.

"There's nowhere to run."

Just like that, the darkness thins from absolute black into night, the nothingness into the Coronado roof. I am racing through the maze of gargoyles, and I can hear Owen behind me, the sound of his steps and the grind of metal on stone as he drags his blade along the statues. The roof stretches to every side, forever and ever, the gargoyles everywhere, and I am running.

And I am tired of it.

I have to stop.

The moment the thought hits me, I slam to a halt on the rooftop. My lungs burn and my arm aches, and I look down to find the full word—B R O K E N—carved in bloody, bone-deep letters from elbow to wrist. I search my pockets and come up with a piece of cloth, and I'm halfway through tying it around my forearm, covering the cuts, when I realize how quiet the roof has gotten. The footsteps have stopped, the metallic scratching has stopped, and all I can hear is my heart. Then, the knife.

I turn just in time to dodge Owen's blade as it slashes through the air, putting a few desperate steps between our bodies. The gargoyles have shifted to form walls, no gaps to get through: no escape. And that's okay, because I'm not running.

He slashes again, but I grab his wrist and twist hard, and the knife tumbles from his grip into mine. This time I don't hesitate. As his free hand goes for my throat, I bury the blade in Owen's stomach.

The air catches in his throat, and I think it's finally over—that I've finally done it, I've beat him, and it's going to be okay. I'm going to be okay.

And then he looks down at me, at the place where my hand meets the knife and the knife meets his body. He brings his hand to mine and holds the knife there, buried to the hilt, and smiles.

Smiles as his hair goes black, and his eyes go hazel, and his body becomes someone else's.

"No!" I cry out as Wesley Ayers gasps and collapses against me, blood spreading across his shirt. "Wesley. Wesley, please, please don't . . ." I try to hold him up, but we both end up sinking to our knees on the cold concrete, and I feel the scream rising in my throat.

And then something happens.

Wesley's noise—that strange chaotic beat—pours into the dream like water, washing over his body and mine and the rooftop, filling it up until everything begins to dim and vanish.

I'm plunged into a new kind of darkness, warm and full and safe.

And then I wake up.

It's the middle of the night, and Wesley's hand is tangled with mine. He's in a chair pulled up to my bed, slumped forward and fast asleep with his head cradled on his free arm on the comforter. The memory of him crumpling to the concrete almost makes me pull away. But here, now, with his hand warm and alive in mine, the scene on the roof *feels* like it was just a dream. A horrible dream, but a dream—already fading away as his noise washes over me softer and steadier than usual, but still loud enough to quiet everything else.

My head is still filled with fog, and the hours before the nightmare trickle back first in glimpses.

*Mom pushing the water into my hand.*

*The tilting room.*

*The breaking glass.*

*Wesley's arms folding around me.*

I look down at him, sleeping with his head on my covers. I should wake him up. I should send him home. I slide my fingers from his, and for a moment he rouses, drags himself from sleep long enough to mutter something about storms. Then he's quiet again, his breathing low and even. I sit there, watching him sleep, discovering yet another of his many faces: one without armor.

I decide to let him sleep, and I'm just about to lie back down when I hear it: the sound of someone in the room behind me. Before I can turn, an arm wraps around my shoulders, and a woman's hand closes over my mouth.

Her noise crashes through my head, all metal and stone, and all I can think as her grip tightens is that it takes a cruel person to sound like this. It's how I imagine Owen would have sounded when he was alive, before his life was compiled and his noise replaced by silence.

When she leans in to whisper in my ear, I catch sight of the blue-black fringe that sweeps just above her black eyes. Sako.

"Don't scream, little Keeper," she whispers as she hauls me backward, out of the bed and to my feet. "We don't want to wake him."

Her hand falls away from my mouth, her arm away from my shoulders, and I spin on her in the dark.

"What the hell are you doing here?" I hiss, almost soundless, still dizzy from whatever Mom put in my water.

"Trust me," growls Sako as she grabs my arm and drags me across the room. "I'd rather be a thousand other places."

"Then get out," I snap, pulling free. "Shouldn't you be hunting down Histories?"

"Haven't you figured it out yet, little Keeper?" she says, driving her Crew key into my closet door. "We hunt down *people* for the Archive. Only some of them are Histories."

I barely have time to pull off my ring before she turns the key, opens the door, and shoves me into darkness.


Agatha is waiting.

She's sitting behind the front desk in her cream-colored coat, her red hair sweeping perfectly around her face. One gloved hand turns through the ledger like it's a magazine, while Roland stands at her side, looking stiff and pale. His attention snaps up when Sako drags me in, but Agatha continues to play with the pages of the massive book.

"See, Roland?" she says, the heavy paper crinkling under her touch. "I told you Sako would find her."

Sako nods a fraction. Her hand is still a vise on my shoulder, but nothing filters in with her touch now. The silent buffer of the Archive surrounds us. Only the Librarians can read people here.

"She was asleep," says Sako. "With a boy."

Agatha raises a brow. "I'm so sorry to disturb you," she says in that milky voice.

"Not at all," I say tightly. "I would have come sooner, but I was indisposed, and my doors were out of reach." Only Crew can turn any door into an Archive door. I turn to Sako. "Thanks for the lift."

Sako smiles darkly. "Don't mention it."

Roland's eyes have locked onto the bandage wrapping around my right hand and up my wrist—*You should see my other arm,* I think—and they hover there as Agatha quietly shuts the ledger and rises to her feet.

"If you'll excuse us, I think it's time for Mackenzie and me to have a little chat."

"Requesting permission to be present," says Roland.

"Denied," she says casually. "Someone needs to watch the front desk. And Sako, please stay. You might be needed." Agatha points to one of the two sentinels by the door. "With me, please." I stiffen.

"I really don't think that's necessary," says Roland as one of the two black-clad figures steps forward. It's the first time I've ever seen one move.

"I hope it's not," says Agatha, "but one should always come prepared."

She turns toward the open doors behind the desk, and I scramble to pull my thoughts together as I follow. Roland catches my shoulder as I pass.

"Do not grant her permission," he whispers before the sentinel gives me a push through the doors.

I pad barefoot through the atrium of the Archive, the white of Agatha's coat in front of me, the black of the sentinel's cloak trailing behind, and for the first time, I feel like a prisoner. As we turn down one of the halls, I catch sight of Patrick standing at the edge of a row of stacks. His eyes follow us—curious, but otherwise unreadable.

Agatha leads me into a room with no shelves and two chairs.

"Have a seat," she tells me, waving at one as she takes the other. When I hesitate, the sentinel forces me down. His hands stay pressed onto my shoulders, holding me in place until Agatha says, "That won't be needed," and then he takes a step back. I can feel him looming like a shadow behind the chair.

"Why am I here?" I ask.

Agatha crosses her legs. "It's been nearly a month since our last meeting, Miss Bishop. I thought it time for a checkup. Why?" she says, tilting her head innocently. "Can you think of any other reasons I'd summon you?"

A pit forms in my stomach as she pulls a small black notebook from the pocket of her coat and opens it with a small sigh.

"Preceding the obvious failure to report when summoned . . ." I bite back the urge to cut in, to call her out on the fact she *knew* I couldn't come. ". . . I've compiled a rather concerning list of irregularities," she says, dragging a gloved finger down the page. "We have nights spent in the Archive."

"Roland's been training me."

"The assault of two humans in the Outer."

"They assaulted *me*. I merely defended myself."

"And the Archive had to clean up the mess."

"I didn't ask the Archive to."

She sighs. "An arrest for breaking and entering a crime scene?"

"I was never processed."

"Then how about crimes more pertinent to the Archive?" she challenges. "Such as failure to return Histories." I open my mouth, but she holds up a hand. "Do not insult me by claiming you were the one to send those lost souls back, Miss Bishop. I happen to know that Mr. Ayers's key was used to access the Returns in your territory. The simple fact is that you have been neglecting your *job*."

"I'm sorry. I was indisposed."

"Oh, I know. Hospitalized. For self-harm." She taps the paper thoughtfully. "Do you understand why I find that so troublesome?"

"It's not what you—"

"This is a stressful job, Miss Bishop. I am aware of that. The mind bears as many scars as the body. But the mind also keeps our secrets. A weak mind is a threat to the Archive. It is why we alter those who leave. And those who are removed." Agatha's eyes hold mine. "Now tell me, what happened?"

I take a deep breath in. Most people do before telling a lie—it's an almost automatic physical preparation and one of the hardest tells to break—but I make sure to let it out before starting, hoping the hesitation passes for embarrassment. And then I hold out my right hand. The cuts from the glass are shallow, but I've made sure they're covered, and the bandages wrap down around my wrist.

"Last month," I start, "when I tried to stop Owen, he broke a few of the bones in my wrist." I think back to my physiology textbook. "He cracked the radius and crushed the scaphoid, lunate, and part of the triquetrum." I point out the rough placement of each. "The last two didn't set properly. There were a few small pieces of bone that never re-fused. They were getting in the way, so I did my best to take them out." Her eyes drift to the bandages that circle my wrist as she leans forward, closing the narrow gap between us. It's exactly what I want, her to focus on the hand. She need never know about the bandages on my other arm.

"Why not go to the hospital?" she asks.

"I didn't want my parents to worry."

"Why not have *Patrick* see to it?"

"He's not my biggest fan," I say, "and I thought I could see to it myself. But I'm afraid the thing about being a teenager is that people tend to notice when you take a knife to yourself, no matter the reason."

A sad smile touches her lips, and I'm beginning to think she actually bought the lie when she says, "Roll up your sleeves."

I hesitate, and that brief pause is enough to give me away. Agatha rises to her feet, and I move to rise, too, but the sentinel holds me in my seat as she leans forward and guides up my sleeve—not my right one, but my left—exposing the bandage that winds around my forearm.

"Tell me," says Agatha, running a finger gingerly over the tape, "did pieces of bone wander into this arm, too?"

"I can—"

But she lifts a finger to silence me.

"I asked you once," she says, "if you wanted to remember all that had happened to you. I gave you a chance to forget. I fear I might have erred in doing so. Bad memories left in weak minds are like rot. They spread and ruin."

I grip the chair even though it sends pain up my arm. "I assure you, Agatha, I am not ruined."

"No," she says, "but you may be *broken*."

I cringe. "I am not. You have to believe me."

"Actually," she says, tugging on the fingers of one black glove, "I don't. Not when I can see for myself."

The sentinel's grip tightens on my shoulders, and Roland's voice rushes in my ears. *Once she has access to your mind, anything she finds there can be used against you. If she found you unfit, you would be sentenced to alteration. . . . Do not grant her permission.*

"No," I say, the words brimming with panic. "You can't."

Agatha pauses, her eyes narrowing. "Excuse me?"

"You don't have my permission," I say, reminding myself that this is law, even though it feels like suicide. Agatha's false warmth dissolves, and she considers me coldly.

"You are denying me access to your mind." It is not a question. It is a challenge.

I nod. "It is my right."

"Only the guilty plead the Fifth, Miss Bishop. I strongly advise you to reconsider."

But I can't. I have chosen my path, and she must respect it. She can't hurt me, at least not right now. It may only be a reprieve, but it's better than a sentence. I roll my sleeve down over the bandages, and she reads the gesture for the denial it is.

The sentinel's grip retreats from my shoulders, and I'm about to push myself to my feet when she says, "We are not done." My stomach twists as she rounds her chair and curls her gloved hands around the back. "You still haven't explained the crime scene or what you were doing there."

*Lie, lie, lie* pounds my heart. But a lie has to be as quick as truth, and the fact I've paused yet again means I won't be able to sell a line. She'll see through it. If I was standing on ice before, my refusal has driven cracks into it.

"Someone I met was abducted," I say, the words coming out too cautiously. "I thought I might be able to see something the cops had missed. The man, Gregory Phillip, went missing from his home.

The room where the abduction took place was trashed, and the police didn't have any leads. They couldn't make sense of the evidence, couldn't figure out how the man had vanished. Because they couldn't see it. But when I broke in, I saw it clearly."

"Saw what, Miss Bishop?"

"Someone had made a void."

Agatha's eyes narrow. "That," she says, "is a very serious accusation."

It is. Voids can only be made using Crew keys, the only people given Crew keys are Crew, and Agatha is personally responsible for every member of this branch, Keeper and Crew alike. Which is why she should be more interested in finding the person behind this than in burning me.

"I understand the severity—"

"Do you?" she says, rounding her chair. "Do you truly know what you're suggesting? Voids are tears in the world. Every time one is created, it puts the Outer and the Archive at risk. As such, the intentional creation of one is punishable by alteration. And you think that a member of Crew would disobey the Archive—disobey *me*—and create such a tear in the Outer in order to dispose of *one human*?"

"Three," I correct. "There have been three disappearances in the last week, and I believe voids were created in every instance. And I'm not convinced the Crew responsible is doing it for themselves. I think it's possible that someone in the Archive has given them the order."

"And why on earth would someone do that?"

"I think"—god, I sound mad; I can barely will the words out—"someone's trying to frame me." Agatha's eyebrows go up as I add, "I crossed paths with each victim before they vanished."

"And who would want to frame you?" she asks, her voice dripping with condescension.

"There are members of the Archive," I say, "who disapprove of your initial ruling. Those who are opposed to my continued service."

Agatha sighs. "I'm well aware of Patrick's feelings toward you, but you honestly believe he would break Archival law to see you terminated?"

I hesitate. I'm not sure I do. It was easy to believe he would send Eric to find evidence, but I have a harder time believing he would *plant* it.

"I don't know," I say, trying hard not to waver. "I'm only telling you what I found."

"You must be mistaken."

"I know what I saw."

"How can you?" she counters. "Voids are not *truly* visible, to anyone. You got a bad feeling, you thought your eyes slid off a bit of air, and you assumed—"

"I *read the wall*. The memories surrounding the creation of the void were all ruined. Whited out."

She shakes her head. "Even if there was a void, how do I know *you* aren't to blame? Do you have any idea how rare a void door *is*? You've already been tied to one—"

"I was doing my job."

"—and now this. You yourself said three disappearances, and you crossed paths with each."

"I don't have a Crew key."

"There was another one, was there not? On the roof? The one belonging to that traitorous History? What happened to it?"

My mind spins. "It got sucked into the void," I say, "along with Owen."

"How convenient."

"I could have lied, Agatha," I say, trying to stay calm, "and I did not. I told you the truth. Someone is defying you. Defying the Archive."

"Do you think I would allow such crimes and conspiracies to happen under my nose?"

I stiffen. "With all due respect, less than a month ago a Librarian plotted to unleash a restricted History into the Outer and tear down an entire branch from the inside, and she nearly succeeded. All of it under the *Archive's* nose."

In a flash, Agatha is upon me, pinning me to the chair, her fingers digging into my wounded forearm. Tears burn my eyes and I squeeze them shut, fighting back the dizzying dark of a tunnel moment.

"Which is more likely?" she says, her voice a low growl. "That a member of the Archive is conspiring against you—out of personal distaste or retribution, fashioning some elaborate scheme to have you found unfit, constituting treason—or that you're simply delusional?"

I take a few shaky breaths as the pain sears across my skin. "I know . . . you don't want . . . to believe—"

Agatha's nails dig into my arm. "My position is not built on what I *want* to believe, Miss Bishop. It is based on truth and logic. It is a very complicated machine I help to run. And when I find a broken piece, it is my job to fix or replace it before it can damage any other parts."

She lets go and turns away.

"I'm not broken," I say under my breath.

"So you claim. And yet the things that come out of your mouth are madness. Am I correct," she says, turning back to me, "in assuming that you still refuse to grant me access to your mind? That you make this *claim* against the Archive, against Crew, against *me*, and yet you deny me the ability to find you innocent or guilty of the charges you put on those around you?"

I feel sick. If my theory is wrong, then I've also signed my execution, and we both know it. I force myself to nod. Agatha looks past me to the sentinel.

"Go get Sako," she says.

A moment later, I hear the door close. Agatha and I are alone.

"I will start with the Crew then," she says, "because none of them would be foolish enough to deny me permission. And when I've scoured their minds and found each and every one of them loyal and innocent, I will tear your life apart, moment by moment, to uncover your guilt. Because you have proven one thing tonight, Miss Bishop: you are guilty of something." She takes my chin in one gloved hand. "Maybe it's the voids, or maybe it's madness, but whatever it is, I will find out." Her hand drifts down my jaw to my collar. "In the meantime," she says, guiding the key out from under my shirt, "I suggest you keep your list clear."

The threat is clear and cold as ice. *If you wish to remain a Keeper.*

The door opens, and Sako stands there waiting.

"Take Miss Bishop home," says Agatha smoothly, her hand abandoning my collar. "And then come back. We need to talk."

Something flits across Sako's face—curiosity, confusion, a shade of fear?—and then it's gone and she nods. She slides her key straight into the door behind her, takes my elbow, and pushes me through.

An instant later, we are standing in my bedroom again, Wesley asleep with his head on the bed and Sako's noise rattling through my body. Her metal and stone clanging become *coiled annoyance waste of space what did she do guarded what does Agatha want now could have a night with Eric his arms wrapped around warm golden and strong and safe*, and when she lets go of my arm, I'm surprised by how strong Sako's feelings are for him.

"Get out of my head, little Keeper," she growls.

I slide my ring back on, wondering how much of *my* mind *she* saw. She turns on her heel and vanishes the way she came, and I'm left standing there in the dark.

My arm aches, but I can't bring myself to inspect the damage, so I sink onto the bed and rest my head in my good hand. I wish that Da were here to tell me what to do. I've run out of his pre-packaged wisdom, his lessons on hunting and fighting and lying. I need *him*.

As the quiet settles around me, the panic creeps in. What have I done? Bought myself a few days, but at what cost? I've made an enemy of Agatha, and even if my theory's sound and the Crew behind the voids is found, she will not forget my refusal. And if my theory's wrong? I squeeze my eyes shut. *I know what I saw. I know what I saw. I know what I saw.*

Music fills my head, strong and steady, and I look down to see Wesley's hand wrapped around mine, his eyes bleary but open. He must misread the shock and fear in my eyes for the echoes of a nightmare—how I wish this were still a bad dream—because he doesn't ask what's wrong. Instead he climbs onto the bed beside me and rolls me in against him, his arms wrapped around my waist.

"I won't let anyone hurt you," he whispers sleepily into my hair. And all I can think as his music plays in my head is that this is how

Sako saw Eric in her mind: like a shield, strong and safe. This is how Crew partners feel about each other. But we are not Crew. We may never be now. But tonight, I let myself pretend. I hold on to his rock sound and his touch. I let it surround me.

Ten minutes later, the first name appears on my list.

# TWENTY

**W**HEN I WAKE UP, Wesley's gone. There's nothing but a dent on the comforter to show that he was ever here. It's late, light streaming in through the windows, and I lie there for a moment, sleep still clinging to me—dreamless, easy sleep, filled only with music—and savor the calm. And then I move, and pain ripples sharply down my arm and dully through my shoulders, and I remember.

What have I done?

*What I had to,* I tell myself.

The Archive paper sits on my side table, tucked beneath *The Inferno*. At least there's still only the one name.

*Abigail Perry. 8.*

I pocket the list. The smell of coffee drags me out of bed, and my hand's on the door before I notice there's dried blood staining my sleeve. I tug out of the shirt; the outline of Agatha's grip is nearly visible in the stain. I unwrap the dressing as quickly as possible—my eyes sliding off the gash as if it is a void, something wrong, unnatural, drawing and repelling my gaze at once—and pull a clean shirt on before heading into the kitchen. Dad's already there, brewing a pot of dark roast.

"I sent Wes home," he says in lieu of a good morning.

"I'm amazed you let him stay," I say, gingerly tugging the clean shirtsleeve down over the stitches. Maybe out of sight will turn into out of mind.

"Actually, he kind of refused to leave." Dad pours me a cup. "After what happened."

I take the mug and drag through my thoughts. Past Agatha's interrogation and Owen's nightmare to the room tipping and the water glass shattering on the hardwood floor. "How could she, Dad?"

He rubs his eyes and takes a long sip. "I don't condone what your mother did, Mackenzie. But you have to understand, she was only trying to—"

"Don't tell me she was trying to help."

He sighs. "We're *all* trying to help, Mac. We just don't know how." I look down at my coffee. "And for the record, that was a one time deal, having your boyfriend stay the night."

"Wesley's not my boyfriend."

He arches a brow over his coffee. "Does he know that?"

My eyes escape to the coffee cup as I remember his arms folding around me, the comforting blanket of his noise.

"Caring about someone is scary, Mac. I know. Especially when you've lost people. It's easy to think it's not worth it. It's easy to think life will hurt less if you don't. But it's not life unless you care about it. And if you feel half of what he feels for you, don't push him away."

I nod distantly, wishing I could tell him that I do feel half, more than half, maybe even all of what Wesley feels, but that it's not that simple. Not in my world. I lean my elbows carefully on the counter. "What are you up to today?" I ask lightly.

"I have to go to the university for a bit. Left some work there that I didn't get to yesterday."

*Because you were playing warden.* "And Mom?"

"Down in the café."

I sip my coffee. "And me?" I ask cautiously. The list is like a weight in my pocket.

"You'll be with her," he says. What he means is, *She'll be watching you.*

"I still have some homework to do," I lie.

"Take it down there," he says. His tone is gentle, but the message is clear. I won't be left unattended. The love is there, the trust is gone.

I tell Dad I need to take a shower first, and he nods for me to go. A small part of me marvels at the fact I'm allowed to bathe without supervision, until I see that they've already taken every remotely sharp object out of the bathroom.

I'm hoping he'll go on ahead to work and I'll be able to make a quick detour into the Narrows on my way downstairs, but by the time I'm out of the shower and dressed and my arm and hand are freshly wrapped, he's waiting for me by the door.

He ushers me down to the coffee shop like a prisoner, passing me over to my mother's care. She won't look at me. I won't talk to her. I know she wanted to help, but I don't care. I'm not the only one in this place capable of losing someone's trust.

For a woman who won't look me in the eyes, it's amazing how she manages to never let me out of her sight. Thankfully the coffee shop is pretty full, and I welcome the lack of eye contact for the first hour as I clear tables and ring up drinks. Berk's working today, too, which helps. He has a kind of infectious cheer and a hatred for quiet, so he makes enough small talk to cover up the fact that Mom and I haven't said a word to each other.

"I hope the guy deserved it," says Berk when I reach out to take a coffee and he sees my bandaged palm and healing knuckles. "Is that the reason you two are fighting?" he asks, gesturing with a pair of tongs to Mom, who's retreated by now to the patio to chat with a woman in the corner table, her eyes flicking in my general direction every few moments.

"One of many," I say.

Thankfully he doesn't ask more about it—doesn't even assume it's all my fault. He just says, "They mean well, parents," and then tells me to take out the trash, adding, "You look like you could use a little fresh air."

I weigh my odds for escaping to the Narrows, but they aren't good. There's a door in the closet at the back of the café, but that's not exactly inconspicuous, and my other two doors— the one in the lobby and the one on the third floor—aren't in easy reach. As for Mom, well, Berk's barely handed me the bag before her eyes dart my way. I hoist up the trash for her to see and point to the back door. Her eyes narrow and she starts heading toward me, but gets snagged by another table halfway. She flashes me three fingers.

*Three minutes.*

Fine. Abigail Perry will have to wait, but at least I'll prove to Mom that I can be left alone. I duck out the back door, relishing my three minutes of privacy and sunlight. As soon as I'm outside, I let my steps slow, savoring every second of freedom.

I've just finished loading the bags into the bin when a hand tangles in my shirt and slams me up against the Coronado wall, *hard.*

*"How dare you?"* growls Sako, her harsh metallic noise scraping through my bones.

"What are you talking ab—" Her other fist connects with my ribs, and I hit the alley floor, gasping.

"You've really made a mess of things. You never should have gone to Agatha."

"What's the matter?" I cough, getting to my feet. "Do you have something to hide?"

She grabs me again and slams me back against the stone side of the Coronado.

"I'm loyal to the Archive, you little shit. A fact Agatha can attest to, because thanks to your cracked little head and its paranoid delusions, I just spent the night letting her claw through my life." She leans in, her face inches from mine. Her black eyes are bloodshot, and dark circles stand out against the pale skin beneath them. "Do you have any idea what that feels like?" she hisses. "Because you *will*. Once she runs out of Crew, she'll come for you. And I hope she tears you apart one memory at a time until there's nothing left."

I'm still reeling from the fact that Sako's innocent when she shoves away from me and says, "She still has Eric. She's been with him for hours. And if she punishes him because of you, I will tear your throat open with my fingernails."

"He shouldn't have been following me," I say.

Sako makes an exasperated noise. "He was only following you because Roland asked him to. To keep you *safe*." The last word comes out in a hiss. I feel like I've been hit again, the air rushes from my lungs as she adds, "Though what Roland sees in you, I have no idea."

Sako smooths her blue-black hair, her Crew key glittering against her wrist. "Maybe I should tell Agatha about your little boyfriend, Wesley. Maybe *he* should be a suspect. Couldn't hurt for her to take a look."

"Wes has nothing to do with this," I say through gritted teeth, "and you know it."

"Do I?" asks Sako. She turns away. "Enjoy your freedom while it lasts, little Keeper. It'll be your turn soon enough. And when it is, I hope Agatha lets me drag you in myself."

She storms away, and I'm left sagging against the wall, winded and worried. Sako and Eric are both innocent?

*Cracked little head,* echoes Sako in my ears.

*Broken,* echoes Owen in my mind.

I squeeze my eyes shut and wait for the voices to quiet. I know what I saw. I saw a void. Voids are made by Crew keys, so it had to be Crew. Eric and Sako are not the only pages in the ledger. I try to picture the book on the Archive desk, turn through it in my mind. There's a master page, a table of contents, and then one page for each person who serves in the branch. How many pages total? A hundred? More? Our branch serves a territory with a diameter of two to three hundred *miles.* How many cities fall within that circle? How many pages of the book could be dedicated to *this* city? And how many of those pages belong to Crew? How many people for Agatha to go through? Four? Eight? Twelve? I crossed paths with the victims, but have I crossed paths with the criminal?

I take a deep breath, checking myself again for blood before I go back inside.

"There you are," says Berk. "I was beginning to think I'd lost you."

"Sorry," I say, ducking behind the counter. "I ran into a friend."

Mom's on the patio serving some new customers, and I catch her stealing a glance through the glass to make sure I'm back. She taps her watch, but my attention shifts past her as Sako saunters down the curb. She's talking on the phone now, her head tipped

217

lazily back as if soaking up the sun, and I realize something. Moments ago she was a monster, an animal, all teeth and bite. And now, impossibly, she looks *normal*. Crew look *normal*. They have the ability to blend in. Even Eric, made of gold. I didn't notice him until he wanted me to. Crew could be anyone. What if whoever's doing this doesn't stand out? What if they blend right in? What if they've slipped into my life unnoticed?

Berk laughs and chats with a customer at the end of the counter. My eyes go to his hands, and I tense when I see that they're bare but for a single silver thumb ring. He's only been here for a couple weeks. But his sleeves are rolled up and free of marks. I scan the coffee shop, searching for regulars. I'm looking for people on the periphery of my life, close enough to watch me without being noticed. But no one stands out. And that's exactly the problem.

Just then, a second name scrawls itself on the list in my pocket—*Bentley Cooper. 12.*—and I start to wish I'd risked Mom's wrath to find Abigail. I'm going to have my work cut out for me later.

"Hey, Mac," calls Berk, nodding at the door. "Customer."

I pocket the paper and turn, expecting a stranger, and find Cash instead.

Wesley may trade in his preppy schoolboy persona for guyliner and silver studs, but Cash's weekend look is still solidly Hyde. His dark-wash jeans and crisp white polo make me feel dingy in my Bishop's apron.

His gold eyes light up when he sees me. He crosses the café and hops up onto a stool. "So this is where you live!" he says cheerfully.

"This is where I *work*," I say, drying a mug. "Upstairs is where I live."

He spins around on his stool and leans his elbows back on the counter while he surveys the café.

"Enchanting."

When he turns back around, I've already poured him a drink.

"And enchanted," he says, gesturing at the cup.

"I figured it was my turn to provide the coffee," I say. "So, what are you doing here?"

He takes a slow sip. "I brought your bike. I saw that you left it at school."

"Wow," I say, "you take your ambassador role very seriously."

"Indeed," he says with a sober nod. "But if I'm being honest, the bike was an excuse to come say hi."

I feel myself blushing. "Oh really?"

He nods. "I was worried. Seniors are in charge of organizing Fall Fest, and Wesley bailed on prep yesterday. When I asked where he was, he said with you, and I was about to give him hell for it, as is my friendly obligation, but he told me you'd had a bit of a scrape. So I thought I'd look you up and come make sure you were all right."

"Oh," I say. "You didn't have to, really. I'm fine."

"We must have different definitions of fine," he says, nodding at my bandaged hand. "What happened?"

"It's stupid, really. This old building," I say, showing him my taped palm. "I put my hand against a window and it broke. It's not a big deal," I add, the fourteen stitches aching under my other sleeve. "I'll live."

Cash brings his fingertips to my hand, so light I barely hear the jazz and laughter in his touch. "Glad to hear it," he says, sounding strangely sincere. He rests his elbows on the counter, looking down into his drink. "Hey, so I've been thinking—"

Someone clears their throat, interrupting Cash, and I look up to see Wes standing a foot away, considering us. Or more precisely, considering Cash's hand, which is still touching mine. I pull away.

"Well, this is a surprise," he says. He looks freshly showered, dressed in simple black, his hair slicked back and still wet, his eyes rimmed with dark.

"Testing out your Fall Fest costume?" teases Cash.

Wes ignores the jab. "Am I interrupting something?" he asks.

"No," I say at the same time Cash mutters, "Not at all."

"Cash was just bringing me my bike."

Wes arches a brow. "The student council is far more involved than it used to be."

Cash's eyes narrow even as he smiles. "Quality assurance," he says.

A moment of tense silence falls over us. When it's clear Wesley is here to stay, Cash hops down from his stool. "Speaking of," he says, "I'd better get back to Hyde. I left a huddle of freshmen hanging ribbons, and I just don't trust that lot with ladders." He turns his attention to Wesley. "Are you coming by later?"

Wes shakes his head. "Can't," he says, pointing upstairs. "Got to look after Jill for a bit. I'll stay late tomorrow."

"You better. Senior pride is on the line." He heads for the door. "Thanks for the coffee, Mackenzie."

"Thanks for the bike," I say. "And the chat."

"Any time."

Wesley watches Cash go. "You like him," he says quietly.

"So do you," I say. "He's a nice guy."

"That's not what I mean."

"I know what you mean." I do like Cash. He's normal. And when he's around, I almost forget that I'm not.

"I would have been here sooner," says Wes, "but it appears my access to your territory has been revoked. Any idea why?"

I frown. Agatha.

"Maybe they decided it was time to hand me the reins," I say as casually as possible. "How did you get here, then? Did you drive?"

"For your information, I took the bus."

I shudder at the thought. So many people in such a tiny box. But Wes has always been better with contact than I am. After all, he's the one who taught me how to let the noise wash over me, how to float instead of drown in the current of people's lives.

"Talk and work, kids. Talk and work," calls Berk from the other end of the counter. Wesley smiles and ducks under the bar.

"So," he asks, softer, "how did you sleep last night?"

The rooftop and the gargoyles and Owen's knife all flash through my mind.

"Awful at first," I say. "But then . . ." I feel my face warming. "I heard your noise, filling my head, and the nightmare just kind of fell apart."

"I wasn't sure what to do," he says, pouring himself a drink. "You called my name."

"Oh," I say, as he takes a sip, "that's because I killed you."

Wes nearly chokes on his coffee.

"It was an accident," I add. "Promise."

"Great," he says, knocking his shoulder against mine, briefly filling my head with rock and bass and drum. "Let's see if we can keep you nightmare-free." He pulls back a little. "Oh, and I talked to Amber. I asked her to let me know if Detective Kinney gets any leads. She said he's gotten really tight-lipped, but that she'll try to keep me posted. I think she thought I wanted to know because of Bethany. . . ."

I'd nearly forgotten about their history. "I'm sorry about her," I say. A void is a rip in the world. It only stays open long enough to drag something—*someone*—through, and then it seals. Once a person is gone . . .

"Yeah. Well. I don't understand the *why*, but you're right about the *what*," says Wes. "I swung by her house to see if anything stood out."

"And?" I ask.

"Something's definitely off. It's in the driveway, right next to the car. I couldn't look right at it."

A breath of relief escapes. I didn't realize how badly I needed someone else to see the voids. Just then, my mother comes over. "Wesley," she says by way of hello as she scoops up two drinks from the counter.

Wes ducks back under the counter and nods. "Hi, Mrs. Bishop."

She seems nervous, and he seems tense, and I remember him growling at her last night, when the world began to tilt.

*What have you done?*

But in the unbalance, I see an opening. "Hey, Wes is going to watch Jill for a while. Can I go with him?"

It's the first thing I've said to her since last night, and I can see the struggle play out across her face as her eyes flick from Wesley to me (or at least to my apron, my collar, my jaw). She doesn't want to let me out of her sight. But if she says no, it'll only cement her as the villain. We're teetering at the edge of something high and steep, and neither of us wants to go over. Part of me thinks that after last night, Mom has already jumped, but I'm offering a rope, a chance to climb back up onto the ledge.

I can tell she wants to take it, but something stops her. I wonder if it's Colleen's voice in her head, warning against the pitfalls of lenient parenting and encouraging vigilance.

"I'm not sure that's a good idea. . . ." Mom looks around the café, but Colleen's an hour away, Berk's staying out of our family drama, and Dad's not here to back her up. If he were, I'm pretty sure he'd side with me.

"I'll keep her out of trouble, Mrs. Bishop," offers Wesley, flashing her a small, genuine smile. If he's surprised by my inviting myself along, he never shows it. "Promise."

Mom shifts her weight, fingers curled around the coffee cups. A man at a corner table flags her over. "Okay," she says at last, still not looking at me. "But be back down in an hour," she adds. "In case it gets busy."

"Sure thing," I say, ducking under the counter before she can see the relief splashed across my face.

"And Mac," she says when Wes and I are nearly to the door.

"Yeah?"

*I'm sorry.* I can see the words on her lips as she looks at the space a foot to my left, but she can't say them. "One hour," she says again for emphasis. I nod and follow Wes out.

# TWENTY-ONE

"**Y**OU'RE IN A HURRY," says Wes once we're on the grand stairs.

"Things to do, dear Wesley."

"I'm intrigued," he says. "But you know, when I said I was going to watch Jill, I didn't intend it as a euphemism. Not that I'm averse, it's just—"

"There are two Histories on my list," I cut in. "And my parents have been playing warden and watch all weekend. I needed an excuse to get away so I could track the names down."

"Is that all my company is to you?" he asks with mock affront. "An excuse?"

We reach the top of the stairs, and I take his chin in my hand, rock music singing through my fingers. "If it makes you feel better," I say teasingly, "you're a very pretty excuse."

His brow crinkles. "I would have preferred *dashing*, but I'll take it."

My hand starts to slide away, but he catches it, holding it gently against his jaw. He gazes down through his black lashes, flashing me a sultry look. Even though I know he's playing, I can feel the heat rising in my cheeks. Finally his hand slips away; but as it does, his fingers graze my forearm and I pull back, wincing.

Wesley's flirting dissolves into a frown. "I don't think you should be hunting."

I sigh and head into the stairwell. "I don't have a choice."

"I could do it for you."

I shake my head. "You no longer have access to my territory."

"You could loan me your key."

"No," I say simply, pushing open the door to the third floor and heading down the hall. "I need to do it myself."

"Wait," he says. "Just wait." I drag myself to a stop beside the painting of the sea. My hour of freedom ticks away inside my head. Wes runs a hand through his hair. "You've been through a lot," he says. "Just give yourself a break."

"I can't," I say simply. "The Archive won't. I have to do this. It's my job. If I can't hunt, then I don't deserve to be a Keeper." I realize with a sinking feeling that it's true. I have to prove that I can do this, that I'm not broken. Agatha's not convinced, and right now, neither am I. But I can't give up. As badly as I want a normal life, I don't want to lose this. Lose myself. Lose Wes.

"I won't be long," I say. As I tug my ring off and pocket it, my senses adjust to the hall, to the keyhole now visible in the wallpaper crease, and to the closeness of Wesley's body, humming with life.

He frowns, tugging off his own ring. "I'm going with you."

"What about Jill?"

He waves a hand. "It's Jill. She's got her nose in some book. She couldn't care less if I'm there to watch her turn the pages."

"You don't have to come," I say, sliding my key over my head and slotting it in the wall.

"But I am," he says matter-of-factly as the Narrows door spreads, stainlike, over the wallpaper beside us. "Listen. I get that you need to do this, but it's been a bad few days, and I don't want you going in there by yourself, okay? Besides, I told your mom I'd keep you out of trouble, and this has trouble written all over it. So if you're determined to go stomping around the Narrows, then I'm going with you." His crooked smile flickers back to life. "And if you try to stop me—well then, I'll scream."

"You wouldn't," I gasp.

"I would. And you'd be surprised how far my voice carries."

"Fine. You can come." I sigh and turn the key in the Narrows door. "But don't get in my way."

Wes starts forward and then stops, remembering something. "What about your summons?" he asks. "Don't you need to report?"

I hesitate. "I already did," I say slowly. "I spoke to Agatha last night."

"And? Did you tell her about the voids? Your theory?"

I nod, half expecting Wes to tell me I should have kept my mouth shut, but he doesn't. He doesn't know Agatha, not the way I do. To him, she is the assessor. The authority. The Archive. It probably wouldn't occur to him to keep it a secret.

"She wasn't very happy," I add.

"I bet," says Wes. "What did she say?"

*I will tear your life apart, moment by moment, to uncover your guilt. Because you have proven one thing tonight, Miss Bishop: you are guilty of something. Maybe it's the voids, or maybe it's madness, but whatever it is, I will find out.*

"She said she'd take care of it."

"Well . . ." Wes rubs his neck. "I guess that's a relief? I mean, this is Agatha. She'll get to the bottom of it, one way or another."

"Yeah," I say, opening the door. I have a sickening feeling he's right.


On good days, the stale, twisting corridors of the Narrows put me on edge. Today, they make my skin crawl. Every little sound twists itself into a set of footsteps. A door knock. A distant voice. My pulse inches up before the door to the Outer is even closed, before the little light that snuck through the boundary between worlds is snuffed, plunging us into the key-lit dark.

My wounded arm hangs at my side, aching dully. I force myself to focus on the task at hand instead of the way the pain creeps through my senses, threatening to drag me into a darker place. I can almost feel Owen pinning me against him, his hands over my hands over the knife. . . .

"Mac?" asks Wes under his breath. I shake myself free of the thoughts. I cannot afford to lose myself here, not with names on my list and Wesley at my back. I can feel him behind me, so close I can almost feel his life radiating off of him like heat. He's keeping his body tensed as if he thinks I'll fall, as if he'll need to catch me.

Two names. Two Histories. That's all. It ought to be routine. Anger prickles through me. If I can't do this, I don't deserve to be called a Keeper.

"I'm okay," I say, pressing my hand to the nearest wall to hide the fact it's shaking. I squeeze my eyes shut momentarily. Taking hold of the thread of time, I turn it back, and the Narrows flickers up again in my mind. I roll it backward until a boy flashes into sight. He's there and then gone just as quickly, but I know where to go next. That's all I need. One step at a time, one foot in front of the other. I pull away and follow his path around the corner, weaving deeper into the Narrows. Soon I find my stride and forget about the pain in my arm and the whisper in my head that says *broken broken broken* in Owen's voice.

"See?" I say, pulling away from another wall. "I told you I'd be—"

I'm halfway through the word *fine* when I round the corner and nearly collide with a body. Instinct kicks in, and I slam the form back against the Narrows wall before I've even registered how small it is, or the fact that it's not fighting back. The girl's shoes dangle off the ground, and she looks at me with wide, terrified eyes, her pupils wavering.

*Abigail Perry. 8.*

The look in her eyes is like cold water. The spell of the Narrows breaks, the nightmarish echoes retreat, and I remember my job. Not to frighten or fight, but to return. To set right.

"Please don't hurt me," she whispers.

I lower the girl's shoes to the ground, loosening my grip without letting go.

"I'm sorry," I say as gently as possible. "I didn't mean to grab you. It's just, you scared me."

Her eyes widen a little more, the pupils settling. "I'm scared, too," she says.

Her gaze drifts to Wesley behind me. "Are you?" she asks him, and Wes, who's always been more of a return-first-talk-later kind of Keeper, kneels in front of Abigail and says, "I am, but Mac here, she's going to show us the way out."

She looks up at me expectantly, and I nod. "That's right," I say, still shaky. "Let's get out of here."

I find the nearest Returns door and send her through. And in that instant before I close the door—when the hall fills with white light—I think of the day I got trapped in that blinding room and my life played all over the walls before folding in square by square, taking my breath and heartbeat with it. I wonder for an instant if that's what it's like to be erased.

But I have no desire to find out.

Two halls away, we run into *Bentley Cooper. 12.* He throws his fists up when he sees us. The kid is all skin and bones and fear, and I can't help but wonder what kind of short life he had to leave him so defensive. The question softens something in me. I know I shouldn't wonder; Da used to scold me for my curiosity, but I'm starting to think he was wrong. Caring is what keeps me human. I know caring is also the reason Owen haunts my dreams—if I didn't let things in, they couldn't hurt me—but maybe Dad was right. It's not life unless you care about it.

I put my hands up, like I'm surrendering, and the boy's come down, and within minutes he's been led into the light. By the time Wes and I step back into the yellow-papered hallway of the third floor, my list and my head are both clearer. The relief I feel at making it through such a small task is sickening—I hope Wes doesn't see it. I slide my ring on and sink back against the wall, feeling more like myself than I have in weeks.

"Well, that was fun," he says casually as he returns his own ring to his finger. "Truth be told, I kind of miss the days when your territory was full of burly knife-wielding convicts. And remember that boy?" he adds nostalgically. "The one who took a jog through the Coronado?"

"Vividly," I say drily. "I picked the broken glass out of your back. Right before we got chewed out for not letting Crew handle it."

Wes sighs. "Crew have all the fun. One day . . ." He trails off, dragging his attention back. "Well, Miss Bishop, your list is clear, and your mother probably thinks we've spent the last"—he checks his watch—"fifty-two minutes engaged in any number of nefarious activities." He reaches out and messes my hair a little, rock music playing through my head with his fingers.

"Wes," I groan, trying to smooth it.

"What? I'm only adding authenticity. Your parents already think we're dating."

"I told them we're not. They don't seem to believe me."

Wes shrugs. "I don't care," he lies. "Gives you a good excuse."

"You're not just an excuse, Wes."

"No, I'm a pretty one," he says with a wink. "I should probably get going, though. Make sure Jill isn't trying to act out any of the things in those books of hers. She's on a pirate kick right now. Made one of Angelli's cats walk a makeshift plank . . ." He turns toward the stairs, but stops after a few feet and casts a mischievous glance back my way. "But I could come by later . . . if you want."

The thought of a full night of sleep, wrapped in nothing but his noise, makes my heart ache, but I force myself to shake my head. "They're not going to let you stay a second time."

"Who says they have to know?" he asks.

"Sneaking into a girl's room?" I ask with mock surprise. "That sounds like something a boyfriend would do."

Wesley's smile tilts. "Just leave the window open."


I make it back to the café with five minutes to spare, catching Mom's eye on the way in. If I'm expecting a smile, a welcome back, or an apology, I'm disappointed. Mom's efficient glance from clock to me to clock to work makes it clear: it's going to take a lot more than an hour without broken promises to piece our family back together.

The first thing I do when I get back upstairs is slide my bedroom window open (if my parents ask, I can say something about needing fresh air, since this seems like the only way I'll ever get any), but when I pause to look out and *down*, I realize there's no way Wes is going to get inside tonight. I rest my elbows on the window and consider the drop until I hear a nervous squeak and turn to see Mom standing in the doorway, looking at me like she thinks I'll jump.

"Nice night," I say, pulling my head back in.

"Dinner's ready," she says, nearly making eye contact before retreating into the kitchen. Progress.

Dad has insisted on cooking, as if that will mend things. He even makes my favorite—spaghetti with meatballs from scratch—but we still spend most of the meal in a silence broken only by scraping knives and forks. Dad won't look at Mom, and Mom won't look at me. All I can think as we sit in silence is that if my life ended right now, there would be this trail of destruction, a wake of ruined trust, and it leaves me feeling empty. Did Da ever feel this way?

*Antony Bishop was a flake, and a criminal, and a selfish asshole who cared more about his secrets and his many lives than his family.*

Is that how Dad really saw his father? Is that what he was? What I am? Something that rends the family instead of gluing it together? Ben was our glue. Have we been weakening without him? Or have I been prying us apart?

Halfway through the meal, I feel the scratch of letters on my list again, and my heart sinks. I excuse myself and escape to my room, my father's command to leave the door open trailing like a weight behind me.

The silence is worse when I'm alone, quickly filling up with *how*s and *why*s and *what if*s. How is Agatha's search going? Why is someone doing this? What if my theory is wrong? I switch the radio on and unfold the Archive paper. Another name.

*Henry Mills. 14.*

I slump down on my bed, tossing my good arm over my eyes. Even if I weren't being watched like a hawk, it would be hard to keep up with names appearing at this rate. Keepers are encouraged to deal with them as quickly as possible, to keep the list from getting long and to keep the Histories from slipping into madness, since they're harder to handle once they have. But they're not expected to spend every waking moment standing near a Narrows door, waiting for the call. Then again, their jobs and their lives don't hang in the balance. Someone else may be able to let the names sit. I can't. Not with Agatha looking for any signs of weakness.

I sit up, considering the open window. Can Wes really get in? And if so, can I get out?

Eventually Mom and Dad go to bed with their door open, but I'm allowed to close mine, probably because they figure the only way I can get out is through the window, and nobody would be crazy enough to try that. Nobody except Wesley, apparently, who appears around midnight sitting like a specter in the window frame.

I look up from the bed as he slips into the room, offering a silent and dramatic bow before crossing to me.

"Color me impressed," I whisper under the music on the radio. "Do I want to know how you did that?"

"I said I was a good climber," he whispers. "Never said I had to climb *up*." He points a finger at the ceiling. "4F is vacant."

"Well," I say, getting to my feet, "I'm really glad you made it."

Wesley's eyes light up. "Yeah?"

"Yeah," I say, tugging on my boots.

Wes's brow knits. "Going somewhere?"

"I assume if you got in, you know how to get back out."

"Well, yeah, in theory. But I kind of thought I wouldn't have to test it till morning."

"There's another name on my list."

"So?"

I go to the window and peer out and up, considering the rock walls of the Coronado. Not the easiest ascent, especially with one good arm. "I need to clear it."

"Mac," whispers Wes, joining me by the window. "I'm all for efficiency, but this is bordering on obsessive. It's only one name. Leave it till tomorrow."

"I *can't*," I say, swinging my leg out the window.

He catches my elbow to steady me, the beat of his life sliding through my shirt and under my skin. "Why not?"

I don't want to lie, not to Wes, but I don't want him to worry, either. I'm worried enough for the both of us, and there's nothing he can do right now except show me how to climb out of this room. "Because it's a test." It's not a lie. Agatha *is* testing me.

"What?" Wesley's eyes darken.

"An evaluation," I say. "After everything that's happened, I guess they—Agatha—wants to make sure . . ." My eyes slide down to my sleeve, the bandages peeking out around the wrist.

"Sure of what?" snaps Wes, and I hear something new in his voice. Anger, directed at the Archive. "Jesus, after everything you've been through, everything you're *going* through—"

I swing my leg back into the room and take Wesley by the shoulders, my eyes sliding past him to the door, worried someone will hear the commotion. "Hey," I say, making sure to talk under the sound of the radio. "It's okay. I don't blame them. But I need to keep the list clear. And to do that, I need your help."

"Is this why they locked me out of your territory?"

I nod, and he lets out a low oath before pulling himself together. "What they're doing," he says, shaking his head as if to clear it, "I'm sure it's just protocol." He doesn't sound like he believes it, but I can tell he wants to.

"I'm sure," I say. I wish I could believe it, too.

He steps up to the window, gripping the sill. After a long breath, he says, "Are you sure you can climb?"

"I'll manage," I say stiffly.

"Mac—"

"I'll manage, Wes. Just show me what to do."

He sits on the sill and brings one leg up, resting his shoe on the wood as he takes hold of the open window over his head and then, in one fluid motion, stands, coming to his feet outside. He keeps one hand curled under the window for support as he shimmies to the side and steps off the sill and onto a thin outcrop of rock, vanishing from sight. When I stick my head out, I see him scaling the side of the Coronado, thin bit of stone to thin bit of stone until he reaches an open window roughly ten feet overhead. He hoists himself up into the window and sits there, elbows on his knees, looking down at me.

"Tell me that was more fun than it looks," I say.

"Loads," says Wes as I take a deep breath and climb out onto the frame, following his lead. My arm aches dully as I grip the bottom edge of the window for support, eyeing the surfacing stones that stand between me and 4F. They are not flat and smooth but jagged, worn away by time and weather like the gargoyles on the roof. Each is somewhere between a brick and a cinder block; as I reach for the first one, a pebble crumbles off overhead and skitters down the wall.

I am going to die. I always thought that if something in the Coronado killed me, it would be the elevators, but no. It will be this.

I take a deep breath and step off the windowsill onto the stones. I will myself not to look down; instead I focus on the number of stones between me and safety, counting down. Eight . . . seven . . . six . . . five . . . four . . . three . . .

"This isn't so bad," I say when I'm nearly to Wes.

. . . two . . . one.

And that's when my toes come down on a moss-slick bit and I slip, plunging a foot before a hand wraps vise-tight around my bad wrist. Pain rips up my arm, sudden and bright, and my vision falters, tunneling. Wesley says something, but his voice is far away and then gone altogether. I feel the darkness folding around me, trying to drag me down, but I cling to his hand and the heavy drum of his noise. I focus on that, not the strange distance or the sense of time skipping like a stone. I focus on the music until I can see the wall in front of me, until I can hear Wesley's words, begging for my other hand.

And just like that, time snaps back into motion, and I grab hold of his arm with both hands, and he hauls me up and through the window. We both hit the floor in the empty apartment and lie there a moment, gasping with relief.

"See?" pants Wes, rolling onto his back on the hardwood floor. "That was fun."

"We really need to discuss your idea of fun." I drag myself into a sitting position, wincing, then get to my feet and look around at the apartment, or at least try. It's pitch-black, the only light streaming in through the window off the street, but I can tell there's nothing here. It has that hollow, echoing feel that comes with empty space, and the only break in the dust on the floor is clearly from Wesley earlier tonight. He brushes himself off and leads me through the bones of 4F.

"It's been vacant for nearly a decade," he explains. "You will appreciate, though, that according to the walls, the last person who lived here had no fewer than *five* cats."

I shudder. I hate cats, and Wesley knows it. He's the one who found me sitting on the floor outside Angelli's place after being assaulted by her feline horde.

"So who are we looking for?" asks Wes, heading for the front door.

"Henry Mills. Age fourteen."

"Splendid," says Wes, opening the door and showering us in hall light. "Maybe if we're lucky, he'll put up a fight."

Wesley gets his wish.

In the short time Henry's been out, he's slipped enough that when he looks at us he doesn't see *us*, he sees something he's afraid of—in this case, cops—and Wes and I end up chasing him through half the territory before we manage to corner him. It's not the most delicate return—we drag him kicking and screaming through the nearest door—but it gets the job done.

It's nearly three a.m. by the time we get back to 4F and make the terrifying descent into my room—this time without incident. I sink onto the bed, exhausted. Wesley makes his way to the nearby chair, but I catch his hand, music flaring through me as I draw him to the bed. I let go and scoot back to make room for him. He hovers there a moment, knees against the mattress.

"Beds are for boyfriends," he says.

"And for people who don't like sleeping in chairs," I say. Something like sadness flashes in his eyes before he smiles, sinking onto the comforter beside me. He snaps the bedside light off, and we lie there inches apart in the dark. Wesley offers his hand, and when I take it, he presses my palm to the front of his shirt. His noise pours through me, loud and welcome.

"Good night, Wesley," I whisper.

"Sleep well," he whispers back.

And somehow, I do.

# TWENTY-TWO

"IT'S A HEAVY burden to bear," says Roland, handing the picture back, "but Crew is worth it."

I look down at the picture of Da and his partner, Meg. I can't imagine fitting with someone the way they do, so close they almost touch, even though they're not wearing silver bands. Is that what love is for people like us? Being able to share space? Without our rings, we wear our lives on our sleeves. Our thoughts and wants and fears. Our weaknesses. I can't bear the thought of someone seeing mine.

"How?" I ask. "How can it be worth it?" I run my thumb over Da's face. This isn't the Da I knew. My Da had far more wrinkles and far less ease. My Da has been in the ground six months. "Letting people in, loving them—it's a waste. In the end it just hurts more when you lose them."

Roland leans back against a shelf, a History's dates printed just above his shoulder. He looks out past me, his gray eyes unfocused.

"It's worth it," he says, "to have someone from whom you hide nothing. The weight of secrets and lies starts heavy, and it only gets harder. You build walls to keep the world out. Crew is the small part of the world you let in.

"It's worth it," says Roland again. "One day, when you're surrounded by those walls, you'll see."

• • •

Wesley is gone by the time I wake up.

It's a good thing, because Mom is bustling around my room, closing the window, tidying stacks of paper, gathering up pieces of laundry from the floor. Apparently privacy went out the window with trust. She tells the desk it's time to get up, tells the laundry in her hands that breakfast is ready. We seem to have taken a step back.

The Archive list is tucked under the phone on my bedside table, and when I go to check it, I see there's a text from Wesley.

> I dreamed of thunderstorms. Did you
> dream of concerts?

In truth, I didn't dream of anything, and the feeling of dreamless sleep on my bones is glorious. No nightmares. No Owen. I look down at my arm and wonder how it went that far. I feel so much closer to sane after a few hours of rest.

I'm about to reply when I see a conversation with Lyndsey. One I never had. It's from Saturday night, when Mom spiked my water and Wes first stayed over.

> Earth to Mac!

> Earth to Mac!

> The HOTTEST boy is in this coffee shop.

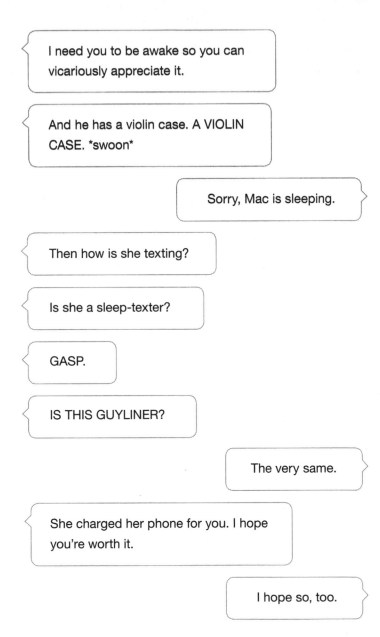

> I need you to be awake so you can vicariously appreciate it.

> And he has a violin case. A VIOLIN CASE. *swoon*

> Sorry, Mac is sleeping.

> Then how is she texting?

> Is she a sleep-texter?

> GASP.

> IS THIS GUYLINER?

> The very same.

> She charged her phone for you. I hope you're worth it.

> I hope so, too.

I almost smile, but then a knot forms in my stomach. *Worth it. Crew is worth it,* echoes Roland.

I put the phone away and begin to get dressed. The cut on my hand is healing well. My forearm, on the other hand, is killing me after last night's adventures; I'm worried I might have ripped the stitches. I flex gingerly and wince, then check my list. There's already another name on it.

*Penny Ellison. 13.*

"Mackenzie." Mom's standing in the doorway. Her eyes get as close as my cheek. "We're going to be late."

"We?" I ask.

"I'm driving you to school."

"Like hell—"

*"Mackenzie,"* warns Mom. "It's not negotiable. And before you go running to your father, you should know that it was his idea. He doesn't want you using the bicycle with your arm in that condition, and I agree."

I obviously shouldn't have left them alone at the table last night. So much for clearing Penny before heading to Hyde.

I get ready and follow Mom downstairs, and we're through the front doors when Berk shows up on the patio and waves her over, spouting something about an espresso emergency.

My eyes go to Dante, leaning up against the bike rack. "I could—"

"No," says my mom. "Stay here. I'll be *right* back."

I sigh and sink against the patio wall to wait, picking at the tape on my palm. Someone casts a shadow over me, and a moment later, Eric sits down on the low wall a few feet away, resting a Bishop's to-go cup on his knee.

"I didn't know about Roland," I say.

"I didn't tell you," he says simply. I look over. He looks tired, but otherwise unscathed. "Agatha is running out of Crew."

I swallow hard. "How much time do I have?"

"Not enough," he says, sipping his coffee. "Are you innocent, Miss Bishop?" I hesitate, then nod. "Then why would you refuse her?"

"I was afraid I'd fail an assessment."

"But you just said—"

"A mental assessment," I clarify. Silence falls between us. "Do you ever wish you'd gone a different way?" I ask after a minute.

Eric gives me a guarded look. "I'm honored to serve the Archive," he says. "It gives me purpose." And then he softens a little. "There have been times when I've wavered. When I thought maybe I wanted to be normal. But the thing is, what we do, it's in our blood. It's who we are. Normal wouldn't fit us, even if we wanted to wear it." He sighs and gets to his feet. "I'd tell you to stay out of trouble," he says, "but it just seems to find you, Miss Bishop."

Mom reappears with two to-go cups, and there's this split second as she hands me one when she finally looks me in the eye. Then she sees the man standing beside me.

"Good morning, Eric!" she says brightly. "How's that dark roast?"

He gives her his best smile. "Worth crossing the city for, ma'am," he says before heading off down the sidewalk.

"Eric's become a bit of a regular," explains Mom as we walk to her car.

"Yeah," I say drily. "I've seen him around."

·  ·  ·

Mom has the decency to drop me off a block and a half from school and out of the line of sight of the parking lot. As the car pulls away, I look down at my arm, hoping I can get through one day without an incident. Maybe Eric's right. Maybe normal doesn't suit us, but I'd be willing to pretend.

I catch sight of Cash, resting against the bike rack with coffee and a smile. Cash, who always makes me *feel* normal. But the moment I reach him, I can see something's off.

His dark hair trails across his cheekbones, but it can't entirely hide the cut beside his eye or the bruise darkening his jaw.

"Looks like I'm not the only one to get into a scrape," I say. "Soccer? Or did you and Wes go a few rounds on the mat?"

"Nah," he says. But he doesn't seem eager to say any more.

"Well, come on," I say as he hands me a fresh coffee. "I told you my clumsy story. It's only fair you tell me yours."

"I wish I could," he says, furrowing his brow, "but I'm not exactly sure what happened."

I frown, taking a sip. "What do you mean?"

"Well, I was heading back from your place yesterday—I was going to take the bus, but it was a nice day, so I decided to walk. I was almost back to the school, when all of a sudden there's this crashing sound behind me, and before I can turn to see what happened, someone pulls me backward *hard*."

The coffee goes bitter in my mouth.

"It was insane," he says. "One minute I'm minding my own business, and the next I'm laid out on the sidewalk." He brings his fingertips to the cut beside his eye. "I caught myself on a bench on the way down. I couldn't have been out for more than a minute or two, but by the time I got up, there was no one else around."

"What did it sound like?" I ask slowly. "The noise behind you."

243

"It was loud, like a crash, or a tear, or a whoosh. Yeah, a whoosh. And that's not even the strangest part." He curls his fingers around the cup. "You'll think I'm crazy. Hell, *I* think I'm crazy. But I swear there was a guy walking maybe a few strides behind me right before it happened. I thought he might have been the one to grab me, but by the time I got back up he was gone." He straightens and chuckles. "God, I sound like a nut job, don't I?"

"No," I say, gripping the paper cup. "You don't."

A ripping sound, a force hard enough to slam Cash backward, and no visible trace? All the markings of a void. Was the man behind him Crew? Or a fourth victim?

"What did the other guy look like?"

Cash shrugs. "He looked normal."

I frown. It doesn't make sense. If someone was trying to attack Cash, they missed, and I don't see why they'd attack him in the first place—not while I was under lock and key. There would be nothing to tie me to this crime, so why do it?

"Did you see anyone else besides the other guy?" I ask, stepping closer.

He shakes his head, and I grab his arm, his noise singing through me. "Can you remember *anything* about the moments before it happened? Anything at all?"

Cash's gaze goes to the ground. "You."

I pull back a fraction. "What?"

"I wasn't paying attention, because I was thinking about you." My face goes warm as he gives a small, stifled laugh. "Truth be told, I can't *stop* thinking about you."

Then, out of nowhere, Cash takes my face in his hands and kisses me. His lips are warm and soft, and my head fills with jazz and laughter; for an instant, it feels sweet and safe and simple. But my life is none of those things, and I realize as the kiss ends that I don't want to pretend it is, and that there is only one person I want to kiss me like this.

Someone by the gate whistles, another cheers, and I pull away sharply.

"I can't," I say, my face on fire. It feels like everyone in the lot is looking at us.

Cash immediately retreats, trying not to look stung. "It's Wes, isn't it?"

*Yes.* "It's life."

"Way to be broad," he says, slouching back against the bike rack. "It's a lot easier to hate a *person*."

"Then it's me. Look, Cash, you're amazing. You're sweet and clever, and you make me smile. . . ."

"I sound pretty awesome."

"You are," I say, stepping away. "But my life right now is . . . complicated."

Cash nods. "Okay. Understood. And who knows," he says, brightening, "maybe one day it will be simpler."

I manage a thin smile. *Maybe.*

And then someone calls Cash's name, and his face lights up as he turns and shouts back, and it's like nothing happened. I have to wonder if he has masks he wears, too. Maybe we all do.

Wes shows up a few minutes later in his senior black-and-gold, looking like he spent the weekend lounging by a pool instead of scaling Coronado walls and warding off my nightmares. Cash gets dragged into a conversation with a nearby group, and Wes knocks his shoulder against mine and whispers, "No nightmares?"

"No nightmares," I say. And that's something to be thankful

for. That is progress—small, fractional, but it is something. It is me clawing my way back to sanity.

The bell rings, and we all head through the gate. Whatever Fall Fest is, it's starting to take over campus. The bones of it are scattered in the stretches of grass between buildings, massive ribbons in black and green and silver and gold are rolled and waiting, and everyone seems oddly cheerful for a Monday morning.

Every moment without the watch and the warden and the constant reminders that I'm *not* okay makes me feel closer to normal. By ten thirty in Lit Theory, I'm feeling positively mundane. And then Ms. Wellson drags her chalk across the board and the sound is too sharp, like metal on stone.

*Metal on stone,* I think. And as I think it, my body stiffens and stops. The rest of the room doesn't. Wellson keeps talking, but her voice seems suddenly dull and far away. I desperately try to move the pen in my hand, but my hand refuses. My whole body refuses.

"Did you really think," comes a voice from behind me, "that a little sleep could fix the ways you're broken?"

*No.* I close my eyes. *You're not real.*

But a moment later I *feel* Owen's arms wrap around my shoulders, *feel* his hand brush the line he carved into my arm.

"Are you sure about that?" He presses down. Pain flares across my skin, and the air catches in my throat as I jerk to my feet, my body suddenly unfreezing. The entire class turns to look at me.

"Miss Bishop?" asks Ms. Wellson. "Is something wrong?"

I murmur something about feeling unwell, then grab my bag and race into the hall, reaching the bathroom just in time to retch. My shoulders shudder as I forfeit breakfast and two cups of coffee, then slump back against the stall, resting my forehead against my knees.

This shouldn't be happening. I'm supposed to be getting better.

*Did you really think that a little sleep could fix the ways you're broken?*

My eyes start to burn and I squeeze them shut, but a few tears still escape down my cheeks.

"Hangover?" comes a voice from the next stall. Safia. "Morning sickness?" I force my eyes open and drag myself to my feet. She walks out of the stall and over to the sink as she adds, "Eating disorder?"

I rinse my mouth out as she joins me, hopping up onto the counter. "Food poisoning," I lie blandly.

"Less exciting," she says, producing a small container of mints and offering me one. "I'm always telling Cash he shouldn't buy that cheap coffee from the corner store. Honestly, who knows what's in it? I guess it's a nice gesture, though."

"I'm sure he's just doing his job," I mutter, splashing water on my face.

Safia rolls her eyes. She hops down off the counter and turns to go.

"Safia," I say as she reaches the door. "Thanks."

"For what?" she asks, crinkling her nose. "I offered you a mint. That's, like, common decency, not social bonding."

"Well, thanks for being commonly decent, then."

The edge of her mouth quirks, and then she's gone.

The moment the door's shut, I slump back against the brick wall beside the sink and wrap my hands around my ribs to keep them from shaking. Just when I think things can't get worse, I feel the scratch of letters in my pocket. I dig the Archive paper out as a second name—*Rick Linnard. 15.*—writes itself below *Penny Ellison. 13.*

Two names, and it isn't even lunch. Could Agatha be doing this

247

on purpose? Would she go that far to prove a point? I don't know. I don't know what to believe anymore. But it doesn't matter how the names got there; I have to handle them. Besides, clearing this list is the only thing still in my control. My mind spins. The class bell rings in the distance. Wellness. I'll skip. I know where the nearest Narrows door is now. The only problem is my key won't work. It's not my territory. And with Wesley's access to *mine* revoked, even if he lets me in to his, I can't cross the divide.

I find a pencil in my bag and spread the paper out on the sink, tapping the eraser several times against it before finally writing a message.

*Requesting access to adjacent territory: Hyde School.*

I stand at the sink and stare down at the page, waiting and hoping for a response. I count out the time it will take to get to the door, cross Wesley's territory into my own, and find and return Rick and Penny.

And then the answer comes. One small, horrible word: *Denied.*

It's not signed, but I recognize Agatha's script. Frustration wells up in me, and I slam my hand into the nearest thing, which happens to be a metal tissue holder. It goes crashing to the floor.

"Mackenzie?" asks a voice from the door. I turn to find a woman standing there. She looks exactly like she did in the hospital, from the messy ponytail to the slacks, but she's traded a name tag that reads *Psychologist* for one that reads *Hyde School Counselor.*

"Dallas?" I ask, crumpling the Archive paper before she can see it. The question and answer have both bled away, but the names are still there. "What are you doing here?"

"We had a deal, remember?" She bends down to fetch the dented tissue box and sets it back on the edge of the counter. "I figured I'd meet you at the Wellness Center, but I ran into Miss Graham and she pointed me in this direction. Is everything . . . ?" She trails off, and I appreciate not having to answer the question when it's obvious that, no, everything's not. "Do you need a moment?" she asks. I nod, and Dallas vanishes back through the door to wait.

I check my reflection in the mirror. Blue-gray eyes stare back at me—Da's eyes—but their once-even gaze is now unsure, the blue made brighter by the red ringing them. My cracks are showing. I splash water on my face to cool my cheeks and rinse away any trace of tears, then smooth out the Archive paper and refold it properly before slipping it into the pocket of my shirt.

A few minutes later, when I step out into the hall, I at least *look* the part of a normal junior. Dallas is eating an apple and pretending to be interested in a Fall Fest flyer on the wall. Cash is front and center in the photo, wearing cat ears, dipping a senior girl with one hand and holding a sparkler aloft with the other.

"When you had me agree to therapy," I say, tugging my sleeves down over my hands, "I didn't realize it would be with you."

"Is that going to be a problem?" she asks, ditching the apple core in the nearest trash bin. "Because it's me or a middle-aged guy named Bill who's nice enough, but kind of smells."

"I'll stick with you."

"Good choice," she says, leading me through a pair of doors and across the quad. The Fall Fest materials are scattered everywhere, and we have to weave through them just to get to the Wellness Center.

"I just didn't realize you worked here, too," I say as we reach the building and go in. Instead of heading toward the lockers, she leads me down a hall to a row of offices.

"Most nights and weekends I belong to the hospital," she tells me as we reach an office with her name on it and go inside. There's a chair and a couch and a coffee table. "During the week, I'm here. As long as we're meeting, I'll be taking the place of your Wellness class, since this is, in fact, addressing wellness of another sort."

"And how long are we meeting?" I ask.

"I suppose that depends on you." She slumps into the chair and retrieves a notebook from the coffee table. "How are the battle scars?"

"Healing," I say as I sit down.

"And how are *you*?"

How am I? Three—possibly four—people have been dragged into voids because of me, my only theory as to why is crumbling, the assessor of the Archive is determined to find me unfit, and my nightmares are becoming real. But of course I can't tell Dallas any of this.

"Mackenzie?" she prompts.

"I've been better," I say quietly. "I think I might be losing my mind." It is the most honest thing I've said aloud in days.

She frowns a little. "Still having bad dreams?"

"These days, everything feels like a bad dream," I say. "I just want to wake up."

# TWENTY-THREE

**B** Y THE TIME I get to lunch, everyone else's trays are stacked in the Alchemist's outstretched arms and they're sitting in a circle, chatting about Fall Fest. I'm surprised to see Safia on the steps, Amber's elbow locked through hers as if holding her hostage.

"Hey, we missed you in Wellness," says Cash as I climb the steps. "What happened?"

"I had a meeting," I say, sitting down in the gap between Amber and Gavin. I pick at my food, watching bits of rice slide through the tines of my fork. "What did I miss?"

"Let's see," says Gavin, who usually spends most of Wellness stretched out on a weight bench, people-watching. "Amber tried to teach Cash yoga, Wesley boxed, and Saf flirted with a senior running on the track and nearly face-planted."

Safia pitches an empty soda can at his head.

"I'm so sorry I missed that," I say with a small smile. And then, in response to her gold-eyed death glare, I add, "I mean *all* of it. I'm having trouble picturing Cash in any of those poses."

"I'll have you know that I do a mean sun salutation." He proceeds to hop up and demonstrate something that I can only imagine is loosely related to yoga. Everyone laughs and cheers him on, but Wesley finds my eyes across the circle and gives me a questioning look, so I dig my phone out of my bag and text him one word.

*Therapy.*

Cash has taken his seat again after collecting a healthy amount of applause, and the group is back to talking about Fall Fest.

"What is it exactly?" I ask.

"It's just a dance," says Wes.

"*Just* a dance?" says Cash with mock affront.

"It sets the tone for the *entire* year," adds Safia.

"It's the official back-to-school party," explains Gavin. "Tomorrow night. It's always the first of September, and the senior class is in charge of organizing it."

"And it's going to be a blast," says Cash. "There's music, and food, and dancing, and we're going to end the night with fireworks."

"Of course it's Hyde," cuts in Safia, "so the dress code's killer strict. Most people just stay in uniform."

"But there are no rules for hair and makeup," says Gavin. "Some people treat it like a contest to see how strange you can get without breaking dress code."

"Last year Saf and Cash both went with bright blue hair," says Amber. "And Wes embraced his inner goth boy."

"Seriously?" I say. Wesley winks at me, and I laugh. "I can't imagine that."

"Crazy, right?" she says. "Anyway, you can wear wacky jewelry or weird makeup or neon leggings."

"It's kind of awesome to see everyone as a stranger version of themselves," says Gavin.

"You're going, right, Mackenzie?" asks Amber.

I shake my head. "Sorry, don't think so." I'm pretty sure my house arrest doesn't have a school dance loophole.

"Hey," says Gavin, addressing me. "Is everything okay?"

"Why wouldn't it be?" I ask.

"I heard you had to leave class."

Wesley's brow creases with concern. "You okay?"

"Wow," I say, glancing at Safia, "word *does* travel fast around here."

"Don't look at me," she says. "To talk about it I'd have to care, which I don't. But I *did* hear a rumor about you and Cash this morning in front of the—"

"What happened?" cuts in Amber. "In class?"

"Nothing," I say. "I didn't feel well, so I left."

"Cash's crappy coffee," offers Saf.

"Hey," snaps Cash, "I only buy gourmet."

"The corner store doesn't *have* gourmet, and you know it."

Saf and Cash start bickering, but Wes isn't so quick to drop the subject. *Are you all right?* he mouths at me across the circle, giving me a weighted look. I force myself to nod. He looks skeptical, but then Cash turns to him and says, "Have you decided yet if you're taking Elle or Merilee or Amber?"

Wesley, still considering me, says, "I'm not taking any of them."

Safia gasps. "Wesley Ayers, going stag?"

He shrugs, finally turning his attention back to the group. "I didn't want to pick just one and deprive the others of my company." He flashes a crooked smile when he says it, but the line rings hollow.

"No one's taking anyone," announces Amber. "We'll go as a group."

"Screw your group," says Safia. "I've already got a date."

"You've been working hard enough to get one," says Cash.

Saf throws a book at his head. It nearly hits Gavin, and the rest of lunch is a blur of chattering, bickering, and festival prep.

I barely hear a word they say.

As the lunch bell rings, I scribble another plea to the Archive.

Again it's denied.


"When did Safia decide to join the Court?"

Amber and I are walking to Physiology, our shoes echoing against the science hall's marble entryway.

"Ah, the migration," says Amber cheerfully. "A time-honored tradition, really. Saf starts the school year determined to make a name for herself, climb the social ladder, build an entourage of minions—god knows enough of the first and second years are willing—and then she realizes something."

"What's that?"

Amber smiles and lifts her chin. "That the Court is, in fact, infinitely cooler than anyone else she'll find at Hyde. She usually comes around before Fall Fest, and we welcome her back as though she never left. I'm sure she'd rather just ditch the act, but she'll never admit she actually wants to hang out with Cash."

*And I'm sure* Wesley *has nothing to do with it,* I think as Amber squints at me.

"Speaking of Cash—" she starts.

"Any new leads on the Judge Phillip case?" I say, changing the subject as obviously as possible. "Or Bethany?" Amber sighs, but takes the bait and shakes her head. "I haven't seen Dad this stressed in ages. They put a new case on his plate this weekend. Another unsolvable. This one doesn't even have a crime scene or a point of departure. Some guy just went for a morning run and never came back. The brother finally reported him missing."

My stomach twists. Jason.

"How can they possibly expect him to solve that?" I ask.

Amber shrugs. "It's his job, I guess. They act like he's some miracle-worker. Trust me, he's not." Halfway up the stairs, she says, "Hey, can I ask you a question?"

"Sure thing."

I expect her to ask why her father picked me up this weekend, but instead she asks, "How long have you known Wesley?"

"A couple months," I say, rounding up. It certainly feels like longer.

"And how long do you think he's been in love with you?"

I feel the heat creeping into my face. "We're just friends." Amber makes a sound of disbelief. "I mean, we're close," I add. Bonded by secrets and scars. "But we're not . . . I don't . . . I care about Wesley, and he cares about me."

"Look," she says as we reach the classroom, "I just met you, but I've known Wesley for ages. I can tell you that 'he cares' is an understatement." Amber steps out of the way to let someone get to class. "Did you really kiss Cash this morning?"

"He kissed *me*," I clarify, "and it ended right there."

Amber waves a hand. "I don't care about the details. The point is, I don't want you playing games with Wes. He's been through a lot, and I think he's finally in a good place, and—"

"And you don't think I'm good for him."

The words hit like a blow, even though they're mine. Because they're true. I'm not good for him. At least, I haven't been. I want to be. But how can I? I feel like a bomb waiting to go off; I don't want him holding on to me when it does. But he won't let go, and I can't seem to, either.

"I didn't say that," says Amber. "It's just . . . Gavin and Saf and Cash and I, we work really hard to *keep* him in that good place. He may live in a big house on a hill, but *we're* his family. I don't know how much you know about his life before you came into it, but he's been hurt by a fair number of people. He may have put himself back together decently, but he's not all the way there. And it's obvious he cares about you *a lot*; so all I'm saying is, don't hurt him, okay? Because it's obvious you're going through some things, too, and I want you to be really sure before you let him fall any harder for you. Be sure that you're good for him."

She opens the door. "And if you're not, don't let him fall at all."


Mr. Lowell's out, and the sub in Government spends the first half of the period reading everything Lowell's already taught us straight off a handout, then decides that revolution is too heavy for a Monday and mercifully lets us go early. There's a text from Mom saying she's going to be late picking me up—I'm hoping I can use it as leverage when the topic of transport comes up again tomorrow morning—which leaves me with half an hour or so to kill. I send a third request to the Archive, then wander out onto the quad to wait for the reply.

Even though the bell hasn't rung yet, a dozen gold-striped seniors are scattered around the quad assembling tents. I spot Wesley at the northern edge of the green, hammering steel rods into the grass.

Not the Wesley who hunts Histories, or the one who lies in bed with me, drowning my nightmares with his noise, but one who laughs and smiles and looks *happy*. It's not that he doesn't look that way when we're together, but there's an edge to him when I'm around. The strain of scars and shared secrets and worry shows in his face even when he smiles, even when he sleeps. I weigh him down.

A bone-deep sadness spreads through me as I realize something.

Wesley may be worth it, worth loving and worth letting in, but I can't do it. I won't. Not as long as there's a target on my back. I can't drag him into this mess. Amber was right. The last time he got pulled into my fight, he lost a day of his life. I won't let him lose more, not because of me.

I retreat through campus, weaving from one path to another, the urge to move stronger than the desire to go anywhere in particular. *Restless bones*, that's what Ben used to call it. I have never been able to sit still. Maybe Eric's right, and being a part of the Archive isn't just a job. Maybe it's in my bones. Maybe I couldn't be normal, even if I had a chance to try. Normal is like stillness: uncomfortable, unnatural. So I walk. And as I walk, a word scratches itself onto the paper in my palm.

*Denied.*

The answer hits like a dull blow as my feet carry me down the path. I don't even realize I've heading for the Wellness Center until I look up and see the stone mantel. I pass through the lockers and into the massive gym.

With everyone either still in class or setting up for Fall Fest, the gym is a hollow white hull—similar to a Returns room, but vast and walled and full of equipment. It's strange being in here alone, and yet it's peaceful. Like the Archive used to be. The quiet here might not be as reverent, but it's all-encompassing, and it reminds me of a time years ago when I was normal—or closer to it—and running was the nearest thing I had to peace.

When I ran, I lost myself.

I have been afraid of losing myself lately. Afraid of pushing too hard. Afraid of letting my guard down. Of letting go.

Now I step onto the track with a kind of abandon and start to run. At first it's a jog, but then I go faster and faster, until I break into a full sprint, giving it everything I have. I haven't run like this in days, weeks, years.

I run until the world blurs. Until I can't breathe, can't hear, can't think. Until Owen is gone and the voids are gone and Agatha is gone and the Archive is gone and Wesley is gone and there is nothing but the sound of my shoes on the track and my pulse in my ears. I run until all my fears—the fear of losing my mind, my memories, my life—have bled away.

Time begins to slip, and for once, I don't try to catch it.

I run until I feel like myself again.

I run until I find peace.

When my shoes finally slow and stop, I bend over my knees, breathing shallowly. Then I pace slowly in a circle, waiting for my heart to slow, my eyes closed in the middle of the empty gym. I focus on the sound of my pulse.

"Miss Bishop?" calls a gruff voice, and I drag my eyes open to find the gym teacher—the one who oversees the sparring ring, I think his name is Metz—trotting over with a clipboard.

"Sorry," I say. "Am I not supposed to be here?"

Coach Metz waves the clipboard. "Whatever. None of the sports have started yet. Speaking of, you're quite the runner. Have you considered track?" I shake my head. "You should," he says. "You're a natural."

"Not sure I have the time, sir."

"Gotta make time for the important things, Bishop. Tryouts are next week. Can I at least put your name down?"

I hesitate. Where will I be next week? Hunting Histories in the Narrows, or strapped to a chair having my memories carved out? What if next week this is all a bad dream and I'm alive and still me?

"We could use someone like you," he adds.

"Okay," I say. "Sure. Count me in." It's so small, but it's something to cling to. A sliver of normal.

Coach Metz passes me the clipboard, and I write out my name and hand it back. He offers me a gruff nod of approval as he reads my name and makes a few notes in the margin.

"Good, good," he grumbles. "Hyde honor at stake, need the speed . . ." And then he trots away, disappearing through a door at the other end of the gym marked OFFICES.

I sink onto the mats to stretch out. My muscles ache from the sudden burst of activity, but it's a welcome pain. I lie down on the mat, going through my stretches; then I stare up at the ceiling and breathe, wondering: If the Archive came for me, would I run? Will it come to that?

My theory is getting thinner by the day. Everything pointed to a setup until Cash. Was the attack on him a mistake? A message? A punishment? Did they miss on purpose? Or were they trying to interrupt the pattern and weaken the theory? Questions trickle through me, and at the heart of all the *hows* and *whys*, the biggest question is *who*.

*You're getting tangled,* Da would say. *Most problems are simple at their center. You just gotta find the center.*

What's at the center of this problem?

*The key.*

You don't technically have to be Crew to make a void—I wasn't—so long as you have the right kind of *key*. But Crew are the only ones issued those keys, so the person making the voids is either Crew or someone who's been given a Crew key. Roland gave me Da's, so I know it's possible. Would a Librarian really smuggle one out? Give it to a Keeper to bury the trail of guilt? What if Owen had other allies in the Archive besides Carmen? Could one of them be trying to get revenge? Librarians are Histories; can they be read like Histories? Is there some kind of postscript that records the time they've been in the service of the Archive after their lives have been compiled?

Would Agatha ever consider reading *them*? Or would she just pin the crimes on me instead? It wouldn't fix the problem, wouldn't change the fact that someone is doing this, but it would give her an out, a person to blame. And after our latest meeting, I have no doubt she plans to find me guilty of something. Why wouldn't she sink me for this? It would be easy. All she has to do is claim I have Owen's key.

I sit up, inhaling sharply.

*Owen's key.* He had it on him when he went into the void. Agatha accused me of having it and I don't, but he did. Maybe he still *does*.

It's the one option I haven't considered. Haven't wanted to consider. Is it even possible? A void is a door to nowhere, but it's still a *door*. And every door has two sides. What if the voids aren't being opened from *this* side? What if someone isn't throwing people in? What if they're just trying to get *out*?

What if Owen's trying to get to me?

No.

I fall back against the mat and force myself to breathe.

No. I have to stop. I have to stop seeing Owen in everything. I have to stop looking for him in every moment of my life. Owen Chris Clarke is gone. I have to stop bringing him back.

I close my eyes and take a deep breath. And then I feel the scratch of letters on the list and take it out, expecting another name. Instead I find a message:

*Access granted. Good luck. —R*

*Roland.* Something untangles in my chest. A thread of hope. A fighting chance. I get to my feet, and I'm nearly to the locker rooms when I hear the crash.

# TWENTY-FOUR

**I**T CAME FROM somewhere across the gym.

The crash was far enough away to sound low, loud enough for it to echo around me, but it started in the far corner, the same direction Coach Metz went. I sprint across the gym floor and through the door marked OFFICES, only to find myself in a small hallway full of trophy cases. None of them seem disturbed, and besides, the crash was deep, like something heavy falling—not high, like breaking glass. Doorways stud the hall, each with a glass window insert; I make my way down the corridor, glancing in each room to see if anything's off.

Three doors in, I look through the window and slam to a stop.

Beyond the glass is a storage room. Inside, it's too dark to make out much more than the metal shelves, half of which have toppled over. I pull my sleeve down over my hand and test the door. It's unlocked.

I step through, flicking on one of the three wall switches, illuminating the space just enough to better see the shelves. Two of them have fallen forward and caught each other on the way down. Balls and bats and helmets are now scattered across the storage room floor.

I'm so focused on not tripping on any of the equipment that I nearly slip on the blood.

I catch myself midstep and retreat from the fresh, wet slick on the concrete. I look up at the air above the blood, and my eyes *slide off* of a new void. The air catches in my throat as I listen for sounds of life around me, hearing only the thudding of my pulse.

But this scene is different from the others.

There was no blood at Judge Phillip's house. None in Bethany's driveway.

An aluminum baseball bat rests on the ground beside my shoe; I crouch and grab it (careful to keep my sleeve between the metal and my fingers to avoid leaving prints), then stand and turn in a slow circle, scanning the darker corners of the room for movement. I'm alone. It doesn't *feel* like it, but that strange sense of wrong must be coming from the void door, because there's no one here. My eyes flick back to the blood. *Not anymore, at least.*

I notice a clipboard resting facedown a foot away from the blood. When I turn it over with my shoe, I see my name written in my own hand, and my stomach twists. With a concerning clarity I realize this is evidence. I reach down and free the paper, pocketing it with a silent apology to the coach.

I clear the debris from the floor and kneel a foot or so behind the bloodstain, setting the bat to the side as I tug the ring from my finger and place it on the concrete. The void door will have burned through most of the memory, but maybe there's *something*. I press my palm to the cold concrete, and the hum drifts up toward my hand. Then I stop.

Because something in the storage room *moves.*

Right behind me.

I feel the presence a second before I catch the movement in my periphery, first only a shadow, and then the glint of metal. I will myself to stay crouched and still, one hand pressed to the floor as the other drifts toward the bat a few inches from my grasp.

My hand wraps around the bat at the same instant the shadow

263

surges toward me from behind, and I spring up and turn in time to block the knife that slices down through the air, the sound of metal on metal high and grinding.

My gaze goes over the bat and the blade to the figure holding it, taking in the silver-blond hair and the cold blue eyes that have haunted me for weeks. He smiles a little as he drags the knife along the aluminum.

Owen.

"Miss Bishop," he says, sounding breathless. "I've been looking for you."

He slices the knife down the length of the bat toward my hand, forcing me to shift my grip. As soon as I do, his shoe comes up sharply beneath the metal and sends it sailing into the air between us. In the time it takes the bat to fall, his knife vanishes into a holster against his back and he catches my boot with his bare hands as it connects with his chest. He twists my foot hard to the outside, knocking me off balance long enough to pluck the falling bat out of the air and swing it at my free leg. It catches me behind the knee, sending me backward onto the concrete.

I hit the ground and roll over and up onto my feet again as he lunges forward and I lunge back. Or at least I mean to, but I misjudge the distance and the toppled shelves come up against my shoulders an instant before he forces the bat beneath my chin. I get my hands up at the last second, but it's all I can do to keep him from crushing my throat. For the first time I see the blood splashed against his fingers.

"Either you've gotten stronger," he says, "or I'm worse off than I thought."

"You're not real," I gasp.

Owen's pale brow crinkles in confusion. "Why wouldn't I be?" And then his eyes narrow. "You're different," he says. "What's happened to you?" I try to force him off me, to get leverage on the bat, but he pins me in place and presses his forehead against mine. "What have they done?" he asks as the quiet—*his* quiet—spills through my head. Tangible in a way it never was in my dreams. No. No, this isn't real. *He* isn't real.

But he's not like the Owen from my nightmares, either. When he pulls back, he looks . . . *tired*. The strain shows in his eyes and the tightness of his jaw, and this time when I try to fight back, it works.

"Get off of me," I growl, driving my knee into his chest. He staggers backward, rubbing his ribs, and I grab the nearest bat and swing it at his head. But he catches it the instant before it can connect and rips the metal from my grip. It goes clanging across the concrete floor, bouncing through the pool of blood on its way and leaving a streak of red in its path.

"The least you could do is ask me how my trip was," he says coldly, twirling the bat still in his hand.

He's not real. He can't be real. This is only happening because I thought of it. This is a hallucination . . . isn't it? It has to be, because the alternative is worse.

Owen stops spinning the bat and leans on it. "Do you have *any* idea how much energy it takes to tear open a void from the other side?"

"Then how did you get out?"

"Perseverance," he says. "The problem with these things . . ." He nods at the rip in the air and makes a small, exasperated sound. "Is they don't stay open very long. As soon as someone gets dragged in, they snap shut. I couldn't seem to get out first. I couldn't go around them. Finally, I decided I had to go *through* them." His eyes flick toward the blood. I think of Coach Metz's body, floating in the void, torn in two by Owen's knife, and my stomach twists. I curl my fingers around the metal shelf behind me.

"Messy business," he says, running his blood-streaked fingers through his silver hair. "But here I am, and the question is——"

Owen doesn't get a chance to finish. I pull the shelf as hard as I can, twisting out of the way just before it comes crashing down on top of him. But even in his current shape, he's too fast. He darts out of the way, and the metal rings out against the concrete. A second later, the lights go out, plunging the storage room into darkness.

"Feistier than ever." His voice wanders toward me. "And yet . . ."

I take a step back and his arm snakes around my throat from behind. "Different." He pulls me sharply back and up, and I gasp for breath as my shoes lift off the floor.

"I should kill you," he whispers. "I could." I writhe and kick, but his hold doesn't loosen. "You're running out of air." My chest burns, and my vision starts to blur. "It's not such a bad way to go, you know. But the question is, is this how Mackenzie Bishop wants to die?"

I can't get enough air to make the word, but I mouth it, I think it, with every fiber of my being.

*No.*

Just like that, Owen's grip vanishes. I stagger forward and land on my hands and knees on the concrete, gasping, inches away from the streak of Metz's blood.

My silver ring glints on the floor, and I grab the metal band

and shove it on as I stagger to my feet and spin. But Owen's no longer there. The signs of him—the toppled shelves, the blood—are there, but I'm alone. A door in the distance closes, and I storm through it into the brightly lit trophy hall . . . but there's no sign of him. No sign at all. I hurry through the outer door and into the afternoon light. Again, nothing. Only the distant laughter of students setting up Fall Fest. The green is dotted with a huddle of sophomore girls. A freshman boy. A pair of teachers.

But Owen is gone.


I spend ten minutes in the girls' locker room, washing the coach's blood off my skin.

I didn't track any of it out of the storage room, but there are traces on me—my arm, my hand, my throat—from Owen's grip, and I scrub everywhere he touched. When I'm done, I wash my face with cold water over and over and over, as if that will help.

I can't bring myself to go back.

There are no prints, nothing to tie me to the room—the *crime scene,* I realize with a shiver—and the longer it's there, the greater chance of somebody finding it. I can't have them finding me with it.

Mom sends a text that says she's waiting in the lot, and I force my legs to carry me away from the scene and through campus, past students who have no idea that Metz is nothing more than a drying red slick on a concrete floor. Or that it's my fault.

Sako is leaning up against a tree nearby, and her eyes follow me as I pass. She's not just watching anymore. She's *waiting.* Like a hunting dog, kept back until the gun goes off. I know how much she *wants* to hear the bang. A new wave of nausea hits me as I realize that if Owen *is* real, she'll get her chance. Agatha *will* run out of Crew. What am I supposed to tell her when she does? That I know who made the void doors? That the History *I sent* into the abyss clawed his way back into the Outer using the key I helped him assemble? The only reason she pardoned me before was because Owen was gone.

He was supposed to stay gone.

He *is* gone.

He wasn't real.

But the blood—the blood is real, isn't it? I saw it.

Just like I saw *Owen*.

"Is everything okay?" Mom asks as I slump into the passenger seat.

"Long day," I murmur, thankful for once that we're not really on speaking terms. Numbness has crept through my chest and settled there, solidifying. I know distantly that it's a bad thing—Da would have something to say about it, I'm sure—but right now I welcome any small bit of steadiness, even if it's unnatural.

I close my eyes as Mom drives. And then to fill the quiet, she starts to sing to herself, and my blood goes cold. I recognize the tune. There are hundreds of thousands of other songs she could sing, but she doesn't choose any of them. She chooses Owen's. He only ever hummed the melody. She adds the words.

". . . my sunshine, my only sunshine . . ."

My skin starts to crawl.

". . . you make me happy . . . when skies are gray . . ."

"Why are you singing that song?" I ask, trying to keep my voice from shaking. She trails off.

"I heard you humming it," she says.

"When?"

"A few days ago. It's pretty. Used to be popular, a long time ago. My mother used to sing it when she cooked. Where did you hear it?"

My throat goes dry as I look out the window. "I don't remember."

I follow the humming through the halls.

It is just loud enough to hold on to. I wind through the Narrows, and the melody leads me all the way back to my numbered doors and to Owen. He's leaning back against the door with the I chalked into its front, and he's humming to himself. His eyes are closed, but when I step toward him, they drift open, crisp and blue, and consider me.

"Mackenzie."

I cross my arms. "I was beginning to wonder if you were real."

He arches a brow, almost playfully. "What else would I be?"

"A phantom?" I say. "An imaginary friend?"

"Well then," he says, his mouth curling up, "am I all that you imagined?"

The moment we are home—safe within the walls of the apartment—I sit down at the kitchen table, pull my phone from my pocket, and text Wesley.

No sleepover tonight.

A moment later he texts back.

> Is everything okay?

*No,* I want to say. *I think Owen might be back and I can't tell the Archive because it's my fault—he's my fault—and I need your help. But you can't be here because I can't stand the thought of him coming for me and finding you. If he's even real.*

Do I *want* him to be real? Which is worse, Owen in my head, or flesh and blood and free? He *felt* real. But real people don't just *disappear.*

*He's not real,* whispers another voice in my head. *You've just lost it.*

*Cracked little head,* echoes Sako.

*Broken,* whispers Owen.

*Weak,* adds Agatha.

Finally I text Wesley back.

> I'm just tired.

> Can't keep running.

> Or hiding.

> Have to face my bad dreams sooner or later.

The grim truth is, I'm not afraid to fall asleep, because my nightmare is already coming true. I sit at the table waiting for his reply. Finally it comes.

> I'll miss your noise.

The numbness in my chest begins to thaw, and I turn the phone off before I can break down and write back. It takes everything I have to sit through dinner, to muster up some semblance of poise and scrounge together words about school. I only bother because skipping would lead to more worry, but the instant the dishes are clear, I escape to my room. My chest tightens when I see the open window, and I move to slide it shut. I hesitate, my fingers still wrapped around the lip.

There are three names on the list in my pocket. Part of me thinks they are the least of my problems, but the other part clings to this last vestige of duty, or at least control. I consider the climb to the apartment above, and then the drop.

"Mackenzie?" I turn to find my mother in the doorway. She's looking directly at me. "Are you all right?"

"Yeah," I answer automatically.

She continues to look me in the eyes. Her mouth opens and closes like a fish, and I can tell she's still trying to form the words: *I'm sorry.* But when she finally speaks up, all she says is, "Better shut the window. It's supposed to rain."

My attention drifts back to the drop—what was I thinking? I barely made it up that wall last night with Wesley helping me— and I pull the window closed, and say good night. Mom surprises me by pulling the door shut behind her. It's a small step, but it's something.

As soon as she's gone, I collapse onto the bed. Beyond the walls of my room, I can hear my parents talking in low voices as they shuffle through the apartment, and past them, the far-off sounds of the Coronado shutting down, the tenants retreating, the traffic on the street ebbing to a trickle and then to nothing. I realize how quiet it is in this room, without sleep and without Wesley. Some people might find it peaceful. Maybe I would, too, if my head weren't so cluttered.

Still, the quiet is heavy, and eventually it drags me down toward sleep.

And then, just as my eyes are starting to unfocus, the radio on my desk turns on by itself.

My head snaps up as a pop song fills the room. *A glitch,* I tell myself. I get to my feet to turn the radio off when the tuner flicks forward to a rock station, all metal and grind. And then a country song. I stand there in the middle of the room, holding my breath as the radio turns through half a dozen stations—no more than a few lines of each piping through—before landing on an oldies channel. The signal's weak, and I shiver as the wavering melody of a staticky crooner floats toward me.

The volume begins to turn up.

My hand's halfway to the power switch when the window next to the desk begins to *fog.* Not the whole window, but a small cloud in the middle of the glass. My heart hammers in my chest as a series of letters writes itself across the misted surface.

*R I N G*

I glance down at my silver band and then back up as a line draws itself through the word.

RING

I stare at the message, torn between confusion and disbelief before finally tugging off the metal band and setting it on the sill. When I look up again, Owen's there, his reflection hovering right behind mine in the glass. I spin, ready to strike, but he catches my fist and forces me up against the window, resting his knife under my chin.

"Violence isn't *always* the answer," he says calmly.

"Says the one holding a knife to my throat," I hiss.

I can see the outline of the Crew key beneath his black shirt. If I can get it away from him and reach the closet door without him slitting my throat, I can—

He presses down on the blade in warning, and I wince, the knife's sharp edge denting the skin under my jaw. A little harder and it will slice.

"That would be a bad idea," says Owen, reading the thoughts in my skin. "Besides, the key beneath my shirt isn't the one you need." He leaves the knife against my throat and uses his other hand to pull the cord free of his collar, so I can see the too-familiar piece of rusted metal hanging from the end. It's not a Crew key at all. It's Da's key. *Mine.*

"Maybe, if you can be civilized, I'll give it back."

The knife begins to retreat, and the moment it shifts away from my skin, I catch his wrist and wrench hard. The blade tumbles to the hardwood floor, but before I can lunge for it, Owen sends it skittering across the room with his shoe. Then he catches my shoulders and pins me back against the wall beside the window.

"You *really* are a handful," he says.

"Then why haven't you killed me?" I challenge. He pulled back earlier and again just now. The Owen in my nightmares never hesitated.

273

"If you really want me to, I'll oblige, but I was hoping we could talk first. Your father is sitting in your living room, asleep in a chair with a book. I'm going to let go of you," he says, "but if you try anything, I'll slit *his* throat." I stiffen under his touch. "And even if you scream and wake him," adds Owen, "he can't see me, so he won't stand a chance."

Owen's hands retreat from my shoulders, and I will myself not to attack.

"What's going on?" I say. "Why can't he see you?"

Owen looks down at his hands, flexing them. "The void. It seems to have a few side effects. You helped confirm that when you first came into the storage room. I was standing right there, and you didn't even see me until you took off—"

"My ring," I say under my breath. It's a buffer, after all. A set of blinders.

"It comes in handy, I suppose," says Owen. "And all that matters is I'm here."

"But *how* are you here?" I growl. "You said you just tore your way through, but I don't understand. The doors you made, they weren't random. Why did you attack those people?"

Owen rests his shoulder against the wall. He still looks . . . drained. "I didn't mean to hurt them. I was looking for you."

My chest tightens. "What do you mean?"

The song on the radio ends and another picks up, this one slower, sadder.

"It turns out," says Owen, "the vast infinite emptiness you pitched me into isn't really empty. It's more like a shortcut without a destination. Half a door. But you can't have half a door," he says, blue eyes dancing. "You have to give it a place to go. Or a person to go to. Someone you can focus on with all your strength. I chose you."

"But you didn't find *me*, Owen. You found *five innocent people*."

Owen frowns. "Five people who crossed paths with *you*. There's a saying in the Archive: 'Strange things shine brighter.' You notice it when you read the memories in objects. But the same thing happens to the memories up here." He taps his temple. "We stand out in the minds of others more than in our own. Whoever they were, you must have made an impression. Left a mark."

My stomach turns. Behind my eyes I see them:

Judge Phillip on the verge of tears when he smelled the cookies in the oven.

Bethany clutching the silver necklace I returned.

A dazed Jason flirting to get my name and number.

Coach Metz with his gruff *good, good* when I agreed to try out for track.

And Cash? *I wasn't paying attention,* he said, *because I was thinking about you. Truth be told, I can't* stop *thinking about you.*

I wrap my arms around my ribs, feeling sick. He could have been taken, dragged through into the dark. Others *were*.

"Is there any way," I say, "to get them back?"

Owen shakes his head. "The void isn't meant for the living. It's not meant for the dead, either." Even in the dim light, I can see the way it wore on him. He looks strangely fragile. But I know better than to trust appearances.

Four people dead, for thinking about me. For caring. And how many others could have been taken? My parents? Wesley? All because of Owen. All because of *me*.

"What are you doing here?" I say through clenched teeth.

"I told you, I came to talk." Owen turns, considering the rest of the room. "I hate this place," he whispers, the words almost swallowed by the melody still leaking from the radio.

And then I remember this wasn't always my room. It was *hers*; Regina's. Owen's sister lived in here. She died in the hallway just outside. Owen looks down at the floor, where faint bloodstains still linger, worn to shadows by time. "Funny how the memory doesn't fade."

His hands, hanging loose and open at his sides, curl into fists. He should slip. If he were an ordinary History, the sight of this room and the memory of what happened here would be enough. The black of his pupils would waver and spread, engulfing the icy blue of his eyes. And as it did, he would go mad with fear and anger and guilt.

But Owen has never been an ordinary History. A prodigy turned prodigal son of the Archive. A brilliant but cunning member of Crew. A manipulator. A boy willing to jump off a roof just to die whole so he could return to punish the system he blamed.

I watch him step around the mark on the floor the way one would a body. "How long was I gone?" he asks, crouching to fetch his knife from the corner.

"Three weeks, six days, twenty hours," I say, wishing the answer didn't come so easily.

"What happened to Carmen?" he asks, straightening.

"She was reshelved," I say, "after she tried to strangle me on your behalf."

Owen turns back toward me, sliding the knife into the holster at his back. "Did she do anything else?"

"Besides waking up half the branch? No."

A grim smile flickers across his face. "And the Archive just let you walk away?"

I say nothing, and he closes the gap between us. "No," he answers for me. "They didn't. Something is different about you,

Miss Bishop. Something is wrong. They may have let you keep your memories, but they haven't given you back your life."

"At least I'm alive," I challenge.

"But your head is full of splinters," he says, his fingers tangling in my hair, his cheek coming to rest against mine. "Broken pieces and bad dreams and terror and doubt," he whispers in my ear. "So jumbled up you can't even tell real from not. Tell me, did the Archive do that to you?"

"No," I say. "You did."

His hand falls away as he pulls back to look at me. "I opened your eyes," he says with strange sincerity. "I told you the truth. It's not my fault you couldn't handle it."

"You lied to me, used me, and tried to kill me."

"And you threw me into the void," he says matter-of-factly. "The way I see it, we both did what we had to do. I didn't enjoy deceiving you, and I didn't want to kill you—I told you that then—but you were in my way. I'm here to find out if you still are."

"I will always be in your way, Owen."

A pale brow arches. "If only your thoughts were as sure as your words, Miss Bishop. But they don't lie as easily. Do you know what's written all over your mind? Doubt. You used to be so certain about your ideals—the Archive is law, is good, is god, trust in them, trust in Da—but your ideals are crumbling. The Archive is broken. Da knew—he *had* to know—and he still let them have you. Your head is full of questions, full of fears, and they are so loud I can barely hear the rest of you. And when Agatha hears them, she's going to treat you like rot in her precious Archive. She'll see you as something to be cut out before it spreads. And not even your beloved Roland will be able to stop her." He brings his hands up to the wall on either side of me, caging me in. "You want to know why I'm here? Why I haven't just slit your throat? Because unlike the Archive, I believe in salvaging what can be saved. And you, Mackenzie . . . Well, it would be a crime to let you go to waste. I want you to help me."

"Help you do what?"

The ghost of a smile touches his lips. "Finish what I started."

# TWENTY-FIVE

**I ALMOST LAUGH.** And then I realize that Owen is serious. "Why would I *ever* help you?"

"Other than self-preservation?" says Owen, pushing off the wall. "I can give you what you want." He wanders around the bed to the bedside table. "I can give you back your grandfather." His fingers trail along the edge of a photo before reaching for the blue bear beside the lamp. "And your brother, Ben."

Owen's fingers close around the bear just before I slam him back against the wall. Ben's stuffed animal tumbles from his grasp.

"How dare you?" I hiss, pinning him there. "Do you think I would actually fall for that a second time? You've played this hand, Owen. It's tired. And Ben is gone. I have no desire to drag him out of sleep again. The only thing I want is to see you on a shelf."

Owen doesn't fight back. Instead he levels his infuriatingly calm gaze on me. "That won't solve your problems. Not anymore."

"It's a start."

Owen's hand flies up and wraps around my bad wrist. "So much misdirected anger," he says, tightening his grip. I gasp at the pain, but the room holds steady around me as I pull back—and to my surprise, he lets go. I cradle my wrist, and Owen crosses his arms.

"Fine," he says. "Let your dead rest. I can give you something else."

"What's that?" I snap. "Freedom? Purpose?"

Owen's blue eyes narrow. "A life."

I frown. "What?"

"A *life*, Mackenzie. One where you don't have to hide what you are or what you do. No more secrets you don't want to keep. No more lies you don't want to tell. *One* life."

"You can't give me that."

"You're right. I can't *give* it to you. But I can help you take it."

One life? Does he mean a chance to walk away? To be normal? No more lying to my family, no more holding back from Wes? But there wouldn't *be* a Wes, because Wes belongs to the Archive, Wes *believes* in the Archive. Even if I could walk away, he wouldn't. I would never ask him to, and it doesn't matter because it's not possible. The Archive never lets you go. Not intact, anyway.

"What you're promising doesn't exist."

"Not yet," says Owen. "But by the time I'm done it will."

"You mean once you've torn the Archive down—how did you put it, Owen? Branch by branch and shelf by shelf? You know I won't let you."

"What if I told you I didn't have to? That the Archive would stay, and you would stay with it if you wanted to? Only no more secrets. Would *that* be worth fighting for?"

"You're lying," I whisper. "You're just telling me what I want to hear."

Owen sighs. "I'm telling you the truth. The fact that you want to hear it means you should listen."

But how can I listen? What he's saying is madness. A dream, and a poisonous one at that. I watch as Owen crosses to the radio and switches it off.

"It's late," he says. "Think about what I've said. Sleep on it. If you're still determined to fight me, you can do so in the morning.

And if at that point I'm feeling merciful, I'll kill you whole before the Archive can destroy you bit by bit."

The Owen in my nightmares does not walk away, but this one does. He gets halfway to the bedroom door, then pauses and turns back, tugging Da's key back out from under his collar. He offers it to me, and it hangs between us like a promise. Or a trap.

"As proof," he says, "that I'm real."

Everything in me tenses when the metal hits my palm. The cool weight of Da's key—*my* key—sends a shiver through me. I loop it over my head, the weight settling against my chest. It feels like a small piece of the world has been made right. Then Owen turns, opens the door, and strides silently away.

I follow, watching light spill into the dim living room as he slips out of the apartment and into the yellow hall. Something thuds behind me, and I spin to find Dad asleep in a corner chair, a book now on the floor beside him. Even in sleep, his face is creased with worry; as I kneel to retrieve the book, I wonder what it would be like to tell my parents why I have nightmares. Why I have scars. Where I vanish to. Why I cringe from their touch.

I hate Owen all the more for planting the thought in my head, because it's not possible. A world without these secrets and lies could never exist.

But as I set Dad's book on the table and tug a blanket up over his shoulders, a question whispers in my head.

*What if?*


I don't remember drifting off, but one minute I'm staring at the door and the next my alarm is sounding. I should be relieved that I didn't dream, and there is a small, rebellious flicker of happiness in my chest, but it dies as soon as I remember Owen: my own living nightmare. Except I'm beginning to suspect he's not a dream.

Da's key is still pressed against my skin, and I force myself to take it off and bury it in the top drawer of my bedside table. My ring is still sitting on the windowsill, but I don't dare put it on if it'll blind me to Owen's presence. Instead I find a necklace chain and loop the band through it, sliding the silver piece over my head and tucking it beneath the collar of my uniform shirt.

It's going to be a long day without a buffer.

My list is holding steady at three names, but I can't push my luck, especially now that I know Agatha's search for Crew will come up empty. Mom's in the kitchen swearing about how she can't find her keys while the news plays out on the TV. I watch, expecting the crime scene at Hyde to be the top story, but it's never mentioned, and all I can think is that the storage room hasn't been discovered yet.

Mom, meanwhile, is still searching under papers, through her purse, in the drawers for her keys. She won't find them because they're stashed in the freezer under a bag of peas.

"I don't need you to drive me," I say. "Really. Just let me go myself."

"This isn't up for negotiation," she says, nearly upsetting a cup of coffee as she scours the mess on the kitchen table.

"I know you don't trust me—"

"It's not that," she says. "I just don't want you riding your bike until your arm's healed."

And just like that, I've got her. Hook. Line. Sinker. "You're right. I'll take the bus."

Mom stops searching and straightens. "You hate the bus," she says. "You called it a tiny box filled with germs and dirt."

"Well," I say, shouldering my bag, "life is messy. And there's a stop a block from school." I don't actually know if this is true. Luckily, neither does Mom.

Her phone goes off from somewhere under the papers she's been searching through. "Fine," she says. "Fine, okay, just please be careful."

"Always," I say, ducking out.

I'd never take the bus. Especially not with my ring hanging uselessly around my neck. The lie does save time, though, since I don't have to worry about stashing my bike before cutting into the Narrows.

Two of the three Histories go without a fight, and the third isn't a match for me, even in my current condition. I approach the boundary between Wesley's territory and mine and slide my key into the lock, hoping it turns. It does. The door bleeds into light and shape before it opens.

I'm in such a hurry that I don't think about the fact that this isn't my territory until I round a corner and nearly run straight into Wesley. I stagger back in time to avoid a collision, and he pulls up short in time to avoid dropping a coffee carrier.

"Jesus, Mac," he says, clutching his chest with his free hand.

"Sorry!" I say, holding up mine in surrender.

"What are you doing here?"

"Hunting," I say as we set off toward Hyde's door.

"I kind of got that," says Wes. "I meant, what are you doing in *my* territory?"

"Oh. Roland granted me access so I could clear my list from school."

Wes nods. "I'm glad they finally cut you some slack. Not that scaling walls isn't fun, but this seems a little less dangerous."

"Only because you don't have your stick out."

"*Bō* staff," corrects Wes. "And it's in my bag. But my list is clear, and my hands were full."

"What's with the coffee?" I ask.

He holds up the carrier. "It's for you."

"You do know my parents own a coffee shop," I say.

"That's never stopped you from taking Cash's," he says with a pout. "And I figured after yesterday's incident, you might be looking for a new supplier." It takes me a second to realize that by "incident" he means Cash's coffee making me sick, and not Cash's kiss. If he's heard about the latter, he doesn't let on, and I don't broach the subject, since it's the least of my problems right now.

He offers me a cup and I take it, careful not to let our fingers touch. The last thing I need is for Wesley to see Owen written all over my mind.

"Any word from Agatha?" he asks. "About the voids?"

The coffee turns to lead in my mouth. I try to swallow. "Not yet."

"Don't worry," he says, misreading my concern. "She'll find whoever's doing this." We reach a door with a green check mark. "How did you sleep?" he adds. "I missed your bed."

"It missed you, too," I say as he opens the door. Unlike the doors that no longer exist in the Outer—the ones tucked in cracks and folds—the Hyde School door opens not onto darkness, but onto the campus. The school is visible even from the Narrows side. I look out, scanning the green for signs of Owen's silver-blond hair. I don't see him, but that doesn't mean he's not there—and I can't afford to lead Wesley to him.

"You coming?" asks Wes.

I reach for the list in my skirt pocket as if I can feel letters writing themselves on the page.

"One more," I say with a sigh and a glance back over my shoulder. "You go on ahead."

Wes hesitates, but nods and steps out onto Hyde's grass. I close the door between us and count to ten, twenty, thirty . . . and then I unlock it with my own key and step through, beelining for the Wellness Center. I half expect to see yellow crime scene tape, but the building is quiet. The trophy hall is empty and perfectly still, and I hold my breath as I make my way toward the storage room door, bracing myself for the scene beyond the glass insert. But when I look through, the air catches in my throat. I push the door open and hit all three switches, showering the room with light.

It's untouched. Immaculate. No toppled shelves, no scattered equipment, no blood on the floor. Nothing except the void, the remnants of which still hover in the middle of the room, snagging and repelling my gaze at the same time, the only proof that anything happened here.

"I thought it would be best to clean up."

I spin to see Owen leaning against the wall, his hands in his pockets. "Good morning."

My fingers curl into fists at my sides. I hate that I'm relieved to see him. I've been dreading this moment since last night, and yet the thought of his *not* being here was in a way more frightening. But now that he's here, I need to figure out what to do. I have to dispatch him, and soon, but the questions that have been filling up my head all night are now trying to climb my throat.

Owen slides the knife out of the holster at his back. "Still determined to fight me?" I hesitate, my eyes flicking from the glinting knife to his face and back. This is not the way to beat him. I force my hands to unclench. "Ready to listen, then?" He arches an eyebrow, feigning surprise.

"You claim there's a way to live without lies," I start. "How?"

Owen smiles, returning the knife to its hidden sheath. "Isn't it obvious?" he says. "Your life is only made of secrets and lies because the Archive is. You exist in the shadows because the Archive does." His blue eyes glitter with excitement. "I am going to drag the Archive out of the dust-covered dark and into the light of day. I'm going to give it back to the world it claims to serve."

"How?"

"By opening the doors," he says, spreading his arms. "By letting the Archive out and the world in."

"The world can't even *see* the doors, Owen."

"Only because it's forgotten how. The whole world is wearing blinders. But if we take them off, eyes will adjust. Lives will adjust. They'll have to." I shake my head. "It's time for change, Mackenzie. It's messy, but the era of secrets must end. The world will adapt, and so will the Archive. It must." His brow furrows, darkening his eyes. "Think about what the Archive's secrets have cost us. Histories only slip because they wake into a world they do not know. They succumb to panic. Confusion. Fear. But if the Archive weren't a secret—if everyone knew what came next—they wouldn't be afraid. And if they let go of their fear and began to understand, then if and when they woke, they wouldn't slip. Ben wouldn't have slipped. Regina wouldn't have slipped. No one would slip."

"Histories aren't meant to wake in the first place," I counter. "And what you're suggesting—a mass awakening—is madness for the living and the dead. Crew will hunt you down before you even start."

"Not if they are with me." He takes a step forward. "You think you are the only one who doubts, Mackenzie? The only one who feels trapped? Do you know why the Archive keeps everyone isolated? It's so they feel alone. So that when one of them feels fear or anger or doubt—and they *all* do—they think they are the only ones. They stay quiet, because they know that one life doesn't matter to the Archive.

"Crew are stronger, paired minds, willing to obey or disobey as a group, but not daring enough to do so. Keepers and Crew all know: if one person or pair rises up, the Archive will simply cut them down. It can always extinguish one voice, Mackenzie. But it can't douse them *all*. Fear. Anger. Doubt. They have been piling up like kindling inside the Archive, and the whole place is ready to burn. The Archive is doing everything it can to keep the fire from starting, but all that's needed is someone to strike the match. So believe me when I tell you that the Crew will go with me. And the other Keepers, too. The question is, will you?"

I open my mouth, but I'm cut off by the sound of steps in the trophy hall beyond the door. Owen falls silent beside me as voices take shape.

"I know the official missing person mark is forty-eight hours," someone is saying, "but what with all the disappearances, I thought it best to let you know."

"I'm glad you did," replies a gruff voice I recognize at once. Detective Kinney. I press myself against the wall beside the door as the footsteps draw closer. Owen doesn't try to hide, but doesn't move, either.

"His wife called me this morning," says the first man. "Apparently, he never picked up their son from preschool yesterday, and he never went home last night."

"Does he have a habit of wandering off?"

"No. And then, when he didn't show this morning, I figured I'd better call. I wish I could tell you more."

The footsteps come to a stop on the other side of the door.

"He was last seen here?" asks Kinney, peering in through the glass.

"Coach Kris saw him in his office before the bell rang."

Kinney pulls away from the door. "We'll start there, then," he says.

The footsteps fade along with the voices as the two walk away. I let out a deep breath, resting my hands on my knees.

"This is all your fault," I say. "If you hadn't dragged those people through—"

"Really it's yours," counters Owen, "since you pushed me into the void. But who's counting crimes?"

The bell rings in the distance, and I check to make sure the coast is clear before pushing the door open.

"The detective is," I say, Owen falling into step beside me. I have to remind myself as I step onto the quad that no one else can see him. And even if they could, he'd blend in. His silver-blond hair glitters in the sunlight, and I can almost imagine what he must have looked like as a student here. His simple black attire lacks any gold piping, but otherwise he'd look just like any other senior. I don't know how much of that has to do with the fact that he is— was—Crew and how much is the fact that, even though he seems old, he's not.

Within seconds of entering the tide of students, I realize how hard it will be to keep my ring off. The path is crowded, and I'm instantly buffeted by a chorus of *what color tights should I wear tonight will Geoffrey even notice I'll never pass x to the ninth is what how many*

*references do I need should have added art Coach Metz better not make us do*
*sprints I'm still sore from Mom is going to kill me I'm going to kill Amelia I*
*hate this place Wesley Ayers better dance with me why did I agree to so weird*
*sometimes metatarsal is connected to the I wish I had cookies get it right*
*empty house Dad is being such an ass stressed silver horns or black streaks*
*can I pull off wings* and it's all tangled up in stress and fear and want
and teenage hormones.

I grit my teeth against the crush of people's lives.

"It's time to let the world in," presses Owen beside me. He
brings his hand down on my shoulder, his quiet pressing through
me, and instead of talking—ostensibly to myself—I *think* the next
question.

*And what happens once you've done that?* I challenge. *The living
would, what? Be free to visit the dead?*

"Why not?" says Owen aloud. "They already do—in graveyards."

*Yeah,* I think, *but in graveyards the dead can't wake.*

I roll my shoulder, shaking him off before he can hear my
thoughts spinning.

*People aren't smart when it comes to the dead.* That's what Da said,
and he was right.

How many would claw their way toward their loved ones, rip
them from sleep to keep them close? How long would it take for
the walls to come down as well as the doors and the world to tear
itself apart?

How can he not see that this is madness? Is he truly that blind
to the consequences? Or is he really willing to tear the world apart
just to get his way? Either way, I have to stop him. But how? Even
in his weakened state, the odds aren't in my favor. Owen cannot
die. I can.

I pause on the path and pretend to look through a notebook.

Owen rests his chin on top of my head, hushing everything but his voice. "Penny for your thoughts?"

*If you're so convinced that everyone else will follow you, why do you need me?*

Owen pulls away, and by the time he comes around to face me, his features have grayed into something unreadable. "Before I can call on anyone, there's something I need," he says. "The Archive has it, and I have a plan to take it—but that plans requires two."

My pulse quickens. But it's not fear that makes it race, it's excitement. Because Owen has just handed me the way to beat him. I might not be able to drag him back to the Archive, but I can follow him in. No one else has to get hurt. No one else has to die.

I start walking again, and Owen follows in my wake, a swell of students carrying us into the building on a wave of *was there a test what was I thinking please let this day be over.*

We move in silence through the crowded hall, and come to a stop outside my class.

"What is it we need to steal?" I ask under my breath.

Owen smiles at my use of *we*. He tucks a strand of dark hair behind my ear. I can feel the quiet spreading through me with his fingertips, feel him reading me for lies, but I've learned his tricks, and I'm learning my own. As he reaches through my mind, I focus on a simple truth: *Something has to change.*

"I'm glad I have your attention," he says, his hand falling away. "And I appreciate the collective pronoun. But before our partnership goes any further, I need to know that your heart's in it."

My heart sinks a little. A test. Of course it wouldn't be as easy as saying yes. Owen Chris Clarke doesn't gamble. He only plays games when he thinks he'll win. Am I willing to play? Do I really have a choice?

I hold his gaze as the second bell rings and the hall empties around us.

My voice is barely a whisper, but my words are firm.

"What do you want me to do?"

# TWENTY-SIX

"**GO TO THE ARCHIVE,**" says Owen, "and steal me something."

"What kind of something?" I ask, clenching my fingers around my backpack strap. Pain flickers through my wrist. It helps me focus.

"Something small," says Owen. "Just a show of good faith. If you succeed, I'll tell you what we're really going to take from them. If you fail, there's no point. You'll just be in my way." His eyes go to a clock on the wall. "You have until lunch," he says, turning away. "Good luck."

I stand there, watching him go, until someone clears his throat behind me.

"Avoiding my class, Miss Bishop?"

I turn to find Mr. Lowell holding the door open for me.

"Sorry, sir," I say, and follow him inside. His hand grazes against my shoulder as he guides me through, and I'm hit with *worry strange girl distant trouble at home I see the bruises quiet clutter ink stains* before I continue forward out of his reach and take my seat. Sixteen people in a classroom without the buffer of a ring make the air feel like it's singing. I sit there, wincing faintly every time a student gets too close, Owen's warped ideas playing through my head while Lowell lectures on the warped ideas of others. I'm not paying much attention until something Lowell says echoes Owen.

"Every uprising starts with a spark," says Lowell. "Sometimes that spark is a moment, tipping the scale. And sometimes that spark is a decision. In the case of the latter, there is no doubt that it takes a certain amount of madness to tip that first domino— but it also takes courage, vision, and an all-encompassing belief, even misguided, in their mission. . . ."

Owen sees himself as a revolutionary, exposing the Archive his cause. That single-minded focus acts both as his strength and his weakness. But is it a weakness I can use?

He's so fixated on his goal that he can't see the flaws. It's proof that even someone as cold and calculating as Owen was once human. People—the living and the dead alike—see what they want to see and believe what they want to believe. Owen wants to believe in this mission, and he also wants to believe that I am salvageable.

All I have to do is prove it.

The moment the bell rings I'm on my feet, moving through the halls and their mess of *sum total of silver or gold silver or gold Saturday school for purple laces if he ever hits me again I'll* out the doors and across the quad to the Narrows door set into the side of the shed, where I pull the key out from under my collar and pass through. Wesley's coding system is different from mine, but I soon figure out that he's labeled Returns with a white plus sign and the Archive with a white *X*, and I slot my key, take a breath, and step through into the antechamber.

Patrick is seated behind the desk, turning through the pages of the ledger. He pauses to write a note, then continues leafing through.

"Miss Bishop," he says, my name little more than a grumble. "Here to confess?"

"Not yet," I say. It's still hard for me to believe he's not the one responsible for the voids. I was sure he was out to get me removed. Erased. But he's not—at least, not this time, this way.

"I need to see Roland. Just for a few minutes." Patrick's eyes move up from the ledger to mine. "Please, Patrick. It's important."

He closes the book slowly. "Second hall, third room," he says, adding, "Be quick about it."

I set off through the open doors and into the atrium, but I don't follow Patrick's directions. Instead of cutting down the second hall to the third room, I head down the sixth hall, following it to the very end the way Roland did when he first showed me to his room. I half expect the corridors to change around me, the way they seem to when I trail him through the maze, but the straight line stays straight. I press my ear to the small set of doors at the end, listening for steps, then slip through into the smaller, dimly lit hall that holds the Librarians' quarters.

Halfway down the hall, I find his simple, dark-paneled door. It's unlocked. The room is as cozy as it was before, but the lack of music whispering from the wall—and the lack of Roland sitting in his chair—makes the space seem too vulnerable. I whisper an apology for what I'm about to do.

I cross to the table by the chair and slide open the drawer. The silver pocket watch is gone—surely Roland has it on him—but the old, palm-sized notebook is there. It sings beneath my fingers as I slip it gently into my back pocket, my heart twisting. I scour the rest of the drawer for a scrap of paper and pen, and when I find them, I write a note. I do not say I'm sorry, or that I will bring it back, only jot down two small words.

*Trust me.*

I don't even look at the paper, since lives are messy and it will be easier to hide this small deviation from the theft if it's subtle.

If Owen goes looking, I want it to be a mere whisper in my head instead of an image. Instead I focus on the very real guilt I feel as I fold the note, put it in the drawer, and duck out. My heart thuds in my chest all the way back into the atrium.

*Wood and stone and colored glass, and all throughout, a sense of peace.*

That's how Da described the Archive to me when I was young. As I walk through the stacks now, I grasp the calm that used to come so easily. These days it feels like a memory, one I'm reaching for and can't quite grab. Wood and stone and colored glass. That's all he told me. He didn't mention the fact I could never leave, or that the Librarians were dead, or that Histories weren't the only things to fear.

*Your life is only made of secrets and lies because the Archive is.*

I smother Owen's voice in my head before it can become my own. I cross back through the doors into the antechamber, sensing that something is wrong the moment I move from wood to stone, but it's too late. The massive doors swing shut behind me, and I turn to see Agatha in front of them, her hair the color of blood and her cream colored coat like a splash of paint against the dark wood.

My eyes flick to the desk, where Patrick is sitting. Of course he would call her.

"My list is clear," I say as calmly as possible.

"But I'm out of Crew," says Agatha. Her voice has lost its velvet calm. "And out of patience." She takes a step forward. "You've run me on a chase, Miss Bishop, and I am sick of it. I want you to answer me honestly. How did you make the voids?"

"I didn't make them," I say, fighting to keep my voice steady even as I take a step back toward the door and the sentinels guarding it.

"I don't believe you," she says, tugging off a black glove as she

295

comes toward me. "If you are innocent, then show me." I shake my head. "Why don't you want me in your head? Afraid of what I'll find? The innocent have nothing to hide, Miss Bishop." She pulls off the other glove.

"You don't have permission."

"I don't *care*," she growls, her bare hands tangling in my shirt.

"Agatha," warns Patrick, but she doesn't listen.

"Do you know how small you are?" she hisses. "You are one cog in one wheel in one corner of an infinite machine, and you have the audacity to deny *me*? To defy *me*? Do you know what that's called?"

"Freedom," I challenge.

A cold smile touches the edge of her mouth. "Treason."

I feel the two sentinels move behind me, and before I can turn, their hands clench around my shoulders and wrists. Their movements are fast and efficient, wrenching my arms behind my back, twisting up hard until my knees buckle. My pulse races in my ears and my vision starts to go dark, but before I can fight back against the men or the encroaching tunnel moment, Agatha's hands are there, pressing against my temples.

At first, all I hear is the quiet that comes with her touch.

And then the pain starts.

# TWENTY-SEVEN

T HE PAIN IS like hot nails in my head, but a moment after it starts it's gone, along with Agatha's touch. The sentinels let go of my arms, and I fall forward to my hands and knees on the Archive floor. When I look up, Roland's hand is wrapped around Agatha's wrist, and Patrick is standing at the mouth of the atrium, holding one of the doors open.

"What are you doing?" snaps Roland.

"My job," says Agatha icily.

"Your job is not to torture Keepers in my antechamber."

"I have every reason to believe that—"

"If you truly have every reason, then get permission from the board." There's a challenge in his voice, and Agatha stiffens at it, the smallest shadow of fear flickering across her perfect skin. Appealing to the board of directors means admitting she's not only allowed more traitorous behavior in the Archive, but that she's failed to uncover the source. "You will not touch her again without approval."

Roland lets go of Agatha's wrist, but doesn't take his eyes off her.

"Miss Bishop," he says as I get to my feet, "I think you'd better get back to class."

I nod shakily, and I'm about to turn toward the door when Agatha says, "She has something of yours, Roland." I stiffen, but he doesn't. His face is a perfect blank as Agatha adds, "A notebook."

I can't bring myself to look at him, but I can feel his gray eyes weighing me down. "I know," he lies. "I gave it to her."

Only then do I look up, but his attention has already shifted back to Agatha. I'm halfway through the door when she says to him, "You can't protect her." But whatever he says back is lost as I slip into the dark.

I don't stop moving until I reach Dallas's office. I'm early, and she's not there, but I sink down onto the couch, my heart pounding. I can still feel Agatha's hands against my temples, the pain of the memories being dragged forward toward her fingers. *Too close.* I pull Roland's journal from my pocket. The memories hum against my skin as I cradle it in my palm, but I don't reach for them—I've taken enough from him already. Instead I close my eyes and lean my head back against the couch.

"I'm impressed."

I look up to find Owen sitting in Dallas's low-back chair, twirling his knife absently on the leather arm while he watches me intently.

"I have to admit," he says, "I wasn't sure you'd do it."

"I'm full of surprises," I say drily. He holds out his hand for the journal, and I hesitate before relinquishing it. "It's very important to someone."

"Everything in the Archive is," he says, taking it from me. His hand lingers a moment around mine, and I recognize the touch for what it is: a reading. His quiet slides through my mind while my life slides through his. I can almost see the struggle with Agatha play out in his eyes, the way they widen, then narrow.

"She's angry because I won't grant her access to my mind."

"Good," he says, pulling away. He pages through Roland's notebook, and I'm surprised by how gentle he is with it. "It's strange," he adds under his breath, "the way we hold on to things. My uncle couldn't part with his dog tags. He had them on him always, looped around his neck along with his key, a reminder. He served in both wars, my uncle. He was a hero. And he was Crew. As loyal as they come. When he got back from the second war, I had just turned thirteen, and he began to train me. He was never the kind and gentle type—the Archive and the wars made sure of that—but I believed in him." He closes Roland's journal and runs his thumb over the cover. "I was initiated into the Archive when I was only fourteen— did you know that?" I didn't. "That night," he continues, "after my induction, my uncle went home and shot himself in the head."

The air catches in my throat, but I will myself to say nothing.

"I couldn't understand," he says, almost to himself, "why a man who'd lived through so much would do that. He left a note. *As I am.* That's all he wrote. It wasn't until two years later, when I learned about the Archive's policy to alter those who live long enough to retire, that it made sense. He would rather have died whole than let them take his life apart and cut out everything that mattered just to keep its secrets." His eyes drift up from the journal. There is a light in them, narrow and bright. "But change is coming. Soon there will be no secrets for them to guard. You accused me once of wanting to create chaos, but you're wrong. I am only doing my job. I am protecting the past."

He offers me the journal back, and I take it, relieved.

"It's rather fitting that you chose to take that," he says as I slip it into my bag. "The thing we're going to steal is not so different."

"What is it?" I ask, trying to stifle some of the urgency in my voice.

"The Archive ledger."

I frown. "I don't under——" But I'm cut off as the door clatters open and Dallas comes in, juggling her journal, a cell phone, and a mug of coffee. Her eyes land on me, and for a moment—the smallest second—I think they take in Owen, too. Or at least the space around him. But then she blinks and smiles and drops her stuff on the table.

"Sorry I'm late," she says. Owen rises to his feet and retreats to a corner of the room as she collapses into the abandoned chair. "What do you want to talk about? Who you're taking to Fall Fest? That seems to be all anyone *else* wants to talk about." She fetches up her journal and begins to turn through pages, and I'm surprised to see she's actually taken notes. I've only ever seen her doodle flower patterns in the corners of the page. "Oh, I know," she says, landing on a page. "I want to talk a little about your grandfather."

I stiffen. Da is the last person I want to talk about right now, especially with Owen in the audience. But when I meet his gaze over Dallas's shoulder, there is a new interest—an *intensity*—and I remember something he said last night:

*The Archive is broken. Da knew——he had to know——and he still let them have you.*

I'm just beginning to earn Owen's trust (or at least his interest). If this is going to work, I need to keep it. Maybe I can use Da.

"What about him?" I ask.

Dallas shrugs. "I don't know. But you quote him a lot. I guess I want to know why."

I frown a little, and take a moment to choose my words, hoping they both read the pause as emotion rather than strategy.

"When I was little," I say, looking down at my hands, "I worshipped him. I used to think he knew everything, because he had an answer to every question I could think up. It never occurred to me that he didn't always know. That he would lie or make it up." I consider the place between two knucklebones where my ring should be. "I assumed he knew. And I trusted him to tell the truth. . . ." My voice trails off a little as I glance up. "I'm just now starting to realize how little he told me."

I'm amazed to hear myself say the words. Not because the lies come easily, but because they're not lies at all. Dallas is staring at me in a way that makes me feel exposed.

I tug my sleeves over my hands. "That was probably too much. I should have just said that I loved him. That he was important to me."

Dallas shakes her head. "No, that was good. And the way we feel about people should never be put in past tense, Mackenzie. After all, we continue to feel things about them in the present tense. Did you stop loving your brother when he died?"

I can feel Owen's gaze like a weight, and I have to bring my fingers to the edge of the couch and grip the cushion to steady them. "No."

"So it's not that you *loved* him," she continues. "You *love* him. And it's not that your grandfather *was* important to you. He *is*. In that way, no one's ever really gone, are they?"

Da's voice rings out like a bell in my head.

*What are you afraid of, Kenzie?*

*Losing you.*

*Nothing's lost. Ever.*

"Da didn't believe in Heaven," I find myself saying, "but I think it scared him, the idea of losing all the things—people, knowledge, memories—he'd spent his life collecting. He liked to tell me he believed in someplace. Someplace calm and peaceful, where your life was kept safe, even after it was over."

"And do you believe in that place?" she asks.

I let the question hang in the air a few long seconds before answering. "I wanted to."

Out of the corner of my eye, I see Owen's mouth tug into a smile.

Hook. Line. Sinker.


"Why the ledger?" I ask as soon as we're out.

Everyone else is going to lunch, and I've chosen a path that rings the campus—a large, circuitous route few students use when they can cut across the quad—so that we can talk in private.

"How much do you know about it?" he asks.

"It sits on the desk in the antechamber. It has one page for every member of the branch. It's how the Archive communicates with its Keepers and Crew."

"Exactly," says Owen. "But at the front of it, before the pages for the Keepers and the Crew, there is one page labeled *ALL*. A message written on that page would go out to *everyone* in the book."

"Which is why you need it," I say. "You need to be able to contact everyone at once."

"It is the only connector in a world divided," says Owen. "The Archive can silence one voice, but not if it's written on that page. They cannot stop the message from spreading."

"It's your match," I whisper. "To start the fire."

Owen nods, his eyes bright with hope. "Carmen was supposed to take it, but she obviously failed."

"When do *we* take it?"

"Tonight," he says.

"Why wait?"

Owen gives me a pitying look. "We can't just walk up to the front desk and rip the page out of the book. We need something to distract the Archive. We don't need something long, but we need something bright." He gestures to the quad, where the stalls and booths and decorations are still being erected.

"Fall Fest?" I ask. "But how will something in the Outer distract the Archive?"

"It will," he says. "Trust me." Trust. Something I will never feel for Owen. Warning lights go off inside my head. The more factors, the less I can control.

"You and I, Mackenzie, we are the same." I attacked him once for that very idea, but this time I hold my tongue. "Everyone in the Archive has doubts, but theirs whisper and ours shout. We are the ones who question. We are the bringers of change. Those who run the Archive, who cling to their rules, are terrified of us. And they should be."

Something sparks inside me at the thought of being feared instead of afraid. I smother it.

"And tonight we will . . ." He trails off, eyes fixed on something down the path. Not something, I realize. Some*one*.

Wesley.

He's standing on the path, holding his lunch tray and talking to Amber. I've been clinging to the hope that even if he saw him, Owen might not recognize Wes—the boy he stabbed on the roof of the Coronado had spiked hair and lined eyes and a different manner—but Owen frowns and says, "Didn't I kill him?"

"You tried," I say as, to my horror, Wesley catches sight of me and waves before turning back to Amber.

"I saw him written on your skin, but I didn't realize the marks were so fresh," says Owen, withdrawing his knife from its holster with one hand, gripping my arm with the other. "You've been keeping a secret," he growls, quiet forcing through my head.

*He has nothing to do with our plans,* I think as calmly as possible. But this time, the plural pronoun does nothing to placate Owen.

"He is a tether to the life you're leaving," he says, tightening his grip. "A rope to be cut." He twirls the knife.

*No.* My mind spins with his blade. *He can be salvaged. If your grand scheme is for the Keepers and Crew to rise up against the Archive, you'll need every one of them you can get. And when the call goes out, he'll stand with me. Killing him would be a waste.*

"I'm not convinced of that," says Owen. "And don't pretend to be pragmatic where he's concerned."

"Fine," I say, pulling free of his touch, "if you don't want to listen to logic, then listen to this: this isn't Wesley's fight. I haven't dragged him into it, and neither will you. If you hurt him in any way, you will *never* get my help. *Trust me.*"

Owen's eyes harden. The knife stops spinning, snapping into his grip. For a second his fingers tighten on the handle. Then, to my relief, he puts the weapon away and falls in step behind me.

"Hey, you," says Wesley, waiting for me to reach him before setting off again toward the Court. My eyes go to his hands to make sure he's wearing his ring. He is.

"Why weren't you in Physiology?" asks Amber.

"Doctor's appointment," I lie.

"We were just talking about the cops on campus," says Wesley. "Did you see them?" He's asking another question underneath the words: *Do you know why they're here?*

I shake my head. "No. Amber, do you know what's up?"

"No idea," she says with a groan. "Dad's not giving me *anything.*"

"The elusive Mackenzie Bishop!" calls Cash as we reach the Court. "No lunch?"

"Not hungry," I say. Owen wanders over to the Alchemist and watches the scene unfold, and it's all I can do to keep from looking at him.

"Missed you again in gym," he says. "Another meeting?"

I'm about to go with "doctor's appointment" again, but Saf cuts in.

"Gee, what kind of meeting forces you to miss gym multiple days in a row?"

"Don't be an ass, Saf," shoots her brother. "You were sent to Dallas, like, *seven times* last year."

"It was three, jerk."

Cash turns his attention to me. "Point is, no big deal. We've all been there. Eventually your parents come up with an excuse, or the school does."

"What did they send you for?" I ask, eager to turn the attention on someone else.

"Hyperactivity," he announces proudly.

"Perfectionism," says Saf.

"Stress-induced anxiety," adds Amber.

"Antisocial tendencies," says Gavin.

All eyes go to Wesley. "Depression," he says, twisting a straw absently around his fingers. My heart aches at the thought of Wes suffering. I imagine us in bed, imagine myself pulling him in against me, wrapping my arms around him and warding off his demons. *He's worth it,* I think. *And I will not—cannot—drag him into this mess.*

"And you, Mackenzie?" asks Cash, drawing my attention back. "What have you done to land yourself in Dallas's office?"

My eyes flick toward Owen. "Apparently I have a problem with authority." I say.

"Is that why you can't go to the dance?" asks Gavin. Owen frowns.

"Actually," I say lightly, "I'll be there after all."

Wesley's eyes light up. "Really?" he asks with a smile. It breaks my heart.

"Yeah," I say, forcing myself to echo his happiness. "Really."

I'm relieved as the conversation turns toward the more innocuous topics of whether Saf and Cash will put gold streaks in their hair and what color glasses Gavin will wear. I'm no longer looking at Owen or Wes, but I can't shake the feeling that both pairs of eyes are still studying me. Wesley's pretending to listen to something Amber says, but every time I look up, I notice him glancing my way, and Owen's watching me like a hawk. And then Wesley's attention starts drifting away from me toward the Alchemist, and it occurs to me for the first time that even though he can't *see* Owen, he might be able to *sense* him. Owen seems to be realizing this, too. He stays quiet and still against the statue, his eyes narrowed in Wesley's direction. Wes returns the gaze without seeing. They both frown.

Mercifully, the bell rings.

I practically spring to my feet. But as I turn toward class, I feel Wes come up beside me. He knocks his shoulder against mine, but instead of his usual noise I'm hit with *something's off what's going on did I do something distant pulling back does she know how much I missed her noise couldn't sleep* before I can put space between us. I keep my ringless finger carefully out of his line of sight.

"Are you really coming tonight?" he asks as Owen appears at my other side.

"Wouldn't miss it," whispers Owen.

"Wouldn't miss it," I echo, stomach twisting.

"I can't believe the watch and the warden gave in."

"Yeah, well"—*they haven't yet*—"I can be very persuasive."

A pair of students calls to Wes across the quad. He hesitates. "Go on," I say. "I'll see you tonight?"

"Can't wait," he says with a smile before taking off across the grass.

"What's going to happen tonight, Owen?" I ask when we're alone.

"Why?" he challenges. "Are you having second thoughts?"

"No," I say before doubt can weaken the word. "As long as my friends don't get hurt." Before he can reach out and read the questions in my skin, I turn and walk away, telling myself I will stop this before it goes too far.

But how far am I willing to go? And how can I possibly stop it when I don't know what *it* is?


Owen shadows me all afternoon. I focus on the clock instead of his pacing form, and as soon as the last bell rings, I make my way toward the door in the shed, thinking that maybe, if I can get him to follow me into the Narrows, then—

"This way," he says, changing course when we're halfway there. My heart sinks as I follow him toward a copse of trees, where he stops and draws a key from a hidden pocket in his sleeve. His Crew key. It takes everything I have not to lunge for it. But we are nowhere near a real door, and I now know that sending him into the void isn't a permanent solution. I have to shelve him, and only one key is going to let me do that, so I still myself as he lifts it to a spot in the air and the teeth vanish into nothing.

No, not nothing. A shortcut. Right here, at the edge of Hyde. Another reminder that this was Owen's campus long before it was mine.

He turns the key and offers me his hand, and I do my best to clear my mind before I let him take it and lead me through.

My shoe hits the ground on the other side, and my heart lurches when I look up and see them. Gargoyles. We are standing on the Coronado roof. I suppress a shudder. How many of my nightmares have started like this?

But if Owen sees the strange poetry of our being here again, he doesn't mention it—only looks out over the edge of the roof and down.

"The day I died," he says, "it was Agatha who gave the order. Alteration. I remember running, thinking for a second how strange it was to be on the other side of the chase. And then I got to the roof and knew what I had to do." He looks back at me. "Would you do it?" he asks. "To stay whole?"

I shake my head. "No," I say, turning toward the roof door. "But I wouldn't go down without a fight."

Owen follows me. "Where are we going?"

"There's still one thing standing in our way," I tell him.

His brow furrows. "What?"

"My mother."


Bishop's is busy. A flock of students from the public school take up half the seats and, judging by Mom's frenetic pace, have been ordering a slew of things. Berk is on the patio, and Mom's behind the counter making drinks. Owen follows me in, his steps slowing as he sees the rose pattern on the floor. He stands there, looking down at it as I head up to the counter.

"Hey, Mom," I say, resting my elbows on the marble.

"You're home early," she says, and I'm kind of amazed she knows what time it is, considering how many orders she seems to be juggling.

"Yeah, it turns out the bus is a pretty efficient mode of transportation. Still dirty, but efficient."

"Mm-hmm," she says, clearly distracted.

"Hey, so, there's a party at Hyde tonight, and I was wondering—"

And just like that, her head snaps up from her work. "You're joking, right?"

"I just thought maybe I could —"

She shakes her head. "You know the answer to this—"

"I know," I cut in, keeping my voice low, "and I wasn't even going to bother asking, but Dallas said I should." For how often she drops *her* therapist's name, mine should carry some weight. And sure enough, Mom quiets. "I know it's a long shot," I say, hoping this doesn't sound as rehearsed as it is. "It's just . . . I want to feel normal. I want to feel *okay*, and this—the house arrest, the hovering—I know I've earned it, but it's the constant reminder that I'm not. And I know I'm not. I haven't been okay for a long time, and I know I have a long way to go before I get there, but for one night I just want to pretend I'm already there."

I watch her begin to falter.

"Never mind," I start to say, adding a small waver to my voice. "I understand—"

"Okay," she cuts in. "You can go."

Hook. Line. Sinker. My chest loosens even as my heart sinks.

"Thank you," I say, hoping my relief can pass for excitement. Then I do something that takes us both by surprise: I hug her. My head fills with *tell her tell her you're sorry can't lose her was only trying to I can't lose her too.*

For once, instead of pulling away, I tighten my grip. "But you have to check in," she adds when I finally let go. I nod. "I mean it, Mackenzie. No disappearing. No antics."

"Promise," I say, turning to go.

"A rousing performance," says Owen as we head back upstairs. I don't reply, because I don't trust myself. Just a few more hours. A few more hours and I will return Owen to the Archive.

A few more hours and this will all be over.

"Not again." Owen's voice is a low growl as we reach the third floor, and I look up from the steps through the glass insert to see what he sees. Wesley is leaning back against my door, holding a box. My stomach twists. Why is he making it so hard to keep him safe?

"Send him away," orders Owen.

I shake my head. "I can't. He'll suspect something is wrong. Just give me some time—"

"No," says Owen. "You said you wanted to leave him out of this, so do it."

"I'm not going to tell him anything. I just want . . ." I trail off. Owen's eyes bore into mine, and I would give anything in this moment to be able to read *his* thoughts.

"How many good-byes did you get to say to Carmen?" I ask. "Please. Give me one."

Owen's hand comes to rest on my shoulder, and I can feel him reading me for defiance, but I'm learning how to bury it. I am not a History. I am a human, and my life is messy and loud. I focus on the truths instead of the lies.

Truth: I am scared for Wesley.

Truth: I do not want to hurt him.

Truth: This is not his fight.

Truth: I cannot protect him from the Archive, but I can protect him from me.

Owen's hand slides away. "Fine," he says. And even if he can't feel the relief in my skin, I'm sure he can see it in my face. "I have a few finishing touches to put on tonight. Have your time with him, but don't be late. The party starts at seven. The show's at eight."

I nod and head out into the hall, feeling his eyes on me the whole way there. When Wesley sees me coming, he smiles.

"What's with the box?" I ask.

"You have a Fall Fest to get ready for," he says. "I've come to help." He clicks a button on the box, and it opens to reveal a dazzling array of makeup.

"Does this make you my fairy godmother?" I ask as I let him in, locking the door behind us.

He considers the term. "Well, yes. In this case I guess that's fair. But don't tell Cash. My cred will go through the floor."

"Where did you even get all this?" I ask, scanning the selection of pencils and shadows.

"Stole it from Safia." He sets the box on the kitchen table and starts searching through, then makes an *aha* sound and emerges with a handful of shadows and a silver liner. "Sit," he says, patting the tabletop.

I climb up, leaning forward until my face is inches from his.

His hair is still smoothed down and his eyes unlined, and at this distance, I can see the gold flecks in his hazel eyes. A strange panic fills me. I don't know what's going to happen; the only thing I know is that I want Wes as far away from it as possible.

"Skip it," I whisper as he uncaps the liner.

"Skip what?"

"The dance," I say. "Don't go. Stay home."

"With you?" he asks, smiling crookedly. I shake my head and the smile falters. "I don't understand."

"I just . . ." I start, but what can I say? What can I tell him without putting him in harm's way? "Never mind." I duck out from under his arms, feeling ill. I go into the bathroom and splash water on my face, then grip the counter and breathe.

"You okay?" calls Wes as I rifle through the medicine cabinet above the sink for some aspirin.

"My arm's just sore," I say, scanning the bottles of pills. My fingers curl around a prescription bottle I don't recognize, and as I read the label, I realize what the small blue capsules are. Sleeping pills. Not your average over-the-counter kind; the kind strong enough to knock you out in minutes. They're practically tranquilizers. These must be what Mom dissolved in my water. I hesitate, weighing the bottle, the contents, the possibility. Is this how my mother felt before she slipped them in my drink? My stomach turns, and I set the bottle back. I would do almost anything to keep Wes safe.

But not that. He would never forgive me.

"Here." Wes appears in the doorway with a small vial. "I keep some aspirin in my bag."

I take the tube with shaking hands and rinse down two while Wes assesses himself in the mirror. He pulls a small disk-shaped container from his pocket and opens it, dabbing his finger in the gel. He starts to spike his hair when someone knocks on the door.

"Coming," I call.

"Is it pizza?" asks Wes from the bathroom. "I would kill for some pizza."

"Wouldn't get your hopes up," I say. "Mom probably forgot a key."

I throw the lock, and the door's barely open before a hand tangles in my collar and wrenches me forward into the hall hard enough that the door slams shut behind me. I'm shoved back against the wood as *about time been waiting can't wait has it coming little Keeper* spills in through my head, and I hardly have time to register the noise as Sako's before a key is driven into the door and I fall back and through.

I hit the antechamber floor hard enough to knock the breath out of me and roll to my feet to see Agatha standing there, smiling grimly.

"Seize her," she says, and I feel the sentinels take hold from either side as she comes forward, holding a piece of paper in front of my face.

"Do you know what this is, Miss Bishop?" The page is written in Latin, with the Archive seal—three vertical gold bars—at the top. "It's permission," she tells me, setting the paper on the desk. I try to pull free as she begins to tug off her black gloves one at a time.

"Now," she says, setting them aside, "let's see what you've been hiding."

# TWENTY-EIGHT

**W**HEN OWEN LOCKED me in the Returns room, my life—thrown onto the walls—began to compile, organize, and fold in. The sensation was strange and dull and numbing.

This is the opposite.

It's like being turned inside out, exposed to things I don't want to see, think, feel again. It's all pulled out of the recesses of my mind and dragged violently into the light.

The pain tears through my head as I see *Wesley in my bed my parents together on the couch looking at me like I'm already lost Cash handing me coffee Sako pinning me in the alley carved a line into my skin beating the thug's face into the park path Roland telling me to lie down and Owen stalking me through the gargoyles killing me in class lifting Ben's blue bear sitting in Dallas's chair.*

Da used to say that if you wanted to hide something, you had to leave it sitting out, right there on the surface.

"When you bury it," he said, "that's when people go digging."

I think about that the instant before it starts. I think about it while Agatha's in my mind, the pain knifing through my scalp and down my spine, all the way into my bones. I think about it after—or between—while I'm lying on the cold antechamber floor, trying to remind my body how to breathe.

There is a moment, lying on that floor, when I just want it to be over. When I realize how tired I really am. When I think

Owen's right and this place deserves to burn. But I drag myself back together. It's too early to stop fighting. I have to get out of here. I have to get back to the Outer. I have to get through tonight. Because one way or another, I *will* get through tonight.

I struggle to my hands and knees. The metallic taste of blood fills my mouth, several drops dripping from my nose to the antechamber floor.

"Get her back up," orders Agatha. The sentinels drag me to my feet, and her hand wraps around my jaw. "Why is that traitorous History streaked across your life like paint?"

*Owen.* I tell the closest thing to the truth that I can manage. "Bad dreams."

Her eyes hold mine. "You think I can't tell the difference between nightmares and memories?"

And then I realize something with grim satisfaction: she can't. Because I can't. She may be able to look inside my mind, but she can only see what I see.

"I guess not," I say.

"You think you can hide things from me," she growls, her fingers running through my hair. "But I'm going to find the truth, even if I have to tear your mind apart to do it." Agatha's grip tightens, and I close my eyes, bracing for another wave of pain, when the Archive door swings open behind her.

"I warned you, Roland," she says without looking back, "that the next time you interrupted me I would have you reshelved."

But the man in the doorway is not Roland. I've never seen him before. There is a kind of timeless poise to the warm brown hair that curls against his temples and the closely trimmed goatee that frames his mouth. A gold pin made of three vertical bars gleams on the breast pocket of his simple black suit.

"Unfortunately, my dear," he says, his accent unplaceable, "you cannot play judge, jury, *and* executioner. You must leave some work for the rest of us."

Agatha tenses at the sound of the man's voice, her hands sliding from my head.

"Director Hale," she says. "I didn't know you were coming."

Everything in me goes cold. A director. One of the Archive's leaders. And one of its executioners. Roland appears at the man's shoulder, and his eyes find mine for an instant, darkening with worry, before he follows the other man—Hale—into the antechamber. The director crosses to Agatha's side with calm, measured steps, each eliciting a small snap.

"Seeing as my presence has a noticeable impact on your vehemence," he says, "perhaps it's best to behave as though I am *always* in the room." His steady green eyes slide from Agatha to me. "And I'd advise you to take a little more care with our things," he says, still addressing her. The sentinels release me, and I will myself to stay on my feet. "Miss Bishop, I presume."

I nod, even though the small motion sends a wave of pain through my head.

Director Hale turns back to Agatha. "Judgment?"

"Guilty," says Agatha.

"No!" I shout, lunging toward her. The sentinels are there in an instant, holding me back. "I didn't make the voids, and you know it, Agatha."

Hale frowns. "Did she make them or not?"

Agatha holds his gaze a long moment. "She didn't *make* the doors, but—"

"I will remind you," cuts in Hale, "that I only granted you permission so that you could determine if she was behind the void incidents. If she is innocent of that, then pray tell how is she guilty?"

"Her mind is disturbed," says Agatha, "and she's hiding things from me."

"I didn't realize anyone *could* hide things from you, Agatha. Doesn't that defeat your purpose?"

Agatha stiffens, caught between outrage and fear. "She's involved, Hale. Of *that* I have no doubt. At least let me detain her until I solve this case."

He considers, then waves a hand. "Fine."

"*No,*" I say.

"Miss Bishop," warns Hale, "you really are in no place to make demands."

"I can solve the case," I say, the words spilling out.

Hale arches a brow. "You think you can succeed where my assessor has failed?"

I find Agatha's eyes. "I *know* I can."

"You arrogant little—"

Hale holds up his hand. "I'm intrigued. How?"

My chest tightens. "You have to trust me."

Hale smiles grimly. "I do not trust easily."

"I won't let you down," I say.

"Do not let her go," warns Agatha.

Hale arches an eyebrow. "I can always bring her back."

"Give me tonight," I say. "If I fail, I'm yours."

Hale smiles. "You belong to the Archive, Miss Bishop. You're already mine." He nods to the sentinels. "Release her."

Their hands fall away.

"Hale—" starts Agatha, but he turns on her.

"You have *failed me*, my dear. Why shouldn't I give someone else a chance?"

"She has a traitor's heart," says Agatha. "She will betray you."

"And if she does, she will pay for it." His attention shifts to me. "Do you understand?"

I nod, my eyes escaping for a moment to Roland. "I do."

And then, before anyone can change Hale's mind, I turn my back on the director, Roland, Agatha, and the Archive, knowing that it won't be the last time I step *through* this door, but if my plan doesn't work, it will be the last time I walk *out* of it.

Sako is waiting. She slots her key and turns it, holding the door open for me. "I hope you know what you're doing, little Keeper," she hisses as she shoves me through.

I stagger forward into the yellow hall of the Coronado before one knee finally buckles beneath me. Pain continues to roll through my head and, desperate for a moment of true quiet, I tug my ring from the chain around my neck and slide it back on for the first time all day. The world dulls a little as I get up and return to the apartment.

"Where the hell—" starts Wes when I open the door. And then he sees me and pales. "Jesus, what happened?"

"It's okay," I say, holding up a hand before I realize there's blood on it.

Wes hurries into the kitchen to get a wet towel. "Who did this to you?"

"Agatha," I say, taking the cloth and wiping at my face. "But it's okay," I say. "I'm okay."

"Like hell, Mackenzie," he says, taking the towel from my hand and blotting my chin.

"It's *going* to be okay," I correct.

"How can you say that? Did she get what she wants? Is it over?"

I shake my head, even though the motion sends pain through

it. "Not yet," I say with a sinking feeling. "But it will be soon." *One way or another.*

"What are you talking about?"

"Don't worry."

Wes makes an exasperated sound. "You come home covered in your own blood two days after cutting yourself and say something cryptic about it all being over soon and expect me not to worry?"

My eyes go to the clock on the wall. "We need to get ready. I don't want to be late."

"Forget about the damn dance! I want to know what's going on."

"I want you to stay out of it." I close my eyes. "This isn't your fight."

"Do you really believe that?" says Wes, throwing the towel down on the table. "That just because you keep me at arm's length, just because you don't tell me what you're going through, that it somehow stops it from being my fight, too? That somehow you're sparing me anything?"

"Wes—"

"You think I haven't gone myself to every one of those crime scenes and searched for something—*anything*—to explain who's doing this? You think I don't lie awake trying to figure out what's happening and how to help you? I care about you, Mackenzie, and because of that, it's never *not* going to be my fight."

"But I don't want it to be your fight!" I dig my nails into my palms to keep my hands from shaking. "I want it to be mine. I need it to be mine."

"It doesn't work that way," says Wes. "We're part—"

"We're not partners!" I snap. "Not yet, Wes. And we'll never be, not unless I get through this."

"Then let me *help* you."

I press my palms against my eyes. Every bone and muscle in my body wants to tell him, but I can't. I'm willing to bet with my life, but not with Wesley's.

"Mackenzie." I feel his hands wrap around mine, his bass playing through my head as he lowers them, holding them between us. "Please. Tell me what's going on."

I bring my forehead to rest against his. "Do you trust me, Wes?"

"Yes," he says, and the simple certainty in his voice makes my chest hurt.

"Then *trust me*," I plead. "Trust me when I say I have to get through this, and trust me when I say I will, and trust me when I say that I can't tell you more. Please don't make me lie to you."

Wesley's eyes are bright with pain. "What can I do?"

I manage a sad smile. "You can help me put my makeup on. And you can take me to the festival. And you can dance with me."

Wesley takes a deep, shaky breath. "If you get yourself killed," he whispers, "I will never forgive you."

"I don't plan on dying, Wes. Not until I know your first name."

He hands me the towel from the table. "You get the blood off. I'll get the makeup kit."

"Okay. You can open your eyes."

Wes holds up a mirror for me to see his work: dark liner dusted with silver and shadow. The effect is strange and haunting, and it pairs well with his own look. "One last touch," he says, rooting around in his bag. He pulls out a pair of silver horns and nestles them in my hair. I consider my reflection, and a strange thought occurs to me.

When I pulled Ben's drawer open, his History was wearing the red shirt with the *X* over the heart. The one he had on when he died. And if things go wrong tonight and I die, I'll die like this: sixteen and three quarters in a plaid skirt with silver shadow on my face and glittering horns in my hair.

"What do you think?" asks Wes.

"You make a perfect fairy godmother," I say, looking toward the clock on the wall. "We'd better get going."

I head for the Narrows door in the hall, but Wes takes my hand and leads me downstairs instead, through the Coronado's door and out to the curb.

There's a black Porsche parked there. My mouth actually falls open when I see it. At first I think it can't be Wesley's, but it's the only car around, and he heads straight for it.

"I thought you didn't have a car."

"Oh, I don't," he says proudly, producing a key chain. "I stole it."

"From who?"

He presses a button on the key and the lights come on. "Cash."

"Does he know?"

Wes smirks as he holds the door open for me. "Where's the fun in that?" He sees me in and shuts the door, jogging around to the other side of the car and climbing into the driver's seat.

"Are you ready?" he asks. There are so many questions folded into those three words, and only one way to answer.

I swallow and nod. "Let's go."

# TWENTY-NINE

"ARE YOU AFRAID of dying?"

Wesley and I are sprawled out in the garden a week and a half before school starts. He's been reading a book to himself, and I've been staring at the sky. I haven't slept in what feels like days but might be longer, and the question slips through my mind and out my lips before I think to stop it.

Wes looks up from his book.

"No," he says. His voice is soft, his answer sure. "Are you?"

A cloud slices through the sunlight. "I don't know. I'm not afraid of the pain. But I'm afraid of losing my life."

"Nothing's truly lost," he says, reciting Archive mantra.

I sit up. "We are, though, aren't we? When we die? Histories aren't us, Wes. They're replicas, but they're not *us*. You can't prove that we are what wakes up on those shelves. So the thought that nothing's lost doesn't comfort me. It doesn't make me any readier to die."

Wes sets the book aside. "This is kind of a morbid topic," he says. "Even for you."

I sigh and stretch back out on my stone bench. "Our lives are kind of morbid."

Wes goes quiet, and I assume he's gone back to reading, but a minute or two later he says, "I'm not afraid of dying, but I'm terrified of being erased. Seeing what it did to my aunt . . . I'd rather die whole than live in pieces."

I consider him. "If you could leave the Archive without being altered, would you?"

It is a dangerous question, one I shouldn't ask. It whispers of treason. Wes gives me a cautious look, trying to understand why I'm asking.

"It doesn't matter," he says. "It doesn't work that way."

"But if it did? If you could?"

"No." I'm surprised by the certainty in his voice. "Would you?"

I don't answer.

"Mackenzie?" he prompts.


"Mackenzie, we're here."

I blink to find the car sitting in the Hyde School lot. Wes is twisted in his seat, looking at me. "You okay?" he asks. I will myself to nod and offer him a reassuring smile, then climb out of the car. With my back to Wes, I slide the silver ring off and loop it on my necklace chain, wishing I could cling a little longer to the buffer and everything that comes with it. But I can't afford to miss Owen.

"Wesley Ayers!" calls Safia from the edge of the parking lot, "you look ridiculous." All four of them are there waiting for us: Saf and Cash with gold streaks in their rich, dark hair, Amber with blue ribbons and butterfly patterns on her cheeks, Gavin in green, thick-framed glasses that take up half his face.

Wes runs a hand over his black spiked hair. "You say ridiculous, I say dangerous."

Cash arches a brow. "Dangerous as in, you could probably impale a low-flying bird?"

"Love the horns, Mackenzie," says Amber.

"I thought you had a date, Safia," I say.

"Yeah, whatever, I bailed."

"She wanted to be with us," says Amber. "She's just too proud to admit it."

"Is that my car?" asks Cash.

On campus, the buildings are dark, but the light from the festival glows against the low clouds, and the air is filled with the distant thrum of music—nothing but highs and lows from here. We reach the front gate with its wrought iron bars and its sculpted *H*—*abandon all hope, ye who enter here*—and pass through. Then we head down the tree-lined path toward the main building and around it, the noise growing louder and the lights growing brighter as we approach. When we pass into the glowing center of campus, Fall Fest rises up before us.

Silver, black, green, and gold. The colors trail in streamers down the building fronts to every side and across the lawn, forming a colorful canopy. Lanterns hang from the trees, lights line the paths, and the grass below the streamers is filled with students and edged with booths. The music seems to come from everywhere, not the way it does when I touch Wes—not filling my bones—but simple and normal and real and loud and all around. A group of girls in brightly colored wigs is perched on a bench eating and laughing, a huddle of boys is playing booth games, and a ton of students decked out in wild makeup and glittering accessories are dancing. The air is alive with their bodies and voices.

Teachers dot the crowd, chatting with one another—none of them with face paint or fake hair, but all in dark clothes like shadows cast around the festival. Mr. Lowell and Dallas hover in front of a booth; Ms. Hill and Ms. Wellson sit on a bench at the edge of the grass dance floor. And there, leaning against a drink stand, is Eric. I tense when I see him, looking grim as he surveys the crowd. I should have known he would be here, watching. But is he still acting as *Roland's* eyes? On the other side of the lawn, Sako sits perched on the edge of another bench. *She* is definitely here for Agatha. I scan the crowd for any other vigilant eyes and spot a third—a man I've never seen before, one with dark skin and Sako's same cold grace—which means that somewhere there's probably a fourth, his partner, but I don't see her. Everyone else looks like they belong. And really, somehow, so do the Crew.

But there is no sign of Owen. Not yet. Even with the whole school here and everyone decked out with crazy hair and strange eyes, I know I'll spot him at a glance.

*The party starts at seven. The show's at eight.*

What is he planning? A cold shiver of dread travels down my spine. What if the gamble's too great? What if I'm making a horrible mistake?

Amber and Gavin link arms and head for the nearest food stand, and Safia grabs Wesley's sleeve and demands a dance.

"It's tradition," she says. "You always dance with me."

Wesley hesitates, clearly not wanting to leave my side. And if I'm being honest, I don't want him to leave, either. I'm struck by the sudden fear that if he does, I won't have a chance to . . . To what? Say good-bye? I won't say that anyway.

"Go on, you two," says Cash. "Mac and I will get along fine."

Safia pulls Wesley into the throng, and Cash holds out his hand. "May I?"

I accept, and my head fills with his jazz and laughter and all of his thoughts, and as we dance I do my best to let them be like music instead of words and listen only to the melody. Cash is full enough of life and energy that, as we spin and twirl and smile and sing along, I almost forget. Even hearing his voice and his music and his life in my head for one whole song, I almost forget. That is the beauty of Cash. Another me in another life would have fallen for this pretty boy who looks at me and only sees a pretty girl and helps me pretend for one song that anything could be that simple.

But even if I believed in Owen's dream of a life without secrets and lies, Cash is not the boy I'd share it with.

Soon the song trails off and a slower one picks up. A senior girl appears at Cash's shoulder and asks for a dance. Wesley appears at my side at the same time.

"Dance with me," he says. And before I can say anything, he wraps his arm around my waist and fills my head with his sadness and his fear and—threaded through it all—his ever present hope. I rest my ear against his shoulder and listen to his heart, his noise, his life. Every moment of it hurts, but I don't let go or push away.

And then, near the end of the song, I see Owen hovering at the edge of the dance floor. His eyes meet mine. My pulse quickens, and I tighten my grip on Wes, gathering up the strength to pull away. I can do this. Whatever I have to do to put an end to this—to Owen—I will do it. I have to. I let him out. I'll return him. I'll lay him at the Archive's feet and earn my life back with his body.

Owen turns and makes his way to the shadow beside the clock tower. The song ends, but Wesley doesn't let go, and I look up into his dark-rimmed eyes.

"What is it?" he asks.

"You're worth it," I tell him.

His brow crinkles. "What do you mean?"

I smile. "Nothing," I say gently. "I'm going to get a drink. Save me another dance, okay?"

My fingers begin to slide through his. He hesitates and starts to tighten his grip, but Amber grabs his other hand and pulls him toward her. "Where's *my* dance, Ayers?" she asks. Our hands fall apart. The music starts up again and I vanish into the crowd, forcing myself not to look back.

Eric's back is turned and Mr. Bradshaw is trying to strike up a conversation with Sako as I slip away into the dark. Owen is humming (*you are my sunshine, my only sunshine . . .*), and I follow the sound of it into the shadows of the clock tower, where I find him leaning against the brick side, turning his knife over between his fingers.

"Hyde School always knew how to throw a party," he says, eyes lost in the glittering lights.

"Will you tell me now what's going to happen here? When do we steal the page?"

"That's the thing," says Owen, putting away his knife. "*We* don't."

I stiffen. "I don't understand."

"There's a reason this plan requires two people, Mackenzie. One of them distracts the Archive while the other steals the page."

"You want me to create the diversion?"

"No," says Owen, "I want you to *be* the diversion."

"What do you mean?"

"You're already on thin ice with the Archive, right? Well, if they're busy dragging you to your alteration, they're less likely to notice *me*."

"Why would they be doing that?" I ask slowly.

"Because you're not going to give them a choice. You're going to make a scene. The Archive hates scenes. I've already staged it for you." He toes the grass, and even in the dark I can see wires. Fuses.

"I said I didn't want anyone to get hurt."

"You have to play your part, Mackenzie. Besides, they're only fireworks. I told you, something short and bright. Flash and show. Once you've lit the match—a literal one this time—all you have to do is be ready to run. I'll take care of the hard part."

"What hard part?"

"All eyes are on you," he continues. "Waiting for you to mess up or make a move. So that's what you're going to do. And then you're going to run, and Crew will chase you. And when they catch you—and they will—you're going to *fight back*, with everything you have, to the very end."

My mind spins. This isn't how it's supposed to go. We are supposed to go into the Archive together. I am supposed to return him. How am I supposed to do that if I'm being executed?

"You don't want a diversion, Owen. You want a sacrifice."

"Don't be dramatic."

"I am not a martyr," I snap.

"I won't let them erase you."

"Oh, well, if you won't *let* them . . ." I say sarcastically.

"I'll save you," he insists. "Trust me."

I scoff. "You want me to put my life in your hands."

In an instant, Owen has me back against the brick wall. "Your life has been in my hands since the moment I stepped out of that void," he growls.

A sickening realization dawns on me. He's already set the scene. He doesn't need my consent to make me a diversion. But the only way he'll come for me is if he thinks I'm worth saving.

But the ledger is on the desk at the very front of the Archive.

What's to stop him from walking in and taking it and leaving without me?

"I won't," he says, reading the thoughts through my skin. "I will not leave you behind. I still need you. We are the bringers of change, Mackenzie. But I need you to be the voice of it."

His hands fall away. He turns toward the festival, and the lights cast shadows across his pale skin. "Change is coming," he says quietly. "Either the Archive will evolve or it will fall."

And watching him in that unsteady light, it hits me.

It's all a lie. His promise of an Archive without secrets, his dream of a world exposed—Owen doesn't expect the Archive to survive this. He doesn't want it to. He wants the same thing he's always wanted: to tear it down. And he thinks he's found a way to do that—by letting this world do the work.

He doesn't want change.

He wants ruin.

And I will do whatever it takes to keep him from it.

My mind is spinning, but I cannot afford to let him see my panic. I take a short, steadying breath. "You should have told me sooner," I say. "For someone who scorns secrets, you sure keep a lot of them."

He frowns. "I didn't want you to overthink it," he says. "But our fates are bound in this. If you fail, I fail; and if I fail, you fail. We are like partners."

*We are nothing like partners,* I think, but all I say is, "Don't you dare leave me there, Owen."

He smiles. "I won't."

And then he crouches and lifts the end of the fuse from the grass. A lighter appears in his other hand. He looks up at the clock tower beside us. Five minutes till eight p.m.

"Perfect," he says, sliding his thumb over the lighter. A small flame dances there. "Five minutes from the spark." He touches the flame to the fuse and it catches, a hissing sound running down the line. *No turning back now,* I realize with a mixture of terror and energy.

"Find the spotlight." Owen steps out of the shadows and onto the path, but I linger against the building and pull the phone from my pocket. There's a text from Wesley . . .

> Where are you?

. . . and I answer back . . .

> Science hall.

. . . hoping I can at least get him out of the way of whatever's about to happen. And then I swallow and dial home. Mom answers.

"Hi," I say. "Just checking in. As promised."

"Good girl," says Mom. "I hope you have a great time tonight."

I fight to keep the fear out of my voice. "I will."

"Call us when it's over, okay?"

"Okay," I say, and I can tell she's about to hang up, so I say, "Hey, Mom?"

"Yeah?"

"I love you," I say, before ending the call.

Four minutes till eight p.m. The clock tower looms overhead, fully lit. I watch a minute tick past as students dance and laugh beneath the colored canopy. They have no idea what's about to happen.

In all fairness, neither do I.

Three minutes till eight p.m. I tell myself I can do this. Tell myself it isn't madness. Tell myself it will all be over soon. When I run out of things to tell myself, I step out of the shadows, expecting to see Owen, but he's not there, so I head toward the quad. I only make it a few strides before a large hand wraps around my arm and drags me back into the dark and *thought you were clever can't get past me thought I wouldn't see the pattern* ricochets through my head. Before I can try to twist free, a metal cuff closes around my wrist, and I crane my neck to see Detective Kinney behind me.

"Mackenzie Bishop," he says, cuffing my hands behind my back, "you're under arrest."

# THIRTY

"**DON'T CAUSE A SCENE,**" he orders, pulling me away from the festival.

"Sir, you're making a serious mistake." The clock strikes one minute till eight, and I twist around, desperately searching for Owen as Kinney drags me down the path.

"Do you know the last name entered into Coach Metz's computer?" he says. "Yours. And the last number to call Jason Pinter's phone? Yours. The prints on Bethany Thomson's necklace? Yours. The only place you didn't actually leave evidence was Phillip's, but you broke into his house, so I'm willing to bet we can tie you to that, too."

"That's circumstantial," I say. "You can't arrest me for it."

"Watch me," says Kinney, pushing me toward the front gates. His cruiser is waiting, lights flashing, on the other side. But the gates are closed. Not just closed, I realize—locked. And I can smell the gasoline from here.

"What the hell?" he growls.

His grip slackens on my arm, and I wrench free, making it three steps back toward the festival before Kinney's hand comes down hard on my shoulder.

"Not so—"

But he never gets a chance to finish. The clock tower chimes eight, and the fireworks start. Not in the air, but on the *ground*.

Several high whistles, followed by the heavy booms as massive spheres of color, light, sound, and fire explode across campus. The blasts are concentrated in the quad, but one goes off much closer to where we stand, and the force is enough to send Kinney and me to the ground. My ears are ringing as a pair of hands pulls me to my feet.

"Can't leave you alone for a moment, I swear," says Owen, soot dusting his cheeks. Behind him, the Hyde front gate is engulfed in fire.

"Where the hell were you?" I snap, ears still ringing as he strides over to Kinney, who's still getting to his hands and knees, clearly disoriented from the blast.

"Busy," he says, pulling the gun from Kinney's holster. He spins the weapon and brings the butt down hard against the detective's temple. Kinney crumples to the path. Back at the quad, another round of explosions goes off. People are screaming. Owen finds the keys on Kinney's belt, unlocks my cuffs, then drags me back toward the blossoming inferno.

We pass through a wave of smoke and into a world engulfed in fire. The blasts are deafening, and the streamer ceiling of the dance floor burns and breaks, dropping flaming strips onto the students below. Everyone is running, but no one seems to know where to run because the blasts keep going off. It's a blanket of chaos.

Owen storms through it, scanning the smoke-covered ground.

"What are you looking for?" I have to shout now over the noise of the falling festival.

"I left him right—"

Just then a body slams into Owen hard, his gun skittering toward me as they both go down. Another blast goes off behind me as I scoop up the weapon, Owen and his opponent a tangle of limbs on the burning ground until he manages to snake his arm around the man's throat and pull back and up, and I see his face.

Eric. One of his eyes is swelling shut, and a bad gash carves a path against his shirtfront, and when he sees me standing there, he tells me to run. And then he sees the gun in my hand and confusion lights up his blood-streaked face.

"Shoot him," orders Owen.

I stare at him in horror. "He's Crew!"

"Right now he's in our way," growls Owen, as if this is just an unfortunate turn of events. But it's not. This was always his plan.

*I'll take care of the hard part.*

The fireworks were nothing but a smoke screen. They could have been an accident. But killing a member of the Archive . . . there would be no question. No hesitation. The Archive would hunt me down. They'd erase me.

"You have to commit, Mackenzie," orders Owen, struggling to gain leverage over Eric. Another firework goes off, showering us in red light. I lift the gun, mind spinning. I've come so far and risked so much. I can't lose Owen, not now. But I can't do this.

"*Commit.*"

I pull the trigger. But I aim wide.

The blast sounds, sharp even in the chaos, the bullet zinging past them both, and between my shot and Owen realizing I missed, Eric twists free and spins. *Run,* I think, *run.* And I'm about to level the gun on Owen—it might not stop him, but it will slow him down—when he slams his fist into Eric's jaw hard enough to crack bone. Eric crumples, and before he can recover, Owen takes his head in his hands and snaps his neck.

The world slows. The smoke thins and the fire dims, and in the instant just after I hear the crack and before the light goes out of his eyes, I see Eric's life unravel. I see him sitting beside me on the patio wall, telling me to stay out of trouble; questioning Dallas in the hospital; leaning up against the yellow wallpaper, chiding me for trying to slip away; checking my hands in the park for broken bones; standing on the sidewalk, nothing but a golden shadow, a glint of light, and then gone.

I stifle a cry as Eric's body slumps lifeless onto the charred earth. No. This isn't happening. This can't be happening.

"Run, Mackenzie," comes Owen's voice as I stare down at the corpse. My fingers tighten on the gun, but by the time I manage to drag my eyes away from Eric's body and up, Owen's already gone, and I'm alone. I look around and realize that I'm standing at the very center of the chaos. There are sirens in the distance, and people are still running, shadows in the smoke and all I can think is *please let Wes and Cash and the others be among them be safe.*

And then, through the chaos, I see her. Everyone else is running *away.* But she is running *toward* me.

Sako.

And I know from the way she's looking at me that she heard the gunshot, that she can see the weapon in my hand . . . and Eric's body at my feet. The gun tumbles from my grip as two more Crew—the third I saw earlier and a fourth—appear behind her. I don't have a choice. There's only one way out now.

I take a stumbling step backward.

And then I turn and run.

# THIRTY-ONE

**THERE'S ONLY ONE** of me and three of them, and they are all *fast*.

The third drops to a knee beside Eric's body but the other two don't stop. I sprint across the quad, not toward the front gates like everyone else, but deeper into campus, cutting through the doors of the language hall only moments before I hear them crashing through behind me. I don't look back, don't sacrifice a single step of my lead as I sprint through the building, all the way to the opposite exit and back out into the burning night.

*You're going to run . . .*

Smoke billows up from the burning lawn as I cut hard down the path toward the Court. I'm almost there when I realize that one set of footsteps has vanished behind me; an instant later, the third Crew steps into my way. I can't change direction before he swings, catching me across the face with his fist.

*And when they catch you . . .*

I go down hard, tasting blood as the world rings in my ears.

*. . . and they will . . .*

Just as I'm getting to my feet, Sako grabs me from behind and throws me down on the dirt path, kicking me hard in the ribs.

*. . . you're going to* fight back *. . .*

The force sends me sprawling onto my back, and a second later she's kneeling on my chest. Hate and anger and images of Eric's corpse roll through me.

"I'm going to kill you," she growls. I throw a punch with my injured arm, but she catches it and slams my hand back to the ground. "I'm going to take my time and make you beg, you little shit."

"Sako," says the other man. "We have orders."

"Hang the orders," she spits.

I bring my knee up hard, catching her in the stomach, but she doesn't even move, only leans forward and forces her hand over my mouth, digging her nails into my jaw. "How could you? How could you?"

All the pain and anger is written over her and pouring through me as her hand slides from my jaw to my throat. And then, out of nowhere, a metal bar appears under her chin and wrenches her back and up and off me. *No.* She rolls to the side, and Wesley puts himself squarely between Sako and me as we both get to our feet.

"Wes, go! Please!"

The fire burns bright in the quad. A few final explosions thunder through Hyde.

"You shouldn't have done that, little Keeper," Sako hisses.

"Get away from her," growls Wes.

He swings his metal bar, and she catches it the instant before it connects with her face, ripping it from his grasp. "You really shouldn't have. . . ."

"Wesley! Don't—"

The third Crew slams into me from behind, wrapping his arms around my chest, pinning mine at my sides as *try to run I'll chase love the hunt little rabbit* forces its way into my head.

"Gotcha," he says, right before I drive my elbow back into his ribs and drop to a knee sudden and hard, jerking forward and forcing him to lose his grip and tumble over my shoulder. He's catlike, up again in a blink, holding something in his hands that looks like ribbon but glints in the uneven light. Metal wire.

"You should surrender," he says, "before this has to get worse."

"I can't," I say. He smiles like he's happy to hear it. And then he attacks. His hand flies forward, and the length of metal wire expands, like he's casting it out. I dodge, avoiding the thread, ducking out of its way. Out of the corner of my eye, I see Wesley go down hard, blood streaking across his cheek. In that instant I feel the lightest touch as the cord loops around my good wrist.

"Gotcha," he says again, and with a single swift jerk the wire cinches, cutting into my skin. I try to pull free, but when I struggle it only tightens, so I grab hold of the thread and use it to wrench him toward me, even though the wire slices into my fingers. My free hand curls into a fist and catches him in the stomach, a solid enough blow to knock the wind from his lungs and send pain up my arm. I realize my mistake too late; before I can get out of reach, he's got the length of wire twined around my other wrist. He pulls, and my hands are forced together in front of me. He grins triumphantly.

*Fight back . . .*

I intertwine my fingers and bring my locked fists across his jaw as hard as I can, splitting his lip—which manages to wipe the smile from his face, but doesn't help me get loose. He keeps his hand around the metal thread and yanks me forward to him, forcing me off balance before driving his fist into my ribs. I double over, and before I can recover he shoves me backward and swings his leg behind my knees, sending me to the hard earth.

He drags me back to my feet, and I have just enough time to see Wesley stagger to his hands and knees—Sako picking up his metal bar and dragging it along the ground toward him—before the

Crew's fist connects with my ribs again. The wind rushed out of my lungs, and I'm left fighting for breath as he hauls me down the path to the nearest building. I try to call out to Wes, but there's no air, no time. The Crew slams me back against a side door, pulls a dark key from his pocket, and jams it into the lock, and a second later, the path and Wesley and Sako all vanish as I fall into the Archive.

I hit the antechamber floor hard. The moment I try to get to my feet, the sentinels are there, forcing me roughly back to my knees.

Agatha is waiting, the other Librarians in line behind her—and clearly they've been told what happened. Their faces are a spectrum of horror and sadness and confusion and betrayal. Patrick is on one side of Roland, Lisa on the other, and they are both holding him back. My eyes flick from his face to the golden key around his neck and back again, willing him to understand, to trust me even if he can't. Again I try to fight to my feet, and again the sentinels force me down in front of Agatha.

"I warned Hale this would happen," she says, cold triumph in her eyes. "A broken mind and a traitor's heart. Do you have *anything* to say?"

*I'm sorry. Listen. Please. Trust me. This isn't what it looks like.* But I can't say any of those things. I have to sell it. Everything in me wants to scream *NO* as I spit blood onto the dark stone floor and say, "The Archive is broken."

Agatha backhands me hard across the face. Pain blossoms against my brow and blood trickles into my vision. "I'll summon Hale. Take her away."

The sentinels wrench me to my feet.

*Fight back . . .*

I jerk forward hard and manage to twist free. It takes every ounce of will and strength, but I run into Roland's arms, pressing my bound hands flat against his shirtfront. It looks like a plea, but only because no one can see my fingers wrapping around the gold key he wears there. The one that turns lives on and off. The one only Librarians are meant to handle. A numbing pain, pins-and-needles sharp, spreads through my fingers and up my wrist, but I don't let go.

*. . . with everything you have . . .*

"Trust," I whisper, closing my hand over it just before they pull me off him. The snap of his necklace is buried beneath the sounds of the struggle as I'm dragged away. I palm the key, slipping it under the edge of my sleeve just before a crushing blow sends me forward to my hands and knees. Two more sets of hands— sentinels both—take hold.

*. . . to the very end.*

A hood is thrown over my head. Everything goes black. Even then, I try to fight.

"Enough, Miss Bishop," orders Patrick as I'm dragged through the Archive. All I can think as I'm led away is that *it will not be enough, it will not be enough, it will not be enough.*

And then I hear it.

Back in the antechamber.

Wesley's voice.

Shouting my name. Arguing with someone loudly as he storms into the Archive.

Everything in me crumples. This was never supposed to be his fight. As I'm dragged down another corridor, I hear the sound of people chasing after him, hear Patrick give a quiet order, and feel one of the sentinels pull away from my side and turn toward the commotion. Patrick's hands—hands I know well because they've patched me up countless times over the last four and a half years— take his place. He and the second sentinel force me through a pair of doors and into a room so empty our steps echo, my name still bouncing on the walls of the Archive.

Then, abruptly, it stops, and I don't know if it's because they've closed a door or because they've caught Wes, but I tell myself he'll be okay even as I try to twist free. The hands tighten, digging into the gash on my arm hard enough to make me grateful for the gold key's spreading numbness as I'm shoved roughly down into a chair. They slice the metal thread free from my wrists, but before I can get to my feet, they're strapping me down, my waist and legs and wrists cinched to the cold arms of the chair. There's no way out. I twist in the binds, but it's no use, and they know it.

"Good-bye," says Patrick, and then a door opens and closes, and the room is silent.

Totally silent.

And totally dark.

And that's when the fear finally hits. It's been chasing me all night, but now it finally catches up.

Fear that none of this is going to work.

Fear that I misjudged, that Owen isn't going to save me, that I was nothing more than a disposable tool.

Fear that he won't come in time.

Fear that he won't make it past the antechamber.

And under all of it, a far worse fear.

A fear that makes me close my eyes, despite the dark.

The fear that maybe, somehow, *Owen isn't real*. That the

nightmare never gave way to reality, that somehow it's been me—and only me—all along. That I've lost my mind. That I'm about to lose my life.

A prickling pain is spreading through my body from the Archive key pressed against my wrist, and I focus on that as I try to twist my arm against the chair, to work the metal toward my hand.

And then I hear it. The door opens behind me, and the sounds of the Archive—of hurrying feet and muffled shouts, none of them Wesley's—pour in for a moment before cutting off again. There's a short, quiet scuffle followed by a sickening crack. I struggle again with my binds, fighting with the chair until someone reaches out and grips my shoulder and the all-too-familiar quiet seeps through my skin.

"Owen?" I gasp.

"Hold still," he orders, and relief spills over me. I coat myself in it as he pulls off my hood. The room I'm in is a glaring white, nearly as bright but not as seamless as a Returns room and completely bare of shelves—of *anything* except the chair and a sentinel slumped in the corner, his head tilted at a very wrong angle. Eric flashes up behind my eyes, but I force myself to focus as Owen frees one of my wrists and drops to a knee, setting to work on my ankles, leaving me to free my other hand myself. He gets my legs unbound and circles behind the chair to find the buckle for the waist strap. The final strap falls away, and Owen rounds the chair again.

"You put on quite a show," he says, offering me his hand.

My heart races as I take it. "I know," I say as he helps me to my feet. "You were right," I add, fingers curling around the metal in my hand.

His brow furrows. "About what?"

I meet his gaze. "I just had to commit."

My grip tightens around his. Confusion flickers across his face, but before he can pull away, I drive the gleaming key into his chest and turn it. For an instant, he stares at me, blue eyes wide. And then the light goes out of Owen's face, the life out of his body. His knees buckle and I catch him, and the two of us sink together toward the sterile white floor.

I can hear the footsteps rushing down the hall, and a strange sadness spreads through me as I ease Owen's body to the ground. He kept his word. He believed in something, however misguided.

I don't know what I believe in anymore.

The only thing I know for sure is that I'm still alive.

And it's almost over.

Almost.

# THIRTY-TWO

**I CANNOT SEEM** to escape this room.

Cold marble floors. Ledger-lined walls. The long table stretching in the middle.

It is the room I was inducted in. It is the room Wesley and I were summoned to after the History escaped into the Coronado. And now it is the room where the Archive will decide my fate.

When Roland and Agatha and Director Hale found me in the alterations room, kneeling over Owen's body, a sentinel slumped in the corner, I said only one thing.

"I want a trial."

So here I am. The remaining sentinel stands beside me, within easy reach, but mercifully hands-off. Roland, Agatha, and Director Hale sit behind the table, Roland's key on its broken cord in front of them.

I flex my hand, still waiting for the feeling to return to my fingertips after using it. Director Hale offers me a chair, but I'll fall over before I sit down in here again tonight. My gaze find Roland's. A minute ago, he paused on his way in and reached out, pretending to steady me.

"Do you regret it yet?" I asked under my breath. "Voting me through?"

A sad smile ghosted his lips. "No," he said. "You make things infinitely more interesting."

"Thank you," I said in a low voice as he turned away. "For trusting me."

"You didn't leave me much choice. And I want my journal back."

Now Roland sits at the table, gray eyes tense as Hale rises to his feet and approaches me, bringing his hands aloft.

"May I?" he asks.

I nod, bracing myself for the pain I felt when Agatha tore through my mind. But as Hale's hands come down against my temples, I feel nothing but a cool and pressing quiet. I close my eyes as the images begin to flit rapidly through my mind: of Owen and the voids and the festival and the fire and Eric. When Hale's hands slide back to his sides, his expression is unreadable.

"Give me context for what I've seen," he says, taking his seat.

I stand before them and explain what happened. How the voids were made. How Owen finally got through. How I set my trap.

"You should have involved the Archive from the start," he says when I'm done.

"Sir, I was afraid that if I did, I would be arrested for the mere fact that Owen still existed, and then Crew would go after him themselves, and everyone would suffer for it. As it is, Eric did suffer. I considered it my job."

*And I wasn't entirely sure Owen was real.*

"It is *Crew's* job to hunt down Histories in the Outer," clarifies Agatha.

"Owen Chris Clarke was not an ordinary History. And he was my responsibility. I gave him the tools he needed to escape the first time, and my crimes were pardoned on the assumption that he was no longer a threat." I'm surprised by the calm in my voice. "Besides, I was in a unique position to handle him."

"How so?" asks Director Hale.

"He wanted to recruit me."

Hale's brow furrows.

"Owen wanted my help. And I let him believe that I was willing to give it."

"How did you concoct the plan to lure him here?" asks Roland.

"I didn't," I say. "He did." I watch the confusion spread across their faces. "I imagine," I add, "that he thought it would end differently, but the seed of the plan was his. He wanted me to be a diversion—to attract the energy and attention of the Archive while he achieved some ulterior goal."

"What was his goal?" demands Agatha.

I hold her gaze. "He wanted to attack the ledger. He promised that, in exchange for my diversion, he would rescue me before I could be altered."

"And you believed him?" asks Hale, incredulous.

"Why would he save you?" asks Agatha.

"*I* believed Owen would attack the Archive. And *Owen* believed I could be converted to his cause. I encouraged that belief in hopes that by insinuating myself into his plan, I would be able to assure his return to the shelves and end the threat he posed."

"Quite a risk," observes Hale, lacing his fingers. "And if your initial plan failed? If you had not been able to obtain Roland's key, if Owen had never come to save you?"

"I weighed it," I say. "Given Owen's skills, I believed my strategy had the highest odds of success. But I hope you understand that I was playing a part. That in order to give myself the best odds, I had to commit to it."

"I hope *you* understand that a Crew member is dead because of your charade," says Agatha.

Behind my eyes, Eric's body crumples to the grass.

"I do. That moment is scarred into my memory. It is the moment I nearly faltered. And the moment I knew I couldn't. I had started down a road, and I had to finish. I hope you can forgive me for the selfish need to end Owen's life with my own hands."

Hale straightens in his seat. "Continue your account."

I swallow. "When I was brought into the branch, I knew I had to introduce as much chaos as possible, a short burst of disorder to help ensure that Owen reached me so that I could stop him."

"I assume that's also why *Wesley Ayers* made such a scene?" offers Roland with a weighted look.

"Yes," I say, leaping on the thread. "He was acting under my orders. Is he all right?"

"He's the least of your worries," says Agatha.

"He's alive," says Hale.

"He'll be okay," adds Roland, sensing my worry.

"You do have a way of inspiring allegiances, don't you?" says Hale. "That boy running around shouting his head off, Roland here claiming he didn't even feel you take his key—"

"I was caught up in the moment," says Roland.

Hale waves him away. "And Owen Chris Clarke. You gained his trust, too. I marvel at that, the way he must have genuinely believed in your commitment."

"Owen believed in his cause," I say. "His focus was greater than my acting."

"So you never actually considered defecting?" he asks, his question close on the heels of my answer.

I hold his gaze. "Of course not," I say calmly.

Hale considers me, and I consider Hale, and silence descends on the room, interrupted only by the director tapping his fingers on the table. Finally, he speaks.

"Miss Bishop, your dedication and sense of strategy are impressive. Your method, however, is reprehensible. You circumnavigated an entire system to fulfill your own desires for revenge and closure. But the fact is, you achieved your objective. You uncovered the truth behind the voids and suppressed a serious threat to the Archive with minimal—albeit upsetting—losses." He turns to Agatha. "Your sentence is overruled."

Relief and hope begin to roll through me. Until Agatha cuts in.

"You forget," she says to Hale, "that there are *two* charges against Miss Bishop. The first is for treason. Clear her of that if you will, but the second is that she is no longer mentally fit to serve. You cannot deny me that claim."

Hale sighs and slumps back in his seat. "No," he says, "but I can consider a second opinion. From someone whose pride isn't so bruised." He waves a hand at the sentinel, who goes to the door and opens it. A woman strides in, her blond hair pulled back in a messy ponytail, blood streaking her hands and the front of her clothes, soot smudged across her forehead and jaw.

Dallas.

"Sorry I'm late," she says, wiping at the soot. "I had to take care of the body."

My stomach turns. I know she means Eric.

"What is the situation at the school?" asks Roland.

"Chaos, but it's calming." Her attention slides to me. She raises a brow. "You look like you've had quite a night."

"Dallas," says Hale, drawing my therapist's attention back. "You've had several days with Miss Bishop. What is your assessment?"

Agatha's eyes narrow at the use of the word.

"Of Mackenzie?" asks Dallas, scratching her head. "She's fine. I mean, *fine* might be the wrong word. But considering what she's been through"—her eyes flick to Agatha and narrow slightly—"and what she's been *put through*"—they shift warmly back to me—"her resilience is astonishing. She was in control of the situation the entire time. I did not interfere."

Roland's shoulders relax visibly, and I take a deep breath, allowing myself to finally believe that I've succeeded, that it's going to be okay.

"There you have it," says Hale. "I think we're—"

"There is doubt in her," snaps Agatha, pushing up from her chair. "I read it."

*"Enough,"* says Hale, rubbing his eyes. "Doubt is not a crime, Agatha. It is only a tool to test our faith. It can break us, but it can also make us stronger. It is perfectly natural, even necessary, and it troubles me to think that you've lost sight of that." He pushes to his feet. "Give me your key," he says softly.

Her gloved hand goes to the gleaming gold below her throat. He snaps his fingers, and her jaw tightens as she gives the gold thread a swift tug, breaking it, and places the key in his palm. He considers it a moment.

And then he drives the metal into Agatha's chest.

He doesn't turn the key, but stands there, gripping her shoulder with one hand and the gold stem with the other, staring into her eyes while the room holds its breath. His lips move as he whispers something to her, so softly I can barely hear.

"You disappoint me."

And then, as quickly as he struck, he withdraws the key, and Agatha gasps for breath.

"Get out," he says, and she doesn't hesitate, but turns, clutching her front, and hurries from the room, her cream-colored coat rippling behind her.

As the door closes behind her, Director Hale sighs and takes his seat, setting Agatha's key on the table before him. The room is deathly still. Roland's eyes are on the table. Dallas's are on the floor.

But mine are on Hale.

"It may be true that nothing's lost," he says, "but everything must end. *When* is in my hands. I'd caution you to remember that, Miss Bishop." He turns to Dallas. "See that she gets home safely."

"Sir," I say. "Please. What about Wesley?"

He waves a hand at the door. "He's out there somewhere. Go find him."


It's all I can do not to shout Wesley's name as I hurry down the hall and into the atrium, breaking into a run as the antechamber comes into sight—and with it, Wesley. He's cut and bloody, swaying a little but still standing, his hands on his head. Patrick waits on one side of him and Lisa on the other, and the Crew who brought me in waits behind him, and I don't care about any of them.

I run, and he looks up and sees me as I make it through the doors, and his hands fall from his head just in time to wrap around me.

We are both bruised and broken, wincing at the other's touch even as we pull each other closer. My arms are tight around his waist, and his are tight around my shoulders. And when he presses his lips into the curve of my throat, I can feel his tears on my skin.

"You are an idiot," I say, even as I guide his face and mouth to mine. I kiss him, not gently, but desperately. Desperately, because he's worth it—because life is terrifying and short and I don't know what will happen. All I know is that here and now, I am still alive, and I want to be with Wesley Ayers. Here and now I want to feel his arms wrapped around me. I want to feel his lips on mine. I want to feel his life tangling with mine. Here and now is all we have, and I want to make it worth whatever happens next.

I tighten my grip on Wes enough to make him break off his kiss with a gasp.

"I'm sorry," I whisper, my lips hovering over his.

"I'm not," he breathes, pulling me closer and kissing me deeper. I'm still afraid of caring—of breaking, of losing—but now there is something else matching the fear stride for stride: want.

"You said you trusted me," I say.

"You said you were in the science hall. I guess we're even." He pulls me back toward him. "What happened tonight, Mac?" he whispers, lips against my jaw.

"I'll tell you later," I whisper back.

I can feel him smile tiredly against my cheek. "I'll hold you to it." His lips brush mine again, but someone clears her throat, and I force myself to pull away from Wesley's kiss. Dallas is standing there waiting.

"All right, you two," she says. "Plenty of time for that. Right now I have to get you back to school." She's standing by the desk, and for the first time I notice the smoldering wreckage of the ledger.

"What happened?" I ask.

"The only thing Owen Chris Clarke achieved was an act of vandalism," says Lisa, gesturing to the book. "He burned it."

Dallas shakes her head and gestures to the door. The Crew who dragged me is standing there, and I tense when I see him.

"No hard feelings," he says.

"I'm sure," I say, Wesley's hand tangling with mine.

"Just doing my job." But he smiles when he says it. It's not a gentle smile, and I'm reminded of the things that filled his noise—the fun of the hunt.

"I'd tell you not to be such an ass, Zachary," says Dallas, brushing him away from the door, "but it would be a waste of my breath. I don't know how Felicia tolerates you." And with that she turns her key, the door opens onto sirens and darkness, and Wesley and I follow Dallas back onto Hyde's campus.

In the Outer, Wesley's noise pours through my head, a tangle of want and love, relief and shock and fear. I don't know what's singing across *my* skin, but I don't pull away. I trust him with it.

Most of the buildings look all right—though the fire ate away a good deal of the ivy—but the field with its streamers and lanterns and booths is a charred black mess.

"Is everyone okay?"

"A few burns here, a few stitches there, but everyone will live."

My eyes slide from her face to her clothing. The black of her cotton shirt is crusted darker with blood, its stain streaking across her exposed skin. "Everyone except Eric," I say as she leads us around the scorched scene and toward the front gate. "That's why you were late."

She nods grimly. "I tried to get his body into one of the flare-up fires before the emergency vehicles got here. Make it look like an accident."

"And Sako?" I ask.

Dallas rubs her hands together, and blood flakes off to the ground below. "She took off. I sent Zachary's partner, Felicia, to find her."

"I think I broke her nose," says Wesley.

Dallas gives him a once-over. "It looks like she got in a few good hits."

"So you're Crew, too?" I ask as she leads us toward the burned remains of the festival.

"No," says Dallas. "I'm what you might call a field assessor. It's my job to make sure everything and everyone ticks and tocks the way they should."

"And if they don't?" asks Wes.

She shrugs. "If they belong to the Archive, I turn them in. If they belong to the Outer, I fix them myself."

"You make alterations," I say. "Wipe memories."

"When I have to," she says. "It's my job to clean up. I already took care of that cop, Kinney. I'll have to send Crew in to get the evidence, but at least I carved you out of his head. As far as he knows, the explosions are what knocked him out."

So many questions are rolling through my mind, but we reach the front gates, which have been pried open. Everyone's corralled there, and two firemen rush over.

"Where did you three come from?" one demands.

"These two got trapped under one of the booths," says Dallas, her tone shifting effortlessly to one of authority. "I can't believe you didn't find them sooner. Better make sure they're both okay."

And before they can ask who *she* is and what she's doing there, she turns and ducks under the yellow tape that's been strung up across the gate and vanishes into the swell of students and teachers and parents that fill the lot. EMTs pull Wes and me apart to check us out, and I slide my ring back on, amazed by how quickly I've become accustomed to the world without it.

The EMT looks me over. Most of my injuries I can blame on the booth that apparently collapsed on top of us, but the wire marks on my wrists are harder to explain. I'm lucky that there are too many people who need looking after and not enough people to do it; the EMT listens when I tell him I'll be okay and lets me go.

But Wesley is either a less convincing liar or he's in worse shape than I realized, because they insist on taking him to the hospital to be safe. The ambulance goes out of the lot before he can say much more to me than, "Leave the window open."

I've barely ducked under the yellow tape when someone shouts my name, and I look up to see the rest of the Court huddled on the sidewalk, a little singed but otherwise unhurt. There is a stream of *where were you*s and *what happened*s and *are you hurt*s and *is Wesley with you*s and *is he okay*s and *that was crazy*s before they finally settle down enough to let me answer. Even then I only get halfway through before Cash makes a crack about how this will go on his feedback card for sure—and Saf elbows him and says she heard that someone *died* in there, and how can he be making jokes? Amber comments on traumatic experiences being optimal times for levity, and then I hear my name again, and turn to find my parents pushing through the crowd toward me, and I get out half of "I'm okay" before my mother throws her arms around my neck and starts sobbing.

Dad wraps his arms around us both, and I don't need to have my ring off to know their minds, to feel their relief tangled with their desperate need to protect the child they have left and their fear that they can't. I can't protect them, either. Not from losing me—not every time—but tonight I'm here, and so I hold them tighter and tell them it's going to be okay.

And for the first time in a very long time, I believe it.

# AFTER

**I**'**M SITTING ON** the edge of my bed that night in my ruined uniform, the silver horns still snagged in my hair, smelling of smoke and blood and thinking of Owen. I am not afraid of sleeping, though I wish Wesley were here with me. I am not afraid of nightmares, because mine came true and I lived through them.

I get to my feet and begin to peel off my ruined uniform, wincing as my stiff and wounded body protests every movement. I manage to tug my shirt over my head, then shed my skirt, and finally my shoes, unlacing them and tugging them off one at a time. I pull the first one off and set it on the bed beside me. When I pull the second shoe off and turn it over, a square of folded paper falls out onto the floor.

I cringe as I kneel to pick it up, smoothing the page. It's blank but for a single word in the lower right corner, written in careful script: *ALL*. I run my thumb over the word.

I wasn't going to take it.

I crouched there over Owen's body, listening to the sounds of footsteps, counting the seconds, and feeling dazed and numb. I didn't plan to take it, but one second I was just sitting there and the next my hands were patting him down, digging the folded page out of his pocket, slipping it into my shoe. The moment was easy to hide. To bury.

Now, as I stare down at the page, I consider burning it. (Of course Owen didn't just burn the ledger; he burned the *rest* of the ledger to cover the fact that this page was missing.)

The thing is, Owen was so wrong about so many things.

But I don't know if he was wrong about *everything*.

I want to believe in the Archive. I *want* to. So I don't know whether it's doubt or fear, weakness or strength, Da's voice in my head warning me to be ready for anything or Owen's telling me it's time for change, or the fact that I have seen too much tonight, that made me take the paper from Owen's pocket.

I *should* burn it, but I don't. Instead I fold it very carefully—each time pausing to decide if I want to destroy it, each time deciding not to—until it's the size it was before. And then I pull *The Inferno* from my shelf, slip the square of stolen paper between its pages, and set the book back.

Maybe Owen was right.

Maybe I am a bringer of change.

But I'll decide what kind.

# ACKNOWLEDGMENTS

They warn you about sequels.

They tell you to stock up on caffeine and pajama pants. They tell you to strap yourself down against the storm. They tell you that it will all be worth it in the end. That you'll get through it.

But they never tell you how.

The answer?

People.

People who keep you grounded. People who keep you sane. Who talk plot. Talk pacing. Talk character.

People who answer hypothetical questions about really strange things without looking at you like you've lost your mind.

People who steal the delete key from your keyboard when you decide at two a.m. that maybe you should hold it down.

People who know when you need to be left alone and when you need to be dragged from the computer into the light of day (or the darkness of a laser tag arena).

People who care. Who believe. Even when you don't.

This was not an easy book, in any sense. It fought back. It dragged me through mud and thistle. There were casualties. Hours. Drafts.

But I had people.

I had my mother, who reminded me to eat and breathe, and my father, who reminded me to swim until the world felt small enough again.

I had my NYC housemates, Rachel and Jen, who knew when I needed noise and when I needed quiet (and when I needed to watch cartoons).

I had Carla and Courtney, who hauled me to my feet and dusted me off and squared me on my path.

I had my agent, Holly, who told me I would find a way, because I always did.

I had my editors, Abby and Lisa, who believed in the books, and in me.

And I had you.